# THE
# BLACK
# BETWEEN
# THE
# STARS

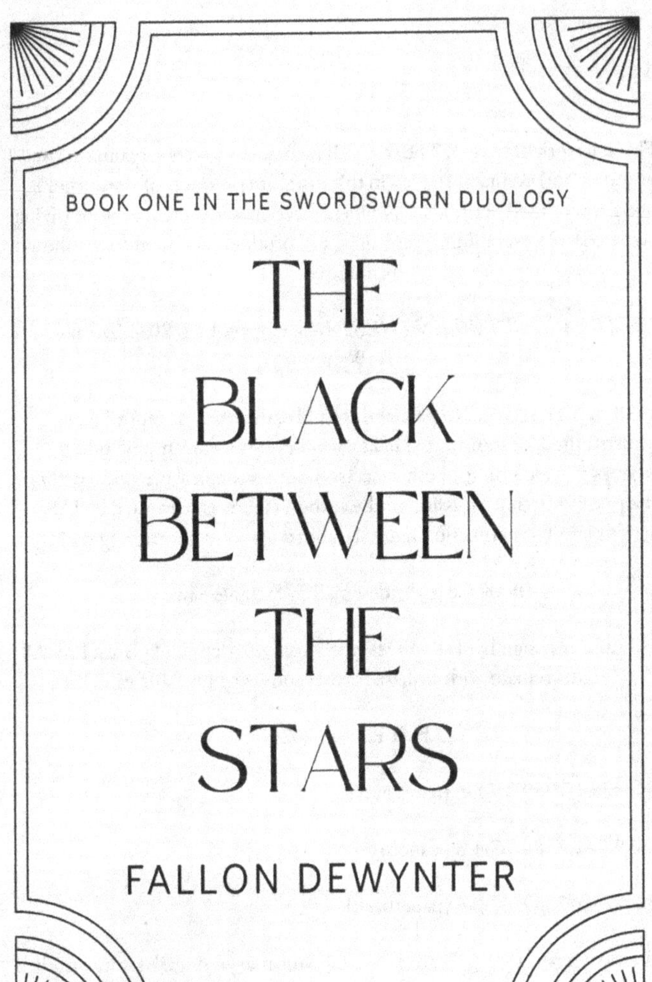



# THE BLACK BETWEEN THE STARS

## FALLON DEWYNTER

Book Cover by designed by Stefanie Saw

Book interior design by: Fallon DeWynter using Atticus and Canva Pro. All rights remain with affiliated artists and programs/software.

First Edition 2024

ISBN: 978-1-7389767-2-0 (hardcover)

ISBN: 978-1-7389767-1-3 (eBook)

ISBN: 978-1-7389767-0-6 (paperback)

Audience: Ages 14+ | Grades: 9-12 | Summary: A girl from an elite women-only warrior clan is chosen to uphold a centuries old-peace treaty and must decide whether to serve the empire that enslaved them or bring it to its knees.

Subjects: women warriors – fiction | fantasy worlds – fiction | magic – fiction | empires – fiction

To the wild girls —
The ones who run with wolves and scream at the moon.
Who would tear out their own souls, and watch the world
burn, if it meant protecting those they love.
Or to anyone who took the time to leave a rating and
review on Goodreads or Amazon =)

# AUTHOR'S NOTE

Writing *THE BLACK BETWEEN THE STARS* was a deep dive into some pretty dark places with both Sinadine's penchant for violence, and Ehrick's sinister machinations acting as a mirror to the more extreme facets of her character. While I do hope that I had taken considerable effort not to contribute to the harmful 'disabled villain trope', I want to preface and clarify that Ehrick is not villainous *because* of his disability. He's villainous because that is the core of his nature. And while his disabilities are not the source of his villainy, the treatment he's endured in a problematic/ableist society have *absolutely* impacted his worldview and motivations.

By the end, I hope you find Ehrick to be a nuanced antagonist you can love to hate, and that the other disabled characters, such as Iereni, help offer a more rounded representation to counter balance his extreme actions.

### **Content & Trigger warnings:**

Hate, Discrimination & Oppression:
- Racial slurs; use of the word savage; slavery; talk of superior race; microaggressions;

prejudice; cultural appropriation; colonization; classism; classism; religious genocide; female oppression/sexism/misogyny; disownment;

Violence:

- Graphic or explicit violence or death (on page – broken nose, severing hand, loose teeth, slit throat, evisceration, burning of skin, cutting of skin); graphic description of violence (blood and internal organs); death (dead bodies and body parts); death of a loved one; animal death/cruelty; animal attack; massacre/mass murder/genocide; murder; execution (beheading); mutilation (cutting off limbs); threatening violence against a child; attempted murder; knife/sword/axe violence; explosions; imprisonment; strangulation;

Mental & physical health:

- Panic attack (minor scene); child abandonment; trauma; cancer (off page); medical treatment and procedures (off page); hospitalization (off page);

Disabilities:

- Lifechanging injury (off page); ableism; chronic illness/chronic pain;

Sexual content:

- Consensual, open door sex scene between main characters; sex workers; sexual assault (implied)

# ACKNOWLEDGEMENTS

They say you should write the book you love because you'll have to read it seventy-five times before it goes to print. While that may be true for traditional publishing, it's more like one hundred and seventy-five for indie (lol!) This path was a long time coming, and admittedly I wish I had reached this point sooner. And while I'm proud of myself for having conquered this hurdle, it still takes a village to make a book come to life which is why instead of putting the acknowledgements at the end I want it front and center so I can thank some very important people without whom this would not be possible:

Starting with my incredible agent, Jim McCarthy. Thank you for fighting for me as fiercely as Sinadine does for her sisters. Your enthusiastic response of *'Sina. Just . . . Sina. Yes. A thousand times, YES!'* after reading only a partial helped keep my head above water. While it was clear I truly had something special on my hands, the traditional publishing world wasn't ready for my bloodthirsty warrior baby girl and knowing you had my back as I took this pivotal step was a gift beyond measure. I am and always will be so thankful for you and look forward to many more chapters in our journey together.

My Hatchlings—the best group of critique partners I could ever ask for: Zabe Ellor, Tiffany Elmer, Caristy (Briston) and Alexandra Overy. Each of you offered such unique strengths when providing feedback from character, to plot, to worldbuilding that has brought TBBTS to what it is today and pushed me to become a much stronger writer. Adalyn Grace, for her thoughtful comments on an earlier draft. I still have the screenshot of your fangirl tweet saved in my phone, and it was something I've held close to my heart any time I hit a wall and started to doubt myself.

My Wattpad4 girlies, L.D. Crichton, Monica Sanz, Rebecca Sky, Erin Latimer and Lindsey Summers. Thank you for always holding space for me to come and scream about all the amazing life achievements or graciously offering words of comfort and encouragement with every setback.

My various author friends: Meredith Ireland, Liselle Sambury, Tigest Girma, Kristi McManus, Sierra Elmore, Deborah Falaye, Roomi Moondi, Deeba Zargarpur, Jessica Cunsolo, Elora Cook, Kess Costales, June Hur, T.A. Chan, Ayana Gray, Kimberly Vale, Angelina M. Lopez, and many who have offered support across the years but most especially as I've navigated this transitory phase in my career, and Stefanie Saw for her AMAZING cover design!! (Like?!)

My Wattpad HQ family. Because of you, I've had some of the greatest years and experiences as an author. I hope I continue to make you all proud.

To the non-writers who tirelessly support me in every way: my sissies – Amanda Anderson and Chelsea Smith. My Sisterhood: Taylor Santos, Kim Sidhu, Alexandra Yuki, Elizabeth Benitez, Moena Gomes, Gaby and Daniella Menjivar, Kayla Harvard, Sophia Cazall, and my boys Maximiliano Pardes, Ricky Diaz, Ishmael Miller, Albert Pierre, and of course, my unbelievably talented and beyond gorgeous cousin, Alexandra MacLean (you know who I'm calling if this ever gets made into a live-action feature!) Thank you for being my village.

My love, you were the first person I told when I decided to go hybrid and I think you were even more excited for this book coming to life than I was. Thank you for your endless support and enthusiasm, and for believing in me as much as you do. But most importantly, thank you for being everything I needed at a time when I needed it most. I never told you this, but I once asked the Universe to *show me something real*. That very same night I met you and whether you know it or not, you've given me something greater than love. You've given me hope.

You've shown me something *real*.

Saving the best for the absolute last (sorry, love :P!), to you—whoever purchased and is reading this book right now—because without you I would have no purpose, and my dreams would not exist.

# THE
# BLACK
# BETWEEN
# THE
# STARS

# PROLOGUE

Berséba de-Hajezhi wiped fresh blood off her hands.

A pair of skinned rabbits lay on a pallet, ready for roasting, with a bowl of ground spices to rub into the dark meat. She tossed a log onto the fire, the bark damp with melting snow. It popped and hissed as it met the flames while her daughter, barely two, slept by the hearth. Dark hair peeking above the thick blanket of wolverine furs, exhausted after a long day of trekking through the woodlands hunting game in the snow.

Sinadine—*of the night*—a fitting name for a child shunned by the stars.

Berséba brushed a hand across the top of her head. She'd taught her to hunt, and fight. To fear nothing. And

Berséba hoped it was enough to leave a mark, rooted deep to the bone.

Because time was running out.

The flap sealing the cave entrance yanked open and Berséba whirled with practiced speed. On her feet and sword drawn, she had the intruder pinned and steel a whisper from a bare throat within a heartbeat.

The older woman released a ragged breath, eyes glassy. "Surely you haven't forgotten the face of a friend, Bersé."

"So, it's time." Berséba lowered her sword and sheathed it. "I'm surprised they sent you for the dishonor of collecting me."

Guida dabbed away a thin trickle of blood with rough fingertips from her throat, the disks of white shells woven within the twisted strands of grey hair sang like windchimes summoning her end. "I asked for it."

Berséba laughed, teeth flashing with the barest hint of fangs. A mark of her ancestry. Her proud lineage. "Why would you do such a stupid thing?"

Shunned for three years, left to forage and fend for herself and her child, Berséba lived in isolation. No one from the clan was allowed to acknowledge her until this day of judgement, when Berséba would have to choose between honoring her clan or something far more precious.

"There was no other way. Or time. I've come to beseech you to see reason."

And though Guida's shoulders were set defiantly, Berséba caught the waver in her voice and smiled. It took a brave soul to challenge her, especially on this matter. The life of her daughter.

"Please, Bersé. Your bloodline—not even your mother—can spare you from the matrons' judgement. Hand over the child. Beg for their mercy and they will grant it."

Berséba unsheathed a dagger from her side and ran the pointed edge beneath her thumbnail, cleaning out blood that the water failed to wash away. "I am Swordsworn," she answered. "I beg of no one."

"You won't be for much longer," Guida pressed, shuffling after her deep into the cave. "If your mother was here—"

"She would respect my decision, as I expect the matrons to."

"It is but one life for the sake of many, surely you must see why the child—" Silenced by a hard slap, Guida pressed a hand to her cheek, flaming bright as her shock.

"Careful," Berséba whispered. "I like you, so consider that fair warning to swallow your tongue before you dare ask me to kill my own child."

"*Why*? Why do this?"

Berséba's eyes flitted across the cave to the fire where Sinadine slept soundly. The night of her birth had been arduous, the pain—nearly ripping Berséba apart. She'd labored for two days and nights before Sinadine came into the world cloaked in darkness. The clan had fallen silent as the stars vanished moments after her first breath, like wisps of candlelight snuffed between fingertips. They didn't disappear behind the filmy haze of clouds or get swallowed up in a storm—they just faded, one after the other, into the impregnable black. Like pearls sinking into shadows.

A harrowing omen.

One that foretold death for the Acharrān way of life and the matrons, in their fear, consulted the bones of the ancients, which only confirmed that Sinadine would herald a bloody ruin upon the world.

*Shunned by the stars. Cursed. Damned.* The proclamation was death.

But as the matrons circled in to make their claim, she'd battled them off and swore a terrible, bloody vengeance upon the head of any who dared lay a blade against Sinadine's tender throat—a vow no one in the clan dared to challenge. But it would take more than fear of her sword to save her daughter's life.

It would take sacrifice.

"Because my heart beats inside her," she said at last. "My rage. My passion and pride. She is of my blood and bone therefore it is my responsibility to protect her, whatever the price." She cut her eyes back to Guida. "*Whatever* the price."

Guida stomped her cane, rattling the beads encased within. "The stars do not lie!"

"No, they don't," she agreed, "but Sinadine deserves a chance to change them. When the matrons look at her they see an end of days, but when I look at her I see she will be the sword that cleaves this world in two, driving the colonizers from our Motherland. She will be the winter before the spring—ruthless and cleansing. I believe she will save us all. *I know it.*" Berséba looked to Guida. "Will you tell the matrons of my words?"

Guida hung her head. "Even if they'd listen it would change nothing."

"Coward." Berséba sneered around a laugh and fastened the belt of her scabbard at her waist. The weight of it settled against her hip, familiar as her own skin, and already her heart grieved for the impending loss. A terrible sorrow, second only to the pain of the daughter she was compelled to leave behind.

Weary, Guida lowered to a flat outcropping of stone, old bones creaking, and closed her eyes. "You've been beyond our walls, Bersé, you've seen for yourself—a woman needs a clan to survive this world," she whispered, soft as smoke.

"That's why I am doing this and why I can't take her with me." A knot clenched in Berséba's chest, squeezing around her heart. "The greatest gift I could ever give her is the chance to prove herself worthy to the stars that shunned her."

As a mother how could she not?

"Take me to the matrons." Berséba pushed steel into her spine. Into her words. "I'm ready."

The assembly gathered in the courtyard of Home Mountain, matrons and daughters, all. Their faces lit by the roaring flames of the star-shaped brazier made of bronze. Smoke spiraled over dancing tongues of red and gold, casting warmth to battle the chill of winter in the air.

The matrons stood proudly, a row of women in kubari robes of deepest indigo like the sky as it bled from day into night. Like the ink of the tattoos marking their skin, and the woad painted across their faces. Elide, her little sister, stepped forward. Their newly appointed leader. The woven bands of leather and gold, signifying her authority were new on her brow, but she carried them with the dignity of ancestry, and the confidence of someone born to lead.

Even though this was a moment of profound sadness, a kindle of pride sparked in Berséba chest, intricately intertwined with frustration. If only Elide could see as she did. If only she could make Elide understand . . .

But Elide was never one for defying the ways of the past, and the stern faces of the elder matrons behind her glowering in contempt, Elide would never set herself apart from their wisdom. She was a staunch advocate for following protocol and maintaining order, and would uphold their ways, unto her last breath.

For that reason, Berséba had no other choice but to play the only hand she had left. *Whatever the cost . . .*

"You were given the grace of two years to be with your child out of respect for all that you have done for the clan, and for our distinguished heritage. A grace we wouldn't have bestowed to anyone else," Elide spoke, always soft. Always measured. Ever proud. "Perhaps that period of isolation has given you adequate time to come to reason."

"If the matrons will not yield, then I am left with no choice. I envoke Raitorēdo," Berséba spoke clear, and loud for all to hear of the stunned gasps rolling like fog across the forum of the gathered clan. "By my honor and rite as Swordsworn, I shield Sinadine from your judgement with my own back, even if it means I must surrender my sword, so be it. Whatever you decide for her, let it fall upon me."

Elide set her chin, furious hands fisted at her side. The only outward expression of her frustration. "One life to save many is a *just* and *noble* course of action, yet you contend to defy our ways. Our judgement. Sisters before self!"

"*Sisters before self!*" the clan echoed.

Berséba assessed Elide and the matrons each in turn. Only her mother, answering a call deep in the Soulands, was missing among them and she was grateful for it. A mother should never have to see such things and the only tempest to brew blacker than Berséba would be the wroth of Avanthi de-Masad.

"Look at you. Trembling where you stand over a *child* when the true threat lies south in a palace of gold and bones," she sneered.

"War is not our way," another said.

"It should be," Berséba answered. Jaw grim.

"If you go through with this," Elide interjected, "you will be disavowed."

"I am aware."

"Then so be it." Elida flagged a hand, calling for silence among the elders and clan. "We've heard enough. As your selfishness affects us all, I call upon a collective vote to determine your fate. Sisters." She gestured to the bowls at her feet. Alabaster for forgiveness. Onyx for judgement. "Cast your stones."

Berséba held her ground as one after the other, each member of the clan came forward. Some cast their vote easily and without hesitation, others lingered over the decision, but eventually conceded, dropping their stones into the onyx bowl until it overflowed with smooth, polished bits of rock. The alabaster bowl remained empty.

None had dared to challenge her decision, once again fearing Berséba's sword more than they did Elide's anger.

"It appears to be unanimous." Elide unfolded her hands and gestured to the pyre, muscle ticking in the side of her jaw. "You know what must be done."

Crossing to the brazier, Berséba removed her dagger from her belt by the elk-bone hilt and passed it to Matron Nnedi who accepted it with a wrinkled hand and nodded gently. Berséba set her teeth as the cool touch of fingers angled her chin and the first pass of the blade sliced across the side of her head, removing the three long braids and the heavy beads adorning them, each one tossed into the brazier to burn.

Then she thrust the dagger into the flames, long enough for the heat to cleanse the steel, before dipping it into a pot of black ink and pressed the point into her skin. And as she carved the left side of Berséba's face her sisters sang, each note, like the stroke of the blade, deep and mournful. This was a funeral of sorts. To the eyes and hearts of her clan, after this ceremony she would cease to exist.

She would be *Osutikāru-da*—Disavowed.

"Speak your words," Elida whispered, a little hoarse, a little empty when Nnedi was finished. "And let them be your last among us."

Berséba gripped the hilt of her sword, drawing strength from it one last time. Blood and black ink trickling down the side of her face in venomous tears. "I, Berséba de-Hajezhi—the Fierce Fang—forsake my place among my clan to my child, Sinadine. By sacred rite, from this moment until her last breath she is a true Daughter of the Acharrā, a bloodkin descendent to the First-of-Us, and you all will *embrace her as such*." She cut dark eyes around her, and some fell away in shame. In fear. "Or, on the Souls of our Sisters, you will answer to me for it. In this life or the next." Last, she turned to her daughter, to Sinadine.

Her sullen mouth set, and hands in fists.

"Behold me, Sina, remember all that I taught you," she whispered. "Remember our words and hold them fast to your heart. Let them guide and fill you with strength. Speak them now."

"We are Acharrān," Sinadine answered, her infantile voice rolling with certainty through the mantra Berséba had repeated night and day for three short years. "We do not bow. We do not bend. We do not break."

The sting of sorrow and pride warmed her eyes and, removing her sword, Berséba handed it to Sinadine. "Feel its weight," she said as her small fingers closed around the scabbard, tentative. "Feel its power. Our legacy. I am part of this blade, as you are part of me. One day, you will be Swordsworn.

"Lead with your sword, Sina, and your spirit will follow."

# CHAPTER ONE

## Sinadine

I REMEMBERED HER MOST WHEN IT SNOWED.

My mother.

The first flakes tumbled from ash grey clouds and I tipped my face skyward to enjoy their cooling touch on my cheeks. Bringing with it distant memories tucked away in the shadowy corners of my mind like forgotten toys covered in dust and cobwebs, but they rattled against the walls of my skull, clamoring for attention.

The last time I saw her was the day she walked beyond the walls of Home Gate. A memory I should've been too young to recall, but I'd latched on to that fragile moment with desperate, greedy fingers. Aching to never let go.

Her smile was the cold majesty of silver mountains. Strong. Proud. Serene. And more than a little cruel. As a child I often searched my face in the placid, reflective waters of the icelake, trying to find a hint of the woman who'd bore me. She was nowhere in my hazel eyes and stubborn chin, but my smile was hers, a secret I coveted—the one piece of her I carried with me.

And I shared it with no one.

Standing alone in the dark, at the edge of a precipice overlooking the vast stretch of rolling mountains, I wasn't supposed to be here, but determination slicked my skin with sweat despite the frigid caress of wind. Winter was coming, and tonight was my last chance to complete a rite of passage I'd waited for my entire life. And if I failed . . . I pushed the thought aside.

*I will earn my mark. I will earn my sword.*

A naked sky, scattered with glistening stars, stretched high above me, crowned with the barest sliver of a sickle moon. Its pale wash of light caressed an obelisk of black granite shaped into a four-sided pillar, topped with a pyramidion, and hewn with white-painted glyphs that glowed like stars trapped in the steady dark. I touched the prayerstone, the surface rough against my fingertips, drawing strength from it, and bowed my head in deference.

"Spirits of my Sisters, give me glory."

"There you are." Rhys' voice floated behind me, sharp as the bite of cold in the air. "You said to meet you at the *entry*way of the mountain pass." Tendrils of white-blonde hair, pale as her skin, danced around her narrow face.

I guested to prayerstone behind me. "I wanted to pay my respects before the ritual."

"You could've told me that. I've been pissing in the wind for ten minutes."

"Well if you want to argue semantics, this is *also* an entryway." I cast her a sly grin. "It's not my fault you chose to wait at the wrong end."

"Swallow your tongue, Sina." Frustration teased out the silver in her narrowed blue eyes before they quickly softened with concern. "Are you sure you want to defy your aunt openly before the whole clan?"

"I don't have a choice."

"But if you wait—"

"For how long, Rhys? Another year? Three? Ten? I'll spend my entire life waiting." My fingers tightened into a fist. "She'll never say my name. Not unless I force her hand."

As Lead Matron, my aunt's word was absolute and challenging her was a risk, but one that had to be taken. I was the last descendant of the First-of-Us and carried a proud heritage that was slowly coming to an end. That precious fact gave me the courage to seize what I coveted most and once I was proven Elide would have no choice but to accept that I'd earned everything she sought to deny me.

My birthright. My legacy.

And when the mantle of Lead Matron passed to me, I'd see my sisters restored to honor and glory as the warriors they were always meant to be, not slaves bled to the bone to serve the empire. Our numbers culled until only a proud few remained. Violence came easy to my mother. A dark gift that much to the chagrin of my aunt—and the unerring pride of my grandmother—I'd inherited. One I intended to put to great use.

"Tell me something, Sina," Rhys demanded, temper infusing color in her cheeks, "if you really believe her to be so intractable, what's to stop her from denying your ascension even if you do complete the ritual?"

"She might. But if I can't be Swordsworn, I may as well be dead," I answered, resolute.

Rhys lowered her gaze. "Then we must hurry."

I followed behind her in the dark. The pale wash of moonlight caressed the jagged plates paving the craggy mountain trail like broken teeth as the path opened to a set of polished stone steps leading to the colosseum. As children we'd scrubbed and mopped all two thousand and forty-seven of them carved with glyphs and inlaid with semi-precious stones.

Voices clamored from within and together we wove around the bodies of the assembled and circled to a break in the front where the eight matrons stood proudly, dressed in kubari robes of deepest indigo with my aunt at their center, crowned with woven leather bands inlaid with gold, turquoise and blue opal. Her hair, more brown than black, was gathered in a high bun and either side of her head shaved to bare skin revealing the deep blue lines of her mark—a roaring cave bear.

"Tonight, our best and brightest, dedicated to their clan and to training, will be tested and only those deemed worthy will ascend," Elide spread her hands wide, commanding the attention of the assembly, her features decorated in a painted mask of her True Face.

Iridescent woad lit by the snapping flames of the star-shaped brazier made of bronze. Smoke spiraled over dancing tongues of red and gold and cast warmth to battle the chill in the air.

"As Swordsworn, we are protectors of the people and administrators of justice," she continued. "For centuries, we have answered calls across the Motherland to oversee trials and executions, to guard villages and homes, to hunt down pillaging renegades or criminals. Those of you prepared for this journey, come forward when I speak your name."

Side by side, Rhys gripped my hand tightly in hers and then she cast a quiet smile when her name rang out across the sands. "Strength and honor," she whispered before joining the growing body of hopefuls.

When my aunt finally fell silent, I counted twelve hopefuls stripped down to their kubi tunic and boots, and knelt before the matrons, heads bowed.

There was about to be thirteen.

Casting off my cloak, I stepped forward and all sound within the shrine fell to a tense hush. Jasz, one of the hopefuls, sneered at the sight of me and our gazes collided like the clash of steel ringing in battle. We'd locked horns for as long as I could remember, not out of fear or hatred, but a simple frustration born of competitiveness. She wanted to be great.

Unfortunately for her I was determined to be better at it.

"Sinadine." A tremor of anger tightened the lines of my aunt's throat. But another name echoed far louder, a whispered curse that circled the arena.

*Dakuwan*. Dark One. The moniker I'd grown up knowing long before my own name.

She gave a cook of her finger and I approached until the light of the fire shone bright in her eyes.

"What are you doing here?"

"I am eighteen. And as bloodkin to the First-of-Us I would like to be tested. It is my right."

"I did not *speak* your name."

"My mother became *Osutikāru-da*," I pressed, my words bright with confidence. "She forsook her place among her clan and relinquished her sword so that I would be allowed all the same rights and privileges as any member of this clan." And I would honor her memory, her name, her sacrifice, by showing them—all of them—that I would be the greatest of us.

The fiercest.

Determined, I cast my challenging gaze to each of the matrons, daring them to drag me away or strip the kubi from my back and cane me until I was a mess of blood and bruises. My grandmother's expression, as always, remained inscrutable. My aunt, on the other hand, trembled like a wolverine about to attack.

I didn't care. I would not be denied, by her or the stars. Not again.

"She speaks true," Matron Nnedi turned into Elide, her voice lowered so it wouldn't carry far. "As your heir, it is up to the stars to decide her fate. We cannot hold her back now."

"She openly defies me. How does that look to those I am expected to lead?

"In time they will forget this grievance and accept the only part that matters." Grandmother's hand closed around Elide's shoulder, quieting her. "Let her try."

Elide's lips scored into a thin line, but finally her chin dipped the barest fraction. "Kneel," she ordered. "And await your turn."

Hope kicked between my lungs, releasing a startled breath of joy even as a distant voice of doubt whispered, *this was too easy.* An unbidden flame I quickly snuffed out with impatient fingers. What did it matter when I was finally getting what I wanted most?

Jasz stiffened at my side, and the blade of her jealousy stabbed between my ribs, twisting in search of a tender heart only to find there was none. My chest was barren. If I had a heart, it had been taken from me the day my mother was cast beyond our gates into exile. The only thing that beat inside me now was cold purpose.

Once the assembly hushed, my aunt released a sharp breath then gave a commanding flick of her finger, signaling the handmaids to approach us, each carrying a small ceramic cup.

"Drink," she ordered. "All of it."

Gathering the bowl, I took a long and slow breath, steadying my senses. Raising it to my lips, we all drank as one and swallowed every offensive drop. The milky alcohol was sharp and pungent enough to melt the hair off a boar, mixed with something else I couldn't put my finger on—but it was *vile.* Coughing, sputtering, I fell to my hands and knees, struggling against the onslaught of gorge.

*Don't vomit.* Even though my body railed to rid itself of the brew, if I did the test would be over. I'd fail. Hands and eyes clenched, I willed the rising bile to settle as warmth poured into my limbs. It pulsed and thrummed in my head, a firm and steady rhythm.

"If the First-of Us deem you worthy, your familiar will present itself." My aunt's voice flowed in the air, thick as honey and black as ink. Faint as a dying breath. "Face your truth and your weakness . . ."

I sat back on my knees and blinked against the stuttering backdrop of the colosseum, weaving in and out of focus taking with it sound and scent and light until I found myself alone in the dim surroundings of a cavern. Stone and snow beneath my hands and knees. I dug in my fingers and scooped up a disbelieving handful.

Cold. Wet. Real.

This made no sense. Panic scored through me like the sharp point of a dagger gliding firmly against my skin, not hard enough to draw blood, but enough so that it hurt.

"Hello?" My voice rang out, faded and heavy as if in a dream. Warning pricked across my nerves in a ripple of knowing long before I heard a soft cackle, deep as winter ice breaking on a mountainside.

I spun on my knees, bracing as a shadowy figure of a woman approached, glowing gilded blue around blackened edges with eyes vivid as lightning in a face so dark I could see no nose or mouth. Only a void so deep and absolute it was like gazing into the face of death, itself.

"Are you spirit?" I croaked. "Or are you flesh?"

She stopped, leaning heavily on a white xhixi wood staff and then lowered before me. A glowing grin split that impregnable darkness like the slice of a sword across a soft, vulnerable belly.

"Who. Are. You?" The staccato of her words reverberated through me, jarring as a foot through my chest.

"I am called Sinadine."

"Sinadine." Fanged teeth flashed as she drew back her hood and the darkness fell away like night yielding to dawn, revealing the weathered face of a crone. Her skin, and eyes a washed-out black like she was made of midnight.

Removing a bone dagger from a sheath around her neck, she held it towards me with gnarled fingers and nails filed to points, clear as diamonds.

"Give us a taste. We shall see what you are made of."

Accepting the dagger, I held it before me. A tiny blade, the length of my palm and thin as a child's finger, the surface hammered and inlaid with glyphs. Pressing the point to my thumb, I stroked it quickly, leaving behind a smear of wet crimson to stain the bronze before offering it back to her.

Smiling, the crone stuck out a grey tongue and licked the blade clean.

"Hmmm." Large eyes narrowed. "You carry the First in you."

"Yes."

"Why have you come?"

"I am the granddaughter of Avanthi de-Mazad, the Stag Heart. I know I'm not supposed to be here," I added, lowering my eyes to the empty space between us. "The stars did not favor my birth, but all I ask is for a chance to prove myself and restore honor to my mother's name."

"Hm." Sheathing her blade, the crone skimmed the tip of her tongue against the sharp edge of her teeth. "Dark, you are. Black as death. Cold as the deepest winter sea. Unyielding as our great steel," she whispered. "You will bring a night without end . . . but there is strength in your shadows." Reaching out, she crooked a finger beneath my chin, angling me to meet her endless gaze.

Harrowing and ancient.

"Can you get blood from a stone?"

Before I could ask what she'd meant she hunched forward with a whimpered groan, eyelids flickering like the beat of an owl's wings and swayed in the sudden rise of a malevolent storm. Wind and pellets of snowy ice funneled into the cavern and whipped around us like a tornado.

She clawed at her chest, overcome by a horrifying mixture of screams and laughter, as clothing and flesh tore in a violent burst that split her down the middle. A stone-cat emerged from the ruins of the crone like a clutch of spiders from their birthing sack.

The twitch of a tail, first, the panting rise of a sleek and powerful body, next.

A female, given her impressive size. She glimmered like starlight that soon faded into a pewter coat that paled to silver around her muzzle, tail and paws—readying for the winter. Mouth open, she flashed long canines wedged in black gums. Large and powerful enough to take down a cave bear or a full-grown caribou by the throat. She could rip me to shreds like I was made of silk, or crack open the dome of my skull, soft as the blue-shelled crabs we ate at a summer feast.

This place might not be real, but *she* certainly was.

Between us lay the crone's xhixi wood staff, white as moonlight and a whip of excitement, of certainty, lashed around my heart—kicking it into a giddy rhythm.

*Can you get blood from a stone?*

"Spirits of my Sisters." I grabbed hold of the staff, my movements careful and calm. "I thank you for this honor and give myself to you, to live or die by your grace or mercy."

The she-cat growled, that deep sound reverberating off the walls of the cavern and the bones in my chest, an echo to the thrumming of adrenaline inside me. As a child born in darkness, I had no fear of shadows, or the beasts prowling in them. Staff braced in my hands, I flashed my teeth. She'd issued her challenge, and I accepted.

Her paw lashed out and I deflected with a quick spin of the staff, lurching to my feet. When she pounced, I jabbed hard between her eyes then charged, aiming for the soft underside of her belly. The joints of her legs. The two of us locked in a sinuous dance of power and speed, but for every hit I landed, I dodged the eviscerating sweep of her claws and followed with a hard crack to the underside of her jaw.

The stonecat roared her pain and frustration and drove the hard dome of her skull into my hip, knocking me down. My head bounced off hard stone and pain flashed behind my eyes as blood swelled in my mouth from when my teeth bit my tongue. I swallowed it down. I hadn't spilled any yet and the test was not over unless I did.

Reeling, I had a second—a breath—to anchor the staff between my hands as she leapt over me, her mouth closing over wood instead of my throat. If the staff hadn't been made with white xhixhi wood it would've immediately snapped between her powerful jaws like a dry chicken bone.

The hard blast of her breath fanned across my face, ripe with the scent of an old kill that seared in my nose and sent bile to churn in my stomach. The muscles in my arms screamed, wood rubbed against my sweaty palms and stone scraped the backs of my shoulders as our eyes locked, twin mirrors of fury and determination. Between the weight of the she-cat and the gnash of her powerful teeth, my staff groaned—a final death rattle—before it cracked clean in two.

Rolling out of the way of her killer bite, I jabbed my knuckles with all the flagging strength of my arms into the space beneath her ribs above the soft side of her belly.

She yowled but leapt off me, and I pushed to my feet, twirling the broken halves of the staff as she braced herself to charge. A plan quickly formed. A dangerous, half-cocked scheme that was just as likely to get me killed, but I was out of options, and, most importantly, time. Exhaustion was sweeping through me, and at this pace I'd tire long before she did. It was now, or failure, and I would return to my clan victorious, or not at all.

The she-cat tensed, the powerful muscles in her back coiled, gathered, and I gave myself to the silence of focus and the calm readiness of patience, my senses honed as the sacred blades of the Swordsworn. A second, a breath, a pause, and I would be dead. My timing had to be exact.

When she pounced—massive paws sweeping wide and fangs bared—I dove forward and rolled low, and as she arced around to pursue me, the weight and momentum of her large body was too much for her to stop with precision. As the she-cat's hind legs scrabbled for purchase, I struck hard, driving the sharp end of the broken staff above the line of her claws, one of the few vulnerable spots on a stonecat's tough hide.

Her anguished cry rang out, an echoing sound that fractured in my ears like shattered pottery. Wrenching her paw away—a clawed knuckle ripped free—she regained her legs and glared at me with burning eyes. Blood dripped from her wound and splattered in steady, fat drops to punctuate her heavy breathing.

Discarding my weapon, I sank to my knees and bowed, head down and hands flat, as I'd been taught. This was it. If I lived, I would become a Swordsworn sister of my clan. If I died, well, my death would be a glorious one. The arms of the First-of-Us would open to receive me, and I'd take my place alongside the Spirits of my Sisters in the stars.

The choice was hers to make. Either way, I welcomed my fate.

The she-cat stalked around me, and I focused on the tread of her steady gait, the clicking of her claws, the fast beat of her heart—and mine—pounding like the wind drums that would sing tonight in my honor. The hot blast of her breath washed over the back of my neck and a chill of excitement rippled across my skin along with the kiss of whiskers.

A soft rumble escaped her throat.

I relaxed, lengthening my neck, and waited as wind whispered over me, cooling the flush of my skin. After the seconds stretched, I released a gentle breath and lifted my head. The she-cat was gone as if she'd been made of nothing more than mist and smoke, leaving nothing but a bloody trail left in her wake . . .

The world swayed, spun, and I roiled against the churning flow. Voices surged—chanting softly, and the shake of my grandmother's hands brought me back to the sands of the coliseum. Warmth burned across my skin. Searing through pores, funneling through veins and burrowing into bone until I was fire, through and through. I crawled out of my mind and back into my body, like fingers clawing at frozen earth. Nails ragged, skin torn and raw.

A shaken breath escaped numb lips, followed by a surge of vomit. The chanting stopped, though weakened I regained my center, my balance, as seeking hands looped under my shoulders and wrenched me to my feet.

My grandmother approached, her expression blank. "Well?"

I swallowed the acrid taste of bile in my throat, scanning my eyes around me quickly in hesitation. What had once been so clear was growing hazier by the second. Not trusting myself to speak, I raised my hand between us, unfurled my fingers, and nearly gasped. There, in my palm, sat the bloody claw of gleaming ivory.

Proud, my grandmother swiped fingers coated in ash across my face. "Worthy!"

Prompted by that proclamation, my grandmother raised my fist and a cry rippled among the Swordsworn—my sisters. The undulation of their voices rose into a roar of triumph matched by pounding drums and fists beating to chests. Their love and pride shared by all, save my aunt. Our leader.

Dark eyes narrowed in her hard face, she was the only one who didn't cry out in celebration. She was the only one who didn't smile.

# CHAPTER TWO

## Sinadine

M USIC SWELLED AND FOR THE REST of the day the courtyard hummed with celebration, all work set aside to dance and feast. Our usually simple but nutritious meals gave way to wonderful, rich array of food that tantalized the senses and had my mouth watering expectantly.

Honeyed goat, roasted caribou, purple rice scented with saffron and coconut milk, wine-soaked olives, pickled peppers, and shaved slices of raw fish, fresh clams and oysters topped with golden caviar. All followed by desserts of sticky lemon cake, dried figs candied in honey, lychees folded into a cold passionfruit pudding.

I gorged and feasted, savoring each succulent morsel as I did my victory—with gusto—as endless casks of sweet red wine, dark rum and gold whiskey flowed like the beating drums and dancing bodies from noon to dusk. Swept into the throes of celebration, the sky flashed a dazzling shade of apricot as the first stars winked faintly in the encroaching blue of dusk.

Fire roared in the star-shaped bronze pit piled with xhixi wood. It would burn for five days and nights, in honor of each of us.

"I can't believe you took a claw from a stonecat unscathed." Rhys folded her arms across her chest. Full and dizzy with spirits, she swayed with a grin. "Had to make the rest of us look bad, didn't you?"

I rolled stiff shoulders and raised a proud brow, high as my chin. "Not my fault you make it so easy."

Cahira and Amparo laughed as Rhys playfully shoved me.

"She has a bruise on her hip that'll be black come tomorrow, I wouldn't call that unscathed," Amparo teased. Her dark brown skin beaded with sweat, and her hair loose in a riot of tight curls. She hooked an arm around Cahira's shoulder, her own hair red as sunset.

"Matron Avanthi killed a stonecat when she was barely fifteen," Jasz sneered. "Snagging a bloody claw at eighteen is hardly noteworthy."

Amparo wrinkled her nose. "Don't be jealous, Jasz."

"Why would I be jealous of *Dakuwan*?" She spat, and drove her shoulder into me, stalking off.

My fingers tightened into a tight fist until my knuckles whined. After a full day of celebration, tonight we would receive the mark of my familiar—a sacred tattoo—and then the forging of our swords would begin.

Spirit of my Sisters, I was impatient to hold it in my hands. To feel its grip against the skin of my palms. To hear the cool whisper of steel drawn from its scabbard.

*Soon.*

And once I had my sword, I'd be allowed to strike out into the world and build up my legacy until I was spoken across all corners of the Motherland, my name whispered reverently on the wind. Then my clan would see me for what I was—the most fearsome and respected Acharrān to ever hold a blade. A legend. And all who'd scowled at me as a child would now see that I had a purpose, that I deserved to live, and my mother was not a traitor for saving my life.

"Come on." Rhys tugged my arm as the horn sounded, calling us to gather near the fire where everyone clamored to wedge into the tight rows of red lacquered seats. "There are still a few open near the front."

"No." I drew away. "You go."

"Sina," Rhys sighed. "You don't have to sit alone."

"I prefer it," I answered. "Go. Before they're all gone."

Rhys sighed again but was swept away by the excitement while I sat on the steps flanking the courtyard. My gaze drifted to Taphne. She leaned heavily on her crutch with twisted legs searching the crowd for a seat. I watched her some mornings from the cool mountain shadows as she trained in the arena with the other children, fighting for what her heart wanted most—a sword of her own.

A sword had to be earned; every single part of it, from the blade to the scabbard, hilt and guard. *Earned*. It took as long as four years of laboring in the quarry to collect enough of the precious ore honed into a steel stronger and lighter than any other.

My palms were thick with calluses from wielding the pickaxe and chisel, hammering away at the dense mountain rock, but it was the struggle that sharpened the hunger in me like a whetstone. As for the crafting of the blade—that was left to the matrons. They alone knew the secrets to forging and inspected each edge, deciding on the sacred words to be carved into the blade. Words we would live by for the rest of our lives.

Guida, the wordweaver, rose on stocky legs and rattled her cane. Hollowed, and filled with clay beads, it sang musically as she walked like the gentle fall of rain against the tiles that shingled the pagodas. Her length of grey hair woven into a thick braid intertwined with delicate shells the children collected from the icelake, tokens given in payment for the thrill of her stories.

She wore them proudly.

Dressed in burnt yellow robes trimmed in black ermine, her worn face was painted with jagged lines of bright blue, red, and dots of white—she was like the sun fading on the horizon, seeking its rest while the stars came out to glisten.

Taphne scuttled to where I sat, her crutch dragging with each hurried step, and plunked down at my side instead of gathering at Guida's feet with the other children.

Across the courtyard, Rhys cast me a satisfied smile.

Smirking, I rolled my eyes.

"What story shall I weave?" Guida waved a hand before her, sweeping from left to right. Her voice thick as pipe smoke and just as soft. Shrieking with glee, the children bounced on their knees, and she cupped that hand to her ear as they shouted their choices to her across the firepit.

*The Grand Tale of Tainumen and the Ghost Snake!*
*The Fallen Sister of Clan Blood Grass!*
*Rise of the Worldeater!*
*She Who Walked Between Worlds!*

I warmed at the excitement of the children huddled as close to her feet as they could manage without piling themselves onto her bent body.

I'd been like them once, perhaps not so full of smiles and glee, but fascinated by Guida nonetheless, and soaked up her stories like river moss did rain and sunshine. Each awe-inspiring word became fuel to the fire burning in my chest, giving me strength, focus and purpose, and now, surrounded by the fire and the fading echo of drums that played and sang in celebration, I felt something I'd never expected to feel.

Joy. The bright, powerful wings of it thrummed wildly inside of me, and I pressed a hand to the flat expanse of my belly. I was happy, truly happy. In this moment I could throw back my head and laugh until my ribs ached. A jarring realization.

Spirits of my Sisters. Sinadine—the *Dakuwan*—laughing. Wouldn't that be a sight?

Guida turned up her nose with an exaggerated grinning grimace that sent the children into fits of giggles and elicited a stoic smile from a few of the matrons also gathered around the fire.

Not all in our clan had a talent for blades. Or the stomach for them, and when Guida spoke the world hushed, aching to catch each skillfully woven word.

"No." She clucked her tongue and wagged her staff. "No, tonight I shall tell you an old story. A powerful and ancient one that flows back to our beginning. How we, the daughters of the Acharrā, came to be Swordsworn."

Taphne settled in closer at my side. Perhaps it was the lull of the fire, the soft rhythm of the drums that joined Guida's grand tale, but I hooked an arm around her shoulders and the breath in her stilled for the barest moment.

"We began with blood, as all life does." Guida wiggled her fingers like the legs of a centipede. "The First-of-Us were skyborn warriors descended from the stars. One tumbled from its place in the heavens, drawn by the cries beseeching for aid, and the Acharrāns answered. Women, eight feet tall, with legs and arms as strong as the xhixi trees that grow at the base of our mountains, they rode into battle on familiars made of moonlight and wielding swords of starfire. Led by their Unnamed Queen against the demons that had taken root. Rising like shadows from the earth.

"Many were lost in this war, and sick of bloodshed, the Unnamed Queen retired her surviving Acharrāns to the safety of our mountains where their star had shattered among the jagged peaks we call home." She waved her hands across the flames and they danced as if guided by the sway of her twisting fingers. Equally enchanted by her words.

I'd heard this story before. Many of us had, aside from a few of the children, but that was the mysterious power of a wordweaver, to tell the same stories and always elicit awe in her audience as each tale spilled from her lips as if anew.

"Over the coming years, they opened their gates to any woman or child in need of refuge and taught them their sacred art of the sword and how to mine the ore to fashion blades. The ore, as well as the land, was imbued with the star's sacred energy, and with it we are given the marks of our familiars, and our steel. Steel we must earn through the sweat of effort and the blood of sacrifice. When the First-of-Us passed on from this life, they became the Spirits of our Sisters, their souls rising to the sky as stars while their surviving daughters, born of this Motherland, pledged to continue their legacy and answer the calls of those in need of protection. To be Swordsworn is to be strong, fierce, loyal, and to value life."

Guida knelt before Padma de-Innesa, and with a cagey grin, she unsheathed her sword strapped to the belt of her kubari. Rising back to her feet, Guida leaned heavily on her staff as she lifted the honed blade towards us. Its curved edge gleamed silvery blue, and my throat tightened with yearning. Desire.

So close. I was so close.

"This is the symbol of the First-of-Us, our legacy trapped in steel. Our vow." She returned the sword to my Padma and bowed humbly before she continued to speak. "We are a clan of found women who needed sanctuary, some with bellies swollen with a babe—victims of violation or circumstance—and all with nowhere to go but a cut-wife to root it out, or an early grave." Guida spat at the fire and the flames popped, spraying sparks to dance like fireflies in the smoke.

"Look at our varying faces. Our many shades of skin. Together we became strong." Her arms flexed at her sides, showing off toned biceps and answering hoots and cries circled the camp, fierce with pride. "We are sisters born not of blood but bond, and so our numbers grew; such was the need of refuge and haven. One clan became many and we scattered across the Motherland, pledging to serve towns, villages, or homes. They were the shield, the sword and the strength of the people, revered and respected. For a thousand years there was peace, for none dared challenge an Acharrān blade or the daughter who wielded it. Such was our strength. Such was our honor. But peace is a fragile thing, easily broken." Guida plucked a shell from her hair, let it fall to the ground and smashed it with the blunt end of her staff.

A saddened gasp rippled among the children and Taphne tensed at my side.

"Conquerors came from the west, a Pale Wolf with a bloody muzzle, sweeping in like a foul plague. The Swordsworn did not take sides on a battlefield, for that was not their way. They did not fight in wars or serve the whims of men whose egos were so easily swayed by pride or politics. Instead, as the rash of this disease spread, claiming city after city, province after province—they guarded the homes, they shielded the innocent. And as the enemy rode in, dripping in Motherland blood, they did not flee nor did they abandon the lives they'd vowed to protect. They fought and died, their souls rising to join the Spirits of our Sisters to watch over and guide us as the stars." She cast a handful of powder into the flames and immediately it burst in a flash of light and pale pink smoke.

Climbing higher and higher.

I followed the rise of those plumes as they faded into black, the stars gazing down upon us in witness. One day mine would rise among them, and when the time came, I'd welcome my death.

"Only when the last of the continent was holding on by a thread, and thousands of our daughters were dead, did the matrons realize the error of their ways, but it was too late. The Pale Wolf rose, a giant on the horizon, howling and fangs bared. What remained of the clans sought haven in the sacred mountains. It was here they held their ground, waiting for the wolf to tire. To show its throat." Guida twisted her cane and the trickling rattle of beads flowed fast as she snapped her teeth and snarled like a beast hungering for a kill.

"But the Pale Wolf was no fool. He did not wish to rule over blood and bones, and he knew the key to winning this war lay not with its people, but the Acharrāns for if they could be brought to heel, who would ever dare challenge him? Gathering his forces, he rode to Home Mountain with a million slaves he'd plucked from cities and villages. Weak and defenseless, he marched them in chains to our gates and beat a bloody fist against our impenetrable xhixi wood doors." Guida fell silent. The weight of sorrow curved her shoulders.

"The matrons gazed from the high walls; hearts heavy with anguish for there was no choice but to bend the knee unless they wished to witness a slaughter of a million souls they'd swore to protect. And so the gates were thrown open and the Pale Wolf entered, his smile smug and armies vast. After seeing what the Acharrāns had done in service of the people, he wanted more than just their surrender, he wanted the secret of our steel, our magic, our essence, our soul. But this we would not give. This, we would not yield." Guida thumped a proud fist to her chest, and sharp cries rippled in the night from the clan gathered to hear her speak.

"For the Heart of the Star holds the power to shape worlds as well as destroy them. Many fell to torture and worse, but none begged, or pleaded for her life. She met her death with valiant tears, and it was then the Pale Wolf realized he had no choice but to stop the killing or lose the secret forever. So he vowed no more daughters would die by his hand, and he would leave them to their mountains in peace. All he asked in return for his graciousness was this: three to be given to him in good faith—one to share his throne and two more with each succeeding generation of his line. Three, for the freedom of many.

"As long as the terms of the treaty are honored, the people would remain safe within the fold of the empire. So the treaty was signed. And for century after century, it has been honored." Guida stomped her cane, rattling the beads encased within, putting an end to the gloomy silence that weighed upon all of us. "You who are proven," she bellowed, "come forward."

The majesty of Guida's story fell away and I wove to the firepit, taking to my knees with my sisters before the wordweaver.

We bowed our heads in deference.

"Children no longer, tonight you are to become women of this clan." She paused as shouts and cries rose around us, and then raised her voice to speak above them. "And while you ascend, we will feast, dance, sing and celebrate in your honor. Tonight, we give praise to the First-of-Us for blessing each of you with the sacred animals chosen to guide you on your journeys, and to shield your backs in time of battle."

Rhys and the others filed away with a few handmaids to guide them to the shrine, boy who'd grown into men and remained to serve our clan.

Guida stopped me before I could follow with the press of her hand against my arm. Her skin, soft and smooth without the calluses of hard fighting or battle but I could feel strength in that easy touch and an eager chill skipped down my spine.

"I knew your mother well," she whispered. "Better than most. I wish she was here to witness this moment." That hand lifted and Guida hooked a finger beneath my chin to meet her watery eyes, meshed behind painted lines of blue, yellow and red with dots of white that scattered across her face like stars. "The stars may have shunned you at birth, but they see you now. May the Spirits of our Sisters light your path to glory."

A gong sounded and we funneled into the cavernous mouth of the shrine, a sacred place of ceremony deep in the mountain.

"Do you think it'll hurt?" Rhys whispered, adjusting the sleeves of her kubari.

"Yes," I answered honestly. My feet padding softly over the cedar path of polished boards laid flush into the stone. Panels of it lined the walls, as well, bringing the scent of forest and trees into the cave, the pathway lit with glass lanterns.

"Are you nervous?"

"No."

She turned to look at me, her soft eyes wide. Uncertain. "Does nothing ever scare you?"

Ready for what was to come, I lifted my chin. "No."

The matrons sat in wait for us. Candles, wedged into every nook of stone, dripped ivory wax as their flames danced with each stir of wind. The curling plumes of incense coalesced into a drugging perfume of flowers and spices that softened my thoughts and spread warmth to hum along my skin.

Overhead, a woman's face was etched into the stone, her eyes hollowed out so that the stars could shine upon us in witness of this moment.

I knelt before my grandmother, and the edge of her lips lifted in a proud smile. She wore the traditional white kubi and red wide legged pants made from woven hemp, belted high at her waist and billowing above her ankles. Her long hair braided for ease as well as ceremony.

Only the Swordsworn had the right to wear them, decorated with beads, gold or silver cuffs for valor, and eagle feathers for leadership, dangling from leather cord.

Removing my satchel from my shoulder, I emptied the contents at her feet. Things I'd collected over the years that would adorn my blade—leather and silk for the hilt, bits of moonstones, mother of pearl and xhixi wood that would be made into its scabbard, white gold for the guard, along with customary gifts for the matrons of dried morning jasmine leaves, tanned buckskin and purple jade veined with gold.

She assessed my offerings. Her kohl-blackened eyes, illuminated by candlelight, shone in the shadows of the shrine like a she-cat against slashing lines of woad. She was terrifying to behold.

Magnificent.

"Welcome, Initiate," she intoned. "Do you know where you kneel?"

"I do," I answered. This was the entrance to the resting place of the Unnamed Queen, wreathed in a crown of star-fire, and the seven surviving Acharrāns from the army that rode with her into battle. After their deaths, leadership was divided among eight matrons. Originally, they were the surviving bloodkin of the First-of-Us, but overtime the lines faded until only one remained.

Mine.

Now they stood as stone, protecting the Heart—an eternal burning white flame kept safe deep below the shrine where the star was said to have shattered. Some whispered that the statues came alive during the night of the last sickle moon, and so in my impetuous youth, I'd snuck down to see these majestic and powerful women made of granite. Their features were lost to time, but the glyphs decorating their bodies were crisp as if carved yesterday.

*We stand.*

*We serve.*

*Speak our true names and we will answer.*

*Only blood of our blood will out.*

If I'd been caught the matrons might've caned me, or worse, but I had to see them. And yet in all my secret trips, never once did they move or speak. But here in this most sacred place I'd felt something radiating from within the walls of the mountain shrine.

A humming energy that reverberated in the core of my teeth almost to the point of aching.

Magic, if I dared believe our stories, once shared and bestowed upon all who ascended to Swordsworn, but as the heart of the star weakened, guttering down from a rioting blaze to a solitary flame, so too did our magic fade into legend and I often wondered what would happen to us when it died.

In her lap, she stirred water into a bowl of dark indigo powder and folded in shimmering powder. "Stardust reveals the true nature of the blood." Grandmother tipped the contents of a clear glass vial, and rusted flakes collected from my bleeding stone-cat claw floated into the inky pool that swirled and moved, churning like stars trapped beneath ink-blue waters of a glittering night sea.

*Impossible.* The smoke, now thick in my lungs, was turning my mind to mist and my sight to vapor.

Finished, grandmother set the bowl aside, an engraved abalone shell, and poured out a tall cup from a ceramic pitcher and handed it to me. Parched, I guzzled down the strong rum, sweetened with honey and spices.

"Are you ready to receive your mark?" she asked when I was finished.

Determination clenched in my belly. "Yes."

She raised her hands skyward, her voice full and proud. "I am Avanthi de-Mazad, the Stag Heart. Matron of Silver Peaks, and bloodkin to the First-of-Us. I call upon the Spirits of my Sisters to bless the initiate knelt before me." Grandmother dragged her braid over her shoulder and lifted the cleaned claw of the stonecat between us.

"Your mark is a powerful token, but claiming it does not make you its master. The tattoo is more than a mark on your skin, it's a connection between you and your familiar, as well as your blade. Steel blessed by the stars. Together they will guide and protect you when you need them most. Lead with your sword, and your spirit will follow."

I swayed on my knees, swept up in the majesty of the ceremony—the rising boom of the matrons' voices, each beseeching the spirits of the Acharrān dead to bless us, and the dense smoke casting a dreamy veil over my eyes and senses.

"We do not seek out battle. We protect those who cannot protect themselves. That is the way of the Acharrā. That is our code. Protect life, unto death." Grandmother crooked a finger beneath my chin, capturing my focus like a fish on a line. "Do you promise to uphold our ways, even at the cost of your life?"

"Yes."

"Will you stand for the weak and shield them from the strong?"

"Yes."

"Will you live and die for your sisters?"

"Yes."

"Then speak your words with a pure heart. Feel them anchor in your soul, a tether that will bind you, now and always." She unsheathed her oathblade at her waist, a dagger made of bone and bronze and pressed the lethal tip against the divot of my throat.

A trickle of blood slithered down my chest as I raised my chin, stretching my neck. "I offer my throat as freely as I do my oath. I will honor the Acharrā, I will uphold their words and wisdom, fight their enemies, and protect the innocent who seek the shelter of my sword. This I swear, until my heart stops beating, and my soul rises from my flesh to join my sisters in the stars."

Grandmother lowered her blade, and gathered my face, pressing the flat of her brow against mine. She held for a moment, then lifted away to collect the bowl of ink and stardust and raised it between us like an offering.

"Great Spirit who roams the mountains and shadows with claws and fangs of stone, lend Sinadine your primal strength, and wisdom. Fierce warrior and friend, walk with her in solitude, roar with her in triumph, and guard her back as you move forth through this world as one." Dipping two fingers into the bowl, she dragged them in bold lines across my face, marking me from brow to chin giving me my True Face. Each of us would have one. The face we would wear into battle.

The last face our enemies would see when we struck them down.

Tilting my head to the right, she grabbed a fistful at my temple and sliced at hanks of black hair. When the bulk of length was cleared away, she smeared an oily paste and, in careful strokes, the sharp blade rasped against the curve of my scalp, shaving the left side of my head clean from temple to nape.

A mark of womanhood and the highest honor.

"Remove your clothes, Sina, and lay down on your stomach," she commanded when finished.

Unfastening the belt of my kubari, I shrugged it off and swayed. My head was weightless on my shoulders, my eyelids heavy as I stretched out on the woven mat at her feet. She sank onto her knees at my side and stroked her hands over my bare skin, her fingertips soft but sure as they traced where the lines of my mark would go, from the back of my thighs and up to the freshly shorn side of my head.

My lids drifted shut, lulled by those delicate touches, and stayed closed long before I felt the first hammer of the needle piercing my skin.

Hours blurred and shifted around me like waves of smoke funneling within the shrine, the steady beat of finger drums, and the crooning voices of the handmaids' hushed singing to punctuate the needle driving into my skin. Little pinches that eventually dulled as I drifted from my body.

Floating in a naked, empty space where there was nothing but a vast blackness and my mother's face.

Square jaw and a warrior's nose—blunt at the bridge from when she broke it on an enemy's skull. Dark eyes strong, fierce and proud. A single red tear rolling down her left cheek, leaving a jagged trail in its wake, following the path of the scarred letters of *disavowed* slicing from brow to chin . . .

*Be the sword that cleaves this world in two. Be the winter before the spring—ruthless.*

*Cleansing.*

*Save us all.*

I shouted for her, but my voice was gone. I reached for her but grasped only air, and when I stared down at my hands, they were small with the stubby fingers of a child.

"Sina." Grandmother's comforting sweet citrus scent wafted around me. "Prepare yourself. This will hurt."

Her hand gripped my shoulders and a flash of heat lashed across my back. Spread. A cry barked from my throat, but I smothered it and bit my arm, seizing against the furious bright burn.

A slow-moving agony like tiny teeth made of fire sinking into my skin, over and over across my body, from the base of my spine to the left side of my skull.

Tears blistered my eyes and I let them fall, unashamed as the pain snatched me from that dark chasm with the floating face of my mother—back into the shrine, surrounded by the handmaids, the matrons and my sisters.

I turned towards the sound of Rhys' weeping. Matron Lucera knelt over her strained body, anchoring Rhys down as white fire flashed across her back, sparking and burning the ink like lit gunpowder into her skin.

Reaching across, I found her hand and held on tight. She turned her face to me, glossy eyes rimmed in red. More sparks, more flashes of light burst around me, more whimpered cries rang out, but I didn't look away.

"Almost there," I whispered, and she nodded, bracing through the worst of it as the white fire slithered across the side of her shaved head. The singing and gentle finger drums continued, weaving a spell around us that I refused to break until Lucera leaned over Rhys' and blew the remaining white fire out.

Smoke shimmered in its wake, rising from her like steam, as it did mine. A cooling salve was applied to our marks that kissed away the heat and Rhys sighed in relief, her grip eased, the corner of her bottom lip bloody from where she'd bit down.

We held steady as a wet cloth wiped away the salve and my skin prickled, but the pain was otherwise gone, quickly fading into a forgotten ache.

"Rise," Grandmother commanded.

Together we did, Rhys' hand still linked with mine, as a dawn of faded purple and blue with gold shone beyond the eyes of the shrine. The matrons formed a line before us with my grandmother at their center and exhaustion weighed on each of them, but so did pride.

A glow almost as dazzling as the rising sun.

"You stand as sisters and have made your vows." My grandmother's smile carried in her voice. "From this day, until your last breath, you are now Swordsworn daughters of the Acharrā. May you live with honor and die with dignity."

# CHAPTER THREE

## Navarre

EACH BREATH WAS A STRUGGLE, a war unto itself, and Navarre de-Nersu blinked back tears, helpless to do anything but watch as his father waged a losing battle.

The last he'd ever fight. After two long years, the emperor was going to die, and no amount of prayer to the One God could save him.

Head hung, Navarre pressed a closed fist to his lips. The caps of bone screamed against the polished marble floors from hours of kneeling at his bedside throughout the night, but these lingering moments of agony were few and precious.

Lights flickered in the gilded sconces on either side of the canopy bed and a priest stood nearby reading from the Great Book while his valet swung a brass ball of burning cloves to purify the soul, and mask the stink of watery bowels.

"The dying must not hear us weep," the physician murmured, a slender man with wisps of hair forking from his chin. "It pulls the soul away from the arms of our Lord and savior. Be still." He set a heavy hand on Navarre's hunched shoulder. "The emperor's suffering is almost over."

One-God, he hoped so.

Injured two years ago, the emperor returned to the Imperial City to convalesce at the urging of his personal physicians, but once at home, he'd taken to bed and never rose from it again. And there he stubbornly lingered for months, clinging to life like withered ivy to stone. Fighting a sickness that ate him through until the chiseled warrior that was his father was nothing but a fish bone picked clean.

The emperor's bedclothes swam too big on his wasted body. Glossy black hair, leached of color, hung limp around the bones of his face in a flat shade of pewter, his skin sallow and so thin that the veins, bulging beneath, shone purple with infection.

Milky puss congealed around the fringe of lashes and even though he hadn't opened them in almost six months, Navarre saw their color every morning when he faced the bronze mirror hung aside the emperor's bed. The silver Torren eyes.

The eyes of the Pale Wolf.

No one could deny the resemblance between them. He was his father's son, even if he was bastardborn. And as much as it pained him, Navarre had prayed for death to come and take him swiftly—if only to end this cruel, prolonged suffering.

"Father," he said, careful to keep his voice hushed so he was barely heard above the priest's nasal reading of the Death Rites.

While it was common knowledge that he was Edvard's bastard, he'd never dared say the word aloud in anyone's presence before. And certainly not to his father directly, but this would be the last time—the only time—to say the words he'd carried inside his chest, tucked close to his heart all these years.

"May the One God keep you in his grace and mercy, may your soul live in the eternal light of heaven. There, I pray you find peace and absolution, and know that I love you, father. I carry no blame, no anger or bitterness, and I will serve the throne dutifully and protect Ehrick with my life. No harm will come to him, and your legacy will not die, so long as I draw breath. I swear this on the love I bear you."

Taking his father's limp, sweaty hand in his, Navarre kissed the golden signet ring as the doors to the bedchamber burst open and Ehrick strode in, a cloth mask pressed to his nose and mouth.

He leaned heavily on the arm of his crutch, iron braces wrapped around his thin, misshapen legs, anchoring him from ankle to hip to provide the support he needed to walk. Each step rattled loudly, like the crash of falling rocks echoing through a canyon.

Ehrick stopped by the edge of the bed.

"How is he?" he asked, lifting the mask only long enough to speak. Fanning vapors of mint oil and something medicinal rubbed into the cloth to clear the soggy mucus in his lungs.

A persistent condition from birth that worsened with the blanketing cold of encroaching winter. But under strict orders, Ehrick also wore the mask when in their father's bedchamber, lest whatever terrible plight that seized the emperor take the last trueborn Torren with him.

"Weak." Navarre's knees whined and popped as he stood, pain flashing up his legs and into his lower back. "Have you come to say goodbye?"

"No." Ehrick stared down at their father's prostrate form. Studying him. "The physicians tell me his bowels are coming so fast and frequent now that there is almost as much blood as there is shit." Hand flexing at his side, he tapped impatient fingers against his slender thigh. "It's a wonder he still breathes."

Navarre sighed. "You should not speak ill of your father."

Ehrick lifted the mask just enough to sneer at his brother. "You know as well as anyone that's a title he hasn't earned and a weight he could never carry."

Navarre couldn't blame his brother for his hatred. Though he'd never been unkind, Emperor Edvard had centered his attention on his other seven hale and hearty sons while Ehrick lay abed, malformed and plagued with a chest cough that often left him struggling to breathe. An affliction that brought crippling pain, and stumped the physicians throughout his youth.

Yet against whatever odds, Ehrick defied their dire prognosis and lived while his elder brothers all perished across the span of a decade until only he remained, at last earning their father's attention. But years of neglect had hardened Ehrick's heart to the man.

"Sire!" Chancellor Prothero hurried to Ehrick, interrupting them. The shaved palette of his perfectly round head gleamed like a fresh pearl with features sucked to the center of his face—all beady eyes and plump, puckered lips. He bowed deeply, flourishing his hands with a twirl. "Pardon my intrusion, my lord, but I must speak with you at once. The privy council received an urgent missive this morning from the vanguard—"

"It is barely noon and already you chase me down to prattle about rebellions and wars." Ehrick flicked cold eyes across the bed to the chancellor before nodding over his shoulder to Navarre. "With me, brother. Our day begins."

The weight of sadness in Navarre's heart was more than he could carry or conceal as he followed close behind Ehrick's lurching uneven steps to the antechamber where the emperor met with his Privy Council to discuss matters of state and war.

A large marble map of the Bridian Empire spread across the far wall of the Tujianese continent and the smaller Sahson Isles where the Bridian's first hailed. A tiny seafaring nation that amassed a naval army large enough to conquer a third of the known world to form the sovereign empire.

"I know the timing is unfortunate." Prothero shifted in silk slippers. "But recent reports are of great concern."

Navarre faced the map, listening absently as Prothero veered on. The blood of his ancestors was seeped into sand and sea, spreading across generations of conquest. All to honor a dream of unity—one nation, one people, and one God.

His father had believed in that dream and waged a war to expand east into Zavora, a large continent rich in gold and diamonds of every color, as well as black oil—the fuel behind the greatest Bridian innovations. But what was supposed to bring prosperity to the empire proved both expensive and difficult, as one year stretched into seven. Costing the empire money, men and stripping the countryside of provisions. Riots bloomed across the continent, breeding discourse as the people that had been promised wealth and prosperity were instead pushed to the brink of financial ruin.

Now, much like the emperor, the war was fizzling out into an old man's death rattle—and the throne had nothing to show for it aside from piling debt.

"I tried to warn him this would happen." Frustrated, Ehrick bounced the end of his crutch to the marble floor in three punctuated beats. "We have no hope of recovering ground, yet we can't retreat—not without losing face. If we did, how long until the Galgoans invaded our shores? The Croy?"

"Send me," Navarre turned away from the map of the nearly liberated world. This was it. The moment he'd been waiting for, though inopportune. As a bastardborn, there was not much he could hope for, save the chance to continue his father's legacy, and if he succeeded perhaps the emperor would look down on him from the heavens and smile at the son he'd never acknowledged in life yet could be proud of in death.

"Ehrick, you know I can do this." Approaching his brother with hopeful energy, Navarre sank to a bruised knee. "Let me go to the vanguard and broker an agreement for peace with the Zavorian officials. I've shadowed Sir Jon and Sir Manderly for three years, entreated with more than one emissary and ambassador, on your behalf while you toured with Uncle Henry during his campaigns. General Reese even said himself I'd make a fine captain one day."

"*Captain*?" Ehrick wheezed through a chuckle. "No. I have another task for you, brother. One you're better suited for," he added before Navarre could give voice to his hurt. "You were saying, Chancellor?"

"Zavorian armies are closing in, and General Voss has requested we withdraw our forces from the continent by week's end. Therefore, I would like to propose requesting all viable ships return in all haste with our senior officers and siege weaponry."

"What about the militia?"

"We need our galleons—what remains of them—to guard our coast. The treasury cannot afford the expense of building more ships or the fodder required to bring them home." He sighed, fingers pinching the bridge of his nose. "Crown coffers are bled thin; we must not allow it to exsanguinate further."

"We can't abandon our men after *seven* years of loyal fighting," Navarre's voice hardened around the edges, like mud baked dry in the sun.

Prothero bristled. "Nor do I wish to," he said with genuine regret, despite clearly affronted at being challenged by Navarre. "But you can't get blood from a stone. The denizens have been taxed into the ground, already. Anymore and I fear the rioting will only escalate." Prothero pushed back his shoulders, hands tucked into the wide, emerald sleeves of his silk Chancellor robes. "We should give notice that the men have a month to seek their own passage, and those who fail to return will have their assets redistributed to the empire. Perhaps that way we can recoup—"

"Sell the crown jewels." Ehrick interrupted, so calmly, so quietly, even Navarre doubted his own ears until Prothro stuttered in disbelief.

"Sire?"

"The Omari and Myzantis collection." He winked at Navarre. "Always found them a bit gaudy."

Navarre's mouth tumbled open. That was at least a third of what was stored in the palace vault; two of the empire's most prized and valuable collections, coveted half the world over for their exquisite craftsmanship. To part with one was unthinkable, but both?

Prothero paled a shade of sickly green. "Sire . . ."

"You're right. Not enough." Ehrick tapped his chin in exaggerated thought. "Let's add the hunting lodge and the summer castle in Cristaine, too. Both are worth several million in gold florin. That should more than do it."

"Sire," Prothero swiped a palm across his sweating brow. "I would caution against liquidating crown assets. It sends a message that—"

"That we care more about our people than plumage. You said it yourself I can't tax my denizens anymore without killing them—and why should I? As their emperling, my position demands sacrifice. See it done, Chancellor. I won't ask a second time."

Prothero worried his hands but swallowed his argument. "As you command, Sire, so shall it be done."

"Good." Ehrick slumped down in a seat and his eyes flickered shut for a moment in relief. Long legs stretched before him, the left one twitched, as it often did when the pain was at its peak.

Navarre's jaw set into a grim line. *He's pushing too hard.*

Reaching into the inner pocket of his vest, Ehrick removed a leather case containing an array of custom steel picks, files, and ivory handled screwdrivers. Ehrick always had a fascination with mechanics. Tearing them apart to learn how they worked only to put them back together better than they were before.

Bedridden for most of their childhood, with little else to do to occupy his mind and hands, he'd devoted endless hours to studying the principles of engineering under the tutelage of the best the Bridian Empire had to offer, creating masterful works, including his leg splints which allowed him to walk after years of never standing on his own two feet.

Hiking his left leg onto the table with a heavy clang, Ehrick opened the kit, plucked out a narrow screwdriver and set to work, tightening and tweaking. "How are the preparations for the escort?"

"Excellent, sire. The men are assembled and will be ready to leave within the hour."

"Is this really the best time?" Navarre braced the table with concern. The emperor and six of his seven legitimate sons had dropped like flies into early graves—claimed by disease, war and tragedy. A line of collapsing dominos, with Ehrick teetering precariously at the end as the last naturalborn son of the Torren dynasty.

If he fell . . .

Navarre shook the terrible thought aside. *No.* Ehrick had great plans to restore the empire by healing the strife of poverty and suffering wrought after seven hard years of war, and Navarre would give his life—his soul—to protect his brother and see his dreams become reality. Whatever the cost. Whatever the risk.

"Brother, I don't think you're in any condition to travel to the mountains."

"I won't be." Ehrick grinned, returning the screwdriver to the kit and tucked it away in his vest.

"Whatever the reason, conscription or coronation, the emperor has always gone to collect the Swordsworn. It's a matter of respect and custom. At the very least a *legitimate* member of your household should be in attendance. Perhaps the Lady Daneysa could—?"

"Send my cousin Iereni."

Prothero paled. "Lady Iereni is far too . . . too . . ."

"Crippled?" Ehrick snorted with derision.

"Sire, I meant no offense, I—"

"She's young, eager for adventure—and my *heir*." Ehrick released a reedy laugh, wet with phlegm. "If anything, I'm more worried you won't be able to wrestle her back home."

"Brother, I'm afraid I must agree with the Chancellor on this. It's a long journey and the woodlands near the Acharrān Mountains aren't exactly safe," Navarre commented, much as he loathed to agree with the chancellor, his stomach turned at the thought of Iereni coming to harm.

"Then it's a good thing you'll be there to protect her, Second Commander."

Navarre jolted. "Me?"

"Am I not always telling you to reach higher, brother?" Ehrick winked.

"*Him?*" Prothero sputtered like he'd sucked back a grape and was choking on it. His eyes fell to Navarre and shone with incredulous disgust. "Why was I not apprised of this decision?"

"You are being apprised *now*." Ehrick waved his hand and a servant, waiting patiently in the far corner of the room, rushed forward and presented a dossier to Navarre. "Here are your patents, seal of office, rank and title. All approved and finalized this morning. I'd stand and knight you myself but . . ." He tapped his left leg where the twitching had worsened.

*Second Commander.* Aside from the rank of First, there was no greater honor. Navarre accepted the patents with shaking hands.

Prothero shuffled closer. "General Maine was already named a forerunner to replace Sir Kevin by the Privy Council last quarter."

"Well, now you can tell him the position has been filled."

"You're denying a seasoned man who served your father—the empire—loyally for many, *many* years."

"General Maine lost the prized city of Aquila, which is the reason my father is dying in the next room. Don't speak to me of what he deserves." Ehrick slammed a warning fist against the table, eyes bright with stoked fury. "He's lucky I don't deny him his head along with this promotion." Beyond the antechamber doors the emperor's breathing sharpened, like rusted steel against rough stone.

Hard. Grating. Difficult.

"Navarre is an accomplished member of the Imperial Guard." Ehrick straightened his spine, the intention of his words bolstering each notch of his vertebrae until he sat as nobly as any emperor. "He has my trust, and I will not be questioned in this matter."

Prothero's cheeks flushed with splotches of red, stark against his pale skin. "Of course, sire. I humbly bend to your will in this regard." He stooped into a stately bow, sweeping out his hands for effect.

Navarre tried not to smile. After a lifetime of everyone speaking over and stepping around his brother, the lastborn son they'd written off for dead and yet somehow managed to live, Ehrick was no longer a child they could ignore. He was the sole surviving heir to the throne, and Navarre—his bastard brother—would stand at this side as Second Commander to the Imperial Guard.

Did wonders never cease?

"You have a lot of work to do, Chancellor, and I've had enough counsel for one morning. But before you go,"

Ehrick added, a coldness creeping into his voice, "I want you to apologize for your impertinence."

"Sire, I—"

"Not to me. To Navarre." Ehrick battled from his seat, leaning hard on his cane to take weight off his left leg as he hobbled forwards. "You've always treated him like filth scraped off your boot, and I won't stand for that kind of treatment. Not anymore. He is my *brother*, a Torren if not by name then by blood, and from now on he will be respected as such."

Prothero paled, his eyes gleaming with incredulous shock. "I am the *Chief* Chancellor of the Privy Council. Your father, the emperor, would *never* dare to demand such a thing."

"I am not my father." Taking hold of Prothero's sleeve, he rubbed the silk between his fingers. "Green happens to suit you, but that could change at a whim. Don't test me."

Prothero puffed his cheeks, weighing his future, before he exhaled then turned towards Navarre. "My lord, please accept my most humble and sincere apologies for any offense I might have caused with my careless tongue. I am also your most humble and unworthy servant," he said, then bowed deeply with such genteel grace for a moment Navarre was stricken incapable of speech.

No one had ever bowed to him before.

"There. That wasn't so difficult, was it?" Ehrick waved him away. "Leave us."

Prothero deepened his bow with another flourish of his wrists, before leaving the chamber as demanded.

Once alone, Ehrick pressed the mask over his mouth and slumped back into the chair with a reedy groan.

Navarre sank into one next to him, concern draped over his shoulders like a heavy cloak. "Was shaming the chancellor like that necessary?"

"More than you know," Ehrick rasped from behind the mask, and took two long, deep breaths before lifting it away. "We have been scorned in the shadows for too long, you think it commonplace, but we are not the bastard and lastborn anymore, brother, we are the future of this empire. If he can so openly disrespect you—as newly appointed Second Commander, then what can I expect from them when I am crowned? No, they must fear us *both*. A wise lesson imparted upon me by our uncle. He'll be back in time for the viewing to lend his voice to the council."

Navarre tensed. Archviceroy Henry Torren was a brutal man. Once he'd held the mantle of First Commander himself, but now as a prince of the church he'd led campaigns across the Tujianese continent, stripping it of its archaic faith and burning heathens to ash in the name of the One God.

Ehrick had always worshiped Henry, who, unlike their father, had always doted on Ehrick and last summer, brought him on one of his campaigns. Ehrick had left bright-eyed and determined, and returned *changed*.

The thought of leaving his brother alone with the man, even if only for a few days, rankled.

"Perhaps it would be prudent to wait for the Archviceroy's return? As your uncle and an accomplished military man, he would make for a suitable alternative for yourself and Iereni." More importantly, it would prevent Henry from slithering into Ehrick's ear like a parasite in Navarre's absence.

"No. The sooner the escort leaves we can get to more important matters. Like my coronation."

"But—"

"Oh, stop with the frown and smile, brother." Ehrick clapped his hands around Navarre's neck and hugged him close. "This is what we've always dreamed of. This is our moment. Together, we will rise from beneath the shadows of great men to rise over them as legends. Together, we will deliver this world into a golden age!"

Navarre's heart leapt in chest, one half too bright, too big for his body and the other sore with grief. God in heaven, if only his mother were alive to see this. And his father—would the emperor be proud of him for reaching so high, or would he look down his nose the way Prothero and the other members of court had all his life?

"You honor me far more than I deserve. I won't fail you, brother."

Beyond them, a single breath rent the air in a swelling beat that stretched like a life cord drawn taut in the hands of Death before it was sliced into silence. The emperor's chest sank, a mountain collapsing under its own weight.

And did not rise again.

# CHAPTER FOUR

## Sinadine

MY FINGERS BRUSHED THE EDGES of the tattoo curving along the side of my head. The healing crackle of scabs flaked away over the passing weeks to reveal the bold metallic blue lines of my mark of a fierce she-cat prowling across my back. Still tender as an old bruise, I'd studied what I could see of it in the polished silver-glass mirror that hung my new rooms in the pagoda.

I had earned my sword along with the privileges and luxuries that came with it. My bed was made from stained xhixi wood and a thick feather mattress in a room with wide windows with lead frames and bubbled glass obscured the view for privacy but still allowed clean grey light to pass. Heat radiated through the walls and floors, rising from the pipes funneling water from hot springs beneath the ground. A blessing in the long winter. The mountains were cold and ruthless as they were beautiful.

Only the strong could survive them.

Outside, the courtyard hummed with activity as the hopefuls trained under the instruction of Padma de-Innesa. She called out drills and my fingers itched to hold my sword.

Last month Tabaa answered a call near the Gulf of Bones, and returned with wondrous tales, and such gifts of tribute. The finest silk kubaris, black lion furs, trinkets of gold and jewels in every color. Ivory combs and gorgeous battle axes with handles of dragon bone.

The year before, Alejandra served the conquered-king of Salorca whose daughter had been captured by rogue bandits. When she'd returned the girl to her father, along with the heads of the men who'd held her for ransom, the conquered-king sent Alejandra home with a hundred prized Tehke horses. Gorgeous blue-eyed creatures with stunning coats of rose gold. I hungered for such tribute, most of which would be shared or sold to feed and clothe the clan. But the glory—the glory would be mine alone.

The next wave of hopefuls bowed as I passed, pausing in their chores, eyes averted in respect, but of them Taphne, caught my gaze. A daring act, and I met her twinkling gaze and tipped my chin the barest notch. Bravery, in all its forms, was to be admired. And acknowledged.

A shoulder rammed into me, knocking me back against a post, and the tender mark on my skin barked in pain.

"Watch where you're going, *Dakuwan*." Rashni gripped the hilt of her sword, facing me like an enemy instead of a sister. It shouldn't have hurt, but it did.

Heat flashed beneath my skin. She'd earned her sword three years ago and had taken considerable delight in tormenting me not long after with scathing whispers and spitting at my feet when I walked past. But things were different now.

I wasn't a child. Not anymore.

"You dare cut your eyes at me?"

I rolled my shoulders. Squared them. "You're the one who needs to learn how to pay attention."

She cocked her head then stepped into my path. "Apologize for the insult before you dare to walk away from me."

My hand flexed. So tight knuckles whined. "Get out of my way."

"Or what?" She shoved me again. Harder.

"Careful," I warned with a low growl. "I am Swordsworn, now."

"I don't care," she sneered. "Even if you're Avanthi's bloodkin, you'll never be one of us and you don't belong here. Just like your moth—"

My fist cut her off cold, snapping her head back in a clean uppercut. She staggered, and before the daze could clear from her eyes, I pounced. Pinned beneath me in the mud, blood roaring in my ears as I pummeled her with furious fists. Knuckles smashing into her face until teeth loosened and came free.

Another final punch, and I slammed them into the back of her throat.

"Swallow," I snarled. Hand fastened over her mouth, I pinched her nose. Her eyes bulged as she thrashed beneath me, bloody bubbles seeping between my fingers, but I held on until I felt the bob of her throat a second before I was hauled off.

"What is going on here?" Iona demanded, her locks of black hair twisted into roped strands away from her dark brown face.

Strung between Anush and Padma, I shrugged as Rashni staggered to her feet, blood and spit trailing from between her swollen and cut lips.

"Nothing," I said, shrugging off the arms that held me. "We're done."

Iona narrowed her wide-set eyes. And looking around, it was more of the same.

Distrust.

Suspicion.

I'd done everything I could to earn the respect of my clan. I was fiercest in training; I won the challenges and matches, again and again, proving my mettle. I'd been deemed worthy by the First-of-Us to call myself a daughter of the Acharrā, and still they gave me a wide berth and wary glares. Especially the eldest members of my clan who remembered my mother best and the night of her disavowment.

Until I returned with the blood of enemies on my blade and the wealth of tribute at my back, they would always see me as Dakuwan. A child, shunned by the stars, destined for death and destruction.

"The matrons want a word with you." Iona stepped forward. "Keep your tongue behind your teeth and follow me."

"Damnable dead." I rolled my eyes. What could she possibly want from me? There was only one way to find out, but being summoned like a child still rankled.

She led the way to the pagodas. Three of them stood proud as the mountains themselves, each spiraling level lined with red lacquered pillars, routed archways and white xhixi walls. Interlocking cedar brackets capped in bronze supported the roofline, shingled in grey tiles that rippled like lapping waves along the bank of the icelake, shielding the terrace balconies from the elements.

Grumbling, my boots clomped as I trailed behind Iona up the spiraling staircase winding all the way up to the summit. Despite recent innovations of electricity and lifts, here, we kept to the old, with only minor modern enhancements. We were forged by the elements every bit as much as our training.

From the mountains and wind, the ice and snow, to the wildness of the feral woods hedging our gates.

Iona rapped a fist against a door, beautifully engraved, and set with turquoise, coral and brass. It whisked open and Iona inclined her head in deference to Matron Liu Fe, skin weathered and age-blotched, with small round eyes set in a wide face accented by a cleft chin. Her hair, so black it was almost blue, was thick and beautiful where the rest of her was as battle-worn as her armor.

She stepped back, allowing us both the grace of entry.

The matrons were all gathered, dressed in indigo dyed kubaris of leather and fur embellished with fine needlework and colorful beads bearing bold patterns that told the story of their great deeds. Grandmother was the furthest to the left, and my aunt sat at the center.

Elide raised her eyes to mine, and in them I saw their usual contempt and mild hatred but joined by something else. Something . . . gentler that almost stopped me in my tracks. I could never recall a time before when my aunt had looked upon me with anything close to tenderness.

In a clan of found women, it was rare to have bloodkin, but that hadn't stopped her from despising me all my life.

My grandmother was the last of a proud line that traced all the way back to the First-of-Us. My mother and aunt, both born from her womb, carried that honor, as did I. Elide was nearly past her bearing years, and I knew it would fall to me to continue the legacy. My insides roiled at the thought of a child growing in my belly, of pushing that life out between my legs and having it latched onto my breasts like a pond leech.

Motherhood was a calling that didn't speak to me, but I respected and embraced my duty, even if the mere thought of it made my breakfast rise into the back of my throat.

Grandmother took in my disheveled, mud-splattered appearance. Arched a brow. "You've been brawling. Again."

"Yes," I answered, unrepentant as blood slid down my fingers, from where Rashni's teeth had torn into a knuckle, and patted softly against the hardwood floors.

"I found her with Rashni de-Gaza." Iona crossed her arms. Muscle flexed, leather groaned. "Sinadine had her on her back."

All eyes shifted to me. "You'd dare to strike one of your sisters in anger?" Her voice remained in its usual graceful tenor, never raised or harsh, even when cross.

A week ago I'd have been dragged to the pit. A dank hole in the cold ground reserved for the most disgraceful of affronts—like striking a sister, even if provoked. It was possible I still would be. She'd tossed me in there several times before for the smallest of infractions, and as always, I accepted my punishment without protest, emerging starved, and freezing, but unbroken.

"Why?" Matron Liu stroked the wisps of hair on her chin.

Sour grief twisted inside me as I repeated Rashni's hateful words. My grandmother's expression remained inscrutable, but when our eyes met, for the briefest moment I thought I saw a glimmer of pride.

"You have been tested and deemed worthy by the First-of-Us," she said. "Rashni should have known better than to challenge their will."

A collective murmur of agreement wove around the room and my bones softened in relief.

"You may leave us, Iona."

Iona bowed, stiff as the rest of her movements always were, and stalked out the door.

"Sinadine," Elide her voice, its usual graceful tenor, never raised or harsh, spoke with the authority of wind moving through the mountains. "Take a knee."

Confused, I sank to the wooden floorboards, and they groaned as I tucked my feet beneath me. Rising from her pallet of cushions, Elide circled the arc of seated matrons and I lowered my gaze. In this position, it was demanded. The beaded hem of her kubari rippled into view, azure, gold and red edged in black mink that also capped the neckline and sleeves.

"Our swords are not weapons; they are shields. Our code is not death, it is the preservation of life." Her hand settled over the crown of my head. "Rise, Sinadine de-Arashi. Wear it with pride and wield it with honor."

Mouth dry, I struggled onto heavy feet attached to bendy legs as Elide held out the length of a sheathed sword. My fingers closed around the hilt of woven navy silk braided over the stingray skin and wrapped over the bronze beneath and joined the white gold guard. Real. Smooth.

*My* sword.

The blade slid free of the black lacquered scabbard, engraved in scalloped detailing inlaid with opal and moonstone, revealing a few inches of gleaming steel that shone almost blue in the grey morning light. Acharrān words were carved into the blade.

*Sisters before self.*

Bright, overwhelming joy squeezed my heart until it screamed between my lungs—sharp with the sting of tears. *Mine.* But this was wrong. This wasn't how it was supposed to be done.

A sword was to be presented before the clan, not hidden away like a shameful secret, though perhaps to my aunt it was. She'd never wanted me to have a blade or the respect that came with it, and I'd done everything I could to defy her wishes.

Returning the sword to its scabbard, I gripped it tight in my hands. "Why are you giving this to me now?"

"Because we're out of time." Elide tucked her hands into the wide draping sleeves of her kubari, the leather supple and soft as velvet. "A missive was sent from the Imperial City," she said in no particular hurry. "The emperor is dead, and the escort is enroute to collect their Swordsworn. They will reach our gates by morning; I've chosen you to be offered in service. The rest may decide for themselves."

No. Terror surged within me, sharp and alarming as the pierce of steel to the heart. No. No. No! To offer myself in service would make me a slave to the empire, and I would not . . . *could not* allow that to happen.

"You can't *choose* for me," I scoffed, shaking the ring of disbelief from my ears like water.

"This is not up for negotiation or debate. You will go, Sina, either willingly or by force."

"How do you propose to *make* me?" And with that bitter challenge, any softness I'd gleaned in my aunt earlier now vanished into the kindling of her waking temper.

"You carry your own blade now, and as a Swordsworn daughter of this clan the protection afforded to you by your mother's disavowment is *gone*." She raised a proud chin. "Therefore, you will do as I command, or I will banish you."

My gaze whipped to the arced row of matrons seated on the cushions silently behind her, without a single ounce of outrage to be hand among them, no one moved to intervene.

Not even my grandmother.

"You'd give me my sword, and then threaten to take it away in the same breath?"

"If needs be."

The bitterness of hurt swam in my blood like venom as I set my jaw, teeth cracking under the strain and lanced my aunt with a piercing glare. The kind of look that would've sent me to the pit for a month if she wasn't already scheming for something far worse.

"I know you hold no love for me, but I've done *nothing* to deserve this."

"Leave us." Wordlessly the matrons acquiesced to Elide's gentle command.

Filing from the room without sparing me a single glance or expression of remorse.

"It's not a question of *deserving*," she said once we were alone. "The treaty demands three lives for the sake of our homes, our children, and our way of life. This is a terrible price, a difficult one, but you've always been fearless. I'm asking you to bravely step forward and set a good example for the others. *Sisters before self*," she said, nodding towards my blade. "Prove to me you are truly a daughter of the Acharrā. Prove to me that you are one of us."

"You knew he was dying," I whispered. "That's why you let me ascend."

Elide remained silent, but the answer was plain enough in the set of her shoulders. I released a scoffing breath as I crossed to the window and braced the sill.

It all became so clear.

Elide never acted without reason, and while I'd wondered as to her motives for finally allowing me to earn my place, after denying me twice before, I hadn't given it much thought beyond her hoping I'd fail in the attempt.

Or die trying.

But here was the truth spread before me like an open field of grass. She didn't want me dead. She wanted me *gone*. Upon succession of a new emperor, those offered were restricted to the newly anointed and in my lust for glory I'd blindly let her play me into a corner. In ten years, I was in line to claim her mantle and with me at the helm, there was only one future I wished for my clan.

Freedom.

To finish what my mother had started. Which made me a threat to all that she'd built here.

"If three don't willingly offer themselves tomorrow the treaty will crumble to ash." Elide settled at my side. "It would be a death sentence for us all."

"Only if we lost," I answered. "Every daughter is worth a hundred imperial soldiers. Let them taste our steel, and they'll fall to our blades before the sun fell from the sky."

Disappointment drew her brows into a hard line. "Oh yes, blood would be spilled, Acharrān and imperial soldiers alike, but the carnage wouldn't end there. It never does. Which is why war is not our way."

"It should be," I answered. Jaw grim. "If slavery or banishment are my only options I'd rather fight and take as many of the *Yatsūan* with me before I die."

"You'd fight very bravely, and die very foolishly, as would any who followed you, but what of those who live should we lose this righteous war?" She wrenched me through the sliding doors to the terrace. "Look to your sisters, Sinadine. Look at them! Look at the children." Her fingers winched at the back of my skull, driving my head towards the glass windowpane overlooking the training arena below where girls sparred with wooden practice swords in the courtyard.

Taphne among them.

"Would you see them pick up swords and follow you into battle? Would you see them robbed of mothers and sisters? Thrust beyond our walls to be sold as fodder for brothels?" She released me with a sound of disgust. "Swordsworn are not assassins and cutthroats. We are guardians and protectors. *Not* aggressors"

"We were meant to serve the people, not an empire that crushes them beneath their boots, leaving blood and shattered bones in their wake," I countered, smothering any hesitation her words had stoked inside me, and turned from the window. Our gaze level. Women ran tall in our family. "We are Acharrān," I said, reminding her of my mother's words.

Anger dimmed from Elide's eyes. A fire gone cold with grief. Regret. "I'd hoped I was wrong about you, but I see my fears were well-founded. I did what I could to raise you to see the error of her ways, and yet you persist to . . ."

she faltered, then swiped a hand between us, scrubbing her words from the air. "You are your mother's daughter, it seems. Wild. And soulless as the night you were born. Like her, you would burn this world to ash and ruin, and us along with you. I won't stand for it. I won't let you."

Pain.

The exquisite burn of it wedged between my lungs like a cobressa, winding around my heart before piercing it with her fangs, pumping me full of venom.

A toxin beneath my skin that bubbled and blistered black.

"Spare me your righteous lectures on the sanctity of life," I spat. "As the last descendant, if you send me away the bloodline to First-of-Us will be severed." And with that threat, I dealt a lethal blow.

Our lineage was too precious to end out of spite and petty grievances, and while I loathed the responsibility of motherhood, compared to the alternative it would be a blessing.

"You won't be the last of us." Sunlight caught in the stones woven in the gold and leather bands, as Elide settled a hand to the flat of her belly. "Not anymore."

My eyes tracked that movement. *Pregnant*. A shattering realization that sucked all hope from inside of me.

"The empire or exile, the choice is yours," Elide continued. "But one way or another, I will be rid of you."

"And that's all you've ever cared about. To be rid of me. As our matron, our leader, you'd rather spill the innocent blood of your kin than that of our enemy—to stand by and do nothing as we're taken as slaves rather than fight to protect what is ours from an empire that rises higher around us, stacking bodies into towering walls that blot out the sun. The stars. Soon we will be forgotten as all we know, and love fades into dust. And it'll be all *your* fault."

I closed in and had the pleasure of seeing the whites of her eyes flash as my words found the chink in her armor, slipping between the bones of her ribs.

"Fear not the darkness in my soul," I said, twisting the blade, "but the weakness in yours."

# CHAPTER FIVE

## Sinadine

DREAMS OF GLORY SHATTERED EASILY as glass and those brittle shards crumbled into a fine, acrid powder that coated my lungs with each, heaving breath as I jogged along the frozen woodland path around the dense cluster of trees, the bark damp and covered in silver moss—the herald of winter.

Too anxious and unsettled to sit still, I'd returned to my rooms enraged, wanting to smash my fist into the walls, to break wood and shatter bone.

I wanted to kill.

To burn off my rage I went for a run, weaving through woodland trails until I reached the watchtower of the aviary. Rhys waved her bow and I eased into a steady walk. My lungs seared and legs shook from exertion as I approached, hands on my hips and gathered my breath as cold wind kissed the heat of sweat and temper from my skin.

The aviary was a large, four-story tower at the top of a foothill surrounded by trees, and housed our hunting birds. Falcons, eagles, owls and osprey, and also received birds sent to us with messages. Most of the empire sent couriers on horseback, or carrier pigeons and ravens, but this close to the mountains only predatory birds made it to us alive.

The woodland was vast, and feral. Home to snow eagles, wolverines big as pack mules, and ice-foxes cunning enough to challenge them.

Few ventured this way unless left with little choice.

I loped up the staircase and met Rhys at the top, her silver-white hair twisted into plaits and tied away from her fine-boned face.

*Tōzai*, the children called her. *Ghost*. Few of our clan were so pale of hair and skin. Her complexion was the colorless hue shared among *Yatsūan*—the Bridian colonizers who struck out from their small dying island to conquer distant homelands they had no right to claim.

"You look like you're in a mood," Rhys said by way of greeting. "What brings you out here?"

"Needed air." I crossed to the balustrade, overlooking the rippling blanket of evergreens capped in white and silver that wound around the base of the blue-grey mountains.

Rhys settled next to me, arms crossed, her gaze pinned to the hilt rising over my shoulder. Her own sword was sheathed at her hip, her scabbard etched with silver lines like rain falling in the night, and a braid of leather dangled from the hilt with a small bronze coin at the end with a square hole notched in the center. The others would've received their blades by now as well. And a fresh burst of anger snapped through me like a bolt of lightning in a blackened sky.

Rhys removed the eyeglass from its holster and extended it with a flick of her wrist as a falcon swooped in an circled above us.

"Not a feral bird," she said. "This one is trained and circling."

"Messenger?"

"I'd say so." Lowering the glass, Rhys lifted the whistle to her lips and blew gently. The sound was too high for our ears, but the bird answered and swooped lower. "Get the bucket. He looks hungry."

Crossing to the aviary door, I wrenched it open and ducked inside. Birds rustled their feathers and a chorus of cries rippled throughout the domed structure. Inside the tower was hollow with dozens of nesting alcoves and narrow walkways slicing across with ladders that ran up and down every few feet.

We owned several snow eagles, the largest of our hunting birds, nearly two dozen silver and red tail hawks, and even more Nimerian falcons—black with a teal sheen to their feathers. They flew higher than any other hunting bird, too high to be clipped down by archers on the ground.

Opening the storage cabinet, I lifted out a covered bucket and mice scratched at the walls of their prison. Removing the cover, I peered inside at the wriggling, little white bodies with blinking red eyes, and plucked out two of the fattest ones by the tail. They screamed and struggled as I handed them over to Rhys to reward the animal for its service.

Putting on the leather gauntlet, she coaxed the falcon onto her forearm and offered him the first mouse. He snatched it by the head with his powerful grey beak and gathered the body in one taloned foot, wings fanning around it as it gorged.

As he tore into the helpless critter, Rhys unfastened the scroll from his ankle and snapped the seal. "It's from Himeco."

I rolled my eyes. "Someone snatching livestock again?"

Ignoring my remark, her eyes raced across the tightly woven text. "Magistrate Tanza is dead and his wife, Uje Oharu, has assumed his mantle, but Dozo Len is challenging her."

A Dozo was a Tujian noble by birth, whereas an Uje was a noble by marriage. It was uncommon for a woman to hold the mantle of Magistrate, so I wasn't surprised to hear a man was seeking to remove her from the table before her husband's corpse was burned.

"She's afraid for her life and worries he will use his influence to have her assassinated so he can claim her seat and obtain complete control over Himeco. She asks for an Acharrān to guard her back for a year until her son can return from his post in the thirty-eighth legion of the Imperial forces."

*A call.* My stomach churned with furious upset at the thought of someone answering the summons and claiming the glory to follow. Rhys whistled, flagging a scout before casting the scroll down the brass shoot to the sentry below and hand delivered to Elide.

"Something's bothering you," Rhys said as the scout raced out of sight, carrying my dreams with her. "Wanna talk about it?"

I snorted. "What good would that do?"

"Unburden yourself. Holding it in serves nothing but to cloud your judgement." Handing the falcon a fresh mouse, Rhys eased the bird onto a stand to fly off and return to its owner once it finished its meal.

I slid my gaze to hers, and unlike anyone else she didn't glance away. I could glare at her unblinking for an hour, let the mask drop and show her my darkest truth and she would never flinch away. She saw me as I was and asked for no apology or explanation.

I don't know what I'd done to deserve such friendship, or loyalty, but at this moment, I was grateful for it.

"The emperor is dead." I bounced a fist against the balustrade, the wood rough and weathered, and as I swiped my palm across the grain I could feel the prickle of splinters aching to lodge into my skin. "The Imperial escort arrives tomorrow and Elide has demanded I offer myself. If I don't, I will be disavowed."

*Like my mother.* And I could not let that happen.

Rhys scoffed a laugh, then quickly sobered. "Damnable dead, you're serious. Are you gonna do it?"

"What other choice is there?" Rhys nodded towards the falcon, head tucked in its wing, and it took far longer than it should have before I grasped her meaning. "You want *me* to answer it?"

She shrugged. "Why not?"

"Because the lead matron must read the call to an assembly of our clan for a volunteer; all she has to do is sit on it until after I'm gone."

"Then don't wait. Just go. You've got your sword, Sina. What's to stop you?"

"If I go to Himeco my aunt will know you helped me." And the thought of Rhys caned then tossed in the pit for circumventing Elide's plans was more than I could bear. She was the only friend I'd ever had, and here she was ready to risk everything for me.

"Rhys . . ."

"Once, a long time ago, you saved my life. Let me do the same."

It felt like a lifetime ago since that distant winter when she'd snuck out with a pair of skates made from varnished bone to the icelake. But it broke from beneath her and she disappeared into a wet hole of liquid black.

Without thinking I dove into the slate water. Into a world of cold and found Rhys floating in that endless dark—ghost-white like she was made of moon dust.

"Think about it, and whatever you decide, I'm with you." Rhys tapped a fist twice to her chest. "Strength and honor."

*

Minutes bled into hours and still I remained too restless to go back and face my clan—my aunt. Following a tight and treacherous path from the aviary, I wove along the side of the mountain. Little more than a goat trail. Only a fool would come this way, but I'd traversed it many times over my youth, and knew it intimately, even in the dark, until I reached the cavernous mouth of rock at the summit.

Before me the Victorious Women roared triumphantly into the night—dozens of noble faces hewn into the mountainside, a monument etched over the centuries to honor the Acharrān warriors of our greatest legends.

This was one of my favorite places to come whenever I needed to quiet my mind, but standing before them in all their triumph, my anger brewed ever brighter knowing that as a slave to the empire I'd never join them. Without stories of valiant deeds or grand tales of glory, I would be lost to chains.

My dreams stripped away like flesh from bones.

Facing them now—our glorious dead—I screamed. Venting my fury to stone and stars until my voice cracked and my throat bled. Slumped on my knees, the sound of my rage fractured and split into the night.

A ringing, violent echo carried with a sharp gust of cold wind that pulled at my braids, rattling the golden cuffs and stone beads. The strain of thin air and restless anger pounded in my skull.

I'd fled to the mountains hoping to find peace, but each breath brought the inevitable closer to my fate and come the dawn I would be trussed up like a pig for a banquet and led to slaughter.

If I went back at all . . .

My eyes skimmed across the rippling peaks to the faded horizon. Rhys was right. How easy would it be to flee north to Himeco?

Less than three days on foot I could be well out of reach before sunup and once I crossed their city gates, my aunt would have no choice but to accept someone else stepping forward in my absence.

Sourness churned in my stomach at the thought of running away from home like a whipped dog under the cover of twilight. Elide would be furious, but after three years, maybe four, the escort long gone with some other poor soul chained in service to the throne, I'd return with wagons of tribute—the greatest gifts the Acharrā would ever see.

And when the time came for my aunt to step down, I'd lead my sisters into glorious battle as my mother had always hoped. Like the Unnamed Queen before me.

I'd save my clan. I'd save us all.

The clatter of falling rocks and sliding stones jerked me to my feet, the sound quickly followed by a sharp cry. Not an animal—a child's voice—calling my name. I rounded the tight corner and rushed to where cries rose over the narrow edge of the path.

Taphne gripped the rock face with thin, white-knuckled fingers. Dropping to my belly, I shot down an arm, but her fingers were just out of reach. "Taphne." Terror gripped my heart with brutal claws, gouging deep. "I need you to reach for me."

"I can't," she wailed.

Beyond the sway of her scrabbling legs, the shattered remains of her crutch lay at the end of a hundred-foot drop on the jagged rocks below. And the image of her body joining it kicked my stomach into my throat.

"Yes, you can. Find your feet and push up."

Terror shone stark in her eyes. "I'm slipping. *Sina*—!"

"Look at me. Nowhere else," I commanded as a stone loosened and clattered down the rock face, almost dragging her with it. "Find your feet, Taphne. You can do this."

Her teeth sank into her bottom lip, and I could hear the scraping of her shoes, scrabbling for purchase. With a grunt of effort, her body shuddered as she levered up in halting increments, her gaze fixed unblinking on mine as I urged her to keep going, to reach me. Her hand shot out and I snatched hold of her by the wrist.

Planting my feet, I drove with my legs and hauled her slight weight up and onto the path. Together we toppled back, her body huddled against mine and trembling with shock, arms cinched around my waist like iron bands.

"Are you alright?" I demanded scooting us further away from the precarious edge.

She whimpered as I sat her on a boulder and scanned her over. The moon gave enough light to examine her twisted legs, scrapped and bloody, but her left ankle was the worst of it. Rapidly swelling inside her boot, it would be thick as a winter squash soon and there was no way she'd manage the hike down the mountain alone.

Spirits of my Sisters, it was a miracle she'd managed her way up it at all.

Furious—my heart still pounding fierce and fast as a wind drum—I seized her shoulders with a deft shake. "What were you thinking? Coming after me was suicide."

"You were running away, and abandoning us! Bringing dishonor to your sword," she said, accusation hot on her tongue. "You didn't even say goodbye."

Releasing her, I brushed a steadying hand over my face. "I wasn't running, Taphne."

"Don't lie." She swiped an angry hand over her eyes, mopping up the glimmer of tears. That was one of the things I admired most about her. Tears came easily to Taphne but she never used them as a weapon or an excuse. "Deserting your sisters is the coward's path!" She thrust out her chin, but it wobbled.

Understanding settled through me and calmed the frantic pulse of my adrenaline.

Taphne had been in the courtyard during the altercation. It stood to reason she'd more than heard what had been said before I laid Rashni on her back, compounded by the sight of me blazing from the pagoda, all fury and despair and knowing how serious an offense it is for sisters to fight each other—Taphne had put far more together than I'd have given her credit for.

"You had no business following me." I snarled. Annoyed by her interference.

"I didn't follow you."

"Then how did you know where to find me?"

"You always come here when you're sad." She dipped her head, gaze flittering off to the horizon. "But you have to come back with me, Sina. Rashni is wrong about you, they all are, but if you run away from your problems then you'll only prove them right. We can't run from the things that make us sad or angry or scared. We have to face them. Because we are Acharrān." She returned her gaze to me. Chin proud. "We do not break."

Surprised gripped me like a hand to the throat, trapping words and breath as something unfamiliar and warm passed through my blood.

Everyone else pushed me away, save Rhys, my grandmother, and now this stubborn and brave little girl. Moved by the glimmer of fierce determination in her eyes, and the soft hint of despair in her voice, I sighed deeply.

Predawn light sparkled in the distance, calling to me like a beacon of freedom, but if I left Taphne alone she was as good as dead. The stonecats and ice-foxes likely heard her cries—tempting as a baby lamb—and scented easy prey.

"You won't get far on that ankle. Come on." I offered her my back and waited until her arms and twisted legs hooked around me. Hesitant at first, but they locked tighter as I rose to stand.

"Must you carry me the whole way?" she whispered, and I knew she was mostly worried about the others seeing her in a position of dependency.

"Yes. But if you're quiet, I'll have you in your hammock before anyone wakes."

"What about my ankle?"

"Say you wrenched it during your evening drills and woke to it troubling you."

". . . and my crutch?"

"I'll find you a new one."

She hummed pensively, and then set her cheek against my shoulder, her warm breath washing along the exposed length of my neck. I set off quickly, picking my way down the rough path wasn't easy, but I managed fairly well.

A line of light broke along the snow-capped mountain tops as we slunk through the Small Gate. Slipping inside the communal hut, my steps masked by hundreds of heavy snores, Taphne slid off my sore back and settled into her hammock, dragging thick blankets around her body. Her ankle now a shade of purple so livid it was a wonder she hadn't sobbed the entire way.

"Wait until I'm out of sight, then call for one of the handmaids." I stroked a hand over her sweating brow and she nodded, her eyes glassy with discomfort but bright with a determination not to fail me.

I pressed my brow to hers—a gesture of respect between sisters—then slithered away as the first of the sleeping girls stirred.

Outside the communal hut, I braced against the cedar wall in the waking shadows until I heard Taphne's voice cry out. But even that painful sound was barbed with a kind of defiant strength, and my lips twisted into a grin as I scurried away, keeping low to avoid the sightlines of the sentries on the walls.

Bounding up the stairs, I thrust open my bedroom door and lurched to a dead stop on the threshold, breath caught in my throat, as my grandmother turned from the windows, hands clasped together and her handsome face bearing a stoic smile of secrets.

"Ah, right on time." She crossed to me, wearing a heavy black fur cloak. Her hair set in twists and woven with silver cuff beads that raced from crown to tips, both sides of her head were shaved into a fresh fade. Unfastening the torc around her neck, made from black gold, the weight of her cloak slid into a puddle at her feet. "Hang that up," she gestured to it, "and join me for tea."

I stood there, a bit dazed, as she lowered to the cushions near the enclosed terrace where a tray sat waiting with an azure pot, matching cups, and a plate piled with fried bread slathered in butter and honey.

Drained from a long night of hauling myself up and down a mountain, I tossed the length of fur onto my untouched bed with a snarl.

"I said *hang that up*, and then come sit down, Sinadine, before the tea gets cold." Her searing tone lashed like a reed across my backside. The kind of tone the matrons mastered in their greying years and brought even my stubborn self to heel.

Gathering the cloak, with more respect this time, I brought it to the rack by the doorway where my own cloaks, shawls and outdoor leathers hung, and tucked hers among them.

Joining her at the mat, I lowered to my knees. Hands on my thighs, my fingers drummed a restless beat as she lifted the lid from the glazed pot, cracked with veins of gold.

The scent of morning jasmine and mandarin rose in a sweet, perfumed cloud as she stirred the steeping leaves and gauged its readiness before pouring the hot tea into bowl cups. Long and slow, her every movement was graceful and elegant with the poetry of focus. Discipline.

Virtues I lacked anywhere else but in combat.

"You look tired," she said gently. "Did you not sleep well?"

I arched a brow at her pointed, knowing smirk. Given my filthy, exhausted state, it wasn't hard to puzzle that I'd been out all night.

"I slept fine. Like a lamb." Plucking up my tea, I rolled the vessel between my numb hands; it burned like fire, but I welcomed the searing heat and the pain it brought. Pain to purge my grief, to remind me I was still alive. And so long as I lived I would fight until my last breath.

"I know you're troubled by Elide's request."

Hooking my tongue along the edge of my teeth, I sucked hard. Apparently Grandmother was in a mood to serve more than tea.

"What gave you that impression?" I flinched when she pinned me with a glare, sharp enough to cut the legs out of my temper. Exasperated, I put down my cup. "Why does she hate me?"

"You're asking the wrong question. Why not ask the wind why it shifts from a simple breeze into a howling hurricane? Or the river why it swells after heavy winter rains? Why is not important so much as *what*. What has been asked of you, Sina?"

"She wants me gone. She's always wanted me gone. Just like my mother."

"Yes." Grandmother raised her cup and sipped carefully.

"Doesn't it *bother* you that your eldest daughter disavowed herself to keep me alive?"

Her eyes flashed to mine without a flicker of emotion. "Berséba made her choice. Trading her place and the respect of her position to allow you the protection of life—you cannot blame your aunt for honoring that, or for demanding this sacrifice of you. You have a chance to become an empress."

"Just a fancier word for slave."

"Is there a greater honor or gift you could give your clan than this?" she set down her tea, so firmly porcelain rattled. *"Sisters before Self."*

Galled, I turned to her, head shaking as she rose to stand before me. "I can't believe you actually want me to do this. To hand myself over to our enemies, to be silent and—?"

"Never be silent, Sina, *never*." She gripped my shoulders with strong fingers and spoke with a gentle whisper. "Be loud, wild and daring, be angry and vocal, but never, ever be silent unless silence is required to slit your enemy's throat."

Stilled by the gentle ferocity of her words, I could only blink in surprise. "What are you saying?"

"I'm saying time has come to reclaim what was once ours. The Acharrāns ruled for a thousand years, and now we have been slaves for almost as long. This marks the tipping point in that balance—and I will not see this overshadow our past legacy as free women." She moved from me to stand before the window, her proud frame silhouette in gilded morning light.

So vivid she glowed as if set aflame.

"The Torren line is at its most fragile. So close to dying out, as are we. The people don't call for us as they once did. Our ways will die and us with it if we don't *act*."

My mind spun with the spark of fresh understanding. There once were many clans, scattered across the motherlands. Now, we were all that was left.

Less than five hundred Swordsworn in a clan of barely two thousand women. We were fading—like the heart of the star—once a fierce fire burned low to embers in snow. But embers, if carefully tended, could rise again.

And burn brighter than before.

"Remember when you were a girl, all those games we used to play?"

A frown ripped across my face, like a scab torn away before it had a chance to heal. "I wouldn't call them *games*."

I was almost five, a sullen thing that never spoke, shunned by most of the clan, when my grandmother had returned from a call. She'd taken one look at me, smiled, and decided to train me by her own hand at all hours of the day and night.

Brutal lessons to pit my mind against the elements. Puzzles and riddles that would lead to my death if I failed to unravel them in time. How to find the weakness in my opponent, to read truth between lies, and to twist either to my advantage.

Things that skirted the boundaries of the Acharrān code, and the principles we stood for.

"Survival and strategy, dear girl. That is what I taught you. Survival and strategy," she said. "To be smarter than your opponent, and far more cunning, for this exact moment. *This.* You are not the first to be called to task, but by the Spirits of our Sisters—you could be the last."

Turning from the window, Grandmother's eyes gleamed like ancient obsidian of the warrior guarding our gates as she gathered my face in gentle hands, but that gentleness belied their strength.

I had seen them shape steel into swords, and use those swords in an elegant, masterful dance of body and blade.

"They banished us to our mountains, like goats herded by wolves," she whispered, "but we will show them we are stonecats with fangs, and claws, and a taste for blood. Our time will come. By your hand a millennium of suffering—of bondage and shame will end. With a stroke of your sword, you will restore peace to your clan and honor to Berséba's name."

Determination flashed through me like fire tempering steel. "When?"

"Soon." Her smile deepened and something inside of me purred and sharpened its claws. "The emperling is weak and sickly—outlive him. *Survive* him, whatever it takes. And when he is most vulnerable, kill him. Then you will be an empress with the power of an empire at her feet."

I snorted. "They'd execute me for treason within a day."

"They will try, but I pity the man who raises a sword to you." A wicked gleam brightened my grandmother's face, and she tipped my chin with a crook of her finger. "You are a leader, Sina, you always have been. So when the time is right—*lead*—and we will follow."

# CHAPTER SIX

# Navarre

The powerful xhixi wood doors of Home Gate shone in the filmy light of the late afternoon sun, their exterior inlaid with bronze, ivory and turquoise, surrounding the carved forward positioned face of a woman screaming into battle. Daring anyone to challenge her might and steel. Her eyes made from fierce orbs of polished obsidian—rounded and smooth as mirror glass—pierced Navarre straight to his soul.

Majestic and terrifying.

His mother had described this place often, and in each rendition, he'd heard her longing for home, for the sisters she'd never see again. Not in her lifetime.

He remembered the first cough and all the ones to follow. How they grew longer, stretching and blending together so there was almost no time to breathe in-between their onslaught. How the sound changed from dry to wet, bringing up gobs of murky phlegm and blood.

*Cancer of the lungs*, the physicians had said. *She's beyond hope.*

A helpless boy of ten, Navarre had stayed by her side, night after long night, and held her hand until it went limp.

The gates opened and as his caravan rolled through every instinct inside him wanted to turn around and flee. He'd come, hoping a missing piece of himself would magically slot into place—something warm and familiar, but all he saw was the desolate grey mountains, the cold blue sky, and the hardened faces of powerful women.

Even the children passing through the courtyard had a warrior's look to them; proud and fierce, though not quite yet stripped of their innocence and laughter.

Iereni bounced in her saddle at his side, exuberant with glee.

"Contain yourself," he said with a smile as he dismounted.

"I can't. It's *amazing*," she sighed as he lifted her down, her thick braid of auburn hair swinging over her shoulder like a wagging puppy's tail. "Must we leave straight away?"

Navarre cocked his eyes to the skyline where bitter grey clouds brewed black on the horizon. Getting caught in a storm in the mountains might see them stranded for days, if not weeks, and Navarre refused to be away from Ehrick's side for longer than necessary.

"Yes." He bounced a finger off her protruding bottom lip that slid down in a pout. "And that's not going to change my mind."

"You're no fun anymore," she teased as he set her down in her wheelchair, quickly assembled by one of the men. A sleek and efficient design made by Ehrick's own hand, the most recent of a dozen models he'd created for her over the last five years.

"We have company." Benj thrust his chin capped in a wiry black beard over Navarre's shoulder.

He turned as eight women approached dressed in deepest indigo robes. Some were comely and others weathered as tree bark, but all were commanding to behold.

"I am Elide de-Brakken, lead matron." A woman stepped forward, her hands linked gracefully.

Both sides of her head were shaved away to bare skin, and she wore the woven bands of leadership made from leather and gold on her brow with bits of polished blue stone.

"This is my mother, Avanthi de-Mazad." She gestured to an older woman at her left with white hair and eyes as dark as the screaming warrior on the gates. "Welcome to our home."

"Navarre. Second Commander of the Imperial Guard." He thumped a fist to his chest. "We are honored to be here."

Elide's eyes skimmed across his men and settled on him last. "The emperling is not with you."

"Emperling Ehrick sends his sincerest apologies and his cousin, Lady Iereni Seford, heir to the throne, in his stead."

The matrons looked to Iereni and, though nervous, she kept her shoulders straight, her chin steady and smile pleasant.

"We are pleased to receive you," Elide said. "Tea has been prepared in the lounge and—"

"I'm afraid we'll have to skip formalities," Navarre interrupted. "The weather is turning for the worst, and we must be on our way quickly."

In part that was true, but a larger part of him wanted to be gone from this place of shadows and ghosts where every pass of the wind echoed with his mother's gasping breath.

An undercurrent of tension rippled among the matrons. Each wore two swords. One that was earned, the other given, and Navarre prayed they wouldn't draw either of them now.

Because if they did—armor be damned—he and his men would be dead before they found the voice to beg.

Or scream.

"Of course." Elide inclined her head. "I'll gather the assembly and we'll begin at once."

# CHAPTER SEVEN

## Sinadine

THE WELCOMING HORN BLASTED FROM the high towers—three hundred feet tall. My grandmother had taken me up there once when I was a child, in the dead of night and brought me right to the precarious edge. Bare toes wiggling in the open air, the woodlands and towering evergreens stretched beneath me like blades of black grass, and I stood above it all, a giant, unafraid as the wind tugged around me, almost begging me to step forward and plummet.

The wild thrill of near death was exhilarating, so bright, I'd faced it all and laughed.

I could face this.

Twenty men entered through our gates, ruthlessly built, and encased in armor of leather and steel, so thick and heavy I wondered how they managed to breathe, let alone wield the two-handed broadswords strapped to their backs. Half a dozen steel wagons rolled through behind them, each loaded with gifts to the matrons.

Kings and Queens had considered it a great honor to come to our gates and pay tribute for our protection, and though tradition had been continued in enslavement, this wasn't an act of respect.

It was an exchange of goods.

We were chattel. Worse, perhaps, because we'd *chosen* this for ourselves.

Sickness settled in my gut. There was no brightness inside me, or the thrill of facing death and laughing. There was only the calm certainty of duty.

My grandmother had entrusted me with a vital task, and I would not fail her, or my sisters. I would kill the emperling, return with his blood on my blade and call them into battle—to face down what remained of the empire and drive the colonizers into the sea from whence they came.

I would free our motherland and restore peace and honor to us all.

I wove down from the pagoda, the staircase thick with bodies descending to join the matrons and our imperial enemies in the courtyard. Catching sight of me, Rhys pushed her way through the slow-moving crowd until she reached my side.

"I thought you would be on route to Himeco by now." She arched a confused brow.

"Sisters before self," I scoffed bitterly.

With a deep breath, her hand closed over my shoulder. Squeezed. "Strength and honor."

"Strength and honor," I echoed.

In the center of the courtyard, the bronze fire-pit roared with flames. A light dusting of powdered snow had fallen in the night, and as the wind stirred in the basin of the mountains, the snow wound around us in flicking waves like white snakes.

The newest of the Swordsworn sank to our knees before the matrons and the rest of our clan watched with heavy hearts.

It was hard to imagine that not long ago we'd all gathered here in celebration, but the arrival of the escort and the weight of knowing what was to happen settled like dense winter clouds across the sky, enrobing us in a muted veil of deepest grey.

Grandmother stood with the matrons, twin swords belted at their hips, all of them elegant and powerfully dressed for the occasion in leather kubaris and heavy fur cloaks. My aunt most of all. A varnished stonecat skull sat like a crown upon her head, its empty sockets mounted with sapphires and the elongated fangs, hooked on either side of her face, were painted in black gold that gleamed like obsidian in the watery light.

We might be conquered, but we were still warriors.

Defiant anger rose in my throat, acrid and bitter, and my fingers ached to unsheathe my sword—to cut them down. Even their armor couldn't withstand Acharrān steel. I'd slice through them like a sharpened xhixi spear through ice, and was confident I'd fell half their number before I drew my final breath.

It would be a short battle, but fierce and bloody and glorious. The ache of temptation scored along my palm, and a distant, defiant voice dared me to make the wish a reality. The leader of the escort approached the matrons, and I tracked him from the corner of my eyes as he bowed before my aunt.

"On behalf of Emperling Ehrick, please accept this humble offering as a token of his gratitude in hopes that we will share in another thousand years of peace between Acharrān and the Empire."

Samples of what they'd brought were stacked by his feet. Bolts of silk in bold, dark colors of aubergine, navy and scarlet, casks of wine and brandy, bags of basmati rice, dates and pistachios, and lastly a small chest filled with gold florin.

Pleased, my aunt raised her hands, palms flashing before us, commanding our attention. "Three must surrender themselves to serve the empire with a willing heart, as is the way," she spoke, her proud chin set high. "The first will bear the honor of future Empress. Those who would stand for us, please do so now."

Silence whispered across stone and snow. I stayed on my knees with the rest of my sisters, and as I gazed out at them, I knew my grandmother was right. They were afraid.

Hesitant.

We'd been raised and trained to follow command, but not to lead. Someone would have to take the first step for the others to fall into line.

It was up to me.

Rising was hard, approaching my aunt—harder still. She unsheathed the oathblade and offered it to the leader of the escort. He removed his polished helm, revealing a young face. Barely twenty, once the scruff was shaved off his chin, with wicked black hair, a poet's mouth and silver eyes, grey as smoked glass right before it shattered. But despite his youth, his hands were thick with calluses, and he moved with a warrior's grace.

"I, Sinadine de-Arashi, stand for my sisters," I said proudly, letting my voice carry for all to hear. "By blood of my blood, I vow to honor the treaty of our ancestors, and offer myself as the first."

Accepting the blade, I sliced my left palm on the sharp bronze edge, spilling drops of blood at their feet. Elide's eyes gleamed with a smug satisfaction that almost made me regret my decision, but the deed was done.

Rhys stood next and a stab of grief lanced low in my belly as she swore her vow and scattered her blood over the paving stones to join mine.

*No*, I wanted to shout at her. *Stay where you are, don't follow me.* My future was set while hers didn't have to be, but whatever my feelings on the matter, Rhys had a right to decide for herself. I couldn't interfere.

No one could.

Two of us stood and bled, and among those on their knees, Cahira and Amparo struggled to decide between them. The sun to the other's moon, they'd never been parted, but to my surprise, it was Jasz who marched forward, her expression determined as she gave her bloodoath, and joined us as the third.

Grandmother poured out cups of sorrel and offered the first to the young man, along with a plate of thinly sliced deer heart, hunted and killed by her own hand. Flakes of smoked salt speckled the grilled meat. We each ate a slice and washed it down with the sweet, spiced rum.

"Sisters, for your sacrifice, we honor you." The matrons bowed at the waist, the only time they would ever bow to anyone, and the entirety of our clan sank to their knees. Brows pressed to the ground in gratitude and respect. When they rose again, the beat of their fists to their hearts pulsed around us like a sorrowful drum.

We would leave here with nothing but our swords and these parting mementos, whatever they may be.

We belonged to the empire now.

Grandmother's handmaid carried a chest, and he held it steady as she touched the ornately carved xhixi wood box, lacquered in red, black, gold and blue, and whispered a soft prayer before giving the nod for him to set it at my feet.

Taking my hands, she kissed the backs, and then squeezed them. "Open it when you've reached the palace. And remember us. *Remember*, Sina." Her lips were featherlight at my temple, the barest trace of skin and warmth as her brow settled against mine.

Love clutched in my chest, seized my heart, and sent its steady beat to scatter like fallen beads. Tiny little orbs of clay and glass, I could be on my knees for a month, and it would be impossible to gather them all. Lost pieces of me left behind with my home.

My sisters.

I didn't want her to pull away, because once she did, the ceremony would be over, and I restrained the urge to latch on to her. A childish impulse that twined my sorrow with anger. Only the strong could call themselves Swordsworn.

Only the brave.

There was no place for weakness among these women, and I would not dishonor them with petulant tears.

The score on my palm ached like a bad tooth, a pulse that matched the fierce rhythm of my heart as my eyes dragged over the moving bodies of my clan. Some swept forward to greet us, offering words of thanks and respect—even tribute—but nowhere among them did I see one, stern little face shining bright with determination.

*You didn't even say goodbye . . .*

I stopped the first child to cross my path. "Where is Taphne?"

The girl blinked up at me and tucked strands of brown hair that had escaped the mess of her braid behind her stuck-out ears. "She's in bed. Idiot twisted her ankle while going to the latrines *alone*. Handmaid Manu instructed her to stay off her feet 'til the swelling's gone."

Of course. Her ankle had been a mess when we'd returned and I thought of her glassy eyes and sweaty brow, how she'd bravely swallowed every single grunt of pain without complaint.

"What is your name?"

"Ro."

I removed a bracelet from my wrist, made from hammered silver, the beaten surface carved with lines that formed intricate knots across the band. It wasn't particularly beautiful or delicate, but my grandmother gave it to me the morning after she'd rode through Home Gate, and I'd worn it ever since.

"Give this to Taphne," I said, holding it between us. My blood smeared across the tarnished silver. "Tell her it belonged to my bloodkin as far back as the First-of-Us. It's too precious to take to the Imperial Palace, and I want her to keep it safe for me."

Ro's face shone with wonder as her thin fingers closed around that circlet of old silver.

Snatching her by the wrist, I arched a brow, stern with warning. "If she doesn't receive this, I'll come back to sort out *why*."

Ro's eyes dropped to the hilt of my sword, and then bowed her head in respect. "Strength and honor." The child scampered off through the crowd, and I tracked her as she raced for the communal hut.

Cool wind folded around my naked wrist, and I tugged my kubari sleeve down, shielding my skin from that echo of emptiness. One more piece of me—gone, but it was worth it as I thought of Taphne in her hammock, tears dry on her cheeks and ankle swollen.

I'd lied about the origins of the bracelet, as had my grandmother when she gave it to me—a truth my aunt had only been too eager to shove in my face when I was older—but the sense of responsibility had given me courage, strength. Maybe it would do the same for her. Even if it was only an ugly bit of silver, it was precious to me, at least.

I hadn't lied about that.

Less than an hour later, the three of us mounted on horseback provided by the Imperial escort. Grandmother remained in the courtyard, long after the other matrons had left, a lone and noble figure—though I knew my aunt would be watching us from the pagoda, smiling at her triumph. I would not give her the pleasure of seeing my frustration, and raised my chin to match the proud line of my grandmother's as I rode away through Home Gate.

Overhead, the slate sky opened in a cascade of wide flaky disks that spun and danced in the air, settling on my cheeks and lashes.

A cold kiss of unshed tears.

# CHAPTER EIGHT

# Navarre

Navarre's thoughts were smoke and ash, obscuring his senses and fogging his sight as the ceremony went by in a haze, his mind too mired in the past—in his mother to take stock of anything.

While the wagons were loaded and prepared, Navarre returned to his mount and removed a wrapped bundle of dark blue velvet bound with thick gold cord, the hilt of his mother's sword jutting from the top.

Returning it to the matrons was a grace not many of the Swordsworn sent to serve the empire were given. The swords were treasured items, and their customs believed that part of the owner's soul remained with her blade and must be returned so that they may rest among their sisters in the afterlife.

It belonged here.

This steel was a gift for a woman's hands alone.

A fact that had frustrated Ehrick when they were boys. He'd demanded their father give him an Acharrān blade, only to be met with disappointment. He'd then commanded Navarre to steal his mothers.

It shamed him now to remember that he had tried, slipping into her room as she slept, sweat running into his eyes. Maybe because he was fascinated by this ancient sword he was never allowed to touch. Maybe because part of him resented her for excluding him from a world he desperately wanted to be a part of, or maybe because he was just a stupid, selfish little boy who couldn't understand that not all things were meant for him.

He'd made it close enough to almost graze the scabbard when his mother sprang from sleep and caught him by the scruff of his neck. She'd demanded to know who'd put him up to it, but Navarre lied and insisted he'd only wanted to see it for himself.

She'd beaten the back of his thighs with the scabbard so hard he'd been unable to sit for a week, but it was the tears in her eyes—the absolute shock and realization of what he had tried to do—that hurt him the most.

Ehrick demanded he try again and when Navarre refused, he'd screamed himself ill and spent nearly a month in his sickbed. A week later his mother's coughing began and when she'd died he'd hid the sword in case Ehrick ever thought to ask him for it.

Mercifully he never did, and now, as he'd promised his mother, he brought what little remained of her soul home so that she would find her rest among the stars.

The other matrons had scattered, only one remained. She watched him approach, wary and wise as an owl, as if she knew the truth of who he was and why he sought her now.

Navarre bowed deeply, folding at the waist in respect. "Matron Avanthi de-Mazad. I stand before you as an Acharrān son here to fulfill his mother's last request."

"Who was your mother, boy?"

"Valan de-Nersu." Navarre bowed his head lower, as he spoke his mother's name.

"I remember her," she said after he straightened.

"She spoke of you often," he said, holding the sword in offering between them. "And asked, should I have the chance, to return her sword to Home Mountain. To you."

Avanthi accepted it gently, her fingers brushing over the weathered black scabbard studded with mother of pearl shaped in cherry blossom petals. Some were broken, a few lost to the years and battle.

His hands felt naked without the weight of the blade, as did his heart. This was the final piece of his mother he'd held onto for half of his life that now slipped through his fingers like a dying breath. And suddenly she was gone.

"Welcome home, sister," Avanthi whispered. Her fingers closed around that hilt and the sleeve of her kubari pulled away, revealing a hint of a tattoo coiling around her left wrist.

*Cherry blossoms.*

Clutching the sword to her chest, emotions swirled in her eyes. Sorrow, regret, but love chief among them.

He wasn't the only one who grieved.

"You honor your blood."

Those words stayed with him long after they'd rode away through the thick winter forest of evergreens and xhixi trees—pale white with leaves red as its blood-colored sap—and entered the vast desert of the Blue Wastes. The sand hardened with ice so the wagon rolled easily, allowing for a quicker pace.

A small mercy.

The sooner they reached the waiting ships docked at Inoken Harbor, the faster he'd be free of his charge. The Blue Wastes was as close as they could pilot them before their equipment scrambled and died. Something in the mountains affected the mechanics.

Walls of dry grass sliced down either side of the desert road, shielding cobressa nests, komodo dens and other desert predators. Grey stalks that swayed and rattled like thin bones with the wind. It was getting worse, and now that they were clear of the woodlands he could see the thickening blanket of clouds overhead.

The storm was going to break soon, and they still had three miles ahead of them.

A horse cantered up to his side, and he recognized its rider as the first girl to offer herself at the ceremony. Sinadine. Her name echoed within him, and Navarre was struck by the full impact of that face he'd only captured a fleeting glance of up to now.

Soft brown skin and eyes like whiskey set on fire flecked with the barest hint of green, a proud chin, and a stubborn mouth to match it, with long, thick black hair in matted twists and braids. Beads were woven throughout with cuffs of gold and bronze. He knew enough of his mother's people to recognize she'd earned every single one through tests and training.

She assessed him coolly. "Your mother was Acharrān." Spoken as a fact and not a question. Her voice stroked up his spine like electricity and velvet, stirring dormant nerves awake.

"She was," he answered, uncomfortable by the scrutiny in her tone. "How'd you know?"

"I saw you return a blade to the matrons before the start of the ceremony. Given your age, I figured you for a son." She returned her eyes to the path before them, and only then did Navarre feel like he could properly breathe.

"You've never come to Home Mountain until now. Why?"

He'd asked himself the same question many times. No one would've stopped him if he'd asked to go, and perhaps that was secretly what he'd feared. That they'd send him on his way and shut the gates to the palace forever.

Up ahead a horse reared, bucking and screaming, almost throwing Iereni from the saddle. Navarre set his heels to his mount with a sharp kick, and loped to her side. Gathering the reins, he struggled to hold the beast steady—its eyes wild with fear and pain.

"What happened?"

"It came from the grass. So fast I couldn't move in time," Iereni wept.

One of the Swordsworn was already on the ground ahead of him, her blade drawn and features severe. "Cobressa," she said.

A long slick scaled body lay at her feet, its severed head the size of a housecat. A hatchling. A full grown one would've dragged the horse into its den, and Iereni with it.

"Sina," she called to the girl—the dark one. "I think the horse has been bitten."

"Let me see." Sinadine dismounted and took hold of the horse's head, whispering words he couldn't understand. The animal calmed considerably, its ears pricking forward instead of lying flat against its head as she stroked a hand down its forelegs, searching for puncture marks.

The line of guards and wagons carried on without them, rolling past the bend in the road behind a high rise of dunes, not caring to stop or look back at what had caused the delay. Navarre set his teeth and tried not to let his annoyance show through. He would've told them to keep moving, as it were. The oxen and wagons were slow and cumbersome, though necessary given the challenging terrain, they needed to reach the ships quickly to break ground to outpace the encroaching storm. But the fact that they had gone on ahead without deferring to him first rankled.

He'd deal with them later.

"The fangs grazed her right pastern." Sinadine straightened. "She'll be lame in a minute. Dead within the hour."

Iereni's shoulders shook with silent tears, and she hugged the horse's neck.

Sinadine stepped forward so Iereni couldn't hear. "Cobressa venom is a bad way to go. Kinder to put the horse down before it spreads."

"You will ride with Rhys." She gestured from Iereni to another of the Swordsworn offered, her pale hair gleaming bone-white as her skin.

"Alright," Iereni agreed when fresh screams rent the air.

Navarre wrenched around in his saddle. "God's mercy, what now?"

Sinadine was already on the move, hand on her hilt and racing towards the dunes. Dismounting, he rushed after her. Near the top they slithered belly down, and peered over the edge.

His men were surrounded in a wide-open flatland of sand. One of the wagons overturned by a panicked ox, they used it to cover their flank, a maneuver that was buying them moments at best. They were up against experienced fighters, at least fifteen, by his count, and more than they could hope to handle.

It was an ambush.

"We need to get back to the horses," he said, voice low. "We're less than three miles from the harbor. We can cut around behind and lose them."

"Run *away*?" Screams rose over the distant clash of steel like smoke in the air. "Your men are down there. Dying."

Navarre's brows lowered in flat, dark lines. "We can't save them."

"Then we *avenge* them."

"We're outmatched."

Her mouth fell open, aghast. Snatching the top of his breastplate, she yanked him forward. "I am Sinadine de-Arashi, the Stone Claw and bloodkin descendant of the First-of-Us. Outmatched?" Her eyes narrowed with disgust as she released him with a shove. "Insult me again, *Otsaidā*, and I'll remove your poisoned tongue with my teeth."

"I have to get Lady Iereni to safety." If anything happened to her under his watch ... "She's the emperling's first cousin—his direct heir until he has children of his own. That makes her life more precious than mine, or any of my men."

"Don't use her as a shield for your cowardice."

"There's no time for this." Frustration blasted through him. "We have moments to act."

"And I intend to make them count." Sinadine rose from the shelter of the dunes, a grinning demon born of shadows, and vaulted onto horseback.

"What's your plan?" he demanded as he returned to the saddle, the other Swordsworn already mounted behind him.

"Strike hard. Kill them all." Fisting the reins, she set her heels hard to flanks and charged to face the enemy with her sword unsheathed and the thunder of hooves beating loud as his heart.

As much as Navarre longed to whisk Iereni to safety, returning without his men was one thing, no one in court would question or lose sleep over the loss of soldiers, but the Swordsworn were important political symbols of conquest, and would not go unnoticed. There were many at court eager to see Ehrick fail and all it would take was the barest hint of weakness to have them swoop in to pick the carcass clean.

Navarre would be damned before he let that happen.

Cursing her name, and for forcing his hand, Navarre withdrew a dagger from his belt and offered it to Iereni. "Take this," he ordered. "Stay in the cover of the grass."

Hands shaking, she clutched the weapon. "What if you don't come back?"

"I will." He met her gaze—steady and assuring. "I promise." Urging his horse into a gallop after the Swordsworn, Navarre didn't waste time counting the dead; he set his sights on the living and charged ahead as Sinadine broke the assassin line.

# CHAPTER NINE

## Sinadine

I WAS EIGHT THE FIRST TIME I took a life.

A Magistrate from Khurdan had brought a man accused of murder to Home Mountain, seeking the wisdom and justice of the matrons, when he'd escaped in the woodlands. I was hunched over one of my rabbit snares, trying to pry the broken neck from the trap, when he'd stumbled across my path. All he saw—when he grabbed hold of me—was a skinny little girl with wild dark hair.

Not the knife I held until it found a new sheath in the center of his throat.

I'd smiled as he died, gurgling by my hand, and acquired the dark taste for killing. Now, as I dragged my sword from its sheath, I hungered to taste it again.

A dagger shot like an arrow, and caught my horse in the chest. The animal slammed to the ground, and I vaulted from the saddle, using the momentum as I dove into a fluid roll, my blade slicing an assassin clean in half before I was back on my feet.

Rhys and I were first to break the line, Jasz close behind. We pushed into the center, forming a row before the surviving men, sweating and exhausted. The assassins had toyed with them to wear them out before sweeping in to slit throats.

"We're outnumbered at least two to one," Jasz observed with a twist of her blade.

A dark grin split my face. "I like those odds."

"Live with honor," Rhys thrust her sword between us.

Jasz and I tapped blades with hers. "Die with dignity," we echoed, and struck with a vicious fury that was met with fluid, precise skill. I gave myself to the violence, and let my sword guide me into a primal dance of blood and bone, my mind void of anything but the gleaming edge of steel as I sliced my enemies through. The assassins fought without fear and died without hesitation as a lethal, impenetrable unit. But for all their skill, they were no match for Acharrān steel.

It was over within minutes.

Those that remained slithered away like shadows over the dunes or into the dense waving grey grass while the dead lay scattered at our feet. A blanket of corpses drenched in blood that shone like spilled ink over dark blue sand.

Navarre settled at my side, his chest rising with heavy breaths—not surprising given the bulk of his armor and heft of his broadsword. "You . . . you fought well."

"I am the *Dakuwan*. I was born for this," I said with a flick of my sword, scattering droplets of blood and gore at my feet. "You fought well, too. For a Bridian soldier."

"I am the Second Commander of the Imperial Guard." Navarre corrected, his shoulders drawing back with impugned authority. "Appointed by Emperling Ehrick, himself."

My eyes narrowed with doubt. "But you're so *young*?"

"I'm almost twenty."

"Still too young to lead seasoned men into battle and expect them to surrender their lives on your orders."

"What about you?" He gestured to Rhys and Jasz, stacking the bodies of the deceased into a tidy pile while his men lagged by the sidelines like useless, lazy swine.

"I don't *lead* them. We fight together, for each other, as sisters not soldiers."

"Is there a difference?"

"Not one that you'd ever understand." Dismissing him, I stooped to examine the body at my feet.

The clothing was dark, but lightweight and mostly made of padded cotton and boiled leather plating which explained why they'd been so quick on their feet, but the style and cut was unlike anything I'd seen outside our grand library.

Raising a sleeve, I cursed beneath my breath.

"Horuēins. Assassins from Tien Nadu," I said, showing Navarre the brand on the left wrist of twin circles emulating an empty gaze, void of sympathy or feeling.

*Hollow Eyes.* Which explained the fearless way they fought. Stripped of their identities as children, they were hammered and beaten until the soul inside of them vanished, leaving only the heart and mind of a killer who obeyed without hesitation.

"*Nadu?*" Navarre scoffed. "That's nearly four thousand miles away. Why would western assassins cross the sea and come this far to the east?"

"They're said to be the best killers in the world." And only the best can be expected to match against us. Horuēins didn't retreat or surrender, so if they slithered away into the dark, it was because they had a greater mission to complete.

Whatever the purpose of this assault, it was only the beginning.

"We should burn the bodies." I wiped my hands clean against my thighs. "But strip them down and dispose of the weapons in a grave. A deep one." Horuēins carried special blades and throwing points, unique to their sect. It wouldn't be hard to identify their origins if found along this desert road, and then gossip would spread like dye in a fast-moving river. "Who knew we were coming this way?" I demanded, facing Navarre.

"No one. I chose this path myself."

"Someone clearly had to." I gestured to the stack of bodies.

"Aside from the emper—"

"Ah, the emperling." I crossed my arms. "I'm guessing his absence was decided last-minute."

The muscle in his jaw clenched. "So what if it was?"

"That's pretty convenient."

Navarre bristled. "Are you accusing the empire of having a hand in this?"

"I don't need to spell out for you what would happen to my clan if he were assassinated on Acharrān lands, do I? Would be the perfect excuse to eliminate the heathen threat and steal what's left that is ours." Our land, rich with xhixi wood, wildlife, and the surrounding mountains full of precious steel—with the treaty gone, they could kill us and claim it all.

"The blade cuts both ways. Your clan also stands to gain from the emperling's death. More, perhaps."

"Only *yatsūan* go about stabbing each other in the back. An Acharrān would look you in the eyes as she ran you through." Hand planted on hips, I held my ground. "When we arrive at the palace, you will say nothing of this to the First Commander. Or the emperling."

Navarre's brows shot to his hairline. "You want me to *lie* to my superiors?"

"Someone is playing a dangerous game and might be closer to the emperling than you think. Until we know who hired the assassins, anyone is suspect, and letting them think they maintain the element of surprise, they'll try again—only this time we'll be ready for them."

Navarre tensed, the instinct to push back warring in his eyes. "I don't appreciate being told what to do, or how to do it," he said after a time. "But you're right. If we do this, we work together. Agreed?" He held out a hand. A tentative offer of truce between us.

One I loathed to accept, but someone either wanted the emperling dead, or my clan, and I intended to find out who. Which meant, for now at least our interests were aligned. "Agreed."

"What're we supposed to say about our fallen?" A guard demanded, removing his helm. "We lost five good men. They had wives. Families who will demand answers. Justice."

Navarre swept a hand through his hair, eyes narrowed in thought. "The woodlands surrounding the Acharrān mountains are dangerous, more so this time of year. I'll tell the First Commander we were set upon by wolverines and suffered unfortunate casualties."

The guard's eyes brightened with horrified rage. "You'd have us disgrace their memories with such lies? And burn our dead with these *heathens*?"

"I am your Second, Benj; you will check your tone and do as I command."

"Like hell I will," Benj spat, and the wooden teeth of his upper dentures capped in steel flashed in the black of his dark beard. "She might've twisted your balls blue, but you can't keep us quiet." The surrounding men echoed his discontent and gathered around him in solidarity.

Before Navarre could put steel into his spine, I stalked up to Benj, and with three sharp moves of elbows and knees, had him down with my sword at his throat in a blurring arc that stopped a kiss away from severing head from body.

"Drop your weapons," I bellowed, voice sharp as the edge of my blade, brooking no challenge, or bluff. I'd kill him as easily as I drew breath, and I'd do it smiling.

Navarre shifted a step but Rhys stopped him with the flat of her blade and offered a warning tilt of her head, echoed by Jasz.

Grudgingly Navarre stepped down. They all did.

Claiming Benj's weapon, I trapped his throat in the lethal vee of steel. "We saved your miserable lives, and honor demands a life debt in return. Instead, I ask only for a vow of silence. Swear it to me now, or I will finish what the assassins started and pile your bodies to burn like kindling among them."

Benj flicked his eyes to Navarre.

"Go ahead. Look to your Second, but you'll be dead before he can try to stop me." A hairline of red bloomed against his skin, and Benj cursed. A tear escaped and cleaved down the left side of his face, quickly chased by another. The bite of Acharrān steel was vicious.

Anyone who had tasted it never forgot its kiss.

"My mother was the fiercest of us. She fought men like you and returned to her clan decorated in their blood, and a vial filled with their tears around her neck. Tears she added to her meals like drops of watery salt. I am my mother's daughter. *Swear*."

"By the grace of—"

"Forget your false god." I set my teeth into a dark grimace. A fierce and unholy thing against the splatter of blood I wore like paint. "Swear on the heads of your fathers, the hearts of your wives, and the lives of your children—all of you swear, and if you break your words know that I'll come for you in recompense."

Each man swore his vow, the wind tearing across them as the storm blew in from the harrowing Norlands. When done, I snatched the lantern dangling from the front of the wagon and smashed it across the stack of bodies and bracken. Oil spilled and caught aflame. Burning brightly in the dark.

"You call yourself 'Second Commander' but you haven't earned your power. Or your status. They'll never follow you if they don't respect you." I shoved the remainder of the broken lantern against Navarre's chest. "So *earn* it."

The storm broke before we reached the banked airships at the harbor, a violent gust of wind and rain. The gale too strong, too fierce to cross the narrow sea, so we set up camp in an escarpment. The horses were tethered to the vehicles, as the Bridian's called them—and a fire built to roast a couple of wild jackrabbits as we waited for the worst of it to pass.

And if it didn't . . . then we had a long trek across the wastes to reach the Imperial City. Four days at least, and from what I could see, we were not provisioned for that kind of journey.

"Here." Navarre thrust an aluminum plate with roasted meat under my nose.

Rhys and Jasz sat out near the fire, and I could hear their distant voices carrying over the scream of wind funneling into the open mouth of the cavern. Navarre sat down across from me and tucked into his own meal, meaty juices running down his fingers as he bit into a gamey thigh.

"The girl." I nodded towards the child who slept in the corner, wrapped in so many furs she was a ball of fluff.

Silver eyes flashed to mine, bright as a wolf in moonlight. "What about her?"

"You love her," I said. It wasn't a question. I'd seen the fear in his eyes for her safety, and after watching him fight it was clear he was not a coward—as I'd accused him—or incapable with a sword. He'd thrown himself before a felled guard, risking his own life to protect the man from a killing stroke. So if it wasn't fear or cowardice behind his earlier decision to leave his men, only love could inspire such stupidity.

There was undeniably duty there as well, but love most of all.

"I do," he admitted, eyes guarded. "You called me *Otsaidā*." Dropping his plate at his side, he linked his fingers, assessing me in the pale wash of firelight. "What does it mean?"

"Someone who doesn't belong." He flashed a smile, bitter as pipe smoke. "That amuses you?"

"It's nothing I haven't heard all my life. You were right when you said my men don't respect me, but it has nothing to do with my age or experience and everything to do with my illegitimacy. Not only am I half Acharrān, I'm bastardborn," he clarified.

"*Yatsūan* are such idiots." I snorted a dry laugh. "All children are legitimate simply because they exist. Why should a babe born of passion be less loved or valued then the one born of duty?" Leaning forward, I set my elbows to my knees. "Yet you call *us* the heathens."

"Finish eating," he said, boosting to his feet. His own meal hardly touched. "I need to arrange lookouts to keep watch during the night. Can't risk losing another mount to a cobressa."

"We can help. We know the terrain better than you or your men."

"And that's exactly why I want you to stay right where I can see you at all times." He left without a backward glance, heavy footsteps stalking down the ramp and into the night.

Despite my annoyance, he was smart not to trust me. I'd agreed to work with him to uncover the persons responsible for the attack, and I would, but not for the reasons he expected. An important lesson my grandmother taught me was to know my enemy, and their enemies, as well.

Time would tell if they would be my friend or foe.

By morning the worst of the rain had passed, but there was still enough wind to send my stomach pitching and reeling along with the hard sway of the ship. A bloated vessel of steel and glass unlike the ones of wood I'd seen in the Norlands. How such things kept afloat was beyond me.

Eyes closed, I sent a prayer to the Spirits of my Sisters we'd live to touch the ground—with our feet—as Jasz vomited into an already half full bucket. Iereni, tucked close at her side, held the strands of her hair away from her face, and crooned softly as Jasz swayed with sickness.

Rhys cursed. "How much longer must we endure this?"

I closed my hand over her white knuckled fist and squeezed. "Why did you do it?"

Rhys opened a bleary eye and winced as Jasz groaned into another wave of sputtering vomit. "Do what?"

I gestured around us, to the guards strapped into seats and snoring loudly, unaffected by the jostling ride.

"You think I could leave you to brave the empire alone?" She gave an incredulous shake of her head. "Never."

"But this is tantamount to slavery."

Her expression softened and her fingers toyed with the coin dangling from a length of braided leather at the end of her hilt. "Do you know how I got this?" she asked.

I nodded. I knew the story well. We all did.

Guida had told the story more than once of the night Rhys' mother had come running in the moonlight to Home Gate, her belly swollen and a mess of blood around her legs. To have made it through the woodlands in her state, few could fathom.

Some saw it as her path had been cleared by the Spirit of our Sisters, and while there were those among the clan who felt she shouldn't have been allowed to pass, the Acharrān code was to welcome any woman who sought shelter and refuge.

She'd faced a difficult labor, and my mother had tended her all the while until Rhys came screaming and strong into the world. Barely a day later men pounded at the gates to retrieve her. She was the daughter of a magistrate, and her father was a trusted advisor to the emperor. She'd shamed him by bedding a man beneath her status and conceived his child in secret.

Her father beheaded her lover while she was dragged before the priests and wed to her betrothed. A brutal general in the Imperial army, who then locked her away in their country estate for months, awaiting the child's birth so he could kill the infant. The same man who'd ventured near a thousand miles to collect his runaway wife, and the child she'd birthed in hiding.

With little choice—unwilling to risk fracturing the treaty for the sake of one woman—the matrons surrendered the mother but not the infant, declaring it died in childbirth and had been burned.

A lie the woman took to her grave as he'd strung her up before our gates and flayed her to the bone. Because she had died so valiantly, the matrons gave her the funeral rites of a true Acharrān.

As for what happened next, few dared speak of, but I'd heard whispers circling a campfire one night that the next morning scouts had returned from a hunt and informed the matrons they'd come across the general and his men, maimed and murdered, with wolverines feasting on what was left.

No one had seen my mother leave or return, but they'd later found her washing blood from beneath her fingernails as she hummed a gentle song with Rhys fast asleep and cradled in a sling against her breast.

I was born less than a day later.

The coin was given in payment and thanks to my mother for her efforts during the difficult birth. And later, before her disavowment, she'd threaded a leather cord through the hole in the center then placed it around Rhys' neck.

She'd worn it every single day, since, and now it graced her sword as a testament of her love for the woman who bore her as well as for the woman who'd brought her mother's soul justice.

"We are bound together, first at your mother's breast and now in blood. We are sisters, Sina, our bond strong and sharp as our blades. Where you go, I will always follow."

"We will not bow," I sighed. And uncurling her fist, she turned her hand around to grip mine, our tender palms fused—scored from the oathblade.

"Strength and honor."

# CHAPTER TEN

## Sinadine

The Imperial City loomed.

A modern marvel, artificial and false, with sunlight that flashed off faceted windows of buildings made of brick and steel. Far less grand in their design compared to the pagodas at Home Mountain, they staggered and spread by the hundreds down paved streets lined with wrought iron posts topped with clear, glass orbs and spinning circular brackets.

The horizon dominated by thin towers stacked atop squat brick buildings that belched ashen smoke, creating sooty clouds that weakened the sun and cast the sky into a somber swath of fouled air.

I pressed a gloved fist to my nose to mask the stench.

"You'll get used to it," Navarre said gently. "The Imperial City was the first to industrialize. More have since followed its example."

"It's a boneyard." Eyes watering, my lungs screamed for air. *Real* air.

Cool, crisp and clean.

"There are no trees here. No soft earth. No grass. Every breath stinks of filth . . ."

I'd known the world had changed beyond our walls, but hearing stories and seeing pictures in printed books had done little to capture or prepare me for the unnatural strangeness of modern innovation. Stripping away the natural character of the Old World for snaking pipes beneath the ground that carried water in and out of the cities, and false light that flicked within glass bulbs strung on wires and cables that slung from one building to another, buzzing like trapped fireflies. Or cobbled roads packed with vehicles rolling on thick rubber wheels, belching ashen smoke as they passed; drivers in the front and their charge lounging comfortably in the back.

In the mountains we honored the land, the animals, and the balance between the two. We lived with integrity and intention, never taking more than we needed and always returning that which we didn't to the earth but here the Bridians had embraced destruction for the sake of industry, excess for the sake of luxury.

*How the First-of-Us must weep at this desecration.*

"You'll get used to it," Navarre repeated.

I didn't want to get used to it. I wanted to rip it all down, brick and stone, with hand and teeth and sword. People scurried by, ambivalent to my rage, men in tailored suits with oversized hats and women in ridiculous gowns that seemed impossible to move in, each paying little mind to our procession through the streets as if we were a caravan of produce instead of sacred warriors from an ancient and respected sect.

My insides snarled at the disrespect.

We were the daughters of the Acharrā—honorable denizens should bow before us as we passed, nobility and commoners alike, on their knees in deference to the might of our swords on which we'd sworn to defend them.

"No one is bowing," Rhys said, as if she read my mind, and shook her head in disbelief. "They act as if we don't exist."

"They have forsaken the old ways." Jasz curled her lip in abhorrent disgust. "They have forsaken *us*."

A rotten tomato splattered against the flank of my mount, tossed by a gaggle of children. Spooked by the assault, my mount stamped at the ground, but I quickly regained control with expertise from years of dedicated training. So that when yet another child raised an arm to toss more rotting fruit, I reached for my hilt in warning and wisely they scampered off, disappearing into the dense crowd that roared with laughter.

"Easy!" Navarre yanked his horse to my side, stopping me from further pursuit. "They're only children."

"They're disrespectful ingrates," I seethed. "We daughters of the Acharrā, and have sworn our swords—our lives—to protect them. We deserve—"

"What?" Navarre interrupted, arching a brow. "Silk banners, flower petals and beating drums? Look around you." He gestured with a nod of his chin. "The empire provides for and protects them now. We have brought modernization and built thriving cities that offer the best in healthcare and education, improving the quality of life for all, regardless of upbringing or status. Why should the people remain beholden to your extinct customs?"

"*We*?" Galled, I shook my head. "You are as shameful as they are."

"Shameful is claiming to be warriors of the people while holding out your hands for gold. Riding into towns and villages to demand quarterly tribute in exchange for the edge of their sword, only to deny those who could not meet that demand." His silver eyes seared to me, blazing in their scrutiny. "What you call noble, others might deem extortion."

If we'd been standing, I might have struck him dead at the impunity of his allegations but beneath my ire I carried my grandmother's words, cautioning me to be silent and still.

So instead, I scored my tongue across the edge of my teeth, temper searing through me so brightly it burned cold as the frost at the summits of my home mountains.

The kind of cold that killed with wicked, vicious ease, but not before it made you beg for the clean mercy of death.

"There was a time, before you Bridian's came to our shores when my clan was near a million strong," I said at last, my voice wavering with the undercurrent of my rage.

"And while our numbers have drastically thinned over the centuries, do you think those mouths were fed on air?" Before he could answer, I yanked my mount to halt, and seized his reins as well, drawing us both a sudden stop. "Tribute is not about decorating our bodies in jewels and silks and finery," I snarled, before he could find the words to protest.

"And it's not about building a horde of treasure for us to preside upon like your noble empire. Our cache ensures the care and wellness of my sisters, not just this generation but those to come. And you dare speak of grand cities as if they were built with your own two hands instead of on the broken backs of the people your forefather's conquered, then judge us for exacting tribute as means for survival yet hold no judgment for an empire that stole a continent from its people. If we're gold hungry extortionists, then tell me—" I released his reins with a disgusted curl of my lip, "what words should I use to define the Torren dynasty?"

Jaw grim, Navarre steered his mount past me and rode on in flaming silence.

As we reached the palace, my blackened mood grew, deep and fathomless.

Lies, grandmother once told me, flowed as easy as water while truth, like sand, could flow just as easily but was much harder to swallow.

The Imperial palace of domes and spires was built on lies, woven like veins of gold within marble. It stood as a symbol of a nation strong, united and whole, but I knew the truth; each pale stone shone like bones picked clean, stacked and mortared with blood and the broken sobs of the innocent lives the empire had slaughtered in conquest.

As we approached those gilded gates I could almost hear the ghostly cries of the dead and damned, calling out to me, their anguish raking over my skin like claws until I bled. The Tujianese people might've gone deaf and blind. But I would not.

I would remember.

And I would bring justice.

We entered the inner courtyard of the palace, surrounded by twin curving colonnades of emerald marble dressed in gold leaf. Steps draped in red carpet rolled down from the gilded doors like a river of blood spilling from an open throat where servants lined the base of the steps in neat rows. They hurried towards us, gathering our reins and helping us dismount. I kicked away the hands that reached for me, and sneered at the ornate stool as I slid from the saddle. I wasn't a child or a frail elder.

"Welcome, welcome." An approaching man tossed up fleshy, pink hands. His large eyes shining with false joviality. "I am Prothero, Chief Chancellor of the emperling's privy council." He swept into a bow with an elaborate flourish. Sunlight bounced off the top of his head as he straightened. "Second Commander. How lovely for you to *finally* join us."

"A storm broke before we reached the harbor." Navarre met the chancellor's chastising tone with surprising grace. Showing little, if any change, in his demeanor. "We had no choice but to wait it out."

I focused on the smaller details of the man—the lines around his mouth as his lips puckered in a soft, sad smile, the pupils of his eyes, the beating pulse in his throat, and the subtle gestures of his constantly moving hands—seeking any hint of surprise at our planned deception.

"Well, at least you haven't missed the gathering. The emperling desires an audience with you at once."

Navarre flicked the barest glance my way before he stalked up the steps into the palace, guided by his own team of servants. Not even the Second Commander moved freely within the palace.

"Well, I imagine you have all had a hellish journey." Prothero turned glittering eyes upon us. "I shall escort you to your chambers so that you may wash and dress for this evening. Tonight you'll each be presented to the emperling and his court. Come." He clapped his hands and the remaining servants formed even rows on either side of us.

Cavernous corridors met with domed ceilings lined with arches, dazzling chandeliers and gilded filigree. It was said Emperor Jaymes had torn down most of the original palace, and built his own atop it.

An opulent gravestone over a desiccated corpse.

We were brought to a vast bedroom, the same pale white and ivory and bleached gold walls dressed in curtains of heavy silk, velvet lined cushions and polished wood furniture. Decadent and luxurious.

Prothero eased to the side and swept out his arm. "May I introduce you to Lady Daneysa, daughter to the Duchess of Seford, sister to the emperling's own cousin."

"Thank you, Chancellor." Daneysa beamed and Prothero bowed with the same ridiculous flourish as he had in the courtyard.

Spirits of my Sisters, everything about *Yatsūan*—from their clothing to their customs—was excessive and ridiculous.

"If there is nothing else, my lady, I shall take my leave." He swept out of the room and a couple of servants scampered at his heels like pups following their master. It turned my stomach. Unlike our handmaids who served by choice and were treated respectfully, these people, forged into objects rather than individuals, had no voice, or autonomy.

"I am most pleased to greet you on behalf of the emperling and to ensure your stay is a pleasant one." Daneysa's smile was bright as the diamonds winking at her ears. "Which of you is to be Ehrick's intended?"

"I am." Bitter words to swallow. I hated the taste of them, like ashes and stale piss.

Her eyes skipped to me, her expression somewhere between surprise and amusement. "Dare I say I hoped as much?" She snapped delicate fingers, and the servants sprang to action. "These are the palace's trusted servants, and each will show you to your rooms." She returned her attention to me. "If you'd be so kind, this way, my lady."

"I am not a *lady*," I said, stalking after her as she disappeared into a smaller room lit with false light and encased in marble tile. A porcelain tub hugged one wall, large enough to fit three grown men. At the other side was a square chamber of glass with a wide disk mounted in the ceiling. "What is that?"

"You've never seen a shower?"

I wrinkled my nose. "No."

Daneysa laughed into her cupped hands. "Oh, darling, you're in for a treat. But let's save that for another day."

Servants hurried around us, preparing the tub, gathering bottles of oil, soap and lotions while hot water spouted from a slender, arcing brass pipe. I felt a slight touch at my right hip and snatched the wrist, so tight the bones rubbed together. The youth whimpered and buckled at the knees.

"Easy." Daneysa splayed her hands. "He meant no harm. In the emperling's presence, all weapons—"

"This stays with me," I interrupted. "Our swords can't be touched by any hand but ours."

"Of course. Simon, please see to our other guests."

I released the youth, Simon, and he scampered out the doors.

"With your permission?" Daneysa approached me carefully, her voice warm as the soft shade of her eyes, green like river moss. She waited until I gave consent before her hands slid along my waist, unfastening knots.

She had to get close.

So close I could smell the perfume of rose oil on her skin and see the scattering of freckles racing down the side of her neck. I jerked my chin up and sneered at the painted mural of bathing maidens and fat babies with white wings across the domed ceiling.

"Is this your first time seeing the Imperial City?"

"Yes." The kubari was thick and lined with many fastenings, but her fingers worked efficiently, as if she was more than practiced with removing this kind of garment.

The remaining servants assisted her with fetching and gathering, but none of them dared venture too close. They were afraid of me, and I preferred it to stay that way.

Here, within these gilded walls, I would trust no one.

"I remember my first time," she said with a sigh, full of wistful memories. "My father brought my sister and me when we were just little girls. I was barely seven, and Iereni all of three, so she doesn't recall that trip quite so vividly. I thought the palace was the most incredible thing I'd ever seen."

I shrugged out of the kubari and she folded the heavy leather and fur garment. "Have this cleaned and the leather properly treated," she instructed before handing it off to one of the servants standing patiently by the sidelines. "I grew up in the sealands of Cadamir," she continued, and to her credit Daneysa hardly turned up her nose as she removed the padded cotton kubi, followed by the fitted undershirt, leaving me naked to the waist.

"They call it the Sinking City, as it stands on stone pillars." Leaning over the tub, she tested the water with a stroke of her hand while I removed the rest of my clothing. "Each year we sink a little lower, so engineers are constantly resetting the foundation. The streets are all waterways so the only way to get around is on the narrow footpaths, or by boat. Beyond the city walls, water spreads all around for miles and miles—you'd swear there was nothing else. And when the sun dances across it, each ripple is like a diamond."

Naked, I climbed into the tub and slid beneath the hot blanket of steaming water, warm as the mountain springs, but it tasted clean as I licked beads of water from my bottom lip.

Daneysa lowered to the flat side of the tub and uncapped a bottle. Raising it to her nose, she breathed in the scent, and her lips skewed to the side.

"No, not quite right. It's too subtle for you, I think." She tried another and another. By the seventh, she sighed. "Oh, this is lovely. Here. What do you think?"

She waved it beneath my nose. Sweet oranges and plum with dark spice. "It'll do."

Pleased, she poured the soap onto a sponge and went to work, gently scrubbing my arms, neck and back. "You have lovely hair," she commented, the length of it wrapped in a sloppy knot atop my head, then brushed the skin along my left temple. "What is this for?"

"My mark? Protection."

"How is a tattoo supposed to protect you?" she asked with sincere curiosity.

Turning around, I pushed wisps of damp hair from my face. "How does a bisected circle of gold with a diamond center protect you?"

She brushed a finger across the pin she wore, the God's Eye, a symbol of their faith. "Fair enough." Rising from the edge of the tub, she handed the soapy sponge to a waiting servant. "I must leave you now to ready myself. With your permission, Caius and Tova will take over."

I nodded and the pair of them silently went to work, a jarring contrast. Daneysa's gentle hands and easy smile were disarming weapons, and under her ministrations I'd almost forgotten my circumstances.

One carefully removed the beads, gold cuffs and leather cords from my hair. Another dragged their fingers through the tangled strands to work out the knots before applying a generous handful of something that smelled like lemon. They scrubbed, rinsed, and lathered in more lotions and oils until my hair was clean and soft as the rest of me.

Finished with the bath, and wrapped in a drying cloth, I allowed a servant to tame my hair into a straight sheet of black with a hot-comb while the other dressed my face with gilded powders.

Daneysa returned to the room sometime later, transformed in an ivory dress. The skirt flared from her hips and creased like the folds of a fan, the neckline capped at her shoulders and bared her arms. She wore a necklace of blue and purple sapphires that was joined with thick gold bracelets at her wrists, and a golden net draped over the coiling waves of her mahogany hair.

"Come, let's get you dressed." Holding out her hand, she took mine and guided me from the bathroom back into the bedchamber, where Iereni spun in circles on the large back wheels of a wheeled-chair.

"Finally!" she huffed. Her thin legs slanted beneath her sunny yellow dress, and feet propped on flat paddles to keep them from dragging on the floor. Sleek and agile in its design, it was far superior to any of the ones we had at Home Mountain.

Taphne had battled her way out of one a few years ago, and a pang echoed deeply in my chest as the soft lines of Iereni's face overlapped with the shadow of Taphne's memory.

"What are you doing here?" Daneysa demanded.

"I was sent to find out what's taking so long."

"Then why isn't Nurse Vanda with you?"

Ignoring her sister, Iereni wheeled around the foot of the bed. "What's in the chest?" She stopped before the lacquered box and looked at me expectantly. "Is it a gift?" I nodded and her eyes brightened. A mixture of green and silver. "Then you must open it!"

"*Iereni*." Daneysa crossed her arms. "Please forgive my sister, she forgets her manners sometimes."

"It's alright," I murmured, my attention fixed on the chest.

*Remember, Sina. Remember us.*

Seated on the bed, I unfastened the latch. Inside was a thin folded wrap of purple silk etched in gold brocade. I parted it and nearly gasped at the bundle of white fur. It was my grandmother's revered stonecat cloak, but she'd had it modified so that the claws that hugged each shoulder were decorated with black gold and dripped with cut rubies like drops of blood from each point. The bottom was layered in blue ermine and the inside lined with more purple silk. The torc of black gold mounted with the stonecat claw I'd received during my initiation.

Iereni's eyes widened to awestruck full moons. "Beautiful," she whispered, her fingers floating through the air as if she ached to touch it.

"It was my grandmother's," I said. "Her most prized possession, made from the pelt of the stonecat she killed when she was fifteen to save her three of her sisters." I gathered it to my nose and breathed deep. It smelled of her. Powerful and proud.

Grandmother had told me the story for years, entertaining my childish fascination, of how they'd tracked a wounded caribou through the snow and were set upon by a stonecat, grey and black in summer, their coats faded to pale silver in winter. A few became pure white, often the largest and most fearsome, and that was how they earned their names, by blending in with the mountains they became invisible amongst the rocky, snow-covered terrain.

Pale shadows of death, their prey never saw them coming.

My grandmother was sending me a message—a stonecat wrapped in imperial colors, with blood on its claws. Not entirely subtle, but the point was clear. She wanted me to blend into my surroundings. To stalk my prey. And though I might be forced to wear their colors and eventually a crown, I must never forget who I was beneath the finery.

*We are stonecats with fangs and claws and a taste for blood.*

*Our time will come.*

"Will you wear it tonight?"

"Iereni, that is enough," Daneysa scolded. "Sinadine has been polite in indulging you. Please return to the gathering and inform the emperling we shall be along shortly."

"I'm not a child, so please don't speak to me like one." Iereni stuck out her tongue at her sister as she spun her wheels and was gone in a few hard pumps of her arms.

"Alright, now we really must hurry. Emperling Ehrick has requested that his intended wear these as tokens of his affection." Daneysa gestured to a couple of new servants, a woman holding a thin midnight blue dress with intricate silver needlework, and an older gentleman carried a velvet lined box bearing a queen's ransom in dazzling sunstones set in a web of white gold. "Does his selection please you?"

"What I think doesn't matter," I said.

"It does to me."

I rubbed the material of the dress between my fingers. "I've never seen anything so fine."

Pleased, she snapped her fingers, and both Caius and Tova rushed forwards, sliding the dress up my legs and hips, guiding the thin straps over my arms. The way it was cut and shaped there was nothing I could wear underneath it and heat filled my cheeks at the thought of being so exposed—not because I was ashamed of my body.

During scorching summers, it wasn't uncommon for the women of my clan to work topless in the fields or quarries if the heat grew too intense. Old or young, our bodies were to be respected, but this was an act of power by the emperling I was bound to serve and marry.

He was showing me, and his court, that he owned every inch of me. Scrubbed and painted, my hair straightened into glossy sheets of endless black, and parted at the center to hide the fade.

And the tattoo.

"You . . . you are truly miraculous," Daneysa sighed, and turned me to face a mirror that Caius and Tova held between them.

I stared hard at my reflection. This powerless, painted slave, and scowled at the stranger I'd become in a dress designed to show off the aesthetics of my body and face. I wanted to hate it. I truly did. But I looked beautiful. A secret that soured in my stomach.

Grandmother was right; the truth was harder to swallow.

Daneysa slid in at my side, our reflections joined in the polished mirror. If she was the splendor of the dawn, then I was the glory of the night, and together, we were a sight to behold.

"What's wrong?" Her head tilted to the side, and her smile dimmed. "You don't like it?"

I huffed gently, at a loss for words.

"There's no shame in liking pretty things, or the way they make you feel."

"This isn't a necklace, it's a collar. The dress and jewels—are chains meant to show that he owns me. Broke me." Like a wild horse to saddle and show off, Ehrick and his predecessors flaunted their Swordsworn before the court as symbols of conquest. Of power. These proud, warrior women, made to bend the knee. That's what the treaty was truly meant to convey. We, the indomitable, the fierce and proud, had been conquered.

"I understand." Her hands closed over my arms, chin resting against my shoulder. Even in her heeled shoes, I was taller. "But I've learned that a dress can be a weapon if you know how to wield it."

"Then I should have armor," I said in jest, but Daneysa's eyes sparkled like sunlight across a field.

"Yes. Perhaps you should."

# CHAPTER ELEVEN

## Navarre

T HE LAST TIME NAVARRE STOOD IN this room his father lay dying. And in the days he'd been gone, Ehrick had wasted no time in making himself at home.

The walls were stripped of tapestries and paintings, the antiques and ornate furniture replaced with more current designs to reflect his modern tastes.

Ehrick sat at the head of a glass table laden with fruit, meat and cheese, but he wasn't alone. Archviceroy Henry Torren stood by the windows, gazing out at the manicured gardens below.

"At last, brother." Ehrick smiled around the grape he popped into his mouth, light dancing in eyes clear of illness. "I was beginning to think you'd abandoned me."

Navarre dragged out a chair at Ehrick's side but, remembering he was still dressed in bulky armor, pushed the seat back in. "You're looking well." And he did, though the cotton mask remained within arm's reach.

"And you look like shit," Ehrick teased, plucking another fat purple grape from the bunch. "Appears the mountains don't agree with you."

"You were expected *yesterday*." The Archviceroy moved from the windows to claim the seat at his nephew's side and folded his hands elegantly in his lap. His silver eyes as familiar as they were cold.

Henry was all slender limbs and hollow cheeks, but strong as a Sahson oak. He'd fought in countless battles for his Holy Campaign on behalf of the One Faith, purging the remnants of heathen religion from empire lands. Tens of thousands burned at the pyre—mostly women.

Navarre smothered a scowl. For as long as he'd lived and breathed, he'd despised the man.

"Your eminence." Saying the words was like chewing glass. "I thought you were set to return to the Holy City after your campaign?"

"My brother is dead," he answered coolly. "More importantly, his All-Holiness, the Grand Patriarch, has requested that I return to oversee the Privy Council as Chief Chancellor."

Navarre flicked his gaze to Ehrick and saw no ounce of surprise or displeasure. Prothero was sure to be thoroughly vexed over the demotion, but what concerned him most was having the Archviceroy within the palace walls, deepening his hooks into Ehrick's skin.

Whispering into his ear like a passing breeze.

"Tell us about your visit," Henry demanded.

"It was uneventful."

"That's not what I asked."

Navarre bit the inside of his cheek, willing himself to maintain composure.

"Forgive our uncle; he's been counselling me for the better part of an hour about Acharrāns." Ehrick eased back into his chair trimmed in emerald velvet. "What do you think of them, brother? Are they a threat to me and the empire?"

Navarre had not missed when the Archviceroy's lips had thinned at Ehrick's endearment, and made sure to compound his displeasure, when he replied, "On my life, brother, no man or woman will live to harm you. I swear it on the bones of our father, One God keep his soul."

"While that is a wonderful sentiment," Henry scoffed, "you did not answer the question."

Navarre braced the chair back with a sigh. "They're a fierce and proud clan, I'll give them that, but since the passing of ecclesiastical laws condemning heretics, the shrines have remained barren. None came to show their respect as we passed."

Ehrick's eyes gleamed with a secret smile, his fingers picking stray fluff from his slender thigh. "And what of the girls? Their manner and disposition?"

Navarre thought of the way Sinadine had sliced through her opponents with a ruthless precision that was all ferocity and focus. "I can't say I've spent enough time to form an opinion. They were quiet and kept mostly to themselves when they weren't united in battle."

"Battle?"

Ehrick perked up in his chair and Navarre cursed his choice of words. "We had a small matter and handled it accordingly."

Henry shifted cool eyes to his nephew. "Do tell."

Navarre hesitated, torn between the plan he'd agreed upon and lying to his best friend and half-brother. His emperling.

Apprehension, a foul worm burrowed into his heart, spreading a painful rot of doubt that quickly overshadowed the echo of promises made to Sinadine. He'd never lied to his brother before, and after a lifetime of sharing every secret and wish, every fear and doubt, he couldn't fathom starting now . . .

If the Archviceroy were not present, the urge to share the truth would've been insurmountable, but Henry was a ruthless man with a taste for violence, and Ehrick's adoration would make him an easy puppet to manipulate.

So Navarre reached for lies, and painted a picture of the cold Acharrān woodlands and the dangerous beasts that lurked within them. His stomach churning with each dishonest word.

"I can see the loss of your men pains you." Ehrick gripped Navarre's shoulder and squeezed reassuringly. "From the depths of my heart I mourn with you, brother, and will ensure the priests give them a poetic benediction when they're finished with the last rites for our father. I'm sorry," a muscle twinged in his jaw, "but we couldn't wait."

"No, of course." Navarre swallowed a bitter lump of sorrow at having missed the burial. "Thank you, brother."

The doors opened and Ehrick turned with a dazzling smile as Iereni whisked into the room. "There's my best girl." Boosting from his seat, Iereni beamed as he noisily kissed both her cheeks. "You look radiant, cousin. Did you have fun on your little adventure?"

"Yes! Oh, I wish you could've seen it for yourself."

"Perhaps one day I will." He stroked a ruffling hand across her head, disheveling auburn tresses. "Go on. Both of you." He set a hand on Navarre's shoulder. "The gathering starts soon. And I want you both looking your best when you stand at my side during the oaths of fealty."

Iereni's mouth tumbled open. "*Really*?"

This was a high honor. Only the Chief Chancellor was permitted by his side during such officious ceremonies.

"There's no one else I want with me then the two people I love and cherish most in this world. I think you'll find something special waiting for you in your rooms for the occassion."

"A present?"

Ehrick winked.

"'Kay." She giggled.

A doting smile brought warmth to Ehrick's pallid cheeks as she glided out the doors. Her wheels barely touching the ground in her glee.

"You've made her incandescently happy."

"What can I say, I have a tender heart. One of my many flaws—just ask the physicians."

Navarre shook his head with a laugh.

This was the brother he knew and loved, the gentle and compassionate. The one who sought to others happiness ahead of his own. Navarre was seeing less and less of him of late—only when Ehrick was free of the Archviceroy's shadow.

"Before you leave, brother, I also have a separate request," Ehrick continued. "I need fifty good men to accompany Sir Rickard and I to the Holy City."

"What?" Navarre jolted where he stood. "Why?"

"Uncle Henry feels it's in our best interests to obtain a blessing from his All-Holiness *before* the coronation. To help quiet any discourse."

It was protocol for emperors to kneel before the Grand Patriarch prior to their coronation and be anointed with the blood and tears of the One God. But if the assassins had been sent for Ehrick, a trip deep into the heart of the Bridian Isles could be perilous, and his heart snagged in his throat at the thought of Ehrick exposed, vulnerable and unaware, while enemies skittered like rats in the shadows.

This was about more than his brother—this was about a billion lives he was bound to protect. If Ehrick fell, the empire would collapse like a mountain to crush the people beneath it in civil war and discourse.

*Protect Ehrick and the empire unto death. That is my vow. My only purpose.* Navarre's fist tightened at his side. "Very well. When do we leave?"

Ehrick shoved Navarre's shoulder with a grin. "You're needed here, to get your bearings as *Second* Commander. Uncle Henry will preside in my absence."

It took every ounce of effort to keep his jaw from clenching at the smug little grin that flickered across the

Archviceroy's face. The man was vile, and Ehrick couldn't see it. "How long will you be gone?

"Three weeks. Perhaps less. Sir Rickard has given leave for you to assemble the retinue."

"As you wish." Navarre would pick the best men he could trust, steering clear of those who'd accompanied him in the escort. While they might've sworn reluctant vows of silence in the Blue Wastes, there was no telling if they'd keep their mouths' shut in the presence of their First.

Two weeks leave to be with their families might be the best recourse to soften foul moods and hopefully quieten any mutinous thoughts.

And if not . . .

Heat blasted Navarre, an angry flush in his cheeks that made him grateful for the haze of black shadowing his jaw. If his father could see him now—a Second who couldn't muster the respect of his men—when he had led with such uncompromising strength . . .

*They won't respect you until you've earned it. So earn it.*

Sinadine was right. He'd been given his position at the grace of his brother—but it was up to him to demonstrate to his men that he would serve them as loyally as the empire. To do so, he would need to solidify his position, as Ehrick suggested.

"Look at him, ready to sleep on his feet." Ehrick clapped that hand to his cheek, jarring him from his thoughts. "Go on. Shower. Rest. You smell like you've lain with pigs."

Navarre knocked his hand aside. "You'd know."

Ehrick wheezed through a laugh, and reached for the cloth mask, breathing deep.

"Before you seek your rest, I'd like a moment of your time, Second Commander." Henry swept out a hand. "Walk with me."

With no polite way to refuse, Navarre grudgingly followed him out into the corridor.

"My nephew is not pleased about his coming nuptials," he said as Navarre retrieved his sword from the standing guards, their footsteps echoing off marble and stone. The Archviceroy's servants had waited dutifully for him and trailed just far enough to give their master privacy.

"From what I've seen, your eminence, arranged marriages are rarely cause for celebration."

Henry curled his lip. "What I am about to tell you is considered privileged information, and as such, will not be shared with any other persons, including the emperling. Is that clear?"

"Yes, your eminence."

"I have reason to suspect the Acharrāns are plotting to assassinate the emperling."

"What?" Henry raised a brow at his bark of surprise, so Navarre lowered his voice before continuing. "How could you know that?"

"I have various spymasters throughout the realm. Very little escapes my notice."

"Then why wasn't I informed of the possible threat *before*hand?"

"Because silence is a weapon, and I needed to know if it was true."

Words Sinadine would heartily agree with, but this was different—the bastard had known an assault was possible, and he'd let them walk into it blind. Navarre curled his hand into a tight first and longed to plough it through the Archviceroy's narrow face.

"Iereni could've died." *Good men already had*.

"Alas, you've returned safely," the Archviceroy grinned, his smile thin and sharp as an assassin's blade. "Minus your little incident with a pack of wolves, of course."

"*Wolverines*," Navarre corrected through clenched teeth.

"Indeed." Henry levelled a cool stare that said he hadn't bought the carefully crafted story before continuing on, his stride even and measured. "As the emperling never left the palace, and the escort has returned mostly intact, some might think the threat is behind us."

"And you don't?"

"Even if the Acharrāns are not at the forefront of plotting, there are always threats close to the throne seeking to ursurp the Torren dynasty. It's not without reason that they could be recruited in the effort. Three Swordsworn reside within our walls. Young and unbroken. We can't be assured of their loyalties. The threat could be more real now than it ever was before."

"Why would they trade one set of chains for another?"

"You're not a worldly man, Navarre, and have not been beyond the capital. My crusade has snuffed out what little influence the Acharrāns had among the people. While a caged animal is no threat, an injured and cornered one could be deadly. And make no mistake—they are cornered. Question is will they tuck tail and be caged, or will they lunge for our throats?"

Setting aside his anger, Navarre considered the facts.

While the Acharrāns stood to gain a great deal from the emperling's death, an assassination attempt defied their code of honor and, even if they succeeded, it would undoubtedly start a civil war. Would the matrons go to such extremes to be free of their Imperial bonds?

Everything he knew about their culture proved they were fiercely proud and loyal. Martyring three girls for the sake of ending an imperial bloodline felt wrong . . . and yet something in Sinadine's eyes stayed with him.

Hidden beneath the polish of honor was the gleam of a soul forged in steel. It was the look of a girl who hungered for blood and retribution. She'd crushed the assassins with a deadly grace that had left him spellbound. And as for her sisters, they might not have approved of her headstrong actions, they were Swordsworn and would follow her anywhere.

Even to Hell.

"I want you to be the eyes and ears of the emperling." Henry stopped at the end of the corridor that split into two. One fanning left—to the Archviceroy's chambers, and the right returned to the barracks. "Get close to our new *guests*. Begin with the tall one. The *very* tall, angry looking one. She might be trouble." He turned towards Navarre. "You know of whom I speak?"

It was hard not to. Sinadine, all legs and brimstone, certainly made a lasting impression. "I have an idea, yes."

"Good. After the introductions at court, I want to know every move she makes. Who she speaks to, when she eats, where she goes. Everything. Maybe we'll uncover something useful before the coronation." Henry didn't wait for his response and sailed down the corridor toward his suite.

So he was expected to play errand boy?

The fact that any servant would've been suited to this task grated his patience to a nub by the time he reached the barracks. But he was used to this sort of thing. Being dismissed, overlooked. No matter what he did or how high he rose, to them he would always be the bastardborn son of a heathen. At least Ehrick was a *legitimate* heir of the Torren Dynasty. No one could turn their nose up at him.

No one would dare.

Eban Rathly waited for him outside his private rooms, adjacent to the First Commander's, hands tucked behind his back and shoulders drawn wide as his smile. "Welcome back, sir."

"Lieutenant." Navarre clapped a hand on his friend's shoulder. Moments after he'd received his promotion from Ehrick, he'd appointed Eban as his Lieutenant because he deserved it, and because a man at the top needed friends he could trust to guard his back. "How were things in my absence?"

"Sweet as a nun's fart."

Despite his sour mood, Navarre laughed. "Glad to hear it. I'll be tied up for most of the gathering tonight, but let's sit down tomorrow to discuss next steps."

"Sir." Eban cast a two-finger salute, and with a click of his heels, resumed his post while Navarre entered his suite.

Tossing his sheathed sword and belt, it bounced off the bed and clattered to the hardwood floor. Barely a second later, the antechamber door opened, and Toddrick hurried out, his pale cheeks flush with a sunny grin.

"Milord, you're back."

Navarre pressed his fingers to his temples and rubbed. "Yes, and for the thousandth time, you don't have to call me that, Todd."

Toddrick's cheeks pinkened further, and the horrible bowl-shaped haircut only enhanced the roundness of his face as he stooped to pick up the sword and set it on the wall brackets. "Sorry, milord."

Casting his eyes heavenward, Navarre prayed for strength. "Help me with this armor."

"Yes, milord." Toddrick went to work, his fingers nimble and quick with practiced ease as he dealt with the straps, hooks and ties. "You have the look of someone who might be troubled, milord. I don't mean to pry but Housemaster Graeme says it's my job as vassal to lend an ear if milord ever needs a confidant to share his burdens."

Navarre tried not to sigh. Having his own personal attendant was as strange and unfamiliar as trying to breathe underwater. For a middleborn son of a distant noble, it was a high honor to serve an imperial commander, but with Navarre at the helm this position was more of an insult than a reward for the poor boy.

Not that Toddrick ever seemed to complain. He was always cheerful as a fresh strawberry dipped in cream.

"Archviceroy Henry has requisitioned me as one of his spies." Probably a stupid thing to admit to someone he barely knew, but Toddrick had an honest look about him, and since he was unable turn to Ehrick, Navarre was sorely in need of someone he could trust.

To his credit, Toddrick didn't falter as he shucked armor and leather from Navarre's body. "And this displeases you, milord?"

"I'm the *Second* Commander of the Imperial Guard. Not a bloody servant."

"Yet you cannot refuse him?"

"No." Refusing would only create more problems than was worth. Ehrick might be his brother at heart, but he'd likely back his uncle in this regard and then Henry would take considerable joy in making Navarre exceedingly miserable. The man had a talent for it.

"Well, if you cannot refuse then you're left with no choice but to see that the Archviceroy gets what he wants," Toddrick said as he carried the armor and placed it on the rack set in the alcove. "Sooner he does, the sooner you will be rid of him, milord."

Navarre swiped a hand through his hair, the strands damp with sweat. It was a hard point to argue. "How long until the Swordsworn are to make their introductions at court?"

"Less than two hours, milord."

Not enough time to close his eyes and rest. "I'm going to shower. Come back at half past to help me dress. I want to go to the church and pay my respects."

Time moved quickly as he scrubbed himself clean beneath a heavy stream of hot water that soothed the ache of travel from his bones—and softened his temper. Regardless of his feelings towards the Archviceroy, if his bother's life was in danger, Navarre would move heaven and earth to protect his family.

Ehrick was all he had left.

Born on the same night; Ehrick arrived almost a month early. According to Acharrān customs, they believed two children sired by the same blood and born the same night were linked as soul twins. Two halves of a whole, and were viewed as sacred in their clan. There was no such regard among Bridians, however.

Despite his parentage, Navarre had faced nothing but ridicule and shame growing up within the palace. Ignored and scorned, only Ehrick had given him an ounce of compassion and when his mother died, it was Ehrick who pushed against his uncle's wishes to have Navarre sent away to a workhouse in some impoverished slum.

Ehrick had never failed to look out for him. Maybe because they were both outcasts. Navarre, the son never meant to be born and Ehrick, the son never meant to live.

But despite the odds, he did.

He battled every single day and Navarre had never known anyone with such bravery and so he used his strength to protect Ehrick, as Ehrick protected Navarre with his wits.

At half past the hour Toddrick returned, prompt as always, with Navarre's garment for the evening. A white shirt, with black tailored pants and polished leather boots. Overtop of that, he wore a sapphire vest with gold brocade, and a black gold livery collar set with sapphires and sunstones.

Toddrick draped a black cape lined with silver fox fur and purple satin around his right shoulder, and fastened it across his chest, knotting it under his left arm.

Standing back, he assessed his work, and nodded proudly. "Perfect, milord."

Navarre felt like a stuffed peacock wearing this much silk and jewels, but the sight of his reflection made him set his shoulders a little more proudly. He looked like a man of worth. Someone to respect.

He looked like his father . . . a realization that brought a mournful tear to his eyes as he reached the church with just enough time to light a candle for his father's soul and say a quick prayer before joining the gathering.

The grand hall was awash with light refracting off crystal chandeliers hanging from the ceiling—shaped like bursting orbs that scattered rainbows across polished wood flooring stained a deep mahogany. Swaths of silk banners hung on the walls—a howling silver brocade direwolf against a desolate purple background. The symbol Emperor Jaymes, first of his line, had claimed after conquering this land for himself.

The Pale Wolf, his enemies called him.

Navarre wove through the sea of courtiers—lords, ladies, and ambassadors of conquered kings and queens—toward the dais where his brother sat on the throne. Thin black hair elegantly combed away from Ehrick's face, showing large silver eyes and a thin-lipped mouth with a hint of color in his cheeks, masking the sallow complexion of his skin. Iereni beamed at his side, glowing brighter than the sun as a line of nobles pledged their allegiance to the emperling heir.

A lengthy and tedious process, but a vital one.

"A moment." First Commander Rickard caught Navarre by the arm, holding him fast before he could reach the base of the short steps leading up to the throne.

To the outside it would appear like he was merely embracing him as a comrade.

Navarre knew better.

Sir Rickard was an imposing man, broad shouldered and stout, and carried himself with the confident swagger of someone infinitely taller than his stout five-eight. While most men in arms preferred a clean, groomed face, Rickard had a long black beard salted with grey that accentuated high cheekbones and a sharp, large nose.

"I've been informed you lost *five* of my men."

"We were—"

"I'm not interested in your excuses," he said, voice low. "I don't like you, de-Nersu," he sneered, using Navarre's Acharrān surname with utter contempt. "If I had my way you'd be cleaning shit from imperial boots, not leading soldiers."

The First Commander had large hands, all wide of palm with thick, blunt fingers, that remained fastened around Navarre's forearm in a grip firm enough for him to feel the true strength and threat that hand was capable of.

"Step a toe out of line and I don't care what the emperling says, I'll put you down like the mongrel you are."

Navarre met Sir Rickard's steely gaze and offered an imperceptible nod before he was finally released, and shook out his hand, restoring sensation to numb fingers. The empress, standing gracefully behind Ehrick's throne, gave him a gentle smile as he made his way up the steps to his brother's side.

"What was all that?" Ehrick gazed up at him with an arched brow.

"Nothing. Just two colleagues exchanging words," Navarre lied, companionably nudging Ehrick's thin shoulder.

This was not the time or place to stoke his brother's mood, especially before the entire court.

"All the nobles have come to pledge. Uncle says it's a sign that we have their support," Ehrick answered. "He was worried my infirmity might've brought out the vultures."

*And still might*, but Navarre kept that to himself.

It was possible someone in this very room had hired the assassins that attacked the escort, and he planned to keep a sharp eye on his brother tonight in case anyone thought to try again.

Chancellor Prothero wove to Ehrick's side and bent close to his ear, light refracting on the bald dome of his head. "Sire, the Swordsworn are ready for their introduction. I suggest we proceed with the formalities."

Ehrick released a weary breath. "Very well."

Pleased, Prothero gave the signal to cut the music and call attention to the court. "Esteemed lords and ladies." His soft hands waved before him like petals floating atop a still lake. "On behalf of Emperling Ehrick, it is my honor to commence the introductions of the Swordsworn." Fleshy palms cracked together, and the courtiers parted down the center, clearing a path from the throne to the wide, ornate doors of wood and brass.

They opened with a groan and the Swordsworn were led in one at a time. The first, pale as a Bridian milkmaid in seafoam silk and the second, dressed in scarlet with ink-black hair and large sloe eyes, much like the empress. Sinadine entered last.

A warrior queen draped in a white fur cloak over her gown of midnight blue. In lieu of jewels, blue lines of shimmering woad streaked across her eyes—transforming her in an almost feline mask, and a collective gasp whispered through the crowd at the sight of the empty scabbard on her hip.

A bold statement, reminding him and everyone else that she was more than a girl—she was a warrior.

And given Daneysa's pleased smirk, Navarre didn't have to hazard a guess as to her accomplice in this brazen display of defiance.

Sinadine joined the line of her sisters, exuding a quiet menace that hummed in the air like a silent threat. She was bright as a sundrenched blade. Fearless as the black between the stars.

And Navarre couldn't take his eyes off her.

# CHAPTER TWELVE

## Sinadine

WHISPERS WOVE AROUND THE ROOM like smoke through ribbon grass, accompanied with lingering eyes and pointing fingers.

Ehrick Torren sat in his gilded throne in the shape of a howling wolf, draped in a coat of deepest purple over a gold embroidered vest. Oiled hair was combed away from his stark face, skin pale from recluse whereas Navarre's shone golden from heritage and frequent sun. Buffed fawn boots adorned his feet joined to bowed legs encased in brackets of steel with pistons and gears bracketing him from hip to ankle.

Even with the support, I imagined walking on such legs was painful.

The empress stood next to her son, eyes downcast and wearing an ivory kubari with diamonds that flashed at her throat and ears. A queen of winter in mourning, her straight black hair draped down her right side, but she wore no fade and beneath the kubari was a high-necked tunic covering any hint of her tattoo.

How easy it would be to kill him. My fingers ached for my sword, but I didn't need a blade to be deadly.

*Kill him. Become fury. Become rage.*

*Become everything we were meant to be*!

The dark urge whispered in my bones. A seductive chill that kissed along my neck, and the temptation, Spirits of my Sisters, was soul deep, and harrowing.

"Your majesty." Daneysa lowered into a curtsy, so low she was almost seated on the ground. "May I present Sinadine de-Arashi, come to offer her hand."

"You should kneel before the emperling," an austere man snapped, cloaked in deepest red. His silvered hair matched the steel of his gaze burning across me.

The empress tensed almost imperceptibly at the lashing tone of his voice and seeing her so cowed lit a fire to my stubborn pride. "No."

"My dear, while I do apologize for Archviceroy Henry's callousness, it is *customary* when presented to the emperling." Chancellor Prothero kept his voice low, but I could hear the hush of the assembly behind me, hanging on every word.

"Your custom." I set my shoulder, pushed up my chest. "Not mine."

"First, she dares come into the emperling's presence thusly dressed, bearing her scabbard! And now she refuses to bend the knee." The Archviceroy curled his lip with indignation. "This is disgraceful. It was your job to ensure she was adequately prepared, Lady Seford, what do you have to say for yourself?"

Daneysa remained in a sunken curtsy, chin tucked in deference. "Your eminence, I—"

"I am the bloodkin to the First-of-Us," I interrupted and had the pleasure of seeing the Archviceroy's knuckles flash white in a fist. "I don't . . . *kneel*."

"Sire, a blood descendent of the original Acharrāns is essentially a princess in the eyes of her clan." Prothero leaned into Ehrick, his soft hands clasped as if in prayer. "As royalty, and for the sake of preventing a scene, perhaps we can extend grace by making an allowance this once?"

Offering a slight nod in acquiescence, Ehrick waved the Chancellor away. "Rise, cousin."

Graceful as a swan, Daneysa did so without a hint of effort or sweat. She must've had strong legs and stronger patience to tolerate such treatment.

Anchoring his hands to the armrest, Ehrick struggled to his feet, pistons pumping and gears whirling as he hobbled forward and faced the whispering crowd with a benevolent grin.

"As the lastborn son of the late Emperor Edvard Torren, eighth of his line, I accept the hand of Sinadine de-Arashi as my future wife and Empress of the Bridian Isles. Let us now feast and celebrate this great honor bestowed upon her and the Swordsworn. Forging another link of unity in a generational chain of peace."

Applause rang out, barely masking the smug whispers. After a few genteel waves, he turned with a grunt, and smothered a fit of coughing into his sleeve.

Navarre closed in. "I told you to bring the mask."

"Using it in privacy is one thing, but here in the face of my courtiers? I will not let them see me as more of an invalid than they already presume I am," Ehrick answered through smiling teeth as he sat back down, his cheeks reddening with effort.

"Away with you," the Archviceroy flicked a hand towards me as if shooing away gnats. "As she insists on dressing and behaving like an uncultured *heathen* she does not deserve the honor of standing aside the throne this evening."

My hand flexed on my scabbard. The only heathen in the room were those who'd forged an empire by spilling innocent blood. He was lucky I didn't have my sword or else I might have decapitated him right there for the insult.

Him and the emperling, both.

Daneysa floated to my side and looped an arm through mine, dragging my fisted hand away from my empty scabbard.

"Careful, darling," she said, steering me away.

"I don't know how you stand it."

"Because I must." Soft green eyes lifted to mine as she led me towards an alcove overlooking the dance floor. "This is one of my favorite hiding spots. You'll be able to see the gala unfold but are removed enough to hopefully remain undisturbed. You might even be surprised what you'll see."

She leaned against the marble pillar, her eyes sweeping the room. "When no one thinks you're looking."

"Why are you being so nice to me?" I demanded, and she turned from the swirling sea of courtiers to smile at me with such tender honesty.

"My father is the secretary of the war council and if there's anything I've learned from him, it is that the key to power lies in making the right friends." She reached for my hand and squeezed. "As women in a world that favors men, we must stand together if we hope to survive it."

Beyond us the ballroom swirled with spinning bodies draped in fine, lush fabrics and silks, but despite the lilting music and tinkle of glassware, I caught more than a dozen probing stares from courtiers goggling like children and doing a terrible job of pretending not to watch our every move.

"Have they no pride?"

"You mustn't fault them," Daneysa sighed. "Courtiers have little to occupy themselves with other than money. If there is anything they love more than wealth, it's controversy. And you are without a doubt controversial. But if you must have their eyes on you," she added covertly from behind her raised hand and winked. "Be sure to give them a show."

Daneysa floated away into the crowd and soon I was joined by both Rhys and Jasz, the three of us equally bored as time flowed, monotonous as the terrible music.

My head throbbed with fatigue after days of hard travel and annoyance of the entire idiotic farce and the balls of my feet screamed from standing for hours in heels. Night pressed in against clear glass windows and servants slid through the dancing or gossiping courtiers, carrying silver trays adorned with delicate bite-sized morsels.

Pretty as jewels, but bland as bathwater.

I spat out a halved boiled egg, with a puffy cloud of creamed yoke at the center into my hand. "*Yatsūan,*" I cursed. "They ruin everything they touch. Are they allergic to *seasoning*?"

"Stay away from the chicken." Rhys smothered a pained grin. "It's dry as an old bone."

I tossed the mushy gob and it hit the wall with a wet smack near a gaggle of ladies. As they sputtered in disgust and stormed off, I caught sight of Navarre and Daneysa near a pillar. Daneysa smiled and laughed at whatever he had to say, but Navarre—judging his posture and tense jaw, wasn't pleased.

"You got her in trouble," Rhys whispered.

"I did nothing."

"Oh?" She swept a finger towards me, gesturing up and down. "As if the scabbard wasn't bad enough. I thought the Archviceroy was going to have a stroke when you refused to bend the knee."

"If only," I grumbled.

"Did you really have to wear your True Face?" Jasz slashed me with a glare.

"Way to antagonize the enemy." Rhys nudged me with her elbow.

"Have you ever known me to do anything else?"

Losing the battle of composure, Rhys smiled—a dazzling flash of teeth and laughter that for a moment

I had to step back and take a breath. I knew her smile as intimately as I knew the whistle of wind through the mountains, or the dance of sunlight on snow atop the jagged peaks, but this was different.

More.

Maybe it was the light and the silk and the jewels woven into her silver hair, but it was like seeing her for the first time. Truly seeing her. And it pained me to think that she was trapped in this gilded cage with me, instead of being free to explore the world and all its wonders.

"You behave like an innocent sent to the gallows for a crime she didn't commit," Jasz muttered, "but our clan remains free because of us—what we've done is an honor. A privilege."

"Slavery is anything but a privilege," I replied, and met her firm glare with one of my own.

"Sisters before self—those are not just words, Sina," Jasz sneered, the set of her jaw mutinous, before stalking off into the swirling crowd.

Little did she know how deeply those words were scored into my marrow. I was here for my sisters. I'd given up everything and was prepared to die for them.

What was more selfless than that?

"Girl! *Psst,* girl!" A hissing voice, followed by indolent snapping tore us out of the moment.

A ruddy man stood, surrounded by a group of men in official vestments of dark green trimmed in gold matched with a livery collar dripping in emeralds. The standard wardrobe of the Chancellors of the Privy Council. He put his fingers to his lips, and released a sharp whistle, even though I was looking straight at him, calling me the way a kennel master did his hounds.

Rhys tensed at my side. "Sina—don't."

Ignoring her whispered pleas, I approached him and his grinning companions eager for a bit of confrontation, and the gleam in their eyes promised I'd have it.

"Aren't you pretty? Even under all that muck," he said, words dulled with wine. "The emperling's chosen, at that. Tell me, girl, why the sullen expression? Are you not awed by the splendor of a party graciously bestowed in your honor?" The Chancellor tugged at the neckline of his vestments where two buttons gleamed at his wide throat.

The third, missing.

"Come now, Reggie, the poor thing was raised in the mountains." One of his rat-faced companions raised his nose high like he smelled something offensive. "You'd sulk too."

"Still, she's a beautiful girl and beautiful girls should smile. Like so." His hand closed around my chin, pudgy fingers pushing my cheeks upwards in a forced grin as if I were incapable of thinking for myself, and pinched there for a moment before he released me to join his consorts in raucous laughter.

A tiny voice warned me to stay my hand but deeper than that, a darker voice urged me to act.

Once again, I was that little girl, exhausted from the quarry being shoved and spat at when I walked by.

Once again, I was being scorned and disrespected and ridiculed. Rashni pinned beneath my weight flashed behind the whites of my eyes, her face bloody beneath my pummeling knuckles as her front teeth came free.

Rolling my tongue unto the pocket of my cheek, I plucked up a tiny gold fork from a passing tray with a fat pink shrimp skewered on the end. Meaty and plump, it bounced off my toe as I thumbed it off—and swiftly plunged the prongs into the fleshy folds of his exposed neck.

His laughter shot into a high keening cry, an arrow arcing above the melodic twang of acoustic guitars and the haunting ballad of the Salorcenish singers.

"She stabbed me! *She stabbed me!*" The pallid man staggered—fork swaying as curses rained from his tongue like weepy snot.

Satisfied, I dragged my gaze from his pitiful wailing to his ashen friends. They were no longer smiling.

But *I* was.

A hard grip cinched around my bicep, dragging me away from the scene.

"Come with me." Navarre moved quickly, his long stride forcing me into a near run just to keep up.

A struggle in heeled shoes. I tried to wrench my arm free but his large hand was too strong, a realization that lit twin flames of fascination and frustration in my chest.

"Let me *go*," I snapped when we were through the ballroom doors and sailing down the corridor.

Silver eyes shot to mine and touched my soul like a brand. "If you know what's good for you, you'll shut up and follow me."

He said nothing more until we reached the barracks. A stone and wooden structure stacked three stories high, long and wide with a flat roofline. I took in as many details as I could, the direction of the stairways, how many doors and windows, possible vantage points, the number of guards we passed, where they were positioned, and gauged the time of night by the positioning of the half-moon.

Little details I'd record later once I was free of the insufferable Second Commander.

Navarre hauled me into a private suite—his, I assumed, given the rack of armor near the wide windows shuttered for the night was the same I'd seen him ride into Home Mountain wearing. He flicked the latch on the door, locking it behind him.

"What is wrong with you? Do you have any idea who that man is?"

"No." I snorted a dry laugh. "And I don't care."

"You should." Navarre stalked to a short table and poured wine from a corked bottle into a brass cup. He drank long and deep, throat rippling with each powerful gulp—draining the glass—before he poured out a second. Holding it in a tight grip, he offered it to me.

I pushed his hand aside.

"Suit yourself," he muttered, then drained that one too, and slammed the cup down with a sigh. "Alright, from the beginning. Tell me what happened."

"Why?"

His silver eyes glittered like sparked flint. "I need to know what happened for when the emperling demands answers."

I thought about ignoring him. Silence was a proficient weapon and one I knew how to employ, burning through my enemy's patience until their rage clouded their judgement, pushing them to make a mistake. But the effort required for such a game was more than I was willing to expend at the moment.

So I told him exactly what he wanted to hear.

"One God, give me strength." Navarre dragged his hands down his face when I was done, and nodded as they fell away. "He shouldn't have tried to humiliate you that way, but as a member of the Privy Council—and a known confidant to the Archviceroy—you've made more than one enemy tonight."

I crossed my arms without apology. "I'm not afraid."

"Then you're stupid." Navarre shook his head, bewildered. "You've no idea what you're up against."

He was right, I knew nothing of these people, nor did I care. The moment the man had put his hands on me all I'd seen was red, and a desire to watch it flow. "He's lucky I didn't aim for the artery. The matrons would've had him caned him for such impudence."

"As I've told you once already, you're far from home and surrounded by enemies who'd rather see you dead than seated on the throne. The archviceroy chief among them." Navarre advanced with each word, menacing and powerful, until we were so close I could see the ring of ebony around the outer edge of his iris and smell the sweet wine on his breath.

I wasn't used to looking up to anyone, but standing this close I had no choice. "Why do you care what happens to me?"

A clash of emotions warred with his features before they settled into impassive stone, locking it all away. Rapid-fire knuckles beat against the door before he could answer. Unfastening the locks, Navarre yanked it open, and a plump youth burst in, his cheeks pink and eyes wide in a startled face.

"Milord," he wheezed like he'd raced a mile chased by cave bears. "Emperling—coming. Now!"

"Is he alone?"

Too winded, the youth shook a furious head, cheeks jiggling.

Navarre snarled a seething curse. "Take her into your room. Quickly, Toddrick."

"Why are you hiding me?" I demanded as Toddrick hurried past me, hands shaking as he unlocked the antechamber door.

"Because if Ehrick sees you right now I can't promise he won't do something extreme." Navarre shoved me into the tiny square of a room, barely big enough for the bed wedged against the wall. "Stay here and keep quiet." His eyes whipped from Toddrick and back to mine. "Please."

It was that single word alone, and the gentleness behind it, which swayed me. "Fine."

He dragged the door shut, and Toddrick threw the latch, his chest struggling with heavy, gulping breaths.

"What's wrong?"

"C-can't b-br-breathe when n-nerv—"

"Sit down," I ordered, steering him to the edge of the cot. He plunked down just as the heavy bang of a door bursting open shook the walls, and voices pushed in after it.

Hard, angry voices.

Toddrick wheezed out a whimper.

"Deep, slow breaths." I shoved his head between his knees and gave his sweaty back a gentle pat before returning to lean against the door, peering through the narrow crack—a sliver of a window into Navarre's quarters.

"Where is she?" Iron splints rattled as Ehrick moved in jerky strides, punctuated by the beat of his cane. "Answer me, damn you!"

Navarre stood in the center of his room, arms straight at his sides like a soldier facing his general. "I'll tell you once you've calmed down, brother."

"Damn your impudence!" Henry slammed a fist against wood of a small side table and Prothero shifted on his feet like he wanted to heave himself out the nearest window. "Chancellor Reginald is with the physicians. They say he'll need sutures to close the wound."

I struggled not to roll my eyes in disgust. Or laugh in recollection of the wailing man.

He'd had it coming.

"I want her dragged to her knees. Beaten." Ehrick seethed, unable to cease his restless pacing, and rounded on Navarre. His twisted features an ugly thing to behold in his petulant rage.

"I can't do that."

The furious red of Ehrick's cheeks flushed white in disbelief. "Did I not make myself clear, Second Commander?" He leaned into him, forcing Navarre to retreat a step, claiming his space, crowding him. An act of intimidation.

Dominance.

My hand curled into a fist against the door, nails scraping the grains of wood.

"Send guards to drag her out to the whipping post and do it *now*!"

"Sire." Prothero wrung his hands. "I must agree that publicly shaming your betrothed would be unwise."

"If a Swordsworn girl can defy the emperling so openly before his own court without recourse, how long until our enemies start sharpening their knives?" The Archviceroy interceded, slapping the back of a chair against the wall I was pressed against.

"Finally, someone here speaks sense." Ehrick thrust a hand towards his uncle in agreement. "Wearing her scabbard in my presence alone was offensive enough, but *this*?" He jabbed a finger into Navarre's chest. "You swore to obey me in all things, and yet here you stand every bit as defiant as she is. Perhaps your Acharrān blood flows stronger than Torren."

Navarre bit his lip rather than shove his fist down the emperling's throat until he choked on it—as I would've. *Arrogant bastard.*

"Strip her to the skin and beat her till she screams, Ehrick." Archviceroy Henry raised an imperious chin. "Let her cries ring through the corridors of the palace."

The line of Navarre's shoulders tensed. "She's to be his *wife*."

"She's unworthy of the throne and the prestige that comes with it. My nephew deserves a bride born of pedigree with both wealth and the backing of a great nation."

"Not this again," Prothero groaned. "Sire, we've discussed the matter a hundred times already. The treaty—"

"*Again* with this miserable treaty." The Archviceroy dashed his hand through the air.

"The Torren line has survived near a thousand years. A thousand years! No other dynasty can make such a claim, and why do you think that is?" Prothero braced the table to shout back at the Archviceroy, his face reddening with agitation. "Because unlike other nations entrenched in political and cultural agendas that would seek to circumvent our authority, the Accharāns possess an unwavering code of honor that ensure they're impenetrable to outside influence from our enemies who would conspire to throw a coup. And as consorts to the throne their prowess as warriors is a proven deterrent to anyone who would dare lay threat to the emperor's life."

The Archviceroy mirrored Prothero's pose, the pair of them facing off from opposite sides of the table like generals about to go to war. "While their ferocity and prowess enhanced our image of superiority once upon a time, the Accharāns are an antiquated symbol of conquest. The people no longer care, and the few that still cleave to them as figureheads I will see stamped out like roaches. Down to the last man, woman and child."

"You forget that our Emperling is half Acharrān? As are you?" Navarre snapped and the Archviceroy's cheeks paled before deepening to a livid shade of red.

"All the more reason to purify the Torren bloodline of heathen influence through an alliance of marriage with a greater nation that will expand our empire beyond the boundaries of this single continent."

"You speak of war like a child playing chess," Prothero shouted. "But this is *not* a game!"

"Stop mewling like an old woman, Chancellor," Henry spat. "The Princess of Oscano would bring with her an army of one hundred and fifty thousand. More than enough to quell any rebellion *and* renew our efforts in Zavora."

"The princess is half a world away," Prothero shot back. "We cannot put our faith in an army so far from home when we stand defenseless. Emperor Edvard's Seven-Year-War, along with your Holy Crusade, Archviceroy, has stripped this land of its wealth and stretched our armies so thin it's threadbare. If anyone were to realize how weak we are in this moment, the empire would collapse under a soft breeze. It is imperative now, more than ever, that we maintain appearances of strength. Fracturing the treaty with the Acharrāns all but screams to the entirety of the world of our fragility."

That caught my attention, and I settled closer to the wall.

Ehrick raised a hand to quell any further discourse. "I told my father—several times over—that conquest doesn't always need to come down to bloodshed, but he would hear nothing of it. Now I am surrounded by enemies on all fronts. Enemies who, once they scent blood, will seek to take away all that my family has accomplished," Ehrick raged, a terrible wheeze punctuating his words. "I need allies and the only ones to be found are in marriage to the princess, yet you insist I bind myself to an Acharrān who dares openly to defy me before my court?" He stomped his cane. "I am to be emperor. I will not abide such insolence!"

"This . . . *grievance* is but a ripple," Prothero lowered his voice, softening each word as if soothing a child nearing the throes of a tantrum. "And those ripples can bleed out. But if you feed into them and they'll build into a wave that can wash away an empire. I must implore you, sire, tread carefully." He pressed beseeching hands together and faced the emperling directly. "The Swordsworn treaty is the glue holding the empire together. The Acharrāns may be few, but they are formidable, and if they ever rose against us, united behind your mother, or even this insolent girl, so too will our enemies—and we would not beat them back. Not a second time."

Ehrick's chest rose and fell with hard, furious pants, but gradually a coolness settled into his eyes. "Thank you, Chancellor, for your keen perspective and wisdom. Uncle. I'd like a moment alone with my brother, please."

"Sire." Prothero swept gratefully from the room, but the Archviceroy lingered. Hesitant, and I gathered, displeased that he'd been dismissed.

Once alone, Ehrick shifted to the edge of the table and slumped against it. "One God help me, I'm so tired of this already and it's barely started. Forgive me, brother, it has been a trying week. I did not mean to lose myself in anger."

"There's nothing to forgive," Navarre answered, the tension leaving the line of his shoulders and rigid planes of his back. Pouring out a cup of wine, he handed it to Ehrick. A gesture of truce between them.

*Idiot.*

"A crown is going on my head in a month, but I won't be able to keep it there if people refuse to respect me. What she did tonight . . . she made me look weak, Navarre. Weak. I saw it in all their faces." Ehrick accepted the cup but only stared deep into the contents. "You don't understand what that's like, brother. You're a bastard, true, and that stain is not easily scrubbed away, but you've always had a presence about you that demanded respect despite your low birth. Yet when I walk into a room, all they see is this." He swept a hand to his legs. "I can't—*can't*—let that happen. Not again. Do you hear me?"

"You're too hard on yourself." Navarre claimed the seat next to him, drawing close.

"No, I'm not. I have inherited a derelict empire, bankrupt of wealth and sons, and somehow I must restore both—quickly—or risk further uprising from the people. The provinces stand divided, and uncle says the north and south are still crying out for the old ways to return. Everyone expects me to fail. Some are eager to make it so. I cannot afford to be so openly challenged, Navarre. Do you understand that? I must be stronger than our father, greater than our legacy. I could be the Torren who lost an empire, or the one who gained the world. I need you on my side. Together—there is hope for success."

"I am with you, brother. You know this."

"I do." The hint of a smile graced his lips, and he weighed a hand on Navarre's shoulder, a companionable gesture full of remorse. "I leave for the Holy City in the morning, but when I return, we should go for a hunt. The gamemaster says the forest is thick with silver stags and boars big as hellhounds. We'll have many fine trophies."

"I'd be honored."

Turning away, I leaned against the wall as the room cleared out, my thoughts spinning fast as my racing heart. Toddrick's limp form hung forward, his arms heavy and knuckles grazing the floor with sleepy breaths. The poor guy had passed out in his terror and missed the entire shouting match.

But I'd soaked up every morsel like it was water after a three day fast.

Grandmother was right, the emperling was vulnerable—in more ways than one, but if I was going to survive to see the next day, I'd have to move soft and silent as a stonecat.

*You are a leader, Sina.* Her words floated around me, thick and warm and powerful as the fur cloak wrapped over my shoulders.

*When the time is right—*lead—*and we will follow.*

# CHAPTER THIRTEEN

## Sinadine

THE FIRST THING MY GRANDMOTHER taught me was to know my enemy.

During the days, I trained with my sisters—it was more than exercise, it was our religion, and the rigors of exertion helped temper my impetuous need for the emperling's blood on my blade.

But my nights were mine to roam.

Slipping out in the cover of dark, I'd explored the outer walls of the palace, and took note of the positioning of the various wings and structures from the aviary, barrack, church, armory and vault as well as studying the guard rotations and posts so I could navigate the shadows unseen. I'd paid particular attention to the aviary but had yet to figure out a safe way inside.

Sending a message to my grandmother would be easy enough. Receiving one, on the other hand, would be near impossible.

A problem that led to considerable frustration as I returned each morning before sunrise, exhausted, and carefully recorded every finite detail in a journal I kept tucked above the ledge of a fat, hourglass pillar. But what little I gleaned wasn't going to be enough.

If I wanted to lead my sisters into a war, then I needed to understand what we were up against. The number of troops in the Bridian army, their weapons, strategies, and strongholds—acquiring that depth of information was going to take time. And I would have to get very, *very* close to Navarre. After what I'd witnessed between him and Ehrick in his chambers, the bond between brothers was strong and my instincts warned me to always be on guard around the Second Commander. However noble, even though he'd given me his word of an alliance, his loyalty was to the emperling, first and foremost.

That made him my enemy.

Rubbing sleep from my eyes, I rose from bed and splashed cold water over my face—shocking me awake. Fatigue weighed on my bones, but determination gave me the strength I needed to keep going.

Sun barely kissed the paved stones of the courtyard by the time I reached the barracks, already packed with imperial guards locked in training. Some with swords, and others with weights. Rhys lingered at the sidelines, putting on her protective gear.

Impatient, I set my hands on my hips. "Why aren't you ready?"

"Almost done," Rhys answered, working into a leather vest and a servant helped her with the ties and straps.

Jasz turned at the sound of my voice, her hair plaited into a tight braid racing down the center of her head like an axe blade. "I am ready, *Dakuwan*." She flexed her fingers in anticipation. Challenge.

We hadn't fought since we were children, and never with edged blades. In our last match, our instructors had to wrench us apart, both bloody—her nose, my lip—and howling with rage. They'd forbad us from fighting ever again, but we were far from home and I hungered to test my steel against hers. Unsheathing my sword, the blade flashed almost blue as I entered the circle, vaguely aware of a few of the imperial guards weaving in on the sidelines, placing bets as to which of us would be victorious.

Rhys joined us in the sparring circle, her face grave, but she held back her reservations and raised her hands. "If you step outside the ring, you lose. You will fight to first blood."

"First blood," I echoed.

"First blood."

We tapped blades—acknowledgement, respect—and an indication the fight was to begin.

Twirling my hilt, I inverted my sword so the flat of the blade ran along the back of my arm, the point skyward as we paced.

Sizing one another.

Sleek and smooth, she lunged, clean as the snap of a heron's beak and I side-stepped, ducking as steel slashed above the line of my shoulders, a move that would've sliced my head clean off. A feral burst of primal hunger roared deep inside of me.

I wanted violence and blood

And here she was—willing to give it to me.

My instincts sang as I danced and dodged the blinding movements of her blade before arcing up my sword to stop her assault. Steel rang, loud as a bell struck in the mountain shrine, and our arms strained. A bead of sweat vanished into the dark line of her brow, and our eyes locked over the cross-section of swords before her knee came up, aiming for my unprotected side.

I jerked out of the way of her strike and a few jibes and cheers rolled in from the sidelines. We weren't the only ones enjoying this.

"You're slower than I remember," Jasz said, pacing from left to right, her sword always positioned to her front, while I kept mine inverted at my side.

"Just moving at your speed."

She laughed and slashed at the air. "Enough small talk." High, low—she pushed in with swift, fluid strokes that gave me little time to think or breathe, and we fell into a lethal rhythm so dangerous if I blinked, I'd lose. Sharp, punctuated beats that met with long, graceful lines.

I gave myself to the violence singing in my blood, and let my body do what I was born to do.

Fight.

Rolling into the next stroke—into the wide arc of her arm and blade—I shot my elbow into her face. Her head snapped back, and she staggered with a hand pressed to her mouth, but her gloved fingers came away clean.

Good. I wasn't ready for this to end so soon, but I had stoked her anger, so the next flurry of slashes lacked her earlier finesse. The sharp crack of our blades rang, loud, thunderous and furious as the ache of effort rippled down my arms and into my back. A glorious burn.

She was good. But I was better.

As Jasz arced into a vicious downward stroke, I dove and hit the ground with a roll. My foot snapped out, tangling between hers and she toppled to her knees.

Springing to my feet, hand fisted in her hair, I pressed the edge of my blade against her throat. Her eyes shot up to my face, sweat slick on her brow and mouth trembling with fury as blood bloomed in a fine line. Lowering my sword, I released her hair and stepped away.

Rhys re-entered the circle, wary. "Tap swords."

Jasz spat at her feet, pacing like a cobressa deciding whether or not to strike, but eventually honor restored sense and the tip of her blade touched mine.

"Well fought, *Dakuwan*."

"You, too." Sheathing my sword, I stepped out of the circle and leaned against a smooth stone pillar.

Navarre stood across from me, in a similar stance, edges of sunlight pushing around him. Casually dressed in dark tunic and britches, he had the kind of face and body that undoubtedly compelled most women—and perhaps a few men—to do stupid and dangerous things. Were it not for the imperial badge and sword on his hip, it would be easy to forget he was the Second Commander. Except for maybe his eyes. Shrewd and sharp silver, they homed in like he could peel away a person's skin and see straight to their soul.

They narrowed on me, discerning, and the urge to advert mine only pushed me to hold his gaze and notch my chin higher. His attention flickered to his men training, and a satisfied grin split my face. Another round won. Not a bad start to the day.

"Wanna fight me next?" Rhys asked.

I shook my head. "You go a few rounds with Jasz. I'm going for a run in the gardens." Morning was when the grounds were quietest, and I wanted another quick survey of the aviary during daylight hours to see how many servants tended the birds and which of them might be easiest to slither around. Or coerce.

Stripping off my gear, I tossed it aside. One of the servants would collect and return it to my room. The sound of swords rang behind me and a fresh wave of cheers rose from the excited guards. If I wanted to sneak away, now was the time, but I didn't make it more than three paces when Iereni rolled herself into my path.

"Where are you going?" she asked, sunlight teasing out the red in her auburn hair, elegantly styled in curls and twists atop her head.

I'd been aware of onlookers even in the thick haze of battle, and not once had I caught sight or sense of her. For a little girl in a wheelchair, she was stealthy.

"To the gardens," I answered, and tried to step around her but she tugged hard on her wheels, and once more blocked my way.

"Can I join you for a bit?"

A hint of exasperation flared inside me. Having her by my side would either make my presence less conspicuous or draw unwanted attention, but I couldn't refuse her company and risk upsetting her, either. Best to give her five minutes of my time and then lose her in the gardens.

"Sure," I said, and she tugged her wheels out of my way. "Where are your servants?"

"I gave them the slip. *Again*." She shot me a rueful grin, whisking quickly at my side. "I've been coming down almost every morning to watch you train. The way you move . . . it's like a dance."

Stepping out onto the pebbled path, the tiny stones shifted under my feet. It had rained last night making the path a little boggy, and I thought about slowing my pace, but Iereni pumped furiously, hands protected with fingerless gloves of beaten brown leather. She was determined to keep up, at all costs, and was so much like Taphne that a twinge panged in my chest.

"Have you never seen the Swordsworn train before?"

"No. The first died before I was born, and Navarre's mother shortly thereafter."

"What of the empress?"

Iereni looked at me, confused. "She had to relinquish her sword the day she married."

Horrified, I stumbled to a halt. "They *took* her sword?"

Iereni nodded. "Once wed, an empress is not allowed to touch any weapons—*ever*—or else she'd be charged with treason. Her sword is kept in the vault with all the emperor's wealth and . . ." her voice faltered. "It has always been the way."

*It has always been the way*. Those harrowing words rattled inside of me like the beads in Guida's wordweaving staff.

There was no way Elide had not known this crucial fact and, oh the damnable bitch, how she must be laughing, pleased with her little scheme. She'd given me my sword knowing full well it would be wrenched away—the one thing I'd craved more than the breath in my lungs.

I'd strike down any who dared try to pry it from my side. All the more reason to kill Ehrick before the damnable deed took place. Then, when I returned to Home Mountain—oh, we would have words, my aunt and me. Violent, *bloody* words.

"Something funny?" she asked as I shook my head with a dark laugh.

"Not that you'd understand."

"So . . . will you teach me, then?"

"You should ask Navarre, or one of the guards."

"He won't. I've begged—*repeatedly*. None of them will." Her lips skewed to the side, as if debating how much to tell me. "After Ehrick I'm next to inherit the throne. My older sister, Daneysa, was born to our mother's first husband, a wealthy man, but one without status. When he died, she remarried my father, the marquisate, and had me. Of the two of us, I'm the one with royal blood, so if anyone harmed me—even unintentionally—the law would not be kind. Naturally, they're afraid." She squinted up at me as a burst of sun flashed from behind a cloud, teasing out the silver in her pale green eyes. "But you aren't."

"No, I'm not. But that doesn't mean I have time to waste on a child." Not with the coronation less than four weeks away.

"Please." Her face tensed with desperation. "I wasn't born this way." She gestured to her legs. "I fell when I was little, and since then everyone treats me like I'm made of glass. My father would keep me on a cushion in a padded room if he could, but the world is dangerous, and I want to be ready to face it. Whatever comes, whatever happens. I don't want to be afraid or dependent."

A sentiment I could heartily agree with, even respect, but with all that was on my shoulders, this was the last thing I needed. "I wish I could help you," I sighed. "I do but—"

"Teach me how to fight, and I'll help you send out messages," Iereni blurted.

Surprise punched in my belly, but I kept my expression neutral. "Why do you think I need your help for that?"

She cast me a baleful stare. "I'm crippled, not blind. I've seen you near the aviary more than once. It's where you're going now, yes? I can help you." She dropped her hands to her wheels, scooting closer. "Sometimes," Iereni whispered, "I do the same for the empress."

Now that was interesting.

If she'd proven trustworthy enough to send and receive confidential messages on behalf of the empress, then perhaps striking a bargain wasn't such a bad idea. If I was going to succeed in killing Ehrick before the coronation, time was against me—I needed allies. The daughter of a magistrate on the imperial war council would make for an excellent start.

Crossing my arms, I pretended to give it thought while Iereni twiddled her thumbs, anxiously awaiting my answer.

"How old are you?"

"Fifteen."

"Don't lie to me."

Her chin sunk to her chest. "Thirteen. And a *half*."

The truth this time. She was fine-boned and undersized, so I'd pegged her for twelve at most. "I'll train you," I said, and she punched a victorious fist in the air, "but on the condition that you send my messages *and* give me information."

Her fist lowered, uncertain. "What kind of information?"

I dropped to my haunches, bringing us level. "Stronghold positions, the numbers of men within each, garrison provisions—and copies of any missives that cross your father's desk. Bring me what I need, and I will train you."

"Why?"

Leaning close, I schooled my features into one of a friend seeking to trade secrets by widening my eyes, softening my smile and brightening my voice. "Because I'm Swordsworn. I have been raised to defend and protect so if this is to be my home now then I will do what I must to ensure its safety, and I can't do that if I don't know all of its strength and weaknesses."

Relieved, Iereni perked up in her chair. "Alright. I can do that!"

"One more thing," I added, rising to my feet, "our training remains a secret."

"Yes! I promise! I won't let you down—when can we start? Now? Can we start *now*?"

The temptation of a smile tugged against the corners of my lips. Foolish, sweet child. So easily led by the nose. "How soon can you get what I need?"

"Tomorrow!"

I dusted my hands, eager to be rid of her. "Then we'll start tomorrow."

# CHAPTER FOURTEEN

# Navarre

"TELL ME THIS ISN'T AS bad as I think it is." Navarre frowned at his notes, then handed the ledger across his desk to Toddrick. Since his return, he'd spent most of his time pouring over the garrison expenses and income, but the numbers had jumbled together, like they could move on the page, until what was simple became impossible to decipher.

It took three days to realize he was in over his head and with little recourse, he'd turned to Toddrick to help him muddle his way through. As Second Commander, it was his responsibility to manage food, weapons and provisions as well as oversee incoming revenue, debt, and taxes. A tedious process as he struggled through endless pages of checks and balances.

Toddrick, ledger in his lap, ran a finger down the columns. "It's worse, milord." Skimming back to earlier pages, his expression transformed from concerned to pale shock. "According to this, the garrison finances have been heavily bled for years. We're in major debt across the board."

"God's mercy." Navarre pressed a weary brow to his desk. "How am I going to clean up this mess?" he mumbled into parchment.

Toddrick closed the ledger and folded his hands over it. "If I might make a small suggestion, milord?"

Still face down on his desk, Navarre waved a hand over his doomed head.

"It's well-known the emperling regards you as his true brother. Let him see with his own eyes the disrepair the former Second Commander allowed the garrison finances to fall, and I'm sure he'll . . . understand."

If he had a head to offer Ehrick, perhaps.

But the former Second Commander died in a drunken brawl, and as far as Navarre could ascertain his hand was the only one pilfering from the pot. It appeared the former Second Commander, Sir Kevin Moore, had a heavy hand with cards and fed his addiction by stealing directly from the garrison's own coffers—then padded the ledgers to account for the missing funds.

Untold years of unchecked filching had dug a hole of debt so deep Navarre could see the fiery grin of the Devil smiling up at him.

Yet for this degree of skimming there must've been an accomplice. Going to Ehrick with this now would only circumvent his efforts to uncover the culprit and prove that Navarre was incapable of handling the mantle. Worse, if he failed to sort out the mess, his men would go unpaid and that worried him most. Barely a week into the position, and he was holding on by a thread.

"Ehrick gave me this responsibility. I can't turn to him at the first sign of trouble and ask him to solve my problems." Navarre took the ledger from Toddrick. "When do the men expect to receive their stipends?"

"Three weeks, by the last count. You might get away with four if you want to buy a couple extra days with the impending coronation as an excuse."

What a goddamn mess. "Let's go over our household expenses this evening and see where we can tighten the belt. Starting with me. We'll work our way down the garrison ranks from there." Navarre wiped sweating palms on his thighs. "The men will grumble, but better that then a full-on mutiny."

Pinching pennies would buy him time, but God help him if he didn't find a solution to this mess before month's end. Ehrick had already liquidated assets to ease the people and return the militia. If it really came down to brass tacks, it was possible he could squeeze out a bit more to stem the hemorrhaging here, as well, but Sinadine was right. If he wanted the respect of his position—his men—he had to earn it, and that meant finding solutions to impossible problems *before* heaping the matter at Ehrick's feet. If only to show his men, his brother, that his faith in him hadn't been misplaced.

A knock split through his dark thoughts and Eban entered, thin sandy hair, greasy at the ends, brushed away from a pock-marked face. But even with his bad skin and questionable hygiene, his smile never failed to make the kitchen maids blush.

"Sir, one of the Swordsworn wants to speak with you."

Navarre didn't need to ask who. Only one would brazenly seek him out. "Send her in."

Eban stepped back and Sinadine entered, flush with sweat that soaked into her padded tunic. According to garden keepers, stable boys, and patrolling guards—she liked to run laps through the garden's labyrinthine maze.

Her eyes sliced across the room, taking in details like a predator marking new terrain.

His office was on the ground level, and modestly furnished. The wall behind him lined with volumes of leather-bound ledgers, accounting records for the barracks finances that rolled back a decade with the rest locked away in the palace archives.

"Hello again, milady," Toddrick said pleasantly as Sinadine claimed the seat next to him.

"Hi," she answered without looking away from Navarre, and inclined her head, a subtle hint.

"Toddrick, please give us a moment."

"Yes, of course, milord. Milady." Toddrick hurried from the room.

The instant the door clicked shut, the walls seemed to shudder and groan inwards, shrinking the space around them until it was all too tight, too close. She had that way about her—commanding as a storm that spread until not a scrap of sky could be seen.

That was Sinadine. A storm.

Powerful. Relentless. Captivating.

*And entirely beyond my reach.*

Galled, Navarre pushed the thought aside like a child shoving away a plate of overboiled vegetables. The hell was wrong with him?

She was Swordsworn, for starters, engaged to his brother, for another, and more importantly a thorn in his side. Sullen, stubborn, brutal, and dangerous as a sword to the gut, if the night of the introductions when she'd stabbed Chancellor Reginald in the neck with a fork had proved little else.

And while Navarre had agreed to a tentative alliance, he couldn't afford to forget one crucial fact: She was his enemy, until deemed otherwise.

As if about to prove his point, she unsheathed the dagger from the discarded belt resting on his desk, she tapped it thoughtfully against the palm of her hand. "What progress have you made with uncovering who hired the assassins?"

"There hasn't been time to devote to it."

She pressed the tip of the dagger into her armrest, and turned the hilt idly, drilling steel into wood. "It's been nearly a week."

"And as you can see, I've been busy." He swept out his hands, indicating the ledgers stacked so high he was drowning in them. "Quarterly expenses are due and stipends to be paid."

"I think this is more important than counting coin." Little curled shavings of wood floated towards the floor like drifting flakes of snow.

"As Second Commander, I'm responsible for overseeing the entirety of the palace garrison *and* city patrol, so forgive me if I can't drop everything at your whim."

Sinadine boosted to her feet and stabbed the dagger into the space between his hands and the jarring thud of impact ricocheted into the floor. By some miracle he hadn't flinched.

"Whoever is behind this, put my clan in danger, *Otsaidā*. Every second we waste is more than my sisters can afford to lose." She leaned across the desk, and her eyes flashed to his. So close he could see the flecks of gold shimmering in them like molten stars.

And perhaps it had been a trick of the light, but he almost swore the blue opalescent gem embedded in the hollow of her throat glowed.

"Very well." He reclined in his seat, arms crossed, putting distance between them. "Where do you suggest we start?"

"With a process of elimination. Who is our biggest threat?"

"This is the imperial city." Navarre spread his hands. "Throw a rock, you'll hit three."

"Generally, the biggest threat comes from those closest to us." Sina sunk back into her chair. "Who is closest to Ehrick?"

"Aside from myself? The Archviceroy."

She crossed her legs, endless and strong, all lean muscle—much like the rest of her. "You don't like him, do you?"

"Not particularly, no."

"Are you sure your personal opinion isn't clouding your judgement?"

"He gave up his claim to join the church as a prince to a Grand Patriarch in his greying years. Ehrick might one day become emperor, but Henry will one day assume the mantle of Grand Patriarch, and Ehrick would then answer to *him*. In a lot of ways, it makes him far more powerful than an emperor. And dangerous."

Sinadine weighed his words in silence. Nodded. "Then I guess we'll start there."

Raking a hand through his hair, he gripped a fistful with a sigh. "Give me a few days to put things into place, then we will begin. Just a few more days, Sina. That's all I'm asking for."

Her eyes narrowed; her lips tightened. "Fine," she conceded. "In the meantime, I have a favor to ask."

"A favor, is it?" It was impossible to contain his surprise, or curiosity.

"I need a sword. A practice one," she clarified after his eyes lowered pointedly to her hip. "Something small, and with enough good steel to be re-forged."

"Why?"

"It's a personal matter." She sighed as he arched a brow. "It won't be used to do harm. You have my word."

The urge to refuse her was an immediate slice across his tongue, but instinct gave way to reason. If he wanted her trust, then he'd have to bend somewhere, and this small ask was perhaps the safest way to do so. Sighing, he called for Eban.

The door popped open and Eban stuck his head inside. "Sir?"

"Take Sina to the armory and let her pick out a practice blade of her choosing, then show her to the palace smithy. Whatever the charge, pay it—and bring me a receipt." It would have to come out of his pocket, but so be it.

"Sir." Eban gave a two-finger salute and smiled a little too warmly at Sina. "This way."

Toddrick re-entered the room and cast a furtive glance as Sinadine vanished through the door with Eban.

"How much of that did you hear?"

Toddrick's cheeks flamed sunset pink, and he wrung his hands. "All of it."

"Excellent."

"Are you going to include this in your report to the Archviceroy?"

Navarre braced his desk in thought. The only thing to hold closer to the chest than a friend, is an enemy. It was in his best interests to keep her as close to his side as possible until he'd figured her out for himself.

And while he might not trust Sinadine, he trusted the Archviceroy even less.

"No. His eminence will likely intervene—and then whatever chances I had of earning her trust will be shot to hell. I'll hold on to this for now. See what comes of it." Wrenching out the dagger still embedded in his desk,

Navarre swiped it across his thigh, cleaning sawdust from steel before sliding it back into its sheath.

The hilt still warm from her touch . . .

"Pull up a chair, Todd. We've got a miracle to perform. And not a lot of time to do it in."

# CHAPTER FIFTEEN

## Sinadine

Grey clouds stretched across the predawn sky, thick as unspun wool and so dense it swallowed most of the light. A gentle mist of rain fell by the time I reached Iereni. She impatiently tapped her hands on the rubber-padded surface of her wheels and perked up with a grin as she heard the crunching footfalls of my approach.

"I thought you might've changed your mind." She'd dressed for battle in cotton pants and tunic, and knee length leather boots. Her golden auburn hair braided in a single plait.

I jerked my shoulder. "I gave you my word, so here I am."

"I found the perfect spot where we won't be seen, but first I want to take you somewhere. We have to be quick though," she added with a head tilt, "because you're late."

"If I apologize, will you stop making an issue of it?"

"Only if you say it sweetly and add 'my lady' at the end." Iereni laughed at my grating snarl. "Kidding."

"What about the rest of our agreement?" I uncrossed my arms as Iereni withdrew a dossier she'd tucked behind her back. Accepting it, I opened the leather cover to scan the contents. Frowned. "What is this?"

"What you asked for. Copies of a missive received from a stronghold outside of Hamsly just last week."

"Where's the rest of it?"

"This was all I could manage on short notice."

Furious, I swiped through pages. "But it doesn't make sense." The words were clearly Bridian, but in a mangled sequence as if written by an addled brain incapable of coherent thought.

Iereni rolled her eyes. "It's in code. You need a cypher."

My eyes flashed to hers, narrowed. "What good is this to me if I can't read it?"

"*You* can't." Iereni smirked. "But I can. And every day that we train, I'll bring you translated pages."

"I'm not in the mood for games."

"Good, because I'm not playing one." Iereni crossed her arms. "You think because I'm young, I'm stupid? I saw your face. You're gonna ditch me once you have it all in hand. I want to learn how to fight. You want information—this is the only way we both get what we want." She pushed up a wobbling chin. "Take it or leave it."

I exhaled heavily. Smart kid. Even if I wanted to wring her neck, I had to admire her for outmaneuvering me so neatly. "Fine." I handed the dossier back to her. "We'll do it your way."

Though her face remained calm, her hand trembled as she tucked it behind her. "Did you bring your letter?" she asked once it was neatly out of sight.

I tapped my chest where the folded sheaf of parchment was hidden.

"Good. Come on." With a sharp pump of her wheels, she sped off down the garden path.

"What are we doing?" I demanded as she rolled around to a secondary service door at the beck-end of the aviary. The tower was made entirely of stone, and forty-seven running strides to circle thatI'd counted twice on my second day and recorded the measurements in my journal. It had six open windows winding up twelve rows for the birds to come and go, and likely housed almost three times the number we had at Home Mountain.

Pulling out a key from her pocket, she unfastened the lock and wheeled inside to a wire cage. "Get in and pull that lever."

Doing as instructed, the cage jolted then slowly rolled up—and my stomach plummeted to my knees. "It's rising off the ground."

Iereni laughed. "Don't you have lifts where you're from?"

I swallowed the wave of vomit rising in my throat. We had something similar but far more substantial in its construction. This was little more than a cage dangling over open air with an inch, maybe two, of steel and rope thin as a prayer, separating me from a fall that would shatter most of the bones in my body. I could face death with a laugh and grin, no problem—but exorbitant pain was another matter.

"How high are we going?"

"Don't worry, we're more than halfway now." Once at the top, Iereni wrenched open the grate and rolled across a gap, big enough for a child to slip through if they were foolishly not paying attention.

"That thing is a death trap," I said, nose wrinkling with a scowl.

"I'll be sure to let Ehrick know you disapprove of his design." She giggled. "Come on." Rolling to a stop, she knocked firmly against an arched door of dense oak and a moment later a towering man popped out, wringing his hands on a stained cloth. White curls circled his head in a cloud, bright against brown skin flecked with moles and rows of dotted scars on his cheeks.

Alert brown eyes fell to Iereni and shone with tender affection.

"Hello, Willem," she said, her tone as warm as his gaze. "Thanks for meeting us. This is my friend I told you about, Sina."

He looked at me and tapped his fingers to the side of his head in greeting.

"If you ever need to come alone, this is the best time of day," Iereni explained. "Only Willem stays on hand while everyone heads to the kitchens for breakfast. He'll keep your secrets, Sina, whatever they are."

I reached into my tunic and withdrew a leather pouch. Inside was the tightly folded and sealed parchment, packed with detailed copies of my notes, as well as a short letter to my grandmother, outlining the assassins we'd killed on route to the palace, and asking her to send out scouts to nearby towns or cities to uncover anything about the arrival of the Horuēins.

"Send this by your fastest bird," I instructed, and the pouch disappeared in a large, calloused hand.

"We have two Jabari hawks," Iereni said proudly. "Willem raised them from hatchlings himself. Add this to the contents, Willem." She slipped off a gold ring from the small finger of her left hand. "It's my personal crest. Your grandmother can use it to mark your correspondence, that way Willem will know it's confidential and to signal you."

Willem answered with swift movements of his hands and fingers, dancing around his face and chest in a language I couldn't follow. We had hand-talkers at Home Mountain, but the gestures were vastly different—its own separate and unique language.

"He says when a letter comes, he'll light a candle before dawn and leave it burning in the top window facing the west wing of the palace. You'll be able to see it from your room."

Meeting his gaze, I nodded. "Thank you."

He smiled, a wide flash of chunky teeth. Iereni thanked him as well, pausing for a bracing hug, before we headed back down. I took the stairs while Iereni rode in the cage. She smirked at me as we exited the aviary.

"How long have you known Willem?"

"As long as I can remember. Father got him the caretaker position after saving him from the execution block." Her hands whisked smoothly over the wheels, gravel spitting behind her. "It doesn't pay much, but it's easy work, and he likes the birds."

We reached a crumbling stone wall, and the ruin of a wooden structure on the other side. Entering through the broken door, I gazed up at the collapsed ceiling to the grey sky above—the clouds had thinned a bit allowing a wash of light to filter through. The damp breeze stirred the musk of moss and rot.

"What is this place?"

"This garden house once belonged to the empress. She came here to read or paint, hence the large windows to the east." Iereni circled a finger towards a dusty shattered pane that ran from floor to ceiling and could slide open to let air pass. "The roof collapsed after a violent storm that brought down a Sahson oak. After the debris and tree were cleared away, the Privy Council decided the cost of repairs wasn't worth the expense."

"This will do." I scanned the space. It was a long square-shaped single room, at least twenty feet across in either direction. The remaining brick walls blocked us from line of sight of the palace and would buffer any noise of our training.

"I thought you'd appreciate the practicality of the location." She gave her wheels a backwards spin, and boosted the front end off the ground. The control of her hands on the wheels kept her balanced. "The guards don't often patrol this way, not so early in the morning, at least. If it were near the evening one or two might sneak in for a quick tryst."

Hands on my hips, I kicked at some loose debris. After years of neglect, the place was a mess. Leaves, twigs, some shattered glass, and broken tiles littered the floor. Ruined remains of furniture were shoved into a corner with a bit of moldy curtains, likely used for padding when a guard had a lover on their back.

"So," Iereni clapped eager hands, "what do we start with first?"

"First, I'm going to sort through this mess while you work on some stretches."

The gleam in her eyes dulled like old brass coins left to tarnish. "Stretches?"

"You have strong arms and hands. But years of sitting in a chair has given you bad posture." I touched her shoulder and traced a line down the curve of her rounded back. "I need to open up your range of motion and build strength into the weaker parts of your body if you're going to wield a sword without tiring or hurting yourself."

"And . . ." she squirmed, "you know how to do that?"

"All Acharrān children do the same before we're allowed to drill with each other."

She lowered her chin, fingers picking at a stray thread in the seam running down her left thigh. "But . . . what if *I* can't do it?"

It wasn't hard to guess at what she was implying, but I couldn't understand why she thought her legs were an issue at all. "Aren't there any heroes in your history who weren't able-bodied?"

She shook her head swiftly. "No. None that I know of."

My brows shot up, baffled that such a thing could be possible. "Well . . ." I lowered to my haunches. "There was Lagida de-Ragan. She was deaf, yet she carried her sword for almost twenty years before she died. Michonne de-Voden lost both legs from a childhood illness, and they didn't have things such as wheelchairs in her day, so she faced down her foes on horseback. And I know a little girl, half your age, named Taphne, born with misshapen legs but that hasn't stopped her from training as hard as her sisters. She is fierce. Determined. And one day her name will join the pages of our history, too."

Iereni's eyes widened with hopeful tears. "Really?"

"There are dozens more. Of all shapes and sizes. I'll tell you their stories if you want. Because this," I gestured to her unmoving legs, "may be an obstacle, but any obstacle can be surmounted if you work hard enough. Lead with your sword, and your spirit will follow."

She swiped an arm across her face, and dried any trace of tears, her smile re-emerging. Bright as morning. "Okay. Show me what to do."

We started gently at first, with long and slow stretches of her arms, back, and neck. She was stiff and rigid and whimpered in pain with each movement, but gradually, as her muscles warmed and loosened, I felt less resistance in her spine and joints.

I showed her a range of exercises for her to do in and out of her chair, to build strength in her chest with pushups from the floor and lying flat on her back and crunching up to target her soft belly. From there we progressed to shadow drills—fighting maneuvers without holding an actual weapon—so she could get a feel for the basic movements and patterns.

Iereni was an eager student, and though she struggled with self-doubt, there was a spark of determination that wasn't easily extinguished. She wanted to prove herself, to be challenged even if it scared her.

And I had to admire her grit.

"Alright, let's stop there," I said, and she sighed in relief. Her thick braid of red and gold hair soaked with sweat.

"How'd I do?" she asked, arms trembling slightly in her lap. She'd be sore come tomorrow, and more so by the end of the week.

"Not bad. Work on those stretches," I added. "Every morning, and every night."

"I will," she beamed, "I promise."

I arched a brow. "And my pages?"

"I'll have the first ones ready by evening."

Because her arms were tired, I wheeled her back to the palace courtyard where a nervous woman paced, her lined face flushed with worry. Her eyes snapped with temper as we approached, and she set small hands onto generous hips, like a mother about to scold a child.

And Iereni gave me an impish wink as she was whisked away.

The stars did not shine down on the Imperial City.

The had sun sunk low by the time I reached my rooms, and only a desolate few that stubbornly refused to be ignored were visible, but even they were soon to fade some nights. Almost as if the Spirits of my Sisters had abandoned this place the way its people had abandoned them.

Most of the calls for aid came from the periphery of the continent and now I understood why. They had eradicated the old ways of faith and tradition. Here, the people didn't light candles for the First-of-Us. The shrines were forsaken for towering churches mounted with the God's Eye at the apex of its pointed roof to honor a false deity that demanded utter obedience and blind faith.

In the distant horizon, visible from the windows in my bedroom, a statue of the First-of-Us loomed on the coast. Her sword drawn against anyone that would dare threaten the Motherland.

A thousand of them circled the continent, forged a century after the first Acharrāns fell from the sky. They stood a hundred feet tall, mounted on great pillars. Age and weather had turned the copper green, and the flame that was supposed to blaze at the edge of her sword no longer burned. She was as neglected as the shrines.

Forgotten.

And I wondered would killing Ehrick change all that, or was the damage so far gone that our demise was inevitable? I pushed the thought aside. If I failed my clan would wither and die, like even the strongest of xhixi trees when deprived of sunlight or water, of that I was certain, therefore failure was not an option.

"You have that look on your face, again."

"What look?" I turned from the single sheet of glass blanketing the windows, so pristine it was like open air. Rhys lay reclined on my bed with her outstretched hand waiting for the dagger she'd lodged into the ceiling to drop. It hung precariously, surrounded by a dozen other little holes notching the elegant plaster.

She rolled her eyes to me. "Like you're up to no good." The dagger dropped and she snatched it without breaking her gaze.

"Just thinking." *About how to kill an emperling, destroy an empire and save our clan . . .*

"The emperling will be back soon." Sitting up, she juggled the blade between her hands.

Yes, he would. Two weeks gone in a blink, and I had little to nothing to show for my efforts. "*And?*"

"And you haven't exactly said much on the subject." She hooked her arms around her bent legs and tapped the flat of her dagger against her shin. "About him, or the fact that you're going to be empress?"

What was there to say?

My first impressions of the emperling—Ehrick on his own was ill-tempered and petulant, but harmless. The night of the introductions at court had shown me he had little respect or influence among his courtiers, but the Archviceroy was a different story.

The man exuded quiet menace and pushed his nephew around like a bull with horns, moving him where he wanted the boy to go.

A decorated general in his youth, and now a prince of the church, once the emperling was dead, he'd be a massive problem which meant I'd likely have to get rid of him, too.

"What's going on in that head of yours, Sina?"

"Why are you interrogating me?" I snapped.

"Because every morning you disappear, and whenever you are around, you're quiet."

"I'm always quiet." And more so now that my mind devoted every waking second to sorting out a stratagem.

"Not like this." Rhys waved the dagger tip in my direction. "We're as good as bloodkin, and you've never been able to keep things from me, but I've never seen you actively try to, either. What aren't you telling me?"

Leaning against the wall, I crossed my arms and shrugged. "Nothing that you need to know."

And she didn't.

There were few secrets I'd ever kept from Rhys—there'd been no point in trying as she always saw straight to my naked soul. And though I had never cared about hiding the truth from her before, this was a dangerous deed that defied the foundation of our Acharrān code. We were not cutthroats and assassins.

We were not mercenaries for hire.

We did not take sides in war or politics.

The daughters of the Acharrā were the hand of truth that meted out justice. If I told her of my grandmother's plan, Rhys would only tie herself into knots with worry and do everything she could to stop me. Or worse yet, she'd do everything in her power to help.

On top of that—she was a terrible liar and the burden of knowing would show on her face for all to see.

And as for Jasz? She would sooner throw me to the wolves then dare let me disgrace our principles. No. This was my mission. My call to arms. A path I had to walk alone. And once the deed was done, I had to hope Rhys, and even Jasz, would come to see reason.

If not—well, that was a problem to solve for another time.

For now, lying was the only way to protect her. To protect all of us. Grandmother had entrusted me with an impossible task, and at the cost of my own life, my soul, I would be the salvation of my sisters.

Not its destruction.

Annoyed by my prolonged silence, Rhys' lips settled into a grimace. "I should head back to the barracks. Navarre has given Jasz and I rotations with the City Patrol. I'm due for mine soon."

A frown ripped across my face. As the emperling's intended, I was confined to the palace grounds, but both Rhys and Jasz were given freedom through responsibility, and it was hard not to begrudge them of it. "I thought that wasn't for another hour?"

"I don't want to be late, and you clearly want to be alone with your *thoughts.*" Boosting to her feet, she sheathed the dagger and collected her sword.

*Don't go.* I hated seeing her angry—or hurt—and both emotions seeped from her like curling plumes of smoke over a dying fire. Maybe I was wrong to keep her in the dark. Maybe I should trust her with the truth and believe that she'd have my back as she always did. But before I could give voice to my thoughts, it happened.

Creaking. *Shifting* in the wall behind me. Slight tremors that hummed beneath my fingertips. I'd heard it a couple days ago after Navarre had escorted me back to my rooms, and paid it no mind, but there it was again. Sharper this time. Louder.

"I know this isn't what you wanted for yourself," Rhys added, pausing on the threshold. "But whether we like it or not, this is our home now." Ice blue eyes flickered to mine. "We need to make peace with that."

She vanished behind the door, and I resisted the urge to go after her to soothe her hurt now diminished by a greater need to uncover the source of the sound. Ear pressed to the wall, I listened, eyes closed and waiting. I'd almost given up when it happened.

*Movement.* My eyes popped open with a gasp.

Something was behind the muraled wall.

Or *someone.*

Rushing to the trestle-table, I grabbed a handful of potpourris and returned to where I'd heard the sound, fingers running across the panel, looking for seams and crevices. When I found one, I tightened my fist and crumbled the potpourri and it floated from my palm in dried flakes of perfumed ash that scattered at the presence of a stray breeze wheezing through the cracks.

My heart soared at the discovery.

There was a doorway here, carefully concealed by a garish mosaic mural of Bridian men deified by the Grand

Patriarchs as saints of the One-God. Finding the latch to open it would be like a puzzle.

Thankfully, grandmother had taught me well.

Tossing the remaining potpourri aside, I dusted my hands clean and went to work. It took effort and careful searching over every nook until my back screamed and thighs ached but finally when my finger pressed against a pair of stern eyes a doorway yawned before me.

Wide and dark and dusty.

Poking my head inside, I grinned as the long corridor of a secret passage spread in either direction, leading to a chasm of tunnels that likely wove around the entire palace and beyond. The faint rattle of pipes sang in the distance, a likely source of the sound I'd heard earlier. Casting a whisper of thanks to the Spirits of my Sisters, I propped a stool in the doorway in case it sealed shut behind me, and slipped inside.

The narrow passage was barely wide enough for me to spread my elbows without scraping along either side. The air was dry and musty but the passageway was fairly clean which meant it was likely still used. By whom was a question for another day.

To the left I could make out the impression of stairs leading down, and to the right a sharp corner. Weaving left, I followed the winding length of stairs as far as they went, the path growing darker and darker with my descent, but I crept comfortably through the shadows. They were as familiar to me as the scent of morning jasmine that bloomed in the pagoda gardens in spring.

There was more than one way to see in the dark.

Using my hands, I traced my fingers and palms across the walls—seamless and gritty. More doorways and passages opened around me, but I followed along in one straight line as the air shifted from dry to damp and the rush of water flowed beneath my feet.

Given the smell, I banked on sewers pushing city waste out to the sea. The corridor followed the direction of the water, so I let them lead me as far as they went until the corridor gave way to a craggy cavern that smelled of salt and brine. This passage had led not only beyond the palace—but the Imperial City—to a vast stretch of midnight waters lapping at a pebbled shore. But it was the sky and wind that called to me.

The moon and the stars so vibrant it brought tears to my eyes.

My knees weakened and I sank to the shore and smiled. There on the pebbled beach, I savored this stolen and forbidden taste of freedom as a blood red sun sunk beyond the hazy edge of the horizon.

The end of another day.

# CHAPTER SIXTEEN

## Sinadine

OVER THE COMING DAYS I LOST myself to the rhythm of training Iereni, and exploring the hidden passages, marking the various routes with bits of phosphorescent chalk until I no longer needed them to guide my steps. My body was a candle burning at both ends, but I was used to pushing through pain and fatigue over years of training with my grandmother.

Iereni returned for our sessions, surprisingly without her nursemaid or attendants in tow, and I never stopped to question how she managed to give them the slip every day. Morning and afternoon, I timed her as she raced her chair up and down the quieter paved garden paths to expand her lungs and push her endurance until she managed fifteen laps without losing breath.

After that she then joined me in the labyrinth where the softer terrain and sharp turns made for a challenge, but she more than kept up. From there we worked on shadow drills—learning the flow and movement so that her body would memorize the rhythm until it became second nature.

True to her word, Iereni gave me everything I needed, translated pages, decoded maps and supply schedules given in bits and fragments, but those fragments gradually came together to form a terrible picture. Each shard, important and vital, brought me closer to victory. I covered each update into several letters sent off to my grandmother—all without response—and the lingering silence from the mountains worried me. I'd sent the last letter, three days ago, and tried not to snarl with impatience, *tried*, when I woke up to yet another morning to find Willem's signal candle unlit.

I wasn't accustomed to failure. From childhood I'd learned that if I wanted to be seen, respected, I had to be the best at everything. Failure was perhaps the only thing that truly terrified me.

Failing my mother.

Failing my clan.

The only thing I hated more than failure was loss of control.

"You're getting better," I said, mopping a cloth across my face, and handed Iereni a water canister.

She guzzled deeply, and swiped a hand across her mouth when finished. "You think so?"

"I do."

"Can I ask you something?" She capped the canister, water trickling from her chin. "What are the beads in your hair for?"

Sitting next to her, I stroked the length of a braid between my fingers. Some were glass, others made of clay or wood, but most were precious stones. All in a variety of colors and shapes, spaced between gold and silver hollow cuffs, bronze circlets. Each special and meaningful. Each earned.

"This square turquoise one is given to all hopefuls at the commencement of training for protection and guidance," I said. "This one," I pinched the next bead of coral red with veins of gold, "was from my first match. The red means I won in less than three moves against all my competitors. As for the braids themselves, three strands woven together are to link mind, body and spirit."

"And this?" She gestured to the hollow of my throat to the blue opal stone nestled in my skin. Perfectly round and encased in gold.

"This is only for the bloodkin of the First-of-Us," I said. "It's to connect me to my ancestry as a descendent of the great Acharrāns who came to the Motherland millennia ago to purge this world from the shadow demons that almost bled it dry. They fought gloriously unto death, so many of them that their blood stained the sands of the Wastes blue until the ancient evil receded back into the earth like smoke where they've remained—too afraid of our wrath to ever rise again."

Iereni's nose wrinkled. "It's a beautiful story but . . . you actually believe it to be true? Women from the stars and demons made of smoke and shadows?"

"You don't believe in demons?" I cast her a disbelieving look. "Doesn't your One God preach of a fiery inferno beneath our feet *full* of them?"

"I don't believe in the One God, either." She skewed her lips with a shrug. "There's too much pain. Too much bitterness. How could a god remain silent in the face of suffering and need? How could he let an infant die of starvation, or a flood wipe out a village's crops? They say near a billion people pray to him across the empire—but never once has he answered."

"The stars do," I replied, my eyes tracing across the sky where they were hidden under the wash of daylight. "So if not the Acharrāns, or your One God, what do you believe in?"

She thought about that for a moment, then smiled. "You. This." She gestured between us. "Everything you're teaching me."

"Fair enough." I twirled my sword before sliding it into my scabbard.

Iereni's eyes tracked it hungrily. "Can I try with a *real* sword soon?"

"You think you're ready for one?" I asked, crossing to the other side of the room.

"Yes!" She bounced eager fists against her armrests. "More than ready. Readier than I've been for anything—*ever*."

"Good. Because I have something for you." I moved aside the mildewed curtains piled on the floor to find the item I'd stashed amid the debris earlier that morning.

The sheath was worn and tough leather, a muted, ugly brown. The sword itself, originally a thick Galgoan short blade that the smithy had re-forged—following my explicit instructions—to mimic the slender Acharrān style.

Turning around, I presented Iereni with the sword and scabbard. "It's not much, but it'll do for our training."

Her eyes popped wide, and her mouth formed a startled 'o'. "It . . . It's mine?"

"You've earned it."

Gentle fingers closed around the hilt and, cradling the sword close, Iereni promptly burst into tears.

It took twenty minutes to console her and, once the tears subsided, I taught her how to clean and care for the weapon.

Afterwards she raced to the aviary to show Willem her new blade while I went off for a run. I followed the familiar garden path through manicured trees, their limbs shorn into blunted shapes instead of sprawling with languid freedom, the leaves gilded red, amber and yellow. In a few days they'd fall to the ground and be swept away by rakes.

Everything about the gardens was forced and unnatural and nothing like running through the untamed woodlands. The sudden grief of memory, an overwhelming ache for the familiar, seized me like a terrible illness in my bones.

I missed the crunch of bracken and the sticky scent of evergreens as my feet pounded over moss so thick it was like running on clouds. If I closed my eyes I could almost smell it. Musky with damp and rot, and the hint of blood in the air from a fresh kill.

I longed for the distant howl of wolverines and yipping ice foxes. The cry of snow eagles and screams of falcons. To feel the sharp cold of ice and snow and stone, the caress wind winding through the mountains and the comforting warmth of a roaring fire. To hear the whisper of swords tangling in the colosseum as my sisters trained beneath the shadow of the mountainous peaks and grand pagodas.

I yearned for *home*.

Here the air was thick with smog and clouds of it billowed endlessly from stacked chimneys and distant industrial factories, staining the sky with a grey-ish cast like rot festering in a bloated corpse.

I tamped down on the sting of tears.

Once the emperling was dead I'd be free of this place.

This disease.

Up ahead, silver-white hair, braided and long, flickered like a banner in the wind. *Rhys*. My heart lurched as she stalked away, back to me, dressed in a dark grey uniform for the City Patrol. Either she had just come off her rotation or was about to start one. She'd spoken little to me since our disagreement, and I'd given her ample space but now my feet pushed faster, closing the distance between us.

She jolted as I swung in front of her, and frowned. "There you are. Navarre's looking for you."

"Why?" I asked, veering left when she attempted to side-step me.

"How the hell should I know?" Rhys danced to the right and dodged to the left but couldn't shake me.

"You're speaking like them now."

Rhys shot up her chin, but otherwise remained silent.

I lowered my hands, sighed, letting her pass but matched her stride. We were deep in the gardens, and that gave me time. "I hate this. I hate you refusing to speak to me."

Her eyes blazed on some fixed point in the distance. "How does it feel?"

"That's not fair."

She stopped suddenly and rounded on me, shoving her hands against my chest. "No, what's not fair is you pushing me out for no reason. I'm not just your *damnable* friend, Sina, I'm blood of your blood." She flashed her palm. To the healing silver line in her pale skin. An echo to mine and Jasz. "That's supposed to mean something."

"It does." *Damnable dead.* Scooping a hand through my hair, I raked it back. Rustling thick, black waves that were tangled and damp with sweat. I had to give her something. A small truth to placate her hurt. "I've been training Iereni in secret."

She rocked like she'd been struck by a fist rather than utter disbelief. "What?"

"Every day," I continued, steering her to a stone bench. "We do stretches and strength training in the morning, and work through shadow drills until the late afternoon. She asked me a few days after we got here."

Confusion wriggled through her silver brows as we sat down. "Why would you hide that from me?"

I dropped my hands to my lap and exhaled heavily, forming more lies through truth. "Because she's worried her father will find out and stop our lessons. And . . . I don't think the emperling would approve, either."

"*Hm*." Rhys shifted her jaw in thought. "People are starting to notice you slipping away for longer and longer durations, Sina, it's why I came to look for you. I've covered as best I can but if your plan was to be discreet, you suck at it."

That was a problem. "Who's been noticing?"

"Navarre, mostly. But a few of the servants are prodding. Some of the guards."

I schooled my face into passive neutrality, but inside my mind spun with frenzy. Was it a coincidence or an indication that despite all precautions, someone was taking notice of my clandestine efforts?

"I'm glad you're doing it, though," Rhys continued, interrupting my thoughts. "I never understood why Bridians arm their boys and disarm their girls, weakening them to the point of total dependency. It's strange. Their entire system is built on the elitism of men. Iereni is right to want to change that for herself." She tipped her head, smiled. "I'm proud of you."

"Why?"

"Because the Sina I know would never teach anyone, let alone have the patience for it."

"I still don't." I snorted. "But . . . she's a good kid. Eager to learn and improving quickly." Clouds passed overhead, casting thin shadows to slither across the path like water in the slow-moving river where I caught fish with my bare hands. "And I needed something to do."

"I could help." She leaned into me, bumping shoulder to shoulder. "That way you can actually stay visible and deflect suspicion."

It wasn't a bad idea.

Diversifying Iereni's training with a different opponent would push her to learn how to anticipate and read someone new. It would also give me more time to focus on my own tasks which I'd reluctantly neglected.

"I think she'd like that."

"You should let Jasz in on this, too." Rhys smirked. "She's also kinda pissed over your vanishing act, and I think this would smooth a lot of ruffled feathers."

A groaning laugh trickled out of me. "Damnable dead, deliver me from Jasz and her foul moods." But Rhys was right. Whatever my feelings, Jasz was a smart, capable fighter, and if this could pacify her in the process—all the better. "Fine. But you talk to her. She's liable to chew my head off if I try."

Rhys closed her hand over mine before I could stand. Though strong and capable of great skill, her small, delicate fingers appeared almost childlike against my larger, scarred hand. "Please tell me there's nothing else you're hiding?"

"No. Nothing else," I answered, without a break in gaze or hitch in my voice.

Relief swam through her ice blue eyes, like sunlight skipping across clear water and I hated how easy it had been to lie while meeting her hopeful gaze.

"I have a shift to get to." Boosting to her feet, Rhys dusted the back of her thighs. "I'll speak with Jasz tonight, and tomorrow we'll sort it all out."

She walked away, head high and her steps light, and the ache of regret burned a hole through my chest, searing straight to my heart.

Returning to my rooms, I tugged off my clothes, tossing them in a sodden heap, and halted by the *shower*. It gleamed invitingly, a chamber of glass and steel. I'd never thought to try it so far, but suddenly I was too impatient to wait for a bath to fill. I wanted the heat of water on my skin, soothing away the burn of aching muscles *now*.

Entering the glass chamber, I fiddled with the knobs. It wasn't all that different from the tub, the left one brought out cold water, and the right one scorching hot. So I spun them both until the faucet jettisoned a comfortable temperature, and when nothing remarkable happened, gave the third knob a hard twist.

Water shot out from above me and I gasped in surprise, then laughed, holding out my hands and tipped my face toward the wide disk as rain poured down like the sky had opened up in fat, heavy drops—warm as a summer storm—soon interrupted by the gentle tap of fingers to glass. Blinking my eyes clear, I instinctively reached for a sword that wasn't there.

"I knocked." Daneysa stood barely visible through the steamed glass. "But when you didn't answer I just—I'm sorry, but the emperling wants to see you. *Immediately.*"

It was a struggle not to roll my eyes, or snarl at the inconvenience.

Turning off the taps, the torrent stopped, and I swung open the shower door. Steam billowed around me, and a hint of warmth glowed in Daneysa's cheeks as I wrapped myself in a drying cloth.

Nakedness was not something Acharrāns were raised to feel ashamed or embarrassed about. We'd often bathed together or swam naked in the still-water of the mountain lakes during the bright summer afternoons, and if there was work to do when the days grew too hot, many of the clan labored topless.

But something about Daneysa's expression made me pause . . . and wonder what lay beyond it.

"I told you it was a marvel." She stepped forward, closing the stall door, her hand brushed ever so slightly against the curve of my bare shoulder, and woke *something* unfamiliar inside of me.

But then I imagined Daneysa could lure the most reticent soul with only a smile and a beckoning crook of her finger.

She was a beautiful girl with skin like sunlight over marble, contrasted by the loose waves of mahogany hair scented with rose oil. A rich plum gloss that matched her gown, enhanced the pillowy shape of her mouth and made her eyes impossibly green.

Amused by whatever she saw in my expression, she eased back and her features transitioned into a mask of gentile elegance with only the barest hint of wickedness dancing beneath the surface, like the flash of a fish's tail before it vanished from sight.

"Come. I've brought you another gift from the emperling."

I followed Daneysa into the bedchamber, and there, draped across my freshly made bed was a gown, but far simpler than the one I'd worn during the gathering.

Deepest blue with long sleeves and a neckline that hugged my shoulders, the trim and hem embroidered in azure, coral and turquoise with hints of gold that matched the thick golden sash around the waist. A pair of heeled shoes with matching gold and ivory earrings completed the outfit.

I ran my hand across the dark blue fabric, soft with a subtle sheen. It was a thing of beauty, but knowing where it came from I wanted to shred the dress with my teeth and send it back to the emperling in a pile of ribbons at his feet.

An omen of what was to come for him and his empire.

The emperling wasn't alone when Daneysa and I arrived. He stood inside the palace's church beneath the God's Eye that hung ominously over the pews where the masses gathered to hear the Archviceroy speak from their books of false deeds. It sickened me to stand and face its empty gaze.

The One God—a lie they created to outshine the stars.

"Ah," Ehrick said with a dramatic roll of his hand through the air, "at last she *graces* us with her presence."

Daneysa curtsied. "Is there anything else I might do for you, sire?"

Ehrick flicked his wrist. "Leave us. You as well, Second Commander."

Navarre's expression was an unguarded canvas of hesitation as he passed, smoke and fog and shadows all wrapped in one. The doors closed behind them and Ehrick lumbered towards me, his iron legs rattling loudly with each lurching step, pistons and gears whirring like a cobressa soon to strike.

"Lovely." He angled his head. "You clean up well once the paint's been scrubbed off."

My fingers clenched into a fist so tight my knuckles whined. "Why am I here?"

"Do you know the histories of the empire? How it all came be?"

"My clan have our stories."

"Stories are far from fact." He thrust up a wagging finger. "Jaymes Torren, my forebearer, was a man with a vision of cohesion and unity. He saw a vast, untamed, brutal world, and sought to bring peace, prosperity, knowledge and salvation. To create a modern age free of ignorance."

"By slaughtering millions, stealing their lands, depriving them of their culture, and profiting off their labor," I spat. "He was a cruel, ruthless, bloodthirsty conqueror who brought nothing but war, death and slavery in the wake of his ignorance."

"If he was such a cruel, ruthless, bloodthirsty conqueror," Ehrick echoed with a mocking whine to his voice, "then why didn't he slay your ancestors when he had them by the throat rather than negotiate for peace?" He swept a hand before my face, as if scrubbing away my very existence. "It's what he should've done. Some beasts are not fit to walk among *civilized* men. Putting them down would've been a mercy."

Rage danced in colorful spots on the edges of my vision, and I strained for every ounce of control I could summon not to succumb to his goading. Smashing my knuckles into his face would feel great, but with his First Commander smirking in the aisle, I realized violence was what he wanted from me.

To prove I was a wild, untamed animal fit for slaughter. He was a playing a battle of wills; a game I couldn't afford to lose.

*The stonecat is silence and strength.*

"Why do you hate your own blood so much?"

Sensing my restraint, Ehrick eased a little straighter, an opponent preparing a new line of attack.

"In truth, I admired them once," he admitted. "When I was young and terribly innocent. I was dazzled by my mother's grand stories of women who wielded swords of starfire, and powerful familiars that leapt from their skin with a thought, carrying them into battle. All I ever wanted, more than anything, was a sword of my own. To be so feared and respected. To be Swordsworn." His jaw tensed, tight as the knuckles in his bony fist. "But when I asked her to take me to Home Mountain so that I might fulfill my little dream, she kissed my forehead and said, '*the mountains are a haven for all, but the gift of our steel is for a woman's hands alone.*" Ehrick sneered. "A haven for all. But men are not worthy to call themselves Swordsworn. Can you imagine?"

"A woman told you no, and your reaction was to destroy her, and all women like her?"

For women becoming Swordsworn was only a small corner in a world that favored men where they could be safe. Where they could grow and thrive. Where they could taste power and claim respect.

"Only to the privileged does equality feel like oppression."

"Spoken like a true Acharrān. Your kind has lived outside of the laws of the empire for too long. Playing judge, jury and executioner. Parading yourselves across the continent like you're disciples of the One-God, Himself. Yet you refuse to submit to a higher authority."

"Why should we when life cannot exist beyond what women birth into being? If you believe your One God is real, then it's because the Acharrān created him, as they've created all things. You want us to kneel to you? It is you who should kneel to *us.*"

A tremor of dark anger scored across his face, but the ice returned, smooth and easy, coating his smile in frost cold enough to burn.

"There's something I'd like to show you. Something to help you better understand your place. Come now, it's not far." He lurched beyond the priest's pulpit to a set of wide doors that yawned at his approach, and I blinked against the wash of evening light as an apricot sun slunk beyond the edge of the imperial wall.

"Six days from now, people will flood into this plaza, so many you won't be able to distinguish faces." Ehrick stood in the center of a terrace, large and open as a stage, facing the wrought iron gates. "This is where the coronation ceremony will take place. As well as the ascension. Acharrāns have two of them, don't you?"

"The first when you earn your sword, and the second when we die," I answered.

He turned back to me, a wicked grin stretched across his narrow face, then his eyes shifted to something beyond me, and that grin stretched wider still.

Confused, I turned to see what he was gazing upon so hungrily, and was met with a devastating sight that split my heart in two.

Skulls.

More than I dared count, stacked in neat rows like beads in an abacus. I staggered forward and brushed cold fingers across one bathed in blue and yellow gold and studded in diamonds. Another at its side, entombed in red and blue gold with yellow emeralds.

On they went, each horrific in its terrible beauty, and the strength in my legs wavered.

These were the skulls of my Acharrān sisters who'd come to serve the empire so that the rest could live free—displayed like garish trophies mounted on a hunter's wall.

*So many . . .*

"Exquisite, isn't it? Took weeks to prepare."

Tears burned my eyes, searing the image into my brain. I would see this for all the days of my life, a memory formed in scar tissue. My hand fisted the gown at my hip and I ached for my sword. To hold it close and weep for the dead.

"Can you hear them?" Ehrick lurched to my side. His voice a venomous, dulcet whisper in my ear. "The screams of your sisters?"

Yes. I could hear them. And feel them, trapped and clawing inside me. We didn't keep the bones of our dead, we burned them, setting their souls free. Here, encased in their prisons of gold and jewels, they were lost to the stars. They were lost to us.

*The stonecat is silence and strength.*

"Such a display is a tad gauche, I admit—though the faux gems and gold are skillfully made replicas by true maestros, but it does send a powerful message. Much like your little display of defiance at the gathering."

A sob wrenched from my throat as a chill of grief tore through me in a searing burn of frost that went to the marrow, shattering bone. My sword. I needed my sword. I needed the comfort and strength of steel.

*The stonecat is silence and* fucking *strength.*

Ehrick reached into the inner pocket of his embroidered vest and waved a theatre pamphlet under my nose, emblazoned with the title *The Swordsworn Bride.*

"You should've seen it for yourself. Such a charming little production that painted you most favorably and me *less* so. Most would expect me to kill the composer for such a grievous insult. Or at the very least, shutdown the opera house." He shook his head absently. "But no. If I kill him, I appear weak of character, more so than I apparently already do. If I shut down the opera house, well then that makes me weak *and* petty. So instead, I've endorsed him, showing the masses I'm both generous and forgiving. With this small act I save face. But be warned." He tossed the pamphlet at my feet then gestured to the monstrous wall. "Make a fool of me a second time and your skull will join them. I'll place it up there, myself, still wet with your blood."

"Maybe I'll do the same with yours first." The muscle around his left eye ticked ominously and I smiled through tears, daring him to strike me. Welcoming physical pain to dull this emotional agony, an excuse to forsake careful planning for quick, easy violence.

"Chain her to the wall," Ehrick ordered. "She needs time to learn her place."

At the snap of the First Commander's fingers, guards seized me, and I didn't fight as fetters were attached to my hands, feet and neck, and even in the chaotic whirl of emotions it didn't escape me that he'd had them waiting for this precise moment.

*Kill him*, a defiant voice roared to end his life along with my grief, and I imagined slicing his throat wide open. Even chained I could disarm a guard and do it long before they could blink. I'd gladly die in glorious combat so long as I carved his black heart from his chest, an impulse almost too great to ignore—but if I failed?

Jasz and Rhys—the thought of their skulls gracing this monstrosity stayed my hand. I couldn't let my anger consume me.

I had to be stronger. I had to survive this anguish to avenge them all.

The guards fastened my fetters to the posts and one of them smiled cruelly, his wooden teeth, a flash against his black beard. *Benj.* The memory of his name sang through my dark thoughts. The guard from the escort. The same one I'd brought to his knees. The scar on his throat shone with a blue-ish tint. The kiss of Acharrān steel left such scars.

We called them brands.

"Not so proud now, bitch," he spat low enough so only I could hear.

"You see?" Ehrick whispered with a lurid grin once the guards stepped back, awaiting further orders. "What need have I for stars, when I have shadows?" He lingered with a laugh before vanishing through the chapel doors.

Alone, I bolted down my rage, a dark, swimming creature in my bones.

*The stonecat is silence and strength. She is the hand of death, come with tooth and claw.*

*And her prey does not see her until they are already dead.*

I wrapped those words around me, a cloak, and cold iron warmed against my skin. Ehrick would die, by claw and tooth, I vowed to see it done.

They'd chained me so I couldn't sit, or bend. After the first hour, my feet started to burn as the heeled shoes put all the stress of weight onto my toes. By the second, the ache flashed up to my knees and into my lower back.

The dainty clasps were impossible to reach, so I wedged the slender heel between the strap and my ankle and tugged until the damnable thing finally broke. The second one was harder to manage, but eventually I was free of the infernal things and kicked them away from me.

Iron chafed my throat, and I gave the chain a vicious yank. Those decorated skulls rattled ominously and for a moment I was tempted to bring it down—all of it—crashing in a heap.

"Careful. If it falls, you'll flatten yourself beneath it," a soft voice said.

I squinted in the dark as the empress emerged, an ethereal figured dressed as always in ivory—the color of mourning for her husband and sons. Smooth dark hair draped over her right shoulder, unadorned with braids or beads, and a smile pushed the apples of her cheeks up against her eyes. In her hands was a steaming bowl atop a polished dinner tray.

"I thought you might be hungry."

"I'm fine," I snarled, but my stomach roared in betrayal. I hadn't eaten anything since breakfast before training with my sisters, and again with Iereni in the afternoon. In truth I was ravenous, but I wasn't about to beg, or show weakness.

Not even to her.

Standing this close, I hadn't realized how tall she was. Not many could look me in the eye without heels, but she did. Something about her soft, submissive nature had made her seem so much smaller when I first saw her next to the throne. After that it was only fleeting glimpses in passing, and she was always surrounded by an army of servants and guards. Spies.

But as I scanned my gaze across the naked terrace, I was surprised to find her alone when Ehrick had clearly gone to such effort to keep us apart.

"I still have a few friends," she said, as if sensing my thoughts. The empresses set down the tray and brought the bowl to my lips. The creamy, pureed soup smelled of lentils, salty ham and spices. She tipped the bowl carefully so I could sip and swallow.

It was warm, but not hot so I drank it fast, draining the bowl, and though it was hearty, my belly kicked for more.

"Have some water." She replaced the bowl at my lips with a canteen.

I guzzled that down, too, not realizing how thirsty I was until the cool liquid touched my tongue.

"There. That's put some color back in your cheeks." She wiped my chin with her sleeve when I was finished and returned the canteen to the tray. "I'm sorry, I would've come sooner, but I had to wait until Ehrick was asleep."

I jerked my wrists, rattling chains and bones. "Are you proud of your son?"

Her smile vanished and she turned away. I thought she meant to leave but instead she wove towards the center of the terrace and faced the empty plaza. Moonlight carved over the edges of her face; skin as pale as her ivory kubari—she looked like she was made of marble.

A beautiful, sad statue.

"The emperor was not a man who allowed for weakness, not in himself or others. That's all he saw when he looked at Ehrick, and ignored him, utterly." She crossed her arms, hands rubbing across her biceps as if trying to keep warm against some unseen chill. "As his mother, I tried to fill that void, but the harder I tried the more he seemed to resent me for it." A silver tear sliced down her heart-shaped face. "You should not anger him so."

"He's a spoiled bully who doesn't deserve the air he breathes."

The empress flinched, but she didn't argue the point, and that seared across my nerves like a branding iron—glowing red and vicious. I wanted her rattled. I wanted her to be angry.

I wanted her to *fight*.

To show me that there was still a hint of the Acharrān warrior buried beneath ashes of the life she'd lost.

"How could you let them do this?" I seethed. "How could you let them do this to *us*?"

Her eyes flashed to me, bright with frustration and shame.

The first spark.

"You have no right to judge me. You don't know what I've endured or why, or what it's been like for me and all the Swordsworn who came before." She shot a hand towards the skulls smiling with false-jeweled teeth. "You've only been here a few weeks—I've weathered twenty-four years. You cannot know the things you will do to survive."

"I know I'd rather die by the sword than live in chains." I tugged mine, rattling the wall in threat.

In promise.

"Is that what you think I've done?" She gave a mournful shake of her head then gathered my face, her touch cool as mountain snow, and leaned in to kiss both of my cheeks. "Soon you will know my burden, sister," she whispered, each word heavy with grief and apology. "For what it's worth you have my sympathy." Her brow pressed against mine and held there.

A mark of respect, from sister to sister.

Tears rolled down her cheeks and splashed on my toes. This wasn't a simple goodbye. This was farewell. Because the next time we were alone together, it would herald her last moments as empress.

And bring me closer to my first . . .

# CHAPTER SEVENTEEN

## Navarre

Helplessness was a brutal poison. It spun in Navarre's head, dizzying his thoughts and rotting through his gut, leeching like acid as it ate him from the inside out.

Ehrick had called him *Second Commander*.

Not brother.

Which meant he'd spoken not as his blood, but as his sovereign lord, leaving Navarre with no choice but to obey his emperling without protest. Especially with Sir Rickard watching him with a smug hatred. So he'd walked away, leaving Sinadine alone with his brother.

Navarre scowled on the other side of the sealed chapel doors, unable to pull his feet away. It was nearly three weeks since the gathering, and while that would've been long enough to cool even the most vicious of tempers, Ehrick had made one thing absolute. He would not abide being disgraced or made to appear weak. Sinadine had done both once already, and Navarre couldn't imagine she'd hesitate to do so a second time.

*Or worse . . .*

"My dear, Second Commander, what's with the face?" Daneysa's voice floated around him, bright as her perfume. "You look fit to go to war."

Hands in fists, he rounded on her with a snarl. "What the hell are you playing at?"

"I don't get your meaning?" she said with a dainty tilt of her chin.

"This." He shot a hand to the shut doors. Teeth clenched. "I told you to keep Sina out of sight until I had the opportunity to gauge Ehrick's mood." *And to soften it if needs be.* But he'd barely gotten a word in edgewise before Daneya arrived with Sinadine in tow.

Daneysa frowned. "I did as my emperling bade me."

"And suddenly you're the dutiful and subservient cousin, bowing to his every whim? Drop the act. There was a time as children when you teased and mocked him along with all the rest. I remember it well."

"We're no longer children, Navarre. He'll be emperor soon."

"I didn't take you for the sort to curry favor."

"Any smart courtier would do the same." Her eyes caught the light and glowed vibrant green. "By his grace, I will rise high and higher still—the world will think the One God gave me wings."

He circled her slowly, giving it careful consideration. "If ambition is your game, then why help Sina deliberately antagonize Ehrick at her introduction? You willfully encouraged her to spit in his face in front of the entire court. Don't deny it—*again*."

Daneysa spread her hands with an easy shrug. "It was only a bit of harmless fun. Aside from the mishap with Chancellor Reginald, which he rightly deserved." She crossed her arms. "God's witness, perhaps now he'll keep his wandering hands to himself. You can't fault me, or Sinadine, for that."

"That harmless bit of fun put a target on her back."

"Oh quit your whining. She's more than capable of handling Ehrick in a snit."

Navarre caught her by the wrist, squeezed hard enough for the amusement in her eyes to fade and the jovial mask to slip. "That's exactly what I'm afraid of."

"If I didn't know better, I'd think you coveted the soon-to-be-empress." Daneysa wrenched herself from his grip. "But she's off limits. Even for *you*."

"Maybe you should remind yourself of that little detail."

There was a flicker of genuine surprise, quickly chased by a bright laugh. "Oh my, how observant you are? A rare talent. I'll confess, I can't help that she draws me; she's bold and exciting." Leaning into him, she walked her fingers up his chest. "Why do you care if I look at her? Are you jealous?" She came closer still, offering the alluring fullness of her mouth that had dragged many to drown in the depths of her seduction.

But she was right. He was observant. And he'd seen what Daneysa had chosen to do with her beauty.

Exuding it like a drug. Wielding it like a weapon.

She preyed on men—young and old, stocky and thin, ugly and handsome. Sharpening her charms until she gleamed with a lethal edge few could resist. Witnessing the calculating truth of her nature had granted him immunity, and for that he was immensely grateful.

Navarre brushed her hand aside. "Your charms don't work on me, Daneysa."

"That's because I never employed them on you." Undeterred, she draped her arms around his shoulders, trapping him within her sugary rose scent. "But if I could own your heart and enslave your soul. I could make you question your own sanity—if that's what I wanted from you, I could take it. Everything. Until you were hollow, empty and broken at my feet." Her eyes seared into him. Through him. "*That* is my power."

"Maybe when I was young and stupid."

"Poor dear, you're still young and stupid," she said, voice gentle and low as he shucked himself out of her embrace. "We all have our gifts, Navarre, and I intend to make the most of mine while I can." Pressing her fingers to her lips, she blew him an airy kiss and spun away, her steps light and head high. Floating down the corridor like a gilded butterfly wrapped in silk.

"Second Commander!"

*For the love of—* "What now?" He turned as a servant girl skidded to a halt.

"Second Commander." She lowered into a deep panting bow.

"Catch your breath, girl."

"Thank you, sir." She sucked in greedy gulps of air as she rose to face him, her gaze pinned to his shoulder. Never looking him, or anyone above her station, in the eye. "The Archviceroy commands a word with you. Please, sir." She bowed again, hands clasped together and trembling. "If you would follow me, quickly, his eminence has been waiting and . . . *please*."

Under other circumstances, Navarre would've ignored the Archviceroy's demands and returned to his office and ever-mounting pile of paperwork occupying his attention. But the sight of a whip-thin and terrified little girl, gave him pause. He'd heard plenty of Henry's penchant for corporal punishment, and Navarre would be damned if a servant back tasted the lash for the sake of preserving his pride.

"Lead the way."

Grateful, she flashed a relieved smile. "This way, sir." She turned and scampered off, forcing him to almost jog just to keep up. And led him straight to where he'd intended to go all along—his personal office.

Toddrick quivered in a corner. His round cheeks flaming red on one side, with a blazing white handprint and a cut at its center. Blood mixing with tears.

Angry heat shot across Navarre's skin, and shocked from boiling to chilled with each breath, like tempered steel.

"Todd, wait for me in the corridor, please," he said and once they were alone, closed the door behind him with slow and lethal control. Ehrick wasn't the only one who knew how to tend a grudge. "You wanted to see me, your eminence?"

Henry turned, orange peels scattered at his feet, dressed in his brooding red vestments, a white chevron across his chest, and a yellow gold livery collar bleeding with rubies and fat pearls—like the blood and tears on Toddrick's cheek.

"Three weeks," Henry said with a shake of his head, "and your reports have been underwhelming, at best. I find that very disappointing."

"She trains during the day and keeps to her rooms at night; what more do you want from me?"

Henry leaned forward, his elegant hands bracing the messy surface of Navarre's desk. Those same fingers that marked his friend's face, and Navarre imagined taking a mallet to each of them, shattering the knuckles.

*Let's see you strike anyone with broken hands.*

"I'm beginning to think you're not taking your assignment seriously."

"Perhaps because I have more important matters to attend," he snapped, not bothering to check his tone.

Henry's cheeks brightened with a hint of color, spilling across the sharp bones like drops of wine in water. "You have until the coronation to get what I need," he said, each word soft as falling snow and colder then late winter winds. "God's mercy be upon you if you fail to deliver."

The Archviceroy sailed from his office, leaving behind a perfumed cloud of patchouli and pure fucking evil. Navarre beat his fist on to his desk, rattling the inkpot and stacked files.

"Milord?" Toddrick shuffled inside and closed the door behind him. "I'm sorry. I tried to keep him out. I tried—"

"Don't," Navarre said gently. Turning to face his friend, he assessed his injuries and sighed. "God, what a mess."

Toddrick's other cheek pinkened with a blush. "S'fine, milord. My father hits harder."

"It needs ice. Sit down."

"I can fetch it, mi—"

"I said *sit down*," Navarre repeated, and Toddrick obediently slammed his butt into the nearest chair, folding anxious hands in his lap. His thumbs racing over each other in fast circles.

Leaving him, Navarre ventured to the barrack's servery where a few guards were tucked into a meal of braised beef and boiled potatoes. He hacked at a chunk of ice in the icebox with a pick and collected the shards into a small bowl, found a clean cloth, and returned to his office. Placing the bowl on the desk, he poured out a cup of strong wine—a Tujianese gold made with pears—and offered it to Toddrick.

"This is gonna sting a bit."

Toddrick accepted the cup and took noisy sips while Navarre wrapped the ice in the cloth and pressed it against his flaming cheek. Toddrick whimpered, sloshing drops of pale-yellow wine on his lap and his brown pants soaked it up like parched earth.

"I'm sorry he did this to you." Navarre held the ice gently in place. "I should've been here."

"He might've done worse if you had been."

Knowing Toddrick was right did little to assuage Navarre's guilt and anger. "Here." He handed him the wrapped ice. "Give the skin a moment to warm up, then put it back on. Hopefully there won't be much swelling, and the cut doesn't look deep enough for sutures."

Toddrick mumbled a shy 'thanks' and gulped down the rest of his wine. "Milord—if I might ask—why is the Archviceroy so concerned about the comings and goings of a Swordsworn?"

"He believes they're a threat to Ehrick."

Toddrick frowned at the bottom of his glass. "I don't think that's all of it."

Seated on the edge of his desk, Navarre crossed his arms. "Why not?"

"Well, milord, if you don't mind me being so bold as to speculate?"

"Please do."

Toddrick cleared his throat, and wiggled in his seat, sitting up a little straighter. "Seems to me, neither the emperling nor the Archviceroy wants this treaty to continue, and you said yourself, he's pressing the idea of an arrangement with the Princess of Oscano. I think he's looking for grounds to annul the treaty."

"But that's impossible."

Toddrick shrugged. "His eminence is a cunning man, and known for removing obstacles, or allies who outlive their usefulness, like the former Second Commander."

Navarre dropped his arms. "What about him?"

"Well. Not to speak ill of the dead, milord." Toddrick drew the circle of the God's eye over his heart. "But Sir

Kevin was once the Archviceroy's creature. I knew his vassal, Sam. He warned me in case I was ever summoned to work for the man."

Navarre's steady heart kicked a little faster. "They worked together?"

Toddrick nodded earnestly, cheeks wobbling. "Yes, milord. I think that is why he's making such a point of pressing down hard on you. The Second Commander was in his pocket, and without him he's lost a valuable playing card in a well curated hand. He needs you."

Navarre's thoughts spun like a dropped coin. "If that's true about Sir Kevin, then perhaps there's a connection to the Archviceroy and the missing money. If I can prove Henry had a part in the thieving, I might be able to rid myself of two problems at once."

"Precisely."

And without his uncle's corrupting influence, Ehrick would hopefully once again become the brother Navarre remembered and the kind of emperor he'd be proud to serve . . . Seizing Toddrick by the shoulders, he kissed him loudly on his good cheek. "You're a genius."

Todderick's round face blazed glorious scarlet. "Thank you, milord."

"Is Sam still in service at the palace?"

"Yes, milord. He's the horse master's apprentice now."

Navarre rounded the desk to his seat. "Bring him to me. Then go to the kitchen and fetch our dinner. We've a long night ahead of us."

◆

If at all possible, Sam was almost as fidgety and anxious as Toddrick, but skinny as a maypole beneath a mop of orange hair. Navarre listened as he told him all about the two years that he served as the Sir Kevin's vassal.

The late-night meetings that often took place outside the palace at a singular gaming-house in the city: *The Crooked Crow.* And how in the last few days before he died, apparently the Second Commander and Henry had come to furious words.

"Now I couldna gather what they were goin' on about . . ." Sam shifted. "But it sounded like he was bein' told ta do somethin' terrible, and his eminence threatened to expose his thievery to the Priv if he dinna *keep to the plan.*"

"Priv?" "Beggin' pardons, sir, Privy Council."

"Are you saying the Archviceroy *knew* Sir Kevin was skimming?"

Sam bobbed an adamant nod, hair flapping over his face. "Aye, that he did. His eminence often used his gamblin' against him. Sir Kevin had a penchant for lasses and cards, but was short on clink, ya ken?"

And a disgraced Second Commander would've been made serious example of by way of the Traitor's Trinity—hung, drawn and disemboweled, all while breathing—and his deeds stricken from the Book of Commanders. The official tome of every Commander that served the Bridian Empire. Erasing his legacy.

"Can you prove this? Any correspondence or records?"

"No." Sam's shoulders bowed. "I'm sorry, but I was afeared and the only reason I tell ya this now is . . . well, I dinna quite know. But if you ask me to stand before the

Priv, I'll swear to the One God t'was all a lie. Otherwise, his eminence will disembowel me f'sure, and I've my Ma to think of. She's poorly and needs the money I send home."

Navarre reclined in his seat, pressed a fisted hand to his lips. *God's Mercy.* The boy was right. Without proof, dragging a stablehand before the council would be tantamount to a death sentence. "Thank you, Sam. You have my word that what you've told me will not leave this room."

Relieved, the youth all but jumped from his seat and shot out the door.

For the rest of the night, Navarre combed through the itemized notes they'd made from the ledgers with Toddrick, diligently reading aloud so he could make sense of the jumbled mess of numbers his brain refused to iron smooth.

The final tally was an astounding four hundred and eighty-seven gold florin unaccounted for over the last ten years, taken in barely noticeable sums at first, but they'd grown considerably larger and more frequent within the final six months, in sums as high as a thousand pounds sterling.

Either Sir Kevin had grown arrogant, or something had pushed him to take a tremendous risk.

Sun seared across the lids of his eyes and Navarre groaned into a yawning stretch. Pain flared down his back and arms. At some point he'd fallen asleep behind his desk, and Toddrick snored loudly across from him. Hunched forward, the girth of his belly kept him from pitching onto his face and a thin line of drool swayed from his bottom lip with each guttural snore.

Nothing aside from sheer exhaustion would've allowed Navarre to sleep through such ruckus. Rising from his desk, he picked up the ledger that lay in a slumped mess at Toddrick's feet, and smoothed out some of the creased pages before snapping it shut with a loud *crack*.

Toddrick jolted awake with a whimpered, *oh my*, and scrubbed a hand over his bleary eyes. "Milord. What time is it?"

"Late morning if I were a gambling man. Fortunately, I'm not."

"Very funny, milord." Toddrick struggled out of his seat and winced at whatever aches and pains that shot through his back and hips. "Shall I get us some coffee?"

"Please."

As Toddrick lumbered stiffly from the office, Navarre set about cleaning up his desk, gathering the sheets of paper with written notes and the tallied sums, and tucked them all inside a single folder he locked away in his bottom drawer. Evidence he planned to later present to Ehrick once he had Archviceroy Henry neatly cornered.

Patience and a steady hand, that's what he needed.

Toddrick returned as he was locking up, and carried a tray with a steaming carafe, a couple mugs and a plate of fresh toast topped with fried eggs. The scent of food brought him fully awake and greedily they both tucked in, without pausing to speak. The coffee was sharp, black—as he liked it, and he could smell Toddrick's, laced with heavy cream and sugar.

"So, milord, what's next?" Toddrick asked while piling their empty dishes upon the tray.

"I'll start with retracing Sir Kevin's last steps at the gambling-house." Navarre licked yolk from his finger. "If I can sort out who he was meeting the night before he died, perhaps I can find a connection to the Archviceroy. In the meantime, I'll need Henry to think he has me in his pocket by keeping a close eye on Sina and join her in the courtyard this morning for training."

"She's not in the courtyard."

Navarre whipped around. "Excuse me?"

Toddrick jerked back in surprise. "Well, milord, I saw her as I was heading to the kitchens to fetch our breakfast, but as I returned—her cadre were still training, but milday Sinadine wasn't among them. She's been leaving them earlier of late."

"Why?"

"Don't know, milord."

Damn, he should've known this. The Archviceroy was right about one thing—he hadn't been taking his assignment seriously and given her far too much freedom. If he was going to sway the man into lowering his guard, then that was something he'd need to remedy.

"Don't worry, Todd, I'll find her. Lock up when I leave and if the Archviceroy comes sniffing around, tell him you don't have the key. We can't afford anyone finding out what we're working on in here."

"Yes, milord," Toddrick said with a bow of his head.

Navarre left him and headed straight to the training courtyard where he found a handful of his men ringed around the edges, watching the sparring match. Jasz against Eban. Sweat flashed on her skin, dampened her straight black, braided away from her long face.

He lingered for a moment, awed by the way she moved.

Jasz was swift and sharp, but there was a difference in her tone and mood compared to when he watched her fight with Sinadone near three weeks ago. That fight had brought something out in both of them. A ferocity and precision. It hadn't been two young women training under a morning sun, but two competitors out to beat their opponent, equally matched in strength and speed, they were two halves of a whole. But Sina carried darkness within her, and sometimes that darkness eked out into others.

Like storm clouds blotting out a sun, that storm had touched Jasz just as he often felt it touch him.

Navarre nudged Rhys with his elbow. "Where's Sina?"

She pulled her eyes away from her sister, palest blue—almost grey. She had the look of a Bridian maid in her slender nose and delicate mouth, but most of all in the white-blonde hair and alabaster skin. "Running."

"Where?"

Rhys tensed and he could see she was deciding how much she wanted to tell him. "The hedge labyrinth in the garden. Something wrong?"

"No." He offered an easy smile as he walked away. Rhys didn't return it.

At least the morning was soft, and he was suitably dressed for a run—it would save him the hassle of turning around to his rooms to get his sword. He kicked into a jog as he reached the pebbled path of the gardens, weaving around manicured bushes and trees groomed in geometric shapes that required garden attendants to maintain daily.

The labyrinth was a hundred feet wide and almost twice that in length. He'd been terrified of it as a child and made the mistake of joining a couple palace rats—children of the servants—as they'd snuck in one summer night, when the moon was full, and got lost.

Those imposing hedge walls swallowed up his cries and in the morning when his mother found him—she'd had the look of a woman terrified and furious. She'd hugged him so tight his ribs ached, and he'd stayed out of the labyrinth for years afterwards but when she died he'd come back to the hedges and sobbed until his voice was gone.

In the morning, she wasn't there to pick him up and hug him.

She was gone.

He'd almost entered the labyrinth when the tangled ring of steel, bright and sharp, interrupted his stride and his thoughts.

Swords.

Someone was fighting nearby.

Navarre whipped around, confused. It was too far from the courtyard to possibly be Jasz and Eban. So he followed the ringing notes, wary as he reached the ruin of the old garden house. Damned if he didn't regret not having his weapon on him now. Rounding the short stone wall, he slunk to the mouth of the open doorway and peered inside.

His heart roared into this throat at the sight of Iereni, panting and straining beneath the weight of steel. Sinadine loomed over her—the arc of a blade lifting and then driving down—*again*—hard as a hammer.

Navarre rushed forward, prepared to lunge into the fray with nothing but his hands, when someone seized him from behind. He caught a glimpse of white hair as Rhys hooked her arm around his neck and slammed him against the wall.

"Easy, Second Commander." Forearm braced to his chest, Rhys twirled her unsheathed sword. "Your cousin is safe."

"But she's—"

"Look again."

And he did.

Sinadine eased up in her movement and stepped back with a nod. "Better. But you're still tight on the right side."

"I'm doing the stretches, I swear!"

Sinadine held out a hand and his cousin reluctantly relinquished her blade.

*I need a sword. Something small, and with enough good steel so that it can be re-forged.*

Sinadine's words echoed back to him as she examined the weapon and said something his ears couldn't hear over the roar of his blood. She was teaching her, not attacking her.

And she'd made Iereni a sword.

Navarre didn't know what shocked or surprised him more? The way his heart had clutched in terror when he thought Iereni was in danger, or that it now warmed with something greater?

"How long has she been doing this?" he demanded once they were sparring again, and now that he was calm, he could see that Sinadine's movements were slow and deliberate—giving Iereni time to assess and react without driving all of her weight onto the girl.

"A couple weeks." Rhys tapped the tip of her sword against the dimple of his throat, capturing his attention. "If I let you go, are you going to behave?"

He nodded. Rhys dropped her arm and his chest groaned with relief. For a slender thing, she was strong, and Navarre rubbed a hand across aching muscles.

"Come on." She sheathed her sword and entered the garden house, whistling to Sinadine. "We have a visitor."

The clashing of steel stopped, and Iereni's smile vanished into a pale mask of fear.

Sinadine sheathed her sword on her hip. "Rhys, take over for me. I need to speak with the Second Commander." Marching towards him, she jerked a head and stormed over to the stone wall separating them from the gardens. "What are you doing here?"

Though he was not opposed to Iereni learning to defend herself, he bristled at her tone. He crossed his arms. "I should be the one asking *you* questions."

Sinadine kicked up her chin, a stubborn gesture that exposed the length of her throat above the neckline of her faded grey kubi. Bruises marred her golden skin.

Concerned, he reached for her, fingers brushing along the abrasions. "What happened?"

"None of your business." She knocked his hand aside. "Why are you here, *Otsaidā*?"

Navarre tucked his hands in his pockets and bit down on the surge of frustration kindling to rage inside of him. First Toddrick, and now this. "I came to find you because I have a lead to investigate."

That got her attention. "Who?"

Navarre told her everything he and Toddrick had uncovered concerning the discrepancies in the financial logs that involved the former Second Commander, and the Archviceroy's potential plot to frame Sina and her cadre for treason.

"So, you're to spy on me," she said when he was done. "Why tell me this?"

"I need your help to expose Henry to Ehrick, and there can't be trust between us with secrets." He held out a hand. "Can we be allies, *Dakuwan*?"

She eyed that hand, then clasped it and shook once. "We'll go to the gaming-house tonight."

"It's only open on Saturday."

Sinadine cursed. "That's three days from now."

"You have a pressing engagement to worry about?" Her lips and brows flattened. Then it clicked. The ascension ceremony was the coming Sunday . . . Navarre scraped a hand over the back of his neck. "Well, this gives us time to figure out a plan, at least." He glanced towards the entryway, towards Iereni and Rhys. "Thank you," he added. "For doing what I should've a long time ago."

"She's coming along nicely. A natural talent. You should be proud of your cousin."

"I am. Very." He flickered his gaze back to Sinadine and swore a hint of pride softened the hard edges of her mouth.

He'd seen her smirk and snarl and shout, but never smile, and it unnerved him how much he wanted to right now. A rogue thought that became a secret wish, burning in the deepest parts of his soul. One that he had to smother.

Immediately.

# CHAPTER EIGHTEEN

## Sinadine

A CANDLE FLICKERED IN THE topmost aviary window. Little over week after sending my second letter and almost three days since the last, she'd finally answered. I raced to the aviary to find Willem pacing at the ground entrance. He smiled broadly as I skidded to a stop and waved me inside.

Sealing the door behind me, I accepted the letter and my hands shook as I broke the deep blue wax seal—too impatient to return to my room—and quickly read the words written in my grandmother's confident hand.

*You've done well, but the work isn't over yet. The cold winds are rising, and before the last sickle moon cradles the sky—the Lone Wolf must die.*

I frowned at the letter.

It offered no explanation behind her extended silence, but she was clear on one point. Ehrick had to die before the winter equinox. The last sickle moon was our New Year.

A time for rebirth. Change. A new beginning.

With less than two weeks to the coronation, if all went well, he'd be dead long before it.

Folding up the letter, I stuffed inside the inner pocket of my kubi and sealed it shut. Iereni was likely already waiting for me so I'd have to return it later. Thanking Willem, I hurried from the aviary, careful to weave around the backend of the gardens. The fewer people who saw me coming and going, the better.

Navarre was there as well, and Rhys with him. Iereni balanced impatiently on her back wheels. *"Finally."* She dropped the front ones down and shook out her hands. "What took you so long?"

"Did you finish your stretches and exercises?" I asked. My grandmother's letter burning a hole in my pocket.

"Yes." Rhys smiled. "I've got her all warmed up for you."

"Excellent." Unsheathing my sword, I tapped my blade to Iereni's. "Let's get started."

Navarre circled around us, cagey as a wolf made of shadows and eyes always on me, palpable as the touch of his hands. The more he stared the more I stared right back hoping to rattle his nerves, but I soon realized watching him didn't bother him to the degree that I'd hoped.

If anything, he made a show of pushing the boundaries into a game, seeing what it would take to break my gaze and enjoying his private victories whenever I did.

By the third day, there wasn't an angle to his face or a whisper of expression I didn't know as intimately as the facets of Home Mountain. The way his eyes changed from smoke to steel to stone, depending on the slant of sunlight and whatever emotion sparked behind them. Bright against the warmth of his skin, more gold than brown, and the shocking black of his hair.

Long and loose, it hung in waves past his shoulders, thick, midnight silk.

"Not bad," he said when Iereni and I broke for a moment to catch our breaths. "Mind if I cut in?"

Iereni lit up like a new sun. "Really?"

Navarre's smile was dazzling and sincere. The kind that warmed the blood to behold. "Only if you promise to take it easy on your poor cousin."

Iereni flashed him a dark grin. "Never."

Navarre unsheathed his sword, and with a devious glance in my direction, he removed his tunic and tossed it at my feet. A gesture I answered with a crook of my brow.

*Game on.*

The steel of his sword rang with Iereni's, pausing only as he explained a move and taught her how to counter his strokes. I remembered how he'd fought in the Blue Wastes. How he'd moved like a shadow, swift and silent, and struck with the ferocity of an avalanche.

I'd seen one as a child, and if I closed my eyes now I could recall it clear as that distant winter afternoon. The crack and boom of snow breaking away from the side of a mountain and roaring in a violent sheet of white that snapped hundred-year-old evergreens like they were dry twigs.

Sweat bloomed across his chest, drawing the eye, but it was the shape of him that held it there. Raw, ruthlessly built as honed granite, but smooth and lithe. His strong arms, corded with muscle and veins, the hard, chiseled expanse of his chest and torso, the wide, powerful shape of his legs.

Finished with Iereni, he planted a loud kiss on her brow, and nodded to Rhys to step back in and take over.

"You were right. She is a natural." Navarre leaned against the pillar, close enough I could smell the sweat on his skin, warmth radiated from him like the inviting lure of a campfire.

"I'm glad you agree. But we can't keep this up for much longer," I said, rolling my empty water cup between my hands. "Not with the Archviceroy breathing down both our necks."

He nodded, thoughtfully, his focus still pinned on Iereni as she worked through cooling down stretches with Rhys. "No, we can't. But if all goes well tonight, he won't be a problem for either of us."

My palm itched with anticipation. "Are you confident we can slip the palace grounds again? Is the Archviceroy not growing suspicious?"

"It's the Night of Souls," Navarre answered. "The streets will be rife with denizens taking in the festivities and the men I've positioned on guard will be less . . . observant." Taking my cup from my hand, he filled it to overflowing, then raised it to his lips.

The seam of his throat rippled with greedy gulps and water slid out the sides. Glistening, wet beads splashed and ran in rivulets down his neck, his chest. And raced lower, dragging my eyes with them, as they navigated the rippling plain of his belly. Every notch and groove. Down—heat flashed across my skin—to where the waist of his pants slung low.

*Damnable dead!*

"Something wrong?" he asked.

I reeled back in horror, attraction doused by the cold lick of mortified shame and wordless in furious disbelief. It was one thing to play our staring game, but somewhere along the way I'd started looking at him—*really* looking at him.

"Seriously," his brow creased with confusion, "what gives?"

Away. I needed distance, space, *air*. I rushed from the garden house and braced the crumbling edge of the stone wall.

*How can I be so damn stupid? Of all people—him?*

Navarre's footfalls crunched over gravel behind me. His fingers curled around my arm. "Hold up a second, I just wanted to—"

Reeling around, I slammed my fisted into his face, the movement too fast, too unexpected, and Navarre staggered back, landing hard on his ass.

"What the hell was that for?" he demanded, rubbing the side of his reddening jaw.

"To remind you to keep your distance from me, *Otsaidā*." Looming over him, I shook out my screaming hand. "We may be allies, but we're not friends." Storming away, my anger twined with the conflicting edge of desire.

A howling hunger deep in my belly that had to be smothered.

I was here to murder the emperling, not succumb to the betrayal of lust and attraction for his bastard brother.

If Navarre was an avalanche—I would not be the trees.

❖

Unlike the wealth and affluence of the High District, the Lows was all muck and mire, and tonight, in honor of the empresses' ascension on the morrow, everyone emptied into streets for the *Night of Souls*—a time to honor her life.

Taverns and teahouses threw open their doors, and music spilled out. Waxed lanterns drifted over the harbor, floating up to the stars as revelers danced in the streets wearing cloaks of blue and red, drunk in celebration. Prostitutes floated among the rabble in gilded masks and gauzy gowns, tossing marigolds for love and peonies for prosperity while the shrines remained empty and ignored. They'd taken a sacred holiday, with its ancient traditions, and made it into a night of defamed debauchery.

"There it is." Navarre gestured to the ship anchored at the end of a bobbing dock. The strap of his sword sheath cut across his chest, accentuating the breadth of his broad shoulders, beneath a hooded vest.

"Why a boat?" I wondered as we boarded the large vessel. *The Crooked Crow* was a barge with a steel belly painted rust red moored at the end of the harbor. Gamblers and drunkards stumbled up the gangway onto the deck crammed with patrons eager to enter her doors.

"Makes for an easier get away," Navarre said, leaning in so I could hear him over the cacophony of voices and music flowing all around us. "Gaming isn't exactly legal, but when the bosses grease the right wheels, City Patrol looks the other way."

I curled my lip. "Depravity and corruption go hand in hand for your people."

He stiffened, and a tick of annoyance pulsed in his jaw. The hint of a bruise visible beneath stubble and the shadow of his hood. "Keep close and your head covered. Last thing we need is anyone recognizing us." Guiding us through the jostling bodies to the two large thugs stood outside the main doors, Navarre offered a roll of sterling coins, and one of the guards stamped his wrist with red ink—a crow drinking from a tipped over chalice.

After I received my stamp, I followed him down a stairway of steel into the heart of the barge stuffed with two hundred patrons, endless rows of tables and a rectangular shaped bar in the center of it all. The back end of the space lined with kegs the size of wagons.

Navarre tapped his fingers against the scarred bar-top and flagged the bartender. "We're in luck."

"You know her?"

He nodded. "Her name is Miego. She worked at the *Opal Garden*. Place is popular among the Imperial Guard. And she's hard to forget."

When the girl was finished serving a large, frothing mug of ale, she whisked over. Limping heavily as she approached. Standing beneath the swaying light, I got a good, hard look at her face.

Yes, I imagined she was hard to forget.

The slant to her nose and jaw said they'd been broken more than once and hadn't set quite right. Her hair was cut in an uneven bob, longer in the front, and did an excellent job of hiding most of the damage. Not that she seemed bothered by it, or the attention it garnered.

Resting slender forearms atop sticky wood, Miego clenched a sodden bar rag in her hands. "You've got balls coming here, Navarre."

"Can't a guy enjoy a night out with a friend?" He reached out to touch me, but quickly thought better of it, and reeled his hand back in. *Good*.

"Not if he's Second Commander." Her eyes slashed to me. "And definitely not if his friend is Swordsworn."

I nodded appreciatively. "You're very perceptive."

"Part of my job. You're just lucky these clods are mostly too drunk or stupid to notice. More than half would love to geld a Commander. The rest would love to get their hands on you. Period." Miego smiled without mirth. "We have an Acharrān themed whore. She's very popular."

My jaw tensed at the abhorrent thought. "I can take care of myself."

Again, she smiled but this time it was genuine.

"Can we talk somewhere private?"

Miego drummed blunt fingers atop the wood, nails bitten to the quick. "Are you paying?" Navarre flashed his purse, and she assessed the weight. Nodded. "Best take this to the back."

Flagging another girl to cover the bar, she opened the flap and scuttled through, limping and swatting aside hands as she led us to the storeroom. Unlocking the door, she waited until we were inside and then pushed it shut.

"Five minutes. That's all you get. And my time doesn't come cheap." She crossed her arms. "Start talking."

"What do you know about the former Second Commander?" Navarre asked.

Miego skimmed her tongue along the edge of her uneven teeth. "Sir Kevin came here every Saturday night for the last six months. A man with a thirst and a heavy purse, as I say."

"Did he meet with Archviceroy Henry while he was here?"

"I can't tell you that."

"Why not?" I demanded.

"Because a large part of our business is discretion. We protect our patrons, and their secrets." She jabbed a finger into Navarre's chest. "Even the dead ones. I'm sorry but if Peyter knew I was speaking to you right now, he'd have my guts for guitar strings."

"Miego, please. I need something. *Anything*."

"I told you I can't and that's the end of it."

"The Archviceroy is known to have spies throughout the city," I said, changing tactics. "Perhaps it's his interests you're really protecting."

"Me? Protect that *snake*?" Miego's eyes scored to me, molten with rage. "After my village was *cleansed* of heathens and witches, all orphans were rounded up and taken to a bawdy house. I was seven. Spent five years training and soon as I bled, they sold me to a pimp who pushed me onto the streets for a shilling an hour. He beat me when I didn't make my quota and let the clients do far worse if they were willing to pay for it." She touched different parts of her body to illustrate all the broken places of her.

"One day I overheard him speaking with a Buck, that's what we called the men. Bucks. Anyhow, he'd said I was getting too old and knew of a doc at some elite medical university looking for a live, female subject to operate on with his students. Cadavers don't allow for the same kind of practical experience as a living, breathing body. It's illegal, 'course, but anything can be bought for the right amount of clink." She rubbed her fingers together. "So I took off, and by some mercy, got away. Been working bar-side at the Crow ever since."

Navarre swore under his breath. "I had no idea."

"You never asked; men rarely do, in my experience." Miego shrugged off his stricken look as if all that she endured were nothing. "Besides, other girls I knew weren't so lucky." She formed a circle with her forefinger and thumb—the God's Eye—and spat through it. "Far as I'm concerned, the Archviceroy and his One Faith can go straight to Hell."

"Tell us what we need to know, and I'll make sure he does."

Miego straightened at my words, interest and a need for justice spinning behind her pupils like a gaming wheel, assessing the risk and reward. "Sir Kevin was scared," she said at last. "Each visit, he got more and more twitchy. I always sent him aloft to the Crow's Nest—Peyter's office—only room in this dump you can guarantee privacy. And precisely ten minutes later a man would show up, aways cloaked and careful, but one evening I did get a hold of something he'd dropped." Reaching into her filthy bar apron, Miego pulled out a notepad with a gnawed-on-pencil, and did a quick sketch, rendering a button in remarkable detail.

Navarre angled it to the flickering storeroom light. "I think this might be from a Chancellor's vestment robes."

"Lord Reginald was missing a button on his collar," I said, my mind flashing back to the night those fat, hard fingers gripped my cheeks and pushed them into a forced smile. "It's how I was able to jab him in the neck, and you *did* say he was the Archviceroy's creature. How much pressure do you think his nuts can take before he sings?"

Navarre grinned. "One good squeeze."

"Another thing," Miego added, wringing her hands. The first genuine glimpse of unease I'd seen in her thus far. "Sir Kevin was in such a state during his last visit that I might've . . . eavesdropped a bit. Only because I was worried things would get ugly and Peyter'd be furious if anyone spilled blood on his new Pysian rug. Sodding thing cost near a hundred florin. I didn't hear much, they spoke too gently, but I did catch two details." Her eyes opened with a sigh. "The name Edvard, and what I thought was an obscure date, until the bells tolled from the Imperial Palace—announcing the emperor's death two weeks later."

"God's mercy," Navarre whispered. "Are you saying Sir Kevin plotted to kill the emperor?"

Miego shrugged. "I can't tell you for sure one way or another, only that the emperor died on the exact date they discussed, and when Sir Kevin next returned to the *Crows*, deep in his cups, he was later knifed in the eye. Mere days *before* those bells rang."

"Someone was tying up loose ends," I said.

Miego nodded. "I'd never seen the man before his meetings with Sir Kevin, and he hasn't returned since."

"Where's the button?" I asked.

"It's pure gold. Figured I could get a bit of clink for it, so I kept it. The girls are bad for stealing, but so far no one's found my cache."

"I need you to get it." Navarre withdrew three gold florins from his pouch. "This is enough to pay a year's tithe on a nice flat in a more established part of the city. Use it, and get the hell out of this dump, Miego."

She palmed the coins and they vanished into the front of her blouse where no straying hands could slide in to pilfer, and no jingle would give them away. "Wait for me by the bar," she said, and pushed us back into the guts of the barge.

# CHAPTER NINETEEN

## Navarre

Navarre took hold of Sinadine's hand, leading her through the dense, jostling mob of unwashed bodies.

God, the stink. He'd forgotten how foul the gaming-houses could be, and the kind of vile crowd it lured.

The *Crooked Crow* was known for shady dealings and bloodshed, which was why the Second Commander's unfortunate meeting with a dagger hadn't seemed out of place.

Perhaps the Archviceroy's hand was in that, as well, ripping out any loose threads from the intricately woven plot to assassinate the late emperor. His own brother . . . Edvard had been near death for a long time; no one would've ever suspected he'd been murdered and with the body cremated, ashes laid to rest in the palace mausoleum, there was nothing left to examine for proof of poisoning.

Intrigue and murder.

The layers to this were complicated and rooted deep. It would all come down to making Chancellor Reginald crack. But if Peyter ever found out Miego had informed against a patron . . . Peyter Shaw—the One-Eyed, was a moniker he'd earned when he was a boy and lost his eye after trying to steal a Marquisate's purse, had turned the name into a kind of signature.

Plucking out the eye of anyone who dared cross him in life or business.

No, he wouldn't find out. Because soon as Miego returned with the button they'd leave without a ripple. Silent and unseen. Which meant blending in was imperative.

Navarre stopped at the corner of the bar and flagged a barmaid. A Tujianese girl with sun brown skin and hair dyed blonde instead of her natural brown. "Two glasses and a bottle of wine."

"Red or gold?"

Navarre arched a brow to Sinadine.

"Gold," she answered.

The barmaid set about filling the order and slapped down two glasses in front of them with an opened bottle.

Navarre paid the tab and tapped his glass to Sinadine's. "Cheers."

"That's a stupid expression," she said, raising her glass for a long swallow.

"What do Acharrāns say in toast?"

"Nothing. We drink."

"Sounds very . . . practical."

"How old were you when your mother died?"

Navarre swallowed sharply, the wine sliding down his throat like acid. "Why?"

"Must've been young for you to know nothing of home, our language, or our customs," Sinadine commented, twisting the half empty cup before her.

"Ten," Navarre answered. "I was ten."

She considered that for a moment, then took another long swallow. "I was three when my mother was disavowed. Do you know what that means?" He shook his head no. "Disavowed is when an Acharrān relinquishes her blade and is banished from her clan. A fate worse than death."

"Why?" he asked gently.

"Because of me," she answered after a time, and topped up her glass to the rim. Wine droplets scattered on her fingers, and she brought them to her lips. "I am the *Dakuwan*."

"The Dark One," he said, echoing her words to him that night in the Blue Wastes. Something moved through her, a kind of sadness that caught Navarre by surprise. In the time he'd come to know her, she was always sharp and dangerous, untouchable as molten steel, but here, for a moment he saw her as she was—not a weapon or a warrior, but a girl.

"I was born on a starless night," she continued. "The stars are sacred. They are the Spirits of our Sisters—the bravest, the worthiest—who rise up to join the First-of-Us, and offer guidance. Judgement. Everything we do is beneath those stars. To be shunned by them is . . . unforgivable. But she sacrificed everything so that I would live. I never saw her again, but I remember that final moment so clearly. It's like a brand." She pressed a fingertip between her eyes.

"Burned right here. I don't even know if she's still alive but everything I've done since that day has been to restore honor to her name. To show my clan her sacrifice was not in vain." Her eyes flickered to him and glowed bright with accusation. "Tell me, *Otsaidā*, what are you willing to do to honor the memory of your mother—knowing that the bones of our sisters have been desecrated? Mounted on a wall like a trophy?"

He listened, horrified, as she spoke of a wall of gilded skulls and shame unspooled inside of him, long, slow and winding. "He showed you that?"

Sinadine revealed the fading bruises around her throat. "He *chained* me to it."

Navarre swore under his breath, weary with grief, and scraped a hand across his face, unsure of what troubled him more—the fact that Ehirck was capable of such a thing?

Or that it happened at all and Navarre had been completely unaware?

"This reeks of Henry's corruption." And knowing he shared blood with such a monster soured his stomach. "Ehrick would nev—"

"Pull your head out of the sand," Sinadine interrupted. "There's a deep rot festering inside of the emperling. A stink that can't be hidden or buried. Yet you choose not to see it."

"You don't know what it was like for him as a kid," Navarre slapped the flat of his hand to the bar-top, his palm searing from the impact. "Every day was a war between life and death—it still is."

"His infirmity does not excuse his cruelty." Sinadine swirled the contents of her glass. Navarre had yet to touch his. "Why are you so beholden to him?"

Navarre scored his thumb across his throbbing palm. "We came into this world together. Born almost to the minute. The physicians were convinced Ehrick wouldn't survive the night. *Too weak*, they said, *let him die*. Then they said he'd never survive the week, the month, the year—again and again he proved them wrong. But that didn't stop our father from ignoring him, or our brothers' mockery. Growing up, all we had was each other. Our weaknesses balanced by the other's strengths. I couldn't read," he clarified.

And damn if it wasn't hard admitting this carefully hidden truth to her.

What would she think of him now? The Second Commander—an imbecile who struggled to understand simple words with letters that tangled like a knot of fishing line he couldn't unravel.

"I do well enough when I'm alone, but my mind mixes things up. Numbers especially. It's worse when I'm under pressure. Tutors and physicians all turned up their noses. I was bastardborn and not worth the effort, but Ehrick never gave up on me. Night after night, he came to my room until finally those strange markings made sense." He chanced looking at her and found nothing in her expression.

No sympathy, or pity. But she was listening.

"Three years ago, he joined his uncle in the Holy Campaign, and when he returned . . ." Pausing, Navarre bounced a fist against his thigh. "If you knew Ehrick . . . if you truly knew my brother, you'd understand he'd never do something so foul. My uncle has preyed on Ehrick's fear of weakness and exploited it for control. Twisting his mind." And that's why he had to pry the villain from his side and root him out. His brother was drowning under his dark influence, and only Navarre could pull him back from this brink of madness before it was too late.

Sinadine arched a brow, but before she could speak a scream broke through the roar of the tavern from a serving girl struggled as she was wrestled down by a couple of hulking men.

She screamed again, quickly silenced by a striking hand that cracked her head against the table.

The servers who worked the floor weren't supposed to be touched, but that didn't deter some men from dragging one off against her will. Provided the establishment saw its share of coin, there wasn't much that was off limits in a place like this.

Navarre clenched his hand into a tight fist, disgust and anger pushing him to rise and reveal himself, but the gaming-den was filled with the worst of the city's dregs, and without reinforcements doing so would only get him and Sinadine killed.

Sinadine gripped the bottle in her hands, rolled it against the grain of scarred wood, the varnish stripping away in some places after years of use.

"Who are they?" she asked without turning around.

"Galgoan mercenaries. Not uncommon in the city this time of year." Pirates who ruled the high and low seas, pillaging and looting ships unfortunate enough to cross sails.

Laughter and music and voices continued, unfazed by what was happening right before their eyes. But the girl put up a hard fight, and when a few of her friends leapt in, the brutes let her go. Their hands and laughter chasing after her as she scampered off, clutching her torn clothes.

"How many?"

"Five," he said, masking the movement of his lips by taking a sip of wine.

A dark grin split her features—a look he'd come to recognize as trouble.

"For the love of God, please don't." But Sinadine was already out of her seat and Navarre shot after her, pushing around jostling bodies.

Slick and fast, she reached the Galgoan's table ahead of him and tapped a hand against the brute's meaty left shoulder. The same one who'd snatched the girl. How she knew when her back turned was a puzzle he didn't have time to piece together.

The brute whipped around with a sneer. "The *fek* d'ya want?"

The noise lowered from a roar to a hum, and Navarre swallowed a foul curse as Sinadine pulled back her cowl.

Shock ripped through to the seedy crowd—given her height and build, with the cowl up she was easy to think her a boy. But the fade, the braids and beads, the ink of her tattoo, there was no mistaking her for anything but Swordsworn.

She braced the head of the table. "I want you and your friends to apologize to the server you accosted. You can start with handing over that heavy purse you're wearing."

The Galgoans exchanged bemused glances. Pushing back his seat, he rose onto legs thick as Navarre's waist. God help them, the man was seven feet tall, a solid wall of muscle wrapped in scarred leather and fur. He stroked his fingers down his waist-length beard braided into two long yellow ropes adorned with polished boar tusks.

"Ye'r a funny *little* girl."

She tipped her chin, facing the brute head on. "Hand over your purse and apologize to your server. You have ten seconds."

Picking up the flagon of beer, he chugged heartily and when finished, belched so loud in her face, Navarre would swear the belly of the barge trembled. The crowd broke into raucous jibes and cheers as he chucked the flagon to an iron support post, shattering clay, then pressed the flat of his hand to the table, and leaned heavily against it.

Mimicking her earlier stance.

"*Fek off.*" He angled his head. Their eyes level. "Before I show ya what happens to funny *little* girls."

In a move, swift as a hummingbird's wing, she snatched up a two-pronged fork from the pile of bones on his plate and drove it into the table. So hard the metal points sank into stained, scarred wood, and vibrated there.

Barely an inch from the back of his veined hand—big enough to wrap all the way around her neck.

The brute barked a booming laugh that echoed among his four equally massive companions. "Y'missed."

Sinadine flashed her teeth. A grin so dark, so vicious, Navarre retreated a step.

"Time's up."

Her foot lashed out, catching the brute at the back of his supporting knee. And as the weight of him dropped, using the momentum to her advantage, she gathered his head in both hands—and yanked down. The loud *thwack* of his skull crashing into the table was joined by the meaty pop of the fork-end lancing through his eye and into the softest part of his brain.

His body spasmed then fell limp in a blink.

*Fucking Hell.*

# CHAPTER TWENTY

## Sinadine

My sword sang from its scabbard, a steel song of mayhem that joined the cacophony of cries and raging curses as the brutes lunged from the table, bright in their fury, to avenge their fallen leader. They attacked with strong hands, crude blades and brutish force.

And didn't last long.

Their blood was a hot, wet spray in the air—as hands and heads rolled, and entrails spilled. It sent the mad dogs loose and the crowd broke into a full out brawl.

"*This way!*" Navarre hauled me around and together we battled to the backend of the barge where Miego stood, ashen.

"I left you alone for *ten* minutes," she shouted and swept us up the clattering steps of a metal stairway. The roars and screams grew louder as a door burst open and more bodies poured into the barge from the main gangway. These ones armed and cloaked in purple and gold.

Navarre's face paled. "The Imperial Guard."

"Sodding hell," Miego whispered. "*Hurry.*" She fumbled with the keyring belted at her waist, hands steady as she unlocked the metal door and calm night air opened on the other side.

She lurched across the threshold, her limping more pronounced, sweat slicked on her brow and neck. Her body wasn't accustomed to the strain of fast movement.

"Take this street and go to the left." She gestured to the thick coil of rope tethering the barge to the dock. "The alley will lead you to the warehouse district."

Voice rose from behind us. The guards. The wildness of the crowd would slow them down, but not for much longer.

I caught her by the arm. "Come with us."

"No. I'll buy you time." A gentle smile touched her lips, and her hand closed over mine. Squeezed. "Strength and honor," she whispered, and disappeared back into the barge, sealing the door behind her.

"We need to move." Navarre tugged his cowl over his head, and I did the same, hurrying down the narrow gangway. Fireworks burst overhead, scattering flashes of light and color as we sprinted through the alley, the echoes of anarchy fading into the sound of frolicking and laughter.

*The Night of Souls* in full swing. The perfect cover.

Navarre lurched to a stop, and I jostled hard into his back. "Turn around," he shouted above the din of voices and music. "Other way. *Quick!*"

Spinning on my heel, I shoved through drunken bodies, weaving down the street, paving stones wet from an evening rain. Over the revelry, the clink of armor and swords rattled. Even in a crowd such as this we'd stand out. Soon we'd be spotted, and if they caught us together—I didn't want to think of the implications for Navarre.

"Here!" Navarre grasped my waist and dragged me into a tight alcove of a darkened doorway, tight as a broom closet. Reaching into his tunic, he withdrew a leather case containing a set of steel picks. "Cover me." Kneeling, Navarre went to work, cursing and muttering obscenities under his breath. "This lock is a rusted mess. Almost there."

"*Hurry.*"

"Not helping."

The picks scrapped, clicked, and finally the lock gave. Pushing the door open, Navarre wrenched me inside, and threw the bolts as the footsteps of the guards rattled past.

A steadying breath pushed through my lips. "That was close." The storeroom was tight, stacked with crates and boxes, all covered in a thick layer of dust, which meant the place had gone untouched for some time. But there was only one way in, or out.

Navarre shot lethal silver eyes to mine. Snatching me by the neckline of my cowl, he hauled me around and pushed against it, forearm planted to me chest, caging me with his fury.

"What in bleeding hell is it with you and *forks*?"

Heat flared across my skin, sending my thoughts to scatter, my heart to pulse in a feverish beat. To my horror it wasn't anger that flashed through me, but something brighter.

Hotter. And for the first time in my life I was grateful for the concealment of shadows.

"Get off me."

"You nearly got us killed." Navarre growled. "And now, thanks to you, all of City Patrol is looking for us."

"The guards were already headed for the *Crows*," I snapped, teeth bared. "Long before I dropped the Galgoan."

The fire tempered the barest fraction in his eyes with understanding. "Henry knows we're sniffing around."

"He knows *someone* is sniffing. I don't think he's onto us, yet." But it wouldn't stay that way if Navarre was caught with the Swordsworn he was supposed to be watching.

Navarre lowered his hands to his side. "He must've had eyes at the *Crows*. Miego is Peyter's right hand. Talking to us likely flagged attention."

"Makes sense," I agreed.

"God's Mercy." Navarre dragged a hand over his face, and I was drawn to the length of his fingers stroking down the bridge of his nose. His lips. Full. Wicked. Daring.

*Damnable Dead, what's wrong with me?*

"Are you alright?"

"Fine." But I wasn't fine. Far from it.

I prided myself on control, but this aching need had a will of its own. My heart was still unsteady, my head a tangled mess of things I didn't want to sort through, and it angered me that it was rising in me *again*. This unwanted, unbidden—yearning.

Why was it happening, where did it come from and why did he, of all people, stir it within me without thought or effort?

"You have that look, again." His eyes narrowed. Assessing. "Like you want to punch me."

"Because I do." My fingers curled into a tight fist, aching to crunch into his granite jaw and pummel that smug, curious expression into dust as he dissected me with those intense grey eyes.

Seeing far too much.

I almost gave into the impulse, but part of me knew the second I touched him I'd do something far worse, like pull him closer.

And devour.

"Why did you punch me earlier?" he demanded. "Why do you want to punch me now?"

My fist bounced impatiently against my thigh. "You get too close."

"Daneysa gets close." He angled his head. "You've never struck her."

"I can handle Daneysa."

"But not me?" Navarre's smile flashed in the dark. Lethal.

"Shut up."

"Make me."

"Keep pushing, and I will."

"If you hit me again, be warned I'll defend myself this time."

A hint of a smile tugged at my lips, but underneath it a shiver of dark hunger shocked up my spine at the thought of us going to blows until we were hot, sweaty and ruined and—

"There it is again."

"What?"

"That *other* look you get right before the one when you want to punch me." He arched a dark brow. "What is it about me that gets you all worked up?"

Cold shame blasted my cheeks. "Don't flatter yourself." He eased closer and my heart seized like a fist. "What are you doing?"

"Proving my point. No—don't look away. At me. Right here." He forked his fingers towards his steely gaze while his other hand captured my chin so I had no choice—nowhere else to turn as he came closer still. A storm rolling in on the horizon. Powerful, inescapable.

Closer. Until our bodies almost brushed. Until the space between us crackled with heat and electricity and need. I pressed my spine hard against the wall, needing friction and pain to ground me.

"There," he said, voice low and gentle but rough around the edges as he released my face, but it didn't matter. His eyes held me captive. Spellbound. His teeth scored along his bottom lip and hungrily, my eyes dipped to it. Held.

Damn that mouth. Damn him.

Damn *me* for wanting them both with the thirst of sun-scorched sands.

"Do we *really* have time for this?"

"There's never time." Navarre whisked a glance towards the windows, shrugged. "But I'm tired of wondering about you. I'm ready to *know*." His hands slid across brick, the skin of his palms grating like a whispered threat, and a promise.

I'd witnessed what his hands were capable of in a fight. It was hard not to imagine what else they could do.

"I won't speak for you. I won't assume. So tell me. Yes or no?" His hands lowered from the wall, giving a bit of space and distance—clarity—but by no means did it diminish the need thrumming in my blood.

My pulse leapt as his fingers encircled my wrists and lifted my hands to his chest, the hard planes of muscle honed from hours of training.

"I'm right here," he said, his voice low and rough as worn leather. "All you have to do is say yes."

This was insanity.

This was impossible.

And I didn't care.

"Yes." The word slipped from me without hesitation. Just pure unbridled need and instinct.

A soft pant of surprise escaped his chest, as if he'd never thought or dared hope, I would give consent. But as that I had, a frisson of something moved through his eyes, a wild and primitive kind of thing that echoed deep inside of me.

My breath held as he eased forward, bracing me between body and wall, sliding against me until every hollow and crevice was matched by muscle and sinew and the heady pulse of desire.

*Yes*, the darkness within me called. *Come to me. Feast.*

I didn't want tender or easy or careful. I wanted the leash of his control to snap between my teeth. I wanted war.

And he gave me one.

His kiss was fast, but thorough. Gentle, but demanding. It was the wildness of horses thundering through mountain valleys, it was reckless as a swollen stream in early spring, racing and ribboning over rocks and earth. It was electric as a storm.

Unbidden. Powerful.

And I unleashed myself to the fury of it. The beauty of it. All lips and tongues, whispers and moans, hot touches and desperate glides.

*More*, my blood sang.

*More*, my lungs beckoned.

*More*, my heart yearned.

The kiss ended with a sigh, with a brush of lips and an unsteady breath, with a wicked glow in hungry eyes and the powerful grip of his fingers fisted at my back, joined by the rigid lines of his body.

He was off balance when he let me go and I was equally off kilter when he stepped away. Torn apart as shouts rang out in the street, followed by the heavy thump and bangs on doors—people rushing away from the chaos and commotion.

Navarre hurried to the window, rubbed grim from a corner, and bit down on a curse. "The guards aren't giving up the search. They're going door to door."

"They'll be on us soon," I said. The only way out was the way we came in. Impossible to escape without being seen. "We should split up. I'll go first and lead them away."

His gaze snapped to me. "Out of the question."

"If we're caught together, then it's over. Alone, I'm just a Swordsworn who slipped the palace. The Archviceroy is already suspicious of me, anyways."

Navarre raked a trembling hand through his hair. Cursed.

More shouts and kicked in doors. They were almost on us.

"The ascension is tomorrow. What's the worst he can do to me before then?" I said, hoping to ease the lines of worry etched on his brow. He was concerned for me, and I didn't know how to feel about that.

"Don't let them catch you. But if they do, don't draw your sword, Sina. Don't give them an excuse to—" Navarre's features tightened. "The button isn't enough to hold against Henry without Chancellor Reginald's testimony. It won't be enough to save you. Promise me."

I nodded. "Strength and honor." Ripping open the door, I ran.

Shouts broke out behind me. Good. If they were following me, then Navarre would have a clear chance to get away. Pumping my arms, I shoved people out of my path as I charged down the street. Women screamed, men cursed, sloshing beer and wine.

Armor was bulky. It made the guards slow and loud. I could hear them clattering for blocks, but where I was silent and agile, they held the advantage of numbers, swarming through the streets like locusts.

The Archviceroy must've cleared out half the barracks. Every turn I made more closed in, pushing me down narrow alleys and darkened side streets. Lungs on fire, the stink of refuse ripe in the briny air, I whipped around, taking a few precious seconds to orient myself in unfamiliar surroundings. Was I heading closer to the palace or further away from it? Trapped in a maze of brick and concrete, I had no way of knowing.

I cursed the infernal city. The weight of the cowl and cloak was hot on my skin, and made it harder to breathe, but it was the only thing keeping my face concealed.

"*There she is!*" A man shouted and a line of them funneled up the tight alley. Kicking back into a run, I vaulted over stacked crates and metal wastebins, climbing up and over a brick wall. Soon as my feet hit the ground on the other side another batch of guards skidded onto the street.

I urged myself down a curved road that flowed into a steep incline. Leaping and twisting around carts, I cut across the path of a vehicle—the driver honked—narrowly missing his front fender—and dove into a narrow alley. A high wall shone at the end. Picking up the pace, I sprang at the last step—reaching, fingers clawing. But the ledge was too high, and there was nothing around me for leverage.

I could climb a mountain without a guide or rope, but this was smooth stone without a single notch for hand or footholds. Backing up, my gaze skimmed the alley, but it was void of windows. Doorways. Drainpipes.

An inconvenient architectural design to protect the inhabitants from vandals and thieves.

A dead-end.

I had to get out of here. Pushing away from the wall, I ran for the mouth of the alley when a figured dipped in, blocking the way out. Small and agile, dressed in a City Patrol uniform. Pale white skin and hair, the hilt of a sword visible over the rise of her shoulder.

*Rhys.* The alley was too narrow for her to draw, so she charged at me. I didn't break my stride. Nor did she. Colliding head-on, we hit the ground, rolled. A tangle of limbs. Head and elbows striking flesh and paving stone. Aching, I pushed to my knees and our eyes locked in the moonlight.

"Sina?"

*Damnable dead.* Even with the cowl covering half my face, it was no surprise she'd still recognized me. Scooting back, I struggled to slow my breathing. Calm my heart.

Rising on shaking legs, she swiped blood from her nose. Gaped in horrified disbelief. "What are you doing out here?"

"Taking in the scenery?" Rhys snarled, but it was the hurt in her features that had me shaking my head. "Doesn't matter what I'm doing." I said, rising to my feet. And winced at the sting in my joints, along with several other places. I'd be as spotted as a stone-cub come tomorrow. "The less you know, the better."

Reeling back, she pressed unsteady hands to her face. "You fucking idiot," she seethed. "You fucking *stupid*—"

"Here! This way—we've got the bastard!"

Rhys jolted as a guard wedged into the alley. Benj sauntered forward, his smile smug and face dripping with sweat that gleamed in his dark beard. His meaty hand closed in the cowl around my throat, hauling me into the wash of moonlight.

*Don't fight. Don't draw your sword.*

*Promise me.*

"Now." His foul breath washed over me and even through the cowl I could smell the stink of his wooden teeth. "Let's see who we're dealing with."

Rhys swung between us and with a sharp jab to the face, brought the man to his knees. His eyes wheeled in his skull before he slumped forward, unconscious into filth.

"Damnable dead," she cursed, shaking out her hand. "Keep off the streets." Leaning against the wall, back to brick, she cupped her hands together. "It's the only way." Clanking armor and heavy footfalls closed in. Rhys' eyes brightened with fear. "Go! Now."

Rearing back a few paces, I charged and sprang. My foot found purchase in her cupped hands, and Rhys swallowed her groan as she boosted me the last few feet. My fingers latched onto the ledge and I strained, hauling myself up each precarious inch. Clearing the top, I hesitated.

"Go," she whispered. Urgent. "I've got this. Go!"

It was all slow moving across the rooftops, careful not to dislodge any shingles. All it would take was one to smash on the streets below to turn their attention skyward.

My feet touched down on the palace grounds as the sky brightened to palest pink. Sirens wailed from the walls throughout the night. Warning all the City Patrol and the imperial guards into high alert.

I ducked into the passageway with seconds to spare as a contingent of guards passed for their morning rounds. Lungs burning, and thighs aching, I ran through the chasm of tunnels I'd studied relentlessly for weeks, but wove to the opposite wing of the palace. Away from my rooms. And slid out into an antechamber.

Startled, Daneysa swung around. "Sinadine," she gasped, a hand pressed to her heaving chest. Her robe hung open over a white sleeping gown. Mahogany hair sleep tousled. "What are—how did you—?"

*Damnable dead.* In my haste I'd entered the wrong room. Iereni was the next one over.

Sirens howled in the distance, and she stiffened. "Is that for you?"

I nodded, jaw tense.

"Then we don't have much time." Clearing her throat, she swept out a hand. "Come on." She sealed the passageway shut behind me, and ushered me over to her closet.

"Why?" I asked as hangers clinked as she whisked through dress after dress. "Why help me?"

Vibrant green eyes found mine, and, pausing in her haste, she touched my cheek. "I told you we would be friends, Sina. Now hurry up and put this on." She shoved a gown at me and only just finished setting my hair as the doors to her bedchamber burst open.

Guards flowed in, followed by the First Commander. Sir Rickard. A surly man with grey stubble and shrewd features. His gaze raked over Daneysa and settled on me.

She'd dressed me in one of her gowns of amber satin—chosen for its high neck and long sleeves to hide any telltale bruises and scrapes. The material was generous on my hips but my broad shoulders filled out the neckline.

"What is the meaning of this?" Daneysa demanded with all the authority of a magistrate's daughter.

"She was reported missing from her rooms." Sir Rickard gestured in my direction. "I was ordered to search the palace for her."

"Well as you see she's here and has been all night." Daneysa swung around, drawing attention to the opened books she'd staged with half eaten plates and empty glasses in her sitting room to make it look like we'd been reading together for hours. "I'd invited her for a late supper, and we got lost in talking about the wonders of Acharrān lore. My servants can also attest to that."

Sir Rickard curled his lip. "Either way, his eminence wants to see her, at once."

"What for?" Arms spread, she blocked the guards from seizing me.

"That's between her and the Archviceroy. Step aside, Lady Seford."

She did, but with great reluctance, and offered a hopeful smile as I was led away.

The Archviceroy's rooms were the closest in position to the emperlings, and far grander than any I'd seen thus far. The ceilings soared like a cathedral with elaborate gold filigree inlaid into the marble. Long velvet drapes of sapphire hung against walls of pale seafoam. Paintings and statuaries adorned every surface.

So much for humility before God.

The Archviceroy sat at his table of polished Sahson oak laden with fruit, cheese and roasted quail. He continued eating as I was pushed to my knees at his side. "Where was she?" he asked while sucking meat off a bone.

Rings gleamed on his fingers. Elegant and long. It was hard to imagine he'd ever raised a sword a day in his life with such hands. No scarring. No broken knuckles. But I did see a hint of calluses on his palms. Fading, like he'd tried to buff them out with power and privilege and pain.

"We found her with Lady Daneysa. Her ladyship claims the girl was with her all night."

Henry dropped the bone and licked grease from his thumb. "I wasn't aware you and Daneysa were so well acquainted."

I met his glare with unflinching silence.

Sir Rickard knocked his fist against my shoulder. "Answer his eminence."

"That's alright." He dabbed the corner of his lips with a linen napkin. His eyes flickered to me. "I think you and I both know the truth. Alas, it will be hard to prove otherwise with the testimony of a lady advocating on your behalf."

A smile tickled against my lips, feather soft, as I imagined Benj nursing his bloody nose. Rhys had a vicious jab. If she hadn't broken it, then she'd certainly come close.

"I suppose you think you're clever," he continued. "Perhaps you are. But all things will reveal themselves in due course. Of that I am certain." Henry angled his head. "Take her to her rooms, and make sure she stays there, undisturbed, until the ceremony this afternoon."

The guards hauled me to my feet, and I smothered a wince as pain shot through my aching knees, and forming bruises whined beneath brutish hands. Only when I was shoved into my rooms did my smile break free. Leaning against the shut doors, I released an easy laugh.

"There you are." Jasz stepped out from the side of my bed, hidden by the drawn curtains. Her cheeks were mottled pink, eyes red-rimmed and furiously bright with tears, still dressed in a City Patrol uniform. So she'd been out scouring the streets for me, too. How differently would things have played out if she'd been the one to corner me instead of Rhys?

"Do you ever think about anyone but yourself?" she demanded, each word raw and grating. "Do you even know *how*?"

Drawing a hand from behind her back, she tossed my journal at my feet. Scattering my notes and detailed recordings from nights of careful sneaking around, the creased parchment of my grandmother's letter among the pages. She'd found and read it.

Anger surged, and as my hand reached for the hilt of my sword, Jasz drew hers—so fast, so sharp—the blade sang. "Explain yourself." Fresh tears slipped free. "Explain *this*."

"I am going to kill the emperling at his coronation," I said, voice low and without preamble. "How or why doesn't concern you."

The bloodshot whites of her eyes flashed, highlighting a jolt of confusion, hurt and the fresh rise of rage. "We are Swordsworn. Bound to serve the emperling *and* each other. Everything you do concerns *me*." Though her words shook, her hand was steady. The edge of her blade caught the morning sun and arched light across her face. "I can't let you do this."

"Don't you understand? I have to! My mother gave up her sword, her sisters, all because she wanted to make a difference. I *am* that difference. I will see our clan restored to its former glory. This is my destiny," I said, hand flexing by my hilt in case I had a need to defend myself.

Her brittle laugh fractured between us. "Your destiny is death and destruction, *Dakuwan*, of us and our *clan*. The stars don't lie." Slamming her sword into her sheath, Jasz swiped a hand across her face, cleaning up the mess of tears. "I won't speak of this because it would mean your head, but if you put our lives in further jeopardy, I'll consider myself relieved of that obligation."

"You'd betray me to the emperling?" I sneered.

"I'll do what I must to protect my sisters," she said, teeth clenched. "I won't let you make us into martyrs. I won't die for *you*."

"You signed up for death the moment you swore the bloodoath to serve the empire that enslaved us. And we'll die that way if I don't do something."

"Oh, you've done enough." The pink of her cheeks deepened to livid red. "Since we arrived, you've spat in the emperling's face with your defiance and disrespect, and never once did it occur to you to think beyond yourself. To us." She thumped a hand to her chest. "Well, there are consequences, *Dakuwan*. Consequences that Rhys has paid for in full."

Cold fear clutched at my chest. "What does that mean?"

Jasz wrenched open the canopy curtains and revealed a gilded box on the end of my bed, the surface carved in an intricate pattern of scrolling leaves, flowers and vines with a filigree latch made from ivory—smeared with a bloody print. "See for yourself." She tossed a hand, and disgusted, stalked out of the room, slamming the doors behind her.

I don't know how long I stood, staring at that box, working up the nerve to move. Each step was a struggle, and the closer I came, the tighter my chest wound until my breaths were no more than stunted, shallow puffs.

My finger grazed the latch, flicking it open—a soft click that echoed like thunder between my ears. I pried open the lid. And staggered back with a groan.

A sob.

There, in a golden box and on a bed of blue velvet was a hand, skin pale as moonlight and still warm . . . her *sword* hand . . . with a string of words carved into the flesh.

Rage blackened the edges of my vision, a growing tempest of fury joined by grey ribbons of regret that wove along the edges like silver moonlight haloing a storm cloud.

Falling to my knees, I gripped the silken duvet in my hands, and bit down into the downy bundle. Tears burned down my cheeks, joined by the muffled wail of maddening screams I could no longer contain as those words scored into my soul.

*If thine hand offends—cut it off.*

# CHAPTER TWENTY-ONE

## Sinadine

I'D ALWAYS LIKED THE FEEL of blood on my hands. The warm and slippery glide of it coating my skin joined by the bright metallic tang in the air. Watching as it dried in the cracks and crevices of my palms and knuckles, slowly fading from a brilliant crimson to rusted brown.

Blood on my hands never bothered me. Until now.

Until *this*.

Exhaustion swept through me, a gentle current of a half-frozen stream that stripped me to the bone. Leaving me numb and entirely void of feeling. I had to be. There was no other way to endure such grief, and no time for me to shed that weight. I could hear the clamor of the people filling the plaza.

They'd feasted and glutted on wine and music throughout the night to celebrate this moment. When one empress would fall, and another would rise to take her place.

Daneysa arrived with servants in tow, and her sorrowful gaze told me she knew what happened with Rhys, but she said nothing as the servants removed my clothes and dressed me in a white silk kubari webbed with diamonds, so many that each movement of silk glittered like fresh snow. My braids were unwound, and beads removed, my hair combed until straight, and parted at the center to cover the fade.

Daneysa touched a soft hand to my cheek and pressed her lips to mine. A lingering kiss, soft with comfort. "I will put them back," she promised.

What did it matter? What did any of this matter, in light of what I'd done?

*There are consequences, Dakuwan.*

Nausea swirled in my empty stomach as we entered the plaza. Jasz' eyes burned through my back, the sharp sting of her anger, her dismay and heartache, but I couldn't look at her. I couldn't bear the weight of her emotions when I was so brittle.

The people roared as I was brought before them, a ghost to stand at Ehrick's side on the edges of a rousing speech to ignite their fervor. Most were still dressed in the revelry from the night, with gilded masks and colorful silks, drunk and swaying, all gathered for the empresses' final ascension.

The Archviceroy's fingers cinched around my arm and the world snapped into focus. All color and contrast and sound, crackling like damp firewood.

"Take her head, present her sword to the emperling on your knees and swear your fealty. Say nothing else. *Do nothing else. And be quick about it.*" He sneered before striding away from me, guiding Ehrick to the sidelines of the terrace.

Acharrāns did not die of old age and sickness, instead when a Swordsworn, deep in her greying years, was ready to seek her rest she was graced with one final battle after a night of celebration—to die with sword in hand and rise to the stars honorably as a warrior. This was a bastardization of the ritual. He'd taken something sacred and turned it into something profane. Entertainment for the masses.

Yet another display of Bridian power.

The empress knelt at my feet and smoothed the fabric of her red kubari beneath her. Head shaved clean to showcase the dome of her skull, and the graceful line of her exposed neck.

"I am Nomi de-Heo. Bloodkin to Timejo de-Dzo. Wife to the late Emperor Edvard of the great Torren Dynasty." Her eyes rose to mine, soft and certain. Ready. "I kneel before you, sister, weary. Humble. And ask that you let me find peace among the stars." Removing her sword from her sheath, she presented it to me.

The wall of skulls smiled behind her with diamond teeth and jeweled eyes; the crowd hushed, as if we were actors in some garish play instead of real life, waiting for my hand to rise and strike her head from her shoulders—with her own blade.

Every instinct inside me screamed and raged. I wanted the empress to rise and fight with honor. She deserved to die with dignity on her feet beneath the stars, not as a slave on her knees when the eyes of the First-of-Us were blinded by the sun. Even after two decades without her sword, I imagined a lifetime of experience rising to the surface of her being, like grass through melting snow, her body moving with a grace that flowed easy as breath and with a strength that I could only hope to match.

It would've been a glorious fight between sisters. And if it were yesterday, I would have given her such a death, but somewhere in the palace Rhys' hand was moldering in a golden box.

*There are consequences, Dakuwan.*

Jasz was right. My impetuousness had already cost them so much. What other parts would Ehrick or the Archviceroy cut off if I defied them again?

My fingers closed around the hilt and drew steel from scabbard. "Please," I whispered, my arm trembling, "forgive me for what I must do."

Empress Nomi smiled. A single tear breaking free. "Be strong where I was weak, sister." She bowed low in deference.

Even in this final moment of her death when she no longer had to bow to anyone, she bowed to *me*.

The edge of the blade found the line of her neck. Long. Elegant. A swan about to spread her wings one last time. And steel went leaden in my unsteady grip, the weight of what I had to do suddenly overwhelming.

I'd killed before, but never a sister. Never a Swordsworn.

And the woman knelt before me was no longer just one, but all. She was my entire clan on their knees, and I was about to cleave their heads from their shoulders all for an empire demanding blood.

Tears flowed, there was no stopping them as I swung true, a flawless stroke. She would've barely felt the sword's kiss before it was over. Blood rained from the stump of her throat, wet scarlet over pale white marble. It misted the air, the scent coating my lungs in a haze of death and anguish.

The crowd roared as the empress' body collapsed. A wave of sound that throbbed against the palace walls, and vibrated in my ears. Music swelled and dancers poured on stage to entertain the mob, but I couldn't take my eyes off the sight of her twitching limbs. Or the blood. A yawning, dark red pool, warm against the edges of my toes. The sides of my feet.

Much like the blood on my hands, for once I didn't care for the sensation.

The empress was dead. Another skull to join the wall. More than a custom or tradition, this was a demonstration to the people of the empire. An act of power, and a reminder that even though I would be their Empress soon, I'd always be a prisoner.

Like the sword in my hands, the dancers spinning on stage, and the rain of fiery sparks shooting into the sky—it was all for show to distract their eyes from the body being carried away.

I turned towards the towering rows of skulls dipped in various shades of gold, from blue to silver, to yellow and black. All etched with decorative whorls and inlaid with gems that glittered darkly in the grey light, and in their growing shadow I shrank beneath the understanding of my own insignificance. Who was I to think I could stop this? Change this? That my own head wouldn't one day be rent from my own shoulders to join them?

So many. A thousand generations wronged.

And in the roar of the crowd, I could hear the dead scream.

❖

Celebration and revelry wound into the night, the palace swollen with nobility and figureheads of state seated at a single table, long enough to seat a hundred, festooned with gold candelabras, platters of honey basted lamb, braised veal, lemon scented chicken, roasted parsnips and potatoes, mushrooms and pearl onions sautéed in wine. They ate and laughed, they toasted and sang praises to the glory of the Bridian Empire.

Glutting themselves on the blood of my sisters.

"Dear girl." A hand stroked across my shoulder. "You're quite flush. Are you well?" The wife of some pompous marquisate, whose name I'd already forgotten, offered me a hopeful smile, makeup decorating her features to emulate a True Face.

And she wasn't even the worst offender.

Women wore beads or feathers in their hair, and gold leaf familiars painted on their skin without knowing or appreciating what any of it meant. Sacred artwork and embroidered motifs used in great ceremonial rituals to commune with the Spirits of my Sisters were transformed into dinner jackets, elaborate dresses, cloaks and jewelry.

My culture. My home and history made into . . . adornments. A shameful parade of textiles, and body art stolen from my mountains, my home, when they had no right to any of it.

"Perhaps she's still reeling from this afternoon," a viscount added, seated across from the woman whose hand was still *touching* me. "I thought beheadings were a common ritual among your people. You should feel right at home among all this." A few of the gentry giggled, amused by his remark.

I slid my tongue along the cutting edge of my smile and my fingers closed around my knife, a short, serrated blade that I imagined plunging into his smug eye, twisting the orb free from its socket. But, over the line of his shoulders, Jasz stood on display like the skull-wall grinning into the night. Rhys remained notably absent, and grief slammed across me—a battle axe splitting me to the marrow.

*There are consequences, Dakuwan.*

I unfurled my fingers, releasing the knife.

Amused, the viscount popped a puff of caramel covered pastry into his mouth. Unaware how close he'd come to losing an eye.

"Excuse us." Navarre rose from his seat and dazzled the nobles with a gracious smile. "I think the emperling's intended has had enough excitement for one day. Allow me to escort you to your room, my lady."

I jerked away from the table, my chair legs screeching across marble floors—the sound barely masked by the swirling music—but no one seemed to care as I stalked out with Navarre at my side. Once inside my rooms, the doors sealed behind us, his hand closed around my arm.

"Don't touch me!" I shouted, wrenching away. Cold. I was so cold. Pain. Grief. Rage and sorrow. I couldn't contain all the fury that swelled inside of me as flashes of the gold box glittered behind my eyes.

*Bloodstained velvet and decaying skin.*

"Hey, easy—"

My sword sang in my hands. I didn't recall reaching for it, or striking, until his own blade clashed with mine.

"Sina!" he panted, eyes wide. "Don't."

I ignored his pleas and snapped into a vicious dance of rage and steel, my movements sharp and unchecked. I wanted blood. I wanted death. I wanted to see him laying at my feet and watch the life ebb from his eyes. We crossed swords. Mine, sharp and true. His, dull as a cracked bell. I could hear the impurities in the metal—the weakness.

*Enemy*, my senses screamed. He was the enemy and as guilty as the rest of them.

Navarre retreated, putting distance between us but I advanced, vaulting across the bed. My foot lashed out, clipping his knee but he rolled into the momentum and sprang to his feet, rounding the pillar.

"Sina," he called out, leaping from side to the side as my sword hammered against marble column, chipping away fragments. "Stop this!"

"No!" Blood pounded in my ears. The haze of it obscured my vision, boiling and black as tar.

Spinning into a kick, Navarre hooked an arm around my leg, anchoring me to him as he whipped me around.

Discarding his weapon, he seized my sword arm. A stupid thing to do. Smashing my brow into the bridge of his nose, Navarre's curse was smothered by a sharp cry of pain, but his grip didn't ease. Kicking off the pillar, he staggered back and I used the momentum to my advantage. We hit the floor in a tangle of striking elbows and knees.

"I don't want to hurt you, Sina."

"You're the one bleeding!" I ploughed my fist into the wall of his kidney. He grunted, and when he instinctively folded in to protect his left, I hooked a leg over and twisted on top of him.

Sword to his throat, I screamed. *Screamed*. All fury and frustration and helpless grief.

"You won't hurt me." Navarre's hands fell away, and his body went lax beneath a swath of crimson sunset that bathed him in the promise of blood yet to be spilled. His eyes, calm silver pools. "I know you won't hurt me."

"I should carve you open," I seethed, "and see what Bridians are truly made of."

"I trust you, Sina."

My hand shook. "Stop it."

"I trust you."

My sword was heavy in my grip. The weight of steel no longer a reassuring comfort. Tears, the betrayal of them seared in my throat and numbness crept into my fingers. Spread up my arms. Into my lungs.

I couldn't think. Couldn't see. *Breathe*.

Panicked, I reeled away from him, staggering to the terrace doors, and pushed outside to breathe—finally breathe in deep, desperate gasps of air for my starving body. I was a corpse thrust back into life—I couldn't get enough. Heart thundering, blood racing and wild, I swayed against the balustrade as a sob ripped from my chest. A wounded, animal sound.

Arms closed around me, and I couldn't shake them off.

"Slow." Navarre anchored me against his chest. "Slow it down, Sina."

"I—I can't feel my hands. I can't—" Chilled to the bone, my body shook with such ferocity my teeth ached. Like I'd been dragged from the icelake and left to die in the snow.

Feeling. So much feeling. My bones rattled with it.

I sank to the floor, dragging Navarre with me, an anchor as I drowned in sorrow.

"Stay with me." His lips whisked against my temple. "Breathe with me." His chest rose, and mine fell. It took a while to find his rhythm, to follow it. For my heart to slow and my lungs to properly expand, but they did, and gradually the numbness faded, starting with my fingertips and spreading upwards.

Navarre swept his hands up and down my arms, warming the unnerving chill in my blood as he cradled me against him. "Tell me. Please. What's wrong?"

I didn't want to, but the words poured out of me, a flood.

Navarre stayed quiet for a long while, with only the distant chirp of crickets and nightingale's song carried on the cold evening breeze.

"Ehrick's always been my brother, my truest friend, but I've never felt true *shame* because of him until now," he said, a whisper against my brow. "I'll find a way to make this right."

Tears blistered the back of my eyes in a relentless wave of guilt that I couldn't stop. Worse, than the grief and sorrow, was this terrible ache of responsibility.

He took her hand. Her *sword* hand. How could I make him understand what that meant? An Acharrān who could not wield her blade was like a setting sun never to rise again. Impossible.

Devastating.

Her sword was more than her heart and her spirit, it was a connection to her sisters—the ones still breathing and the ones in the stars.

Killing her would've hurt less than this.

"It's not your wrong to make right. It's his. And it's mine."

His fingertip stroked the line of my jaw still wet with sorrow. "I never expected softness from you. I never expected tears."

"To my people . . . our people," I amended gently, "crying is necessary medicine. Denying yourself their comfort and release allows the poison of anger, anxiety, and sorrow to rot inside of you until you're consumed by it. Straight to the bone."

We called it zovesh. The living death.

"They say my mother could taste the truth in tears. That's why she collected them, she liked to know what lay behind the eyes of her enemies in that final moment of life." I dabbed at the fresh beads of grief rolling down my cheek and rubbed it between the pads of my fingers.

What would my tears reveal about me?

Navarre's pressed his lips to my temple, a lingering and gentle touch, but when I gazed up at him, his eyes blazed. Desire and duty warred within him.

I could see which side was losing and something in me echoed that flame.

Reaching between us, I stroked my fingers across the daring, wicked curve of his bottom lip, and a violent tremble shook through his chest.

"Don't do that."

"Why?"

Dappled moonlight cascaded in silver highlights across the hard line of his jaw and glinted in the dark grey pools of his eyes. He was an animal caged, and I was threatening to set him free.

"Because you fascinate me. And infuriate me." Softly spoken, his voice rolled between us, gentle as smoke spiraling over candlelight. "To want you like this is treason."

The sane part of my brain urged me to pull away. He was the enemy. He was dangerous. He was a threat. But in this moment—compelled by the beckoning fullness of his mouth—desire outweighed my need for self-preservation or common-sense. I needed to feel something. Anything but this cold, emptiness. And the wicked thrill of his darkening gaze shot through me like a lit arrow.

"Then we're both traitors," I whispered. And tugged him forward.

His mouth clashed against mine, urgent and demanding at that first heated kiss, stolen in the shadows of the warehouse, and now here out into the open air and moonlight. My hands slid up his arms, across his shoulders and tangled in his hair, dragging him down with me. The shock of his body sliding over me was like fire licking across an already burning log and I groaned, hungry for more.

For this. For him. A distraction from the misery.

A balm for the pain.

*Touch me*, my thoughts commanded. And his hands obeyed. Rough palms and long fingers gliding over my thighs, my hips and breasts, gathering, cupping, squeezing. Mine were no less ruthless. No less impatient.

A moan slipped out of me, my voice harsh and gritty as I arched into him, and begged. Needing friction and contact and more of whatever it was he was doing to my body. Our mouths fast and fierce where our bodies were so slow, the contrast was maddening but I sank into it, surrendered to the need until I was lost in the sensation.

Lost in him.

"Wait," he panted between my assault and drew back on his knees. My groan of frustration tangled in his answering laugh. "My. *God*," he sighed. "How do you do this to me?"

"I don't know what you mean. I've never kissed anyone before you."

Navarre's brows winged up in surprise. "Never?"

Only once. Cahira had pressed her lips to mine when we were almost twelve. A game, I'd thought, until I saw her eyes afterwards, filled with the dewy sheen of awe and a kind of primal knowing suddenly confirmed in that singular moment. A knowing I'd apparently lacked until this moment.

I shook my head. "Not like this."

"That's a shame. You have the kind of mouth made for it." His fingers stroked up my throat, over my leaping pulse, and cupped my cheek.

Tender. Trembling.

"Enough," I whispered beneath the stroke of his thumb across my lips. The moment of pause between the war of lips and tongues had given me a fresh wave of clarity to douse the embers of passion he'd so effortlessly stoked.

This couldn't happen. Not when there was a line drawn between us, and we stood on opposite sides.

Navarre with his brother, and I with my sisters.

Understanding, his hand fell away and he rocked back onto his knees. "I should let you rest."

"No." I rose to my feet as he did. "I want to see where my sisters are buried."

His eyes searched mine. Careful. Patient. Understanding. "Okay."

The door to the mausoleum was a heavy bolt of iron, rusted around the edges, deep beneath the bowels of the palace. The way lined with unlit torches. Navarre collected one, sparked a match and it lit with a dancing blue flame. Kraken oil. Nearly a thousand florin an ounce, but a few drops would burn for a day and a night.

The door was unlocked, and he wrenched it open.

"This is where the empresses and her cadres are laid to rest," he said, slotting the torch into the notch by the door. "After the heads are removed, the bodies are burned and the remains stored here."

The mausoleum was a massive underground chamber made of gleaming white stone, with soaring ceilings braced by endless rows of columns painted in blues and gold.

The God's Eye, made of faceted crystal, was suspended over a large, capped well.

Hands set to the brass wheel, Navarre groaned, muscles straining he wrenched and turned the wheel. Stone screamed against stone and a cloud of ashes spiraled into the air through the yawning crevice.

The bones of my sisters. Their hearts and flesh trapped in the earth when they were supposed to be scattered to the four winds.

I couldn't leave them this way.

Fresh rage sparked inside me at the thought of Rhys' remains being locked away in the dank bowels of the imperial palace. To know she was chained to such a fate because of me. But none of us would've been here if it wasn't for the treaty. We would be home in the mountains, safe and happy, living our lives instead of as slaves to the crown.

Renewed hatred—for the empire, for my aunt—all of it, flared inside of me. Grounding my pain with purpose.

"I need something. A bowl or an urn."

"What are you going to do?"

Sliding my hand inside, I grabbed a fistful of milky grey dust. "Honor them."

❖

The terrace had been scrubbed clean and it shone a terrible white, like gleaming bone. Bright as the grinning skulls. Most of the guards were kept busy by the festivities, either posted within the palace or patrolling the walls in case of threat. The plaza was of less concern or risk, but Navarre dismissed the closest guards from their post to afford me privacy, and they were happy to obey the command.

It wasn't every day an empress was laid to rest.

Navarre kept watch from the periphery, and I was grateful he understood my need for distance. Cold night air raced over my skin, and I shivered against it. Winter was in the wind, and the impending promise of snow. Too shaken by grief, I hadn't noticed earlier on the balcony of my chambers, but it slid over me know.

Cold and familiar as the mountains.

Setting down the bowls, I dipped my fingers first into water, then the ashes, and smeared the paste in bold lines across my face, over my neck and arms.

Finished, I rose and faced the skulls of my sisters, and touched a hand to one at eye-level, encased in black gold and studded with sapphires. Her name carved in imperial lettering on her brow. *Zaran.* Soon Nomi's would join them, her gentle eyes replaced with fake jewels and skin with gilded metal.

This was not right. Our bones were not to be desecrated for decoration like trophies set on display as a show of strength and dominance to the masses. The treaty had been meant to keep our sisters safe. A few sacrificed for the sake of many. But as I stood there now, I couldn't escape the bitter truth that none of us we're free. We'd failed them. All of them.

The sound of an opening door cut through my grief and Navarre tensed as Jasz strode across the far end of the terrace. She inclined her chin as she approached, Rhys not far behind, her left arm bandaged and bound across her chest.

Jasz faced the wall. Her chin wavered but she put steel into the muscle and bone. "I didn't know this is what they did to us." Grief made her words brittle, and they sliced their way out like claws to her throat.

"None of us did," I answered.

"They deserved *better*." Tears flowed down Rhys' cheeks, splattering on her bare toes.

"Forgive me," I whispered. Taking a knee before her, I bowed low in grief and apology. "It should've been me. Not you." *Never you...*

"The shame is not yours to carry," Rhys answered, voice raw after the hours she must've spent weeping. "But you should've told us, Sina. You should've trusted us with the truth instead of thinking you had to face it alone."

The miserable ache of grief shocked me to the bone but I nodded in agreement and accountability. I wasn't alone. I was part of a clan, and it was time I started acting like it.

"No more secrets," I vowed. "No more lies." My breath trembled as the blaze of tears lit a scorching fire in my throat and behind my eyes as I looked to my sisters. Strong, fierce and proud. "Tonight, we honor our dead," I said. "And tomorrow we avenge them."

"I stand with you, *Dakuwan*." Jasz's eyes glittered, dark with promise.

Rhys tapped the blunted end of her bandaged arm to her chest. "Strength and honor."

Jasz marked herself first, and then Rhys, with the ashes of our dead. Barefoot, we formed a line before the skulls. This was a pitiful funeral. They deserved the grief of our entire clan. They deserved singing and drums and the beat of a thousand feet pounding their misery into the earth, but all they had was us three, and this one night.

"Spirits of our Sisters, we are daughters of the Acharrā," I said, raising my voice so it carried proudly in the still and steady dark. "And we have not forgotten you."

Eyes closed, Jasz released a soft breath as the first wailing note tore from her throat and flowed into a haunting song sung only for the honorable dead. I'd never been much of a singer, but Rhys and I tipped our faces towards the stars and joined her. Our voices rising in undulating harmonies that sounded hollow as old bones without the beat of wind drums to carry them.

Once the song was over, we danced. Heads bouncing, heels drumming and arms twisting at our sides as we wove in alternating pattern of circles. We danced, for the dead—our sisters, slain. We danced for their souls. We danced for their honor, until our thighs ached and feet throbbed. As the moon slid across the sea of black, a glowing silver orb to vanish beyond the horizon—we danced.

And when the first spear of sun flashed, we faced the rising dawn—arms outstretched—and released the trapped souls of our Acharrān sisters to the morning light.

# CHAPTER TWENTY-TWO

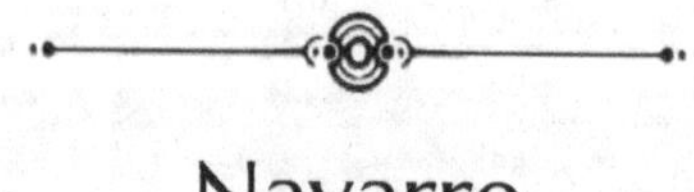

## Navarre

"Aren't you going to open it, milord?" Toddrick shifted eagerly at his side.

Removing his cloak, Navarre set the parcel down on his desk. It had taken three days, a considerable sum of his own money and calling in some impressive favors to ensure to both impeccable quality and expedited delivery, but finally it was ready. "It's not for me."

"Oh, come on," Toddrick wiggled like a giddy pup, "just a peek. It's not every day we get to see the work of a genuine *maestro*." A wide smile pushed up his round cheeks. The cut on the right one faded to a pink crescent that dented his skin like a bright dimple, and somehow made him appear even more innocent.

"Alright." Navarre winked. Unfastening the knots of ribbon, he peeled away the cloth to reveal the elegantly shaped case inscribed with a flourishing monogrammed stamp.

"Oh my." Toddrick gasped as he cracked open the lid. Dewy eyed, his hand fluttered to his heart. "It's beautiful, milord."

It was more than beautiful. It was breathtaking. Art and science melded together so intricately, Navarre wondered how such a thing could be possible. The hand was shaped from Tujianese bronze—the strongest in the world, next to Acharrān steel—and met a leather cuff that hugged the arm to the shoulder with sensors that would read shifting in the muscle and send pulses to the fingers, guiding them in simple movement.

Rhys would never have the dexterity of a grand pianist or a physician surgeon, but she'd absolutely be able to wield a blade. And throw a punch.

Only one man in the Imperial City could do such work, and it had cost him an expensive favor, but Navarre would've paid any price his pockets could afford. The memory of Sinadine and her sisters, their harrowing grief and misery as they tirelessly danced until dawn before the wall of gilded skulls had haunted him for days afterwards.

Guilt didn't sit easy with Navarre, but there was no shaking the disquiet of the foul emotion running rancor in his system like a poison, leaching to the bone until he wanted to fall to his knees and scream.

Once he renounced the Archviceroy, Navarre hoped to convince his brother to peacefully dissolve the treaty—freeing the Swordsworn from their obligation to serve. Sinadine and her sisters would return to the mountains. Ehrick would be free to pursue an alliance with the Princess of Oscano. Everyone would get what they wanted most.

But Henry had to be dealt with, first.

"Any word on Chancellor Reginald?" Toddrick asked, as if Navarre's dark thoughts were etched plainly on his face.

"None." The morning after the ceremony, Navarre had gone to Reginald's apartments on High Street to interrogate the official regarding his clandestine meetings at the *Crow* and connection to the Archviceroy, but to no avail.

The man had absconded from the Imperial City, it seemed, likely hiding in fear of his life. Which meant Navarre had to find him and fast, or risk losing the only chance he had to wrench the Archviceroy from his seat of power once and for all.

They both turned as Eban entered the office, his features drawn. "Sir, I—"

"Oh, don't fuss on my account," Ehrick pushed around the boy, and shuffled into the room, iron legs clanking around the hiss of pistons and pumps. "Leave us," he commanded.

Toddrick, red as a sliced pomegranate, skittered out fast as he could manage. Eban lingered a moment on the threshold, his gaze swimming with apology as he shut the door.

"Smile, brother," Ehrick spread his hands with a beaming grin, "I've come with fortuitous news."

"Do tell."

"Uncle Henry has suggested we invite the Princess of Oscano to attend my coronation. He hopes that with her and her father visiting the Imperial Palace that we might broker some kind of alliance. I'd like you to sail to Zavoria as my personal envoy, carrying the request."

Navarre's chest seized. "I can't."

"You can't?" Ehrick frowned. "Barely a month ago, you were chomping at the bit for such an opportunity. Why the change of heart?"

*Because our uncle plotted to kill our father and your life may be in danger.* The words burned inside of him, searing and with no place to go.

"Seems you were right, brother, when you said that as Second Commander I would have much to learn. My place is here, at your side." Between his brother and the Archviceroy. "Sir Rickard should go. As your First, he is highly decorated, and deserving of the honor."

"You feel unworthy to the task?"

"She is a princess." Navarre cleared his throat. "And though your brother, I am a bastard. Sending me might be perceived as an insult."

"Is that the only reason?" Ehrick narrowed his eyes. Then lowered them to Navarre's desk.

Understanding too late, he tried to brace himself between his brother and the case, but Ehrick touched a hand to his shoulder, and reluctantly he stepped aside.

"Uncle told me about this little secret of yours. Remarkable."

*Goddamn the Archviceroy and his* spies. Navarre tensed as Ehrick lifted the hand, all the mechanisms and gears, the movements of the fingers—so lifelike.

"Tujianese bronze," his voice rose with interest. "Made by the skilled Maestro Ignotus, no less. Very expensive."

Ehrick had studied under Ignotus for a time, soaking up his knowledge with avid interest until he'd resigned from teaching. It was why Navarre thought of the man.

"Ignotus is General Hiro's husband," he said, struggling against the urge to snatch the hand from Ehrick and hide it away.

"*Ah*, yes. General Hiro. I suppose he can consider his personal debt to you paid in full after this." Ehrick waved the bronze mechanical hand, and those fingers moved in a macabre wiggle. He returned it to the lacquered case, and gently stroked the polished surface. "Tell me, brother, what am I to make of this gesture?"

Panic kicked him square in the chest. "A Swordsworn without a sword hand is a useless asset," Navarre answered.

Ehrick lowered to the desk, his swaying foot clanked against the table leg. A hammer to nail. "So, it's a vested interest in their skillset that motivates you to undermine my authority?"

"It was a bit harsh, brother."

"Harsh, but necessary." Ehrick plucked a grape from the bowl of fruit laid out on desk from Navarre's untouched breakfast. "Uncle Henry told me about Sinadine slipping the palace grounds, and the mess she caused in the Low District fractured delicate trade agreements with the Galgoans. She's wild and willful." He popped the grape into his mouth, and bit into it firmly. "We agreed such defiant behavior can't go unchecked."

"But Daneysa—"

"—shouldn't put her nose where it doesn't belong," Ehrick interrupted. "Fortunately, her status protects her from serious reprimand. *This* time."

"And Rhys?" Navarre spread his hands, let them fall. "She was innocent of any wrongdoing."

"Innocent?" Ehrick scoffed, bemused. "Tell me, brother, why do you think our predecessor asked for three girls, and not one? Because a single Acharrān would never submit. But put her sisters to the knife and it's surprising how easily they come to heel. *Sisters before Self*, as they say." A soft laugh eased out of him, like the wind whispering between the cracks in the windowpane. Gentle, almost inaudible.

But Navarre felt it slithering through the air and across his skin all the same.

Ehrick cocked his head. "You think me cruel?"

"I think you've been corrupted." Tears seared the backs of his eyes and Navarre struggled to hold them at bay. The misery suddenly too great for him to contain in the face of his brother—the last of his family, becoming a stranger he hardly recognized. "I know what atrocities the Archviceroy committed during his campaigns, and I fear his influence has taken ahold of you." *I fear that I'll never be able to root him out.* "I can't stand before you and pretend that I understand or approve of your actions. Not anymore."

Ehrick eased from the desk. Rising slowly. "I do what I must, because I am the last. Because I am all that lies between the future of our family and failure. It's a terrible weight you are fortunate not to have to carry." The anger in him softened to quiet disgust. "You think I like the things I've had to do? Until I am crowned, and bear the full authority of my birthright, I must be swift, decisive, and without weakness. I cannot give my enemies a moment to doubt my ability to rule." Releasing a scoffing breath, he shook his head. "You know me, brother. You know my heart and mind better than anyone; how could you question me, so?"

Wounded hurt strained his voice and glistened in eyes Navarre couldn't bring himself to meet. "I'm sorry."

"Don't be sorry, be on my *side*. Remember all that's at stake, our legacy. Our future. The moment you start to doubt me—everything we're working towards will shatter."

Ehrick was right. They'd always stood together, united as one. To doubt him now when Ehrick needed faith in him the most . . . Navarre hung his head.

Ashamed. Aggrieved.

"My brother." Sighing, Ehrick clasped his hands around Navarre's neck, hugging him fast. "Let us not quarrel. The worst is behind us now. Once the crown is on my head, we will both fulfill our true purpose. As my right hand, with your strength and my wits, this world will be molded to our making like wax pressed beneath a seal. We will make our mark that I promise you."

"I look forward to the day," Navarre answered, holding his brother close. "I don't know what came over me."

"You've a tender heart. Always have," Ehrick laughed, and easing back, those hands gathered his shoulders. "I am moved by your compassion. Take your gift to the Swordsworn girl if it puts your mind and conscience at ease. This once, I will allow it. But know this," those hands gave a hard, bitter squeeze, gripping him like the teeth of a scolding mother to the scruff of an errant pup, "my actions are not for you to understand. Nor do they require your approval. *Brother*."

# CHAPTER TWENTY-THREE

## Sinadine

DAMP MISTED THE AIR, MORE like smoke than rain, and dusted the ground in frost. Each breath, soggy and bitter, escaped my lips in white plumes. Ghostly snakes. A cruel morning, but it suited my mood.

Three days had passed since the execution, and my anger wasn't abating or easier to manage. Instead, it eked out into every part of me, a cancer that I tried to purge through preparation. The coronation was a week away. I had seven days to kill him, but now I wasn't planning to do it alone.

Sweeping in, I pushed Iereni from offense to defense. Steel sang and she gritted her teeth, sweat beading into her eyes. "Keep your sword arm steady," I commanded with a warning point of my blade.

"Slow down," she grunted, struggling to meet my driving blows, her left hand dropping to guide her wheels as I forced her where I wanted her to go.

"Control the fight," I demanded without relenting. "Drive me back."

"I'm trying!"

"Try *harder*!"

"Stop shouting at me," she cried, cheeks pink with anger and frustration.

"Your enemies won't be slow. Your enemies won't let you breathe or think. They won't care if you're tired or sick." Dropping my sword, I reared back and kicked her straight in the chest—her wheels lifted, and she tumbled over—smacking her head into the ground with a hard grunt, and her sword skittered out of reach. Sobbing, she scrabbled for her chair.

I wrenched it away. Tossing it aside. "Pick up your sword."

Iereni dragged herself back on shaking arms. After what had happened to Rhys, I'd ordered my sisters and Navarre to keep their distance so now there was no one to stop my advance and she quaked beneath my glare. Gone was the spark of strength and determination, carefully nurtured through weeks of training, leaving behind nothing but a wide-eyed little girl—lost, and terrified.

"I can't."

"Pick it up."

"I need my chair."

"Forget your chair, I'm about to run you through." I slapped the flat of my blade to her shoulder, hard enough to sting. "Stop me!" Fresh tears bloomed. So I struck her again.

"I can't!"

"Why?"

"Because you're not fighting *fair*," she shouted, cheeks flaming and damp.

Lowering to my haunches, I set the tip of my sword to stone, ignoring the way she flinched. "Your enemies won't fight fair. They'll take one look at you and aim right where you're weakest." I nodded to her chair laying askance, the left wheel spinning slowly on its side. "Anything to disarm you."

She glared at me with furious, upset. "You could've warned me."

"There are no warnings in a combat. Only action and reaction. It's one thing to know how to fight; it's another to know how to *survive*. If you can't face your fears, you won't overcome them."

Iereni dipped her chin with a bracing breath. "I . . . I thought you were mad at me, too. For the empress. For all of it." A skittish hand brushed across her shoulder where I'd struck her. "I thought you hated me."

"I hate everyone. Ask Rhys or Jasz," I teased but worry and pain still cast a sheen over her features and rattled through her arms.

I'd hurt her. Worse than that, I'd scared her—pushed her beyond comfort and into a state of utter helplessness. A vital lesson for every warrior, but one I'd poorly handled because in all honesty, I was angry, even if I didn't wish to admit it, and a small part of me had taken it out on her.

"I don't hate you," I added gently. "I'm sorry if I made you think so."

Sniffling, Iereni swiped at her reddening face. "I'm sorry too," she whispered. "For what he did. What he *made* you do."

Capturing her chin, I pushed her gaze up to mine. "You played no part so don't you dare carry the shame."

Iereni nodded stiffly, fresh tears rolling thick down her cheeks. "I'll try."

Straightening, I towered over her with a twist of my sword, angling the blade along the line of my arm. "So here you are. The enemy has you on the ground and they'll think you're helpless. Together—we'll show them you're not."

There were several strike points below the waist. The knee. The inner thigh. Sever the tendon behind the ankle and a three-hundred-pound man would collapse and scream like an infant ripped from the breast. All areas harder for them to protect, and easier for her to strike. I'd make sure she knew them all because once I was gone, in a world where men held absolute power and women were forced to serve their every whim, Iereni would have to protect herself.

I nudged the hilt against her knee with the toe of my boot. "Pick it up."

My footsteps shuffled in the dark. Not trusting a torch to light my way, I crept down to the mausoleum, the only place I could safely meet with my cadre to talk about what would come next. As promised, there were no more secrets. The coronation was fast approaching. If Ehrick was going to die, then we would all have knowledge and part to play in his assassination.

Jasz rose as I entered and sealed the iron door behind me. "Where's Rhys?"

I jerked to a stop. "Isn't she with you?"

"Navarre pulled her aside earlier."

"Did he say *why* he wanted to speak to her?" I demanded, hands on my hips.

"No. I didn't detect anything amiss at the time, but she should be here by now."

A dizzying spin of terrified panic swirled in my belly, and I pressed a hand there, smothering it along with the harrowing image of Rhys' hand rotting in a gilded box. "He won't hurt her," I said, more to assure myself than Jasz. And may his God protect him otherwise, because if another piece of her went missing I'd start collecting my own.

"Any word from your grandmother?" Jasz demanded, pulling the attention where it needed to be given our narrow window of time. To avoid raising suspicion, we kept these clandestine meetings to twenty minutes or less and always during midday when most of the guards were shoveling food into their gullets.

"None."

Jasz worried the edge of her thumbnail between her teeth. "Should we be concerned?"

"Her last letter said she was going to rally support from the Norlanders. It's only been a couple weeks. She's likely not returned from those efforts, yet." Because killing Ehrick was just the start. A war would undoubtedly follow, and we'd need numbers to quell it immediately.

"We're cutting close." She shook her head. "The coronation is in two days, and we still have no idea what pieces are in play."

"Then we focus on the pieces we can see," I said. "Us. And Ehrick."

Jasz nodded stiffly. "Well, once you kill the emperling we'll have *minutes* to get clear of the imperial walls before the alarms sound," she said, rolling out a sheet of parchment. A map she'd copied from the one in Navarre's study of the City Patrol.

This one showed not only the detailed workings of the hidden passages within the palace walls, but the catacombs and sewers that webbed beneath the city. All pinned and flagged with guard posts we'd pieced together between my excursions and their patrol schedule, highlighting which paths to avoid and which would be unattended. Unfortunately, the most direct routes, already under heavy surveillance, would be more so during the coronation. Which left only two far more complicated options.

One wrong turn and we'd never find our way out alive.

"The chapel is our best strike point," Jasz began. "It's a narrow structure—far from the barracks and with only two ways in or out. The nobles and clergy will enter through the main doors, here—heavily guarded." She jabbed the point on the map and my eyes followed.

"Which means the second doors, leading out towards the plaza, are the one we should take."

Less guards, but more bodies. The plaza would be flooded with people, but that would also play in our favor. A panicked mob would create chaos and distraction, making it easier for us to disappear.

"From the moment you take his head, we need to get here," Jasz continued. "To this cross-section of the catacombs leading from the sewers to the Narrow Shore. Once we're on horseback, we ride hard for the Blue Wastes. They won't be able to track us there, and it'll take at least three days, maybe more, to get a battalion ready to march. We'll reach Home Gate long before they can catch up."

"There's an easier way," I said, pushing hair away from my face. "We keep to my earlier plan."

The passages wound all around the palace, including the emperling's rooms. I could slip in and kill him and be gone with my cadre while his body was still warm. There was little honor in it, but he didn't deserve the grace of a clean death. By the time the bells tolled we'd be racing for Home Mountain and if grandmother had done her part, an army would be waiting for us.

Ready with swords and steeds.

"There are too many unknown variables," Jasz interceded. "What if he's not alone? What if he's not asleep—or even in his rooms at all? What if a servant sees you and calls for the guards? All it would take is one fallen glass, one short cry and it's over. The coronation is complicated and layered, but it has the most certainty for success. Rhys and I patrol at night, which means if anything goes wrong, we *can't* help you." Grim determination hardened her jaw. "We do this together, or not at all."

Sighing, I shook my head. We had one chance to pull this off. Or die trying.

For the next ten minutes, we sorted out how to move from the chapel to the catacombs. Horses and provisions for the race home wouldn't be hard to come by but getting them to the Narrow Shore was another matter. We'd only just worked out a solution when the iron door screeched open, and both of us had our swords half drawn before Rhys poked inside.

"You're crying," Jasz gasped with accusation, boosting to her feet. "What happened?"

"Sorry. I'm sorry I just . . . you won't—*Look*!" Rhys removed the cloak draped over the left side of her body and extended a mechanical hand with fingers—Spirits of my Sisters—that *moved*. Her sobbing laugh fractured off the stone walls. "Can you believe it?" Cheeks shining and wet, Rhys threw her arms around my neck and held on. Tight and fast.

"Who did this?" I demanded, but deep down, I knew the answer. Only one person in this damnable place would be so gracious and compassionate.

Rhys looked to Jasz who shared her knowing expression. "You should go to him. I think he's waiting for you."

I expelled a heavy breath, my throat tight with frustration. I'd avoided him after our stolen kiss and he'd given me ample space, as well. His absence, though necessary, left a terrible void but I had to resist. For Rhys.

For my sisters. I had to be stronger than my desire. "I can't."

"Sina . . . none of us know what is going to happen tomorrow. All that's guaranteed is here and now. Don't waste it."

"Rhys is right." Jasz gestured to the doorway. "You should enjoy the time you have left, *Dakuwan*."

"Navarre will have to wait." I argued, pushing everything aside. "Tomorrow, we start a war and every second we have to prepare counts."

Hours later I emerged from the catacombs exhausted by exhilarated. I found Navarre at the far end of the training yard, drawn to the heavy breathing and clang of metal to stone. I moved around the pillar for clear sightlines as he rolled through a series of lifts with a bar weighed down with two hundred pounds of steel plates, his torso a ruin of sweat, and his face a mask of focused intent. The muscles in his arms strained and rippled, his movements powerful and clean.

On the fifth rep he racked the bar and it clattered. Breathing heavily, he walked away and mopped his face with a towel.

His head popped up, halfway through buttoning a clean tunic, silver eyes focusing. "Hey."

"You don't seem surprised to see me."

"I am." He tossed the cloth aside and crossed to me. "But I hoped you'd come . . . eventually."

"Have you found the chancellor?"

Tugging on a shirt, Navarre shook his head. "Not yet. But Toddrick is putting the word out among his network of household servants and vassals. I'll find him soon enough. Once we secure his testimony, and the Archviceroy is remanded for treason, I'll make sure that Ehrick agrees to absolve the treaty." His hand reached out, a slow, gentle stroke of fingers to the line of my jaw. "You'll be free, Sina."

Close. So close I could smell the sweat and feel the warmth radiating from his skin. "What you did for Rhys . . . I don't have the words to thank you."

"I have something for you, too." Reaching inside his tunic, he withdrew a small, leather pouch. Opening the drawstring, he poured out a pair of pearl earrings that shone like milky stars in the daylight.

"They were my mothers." He set one into my cupped palm. "Pearls from Salorca. They form in pairs. Perfectly matched and balanced. It's said that when separated they are drawn to each other. No matter how far apart."

"Sounds like an old fable."

Navarre pursed his lips. "There was truth in them, once."

My eyes lifted as he pinned one to his lobe and then fastened the other to mine. "What if I never want to think of you?"

"I think you will," he said. "I *hope* you will." And those eyes sharpened. Smoke turned to steel, a shade of grey so dark they were almost black and in them I saw myself as he saw me.

Something beautiful and dangerous.

Fisting his shirt, I jerked him forward and pounced. All hands and mouth and ravenous need that he met and matched with lips and tongue, power and fury. A glorious, violent tangle that brought my pent-up desire surging to the surface like a storm, aching for the ravage and ruin.

Boosting me in his arms, he planted me against the door to feast. Fingers tangled in his hair I lost myself in him, in deep, long, drugging kisses that left me dizzy and gasping. So sharp, so bright it was like being struck dead and snapped back to life. Helpless to do anything else, I took and gave all I could while my soul cried out his name.

*My warrior. My heart. Mine.*

"I woke up this morning—aching for you. I could almost smell your skin on my sheets. It drove me wild," he panted between kisses, voice low and rough as worn leather. "Come to me tonight." His teeth closed around the curve of my breast, biting through the fabric of my kubi and I smothered a gasp. "Please, God, say yes."

"No," I answered, nipping the tempting, wicked curve of his irresistible bottom lip. "*You* come to me."

Relief escaped him in a featherlight laugh. "I can do that," he agreed, and kissed me again.

Slower and deeper in that maddening way of his, with one hand tangling in my hair and the other cupping my throat with a demanding, dangerous squeeze. Hard enough to thrill. Excite. But not enough to mask the ache pulsing there tender and raw with regret.

His eyes traced over me before I left as if remembering every detail when we said goodbye. And maybe he was.

Time was running out and tomorrow, one way or another, this was going to come to an end. These were stolen moments, for both of us and for vastly different reasons.

The weight of my sword swayed with the rhythm of my stride, timed with my pulse as I returned to the palace with the sun already low on the horizon.

Slumped against my bedroom door, I pressed my brow to painted wood, weary but resigned. My clan was counting on me, and I would not fail them.

Come tomorrow, when I stood before the denizens of the Bridian Empire—in the moment I was expected to relinquish my sword and I shed my Acharrān heritage to embrace the crown of empress—I would kill Ehrick and if necessary, I'd kill Navarre, too.

Regardless of his feelings. Or mine.

A flicker of movement—fast as the snap of a wolverine's jaws—and then I was jerked clean off my feet, toes scrabbling for purchase. Gasping. A thin, metal cord bit into my throat, held by strong arms of a towering figure.

*Huge.*

I jabbed an elbow back. Once. Twice. Aiming for his ribs. His kidney. My assailant grunted but didn't let go and the scream for air seared in my chest, igniting a forest fire in my lungs as wire scored into the skin of my throat. Eyes wheeling—seconds—I had seconds before I blacked out.

Kicking off from the wall, we tumbled backward, and his grip loosened enough for me to use the momentum to flip up and roll over him. Freeing my throat. The first searing breath left me dazed, but my body was trained for this, and moved of its own volition as I drove my knee into his face, stunning him long enough to hook my legs around his neck and lock his arm in a painful hold, wrenching his shoulder out of his socket—a wet pop, and my thigh smothered his muffled wail as, with a hard twist of my legs, I broke his neck.

A clean snap of bone that sang through my blood.

The doors to my room burst open and Rhys spilled inside, face ashen and sword drawn. "Are you alright?"

"Horuēins," I wheezed around the rawness of my throat.

"I know. I found servants dead at the end of the hall—that's when I knew something was wrong." She sheathed her sword, eyes bright. "How'd they get into the imperial grounds unseen?"

"There's no guards." I swept my eyes down the length of the corridor to find it uncharacteristically empty. And even then, all the commotion should have brought more than a few guards running. "Someone's cleared the palace . . . I—" Words vanished as my heart stopped cold in my chest. "Where's Iereni?"

"I don't know. Her rooms, I guess."

Struggling to my feet, I drew my sword, steel singing with dark promise. "Go to the barracks. Find someone. Get help!"

"I can't," Rhys stammered. "I can't leave you."

"There's got to be a dozen or more to take out this many servants. *Get help.*" I didn't wait for her response and ran as fast as my legs could carry me, passing body after body on the way.

A male servant, sprawled facedown, his innards tangled around his feet. Another, not far beyond him—and Iereni's nursemaid. The old woman struck down by a blow so vicious her neck was almost severed. Her body lay in a pool of blood, still twitching . . .

The cold shock of bone deep terror pulled me onward, and I crashed through Iereni's bedroom doors. She had her guard up, as I'd shown her, and was surrounded on nearly all sides.

Horuēins. Seven of them, men and women. Acting on surprise, I lunged, shoving my sword deep through the back of one. His blood slicked my hand. *Six.*

Kicking the dying body from my blade, I plucked up a hatchet from the corpse and flashed my teeth. A hiss of rage rattled between them as they assessed the new opponent on the field, and then they broke as one. Fluid and precise.

Four lunged for me and I dove beneath the first strike, then swept out with hatchet and sword, slashing two. Shallow cuts that would slow them down. Pivoting on my knees I sent the hatchet sailing. It found its mark—deep in a Horuēin's skull—and the impact took her clean off her feet, then slashed up with my sword to block a twin strike of sais.

They were fast. Sharp. But I was rage and fury. I was death and blood.

I was the *Dakuwan.*

The soft, wet gasps and strangled groans—a glorious symphony. I turned, panting. The remaining Horuēin had

Iereni in his arms. Her unmoving legs hung limp as she struggled against the band of his arm at her waist.

One lay dead by Iereni's hand with a deep score to the thigh. He'd bled out in seconds, but her sword had gone too deep and got stuck in bone. Disarming her. Otherwise she might still be fighting for her life instead of watching with hopeful fear. If the sword had been true Acharrān steel, it never would have betrayed her.

"Sina . . ." My name was a plea as the edge of a curved dagger pressed to her throat.

I raised my sword, blood raining from the tip. "Release her and I'll let you live. Harm her and you'll die. Slowly."

"We, the servants of death, do not fear our Master." His dagger sliced into her skin and blood sprayed—bright as the terror in Iereni's eyes.

I lunged, so fast, so fierce, the assassin was forced to drop her body to stop the vicious arc of my sword. No match for an Acharrān blade and my rage, steel snapped, and I split him wide open. His eyes bulged, blood and guts sloshing at my feet, a flood of entrails.

I screamed in his face as he died—*slowly*, as promised.

Iereni lay in a crumpled heap, chair cast aside, and blood pooling around her head. A wet, red cloud. Her body lay still. Too still. I sank to my knees at her side, her name a weakened croak, as I pressed a hand to her throat and almost sobbing in relief at the featherlight beat of a pulse, weak, but defiant.

She was alive. Barely.

Ripping the sleeve from her dress, I tore it into long strips. The Horuēin hadn't cut clean across so the wound was deep but jagged. Her struggling had thrown off the blade and when he'd dropped her, the pressure of her shoulder against her throat had staunched it enough to buy her time. But she'd die if I didn't get her to the infirmary near the barracks.

"Hold on, little sister," I whispered, knotting the cloth around her throat. "Don't you dare stop fighting now." Gathering Iereni in my arms, I ran and, *damnable dead*, she was so slight, so insubstantial.

A dying leaf that would crumble under a heavy touch.

Near the courtyard, voices closed in with the clang of footsteps and armor. The guards Rhys roused from the barracks swarmed around me, swords drawn and faces severe.

"Seize her," the Archviceroy shouted, his face a livid purple against the red of his vestment robes. Eyes wild with accusation. "Seize the traitor!"

# CHAPTER TWENTY-FOUR

## Navarre

P ANIC WAS A FOG IN Navarre's skull, dense and impossible to see through as guards surrounded Sinadine in the courtyard. Iereni's prostrate body lay a few feet away. Daneysa was shouting, sobbing above it all, her face, tear-soaked and splotched pink. A vision of terrible beauty.

Toddrick had come to him so out of breath he could only stammer three heart stopping words.

*Sinadine.*

*Traitor.*

*Arrested.*

Standing here, amid the chaos, her sword splattered with gore and face bloody as the bodies of his men were hauled from inside the palace to pile up like kindling—Navarre couldn't believe it.

Refused to believe it.

"What happened?" he demanded as the First Commander barked for chains.

"She says there were assassins in the palace," Eban answered. "Horuēins."

"Lying, treasonous little *bitch*." Sir Rickard drove a hard boot into her side, and she grunted, bowing over with pain, but she smothered any cries.

"She's not lying," Rhys stepped forward, her skin so pale with worry she shone bright as the moon. "I saw the assassins before Sina ordered me to come get help."

"There's no evidence of a breach." Rickard gripped the pommel of his sword. "We swept all rooms, all corridors, and found no bodies, aside from our own slain." Lowering before her, he grinned into her face. "Thirty men. I'll see you suffer for each and every single one of them."

"That's not possible. I *saw* them," Rhys argued. Helpless.

"You're not a credible witness," the Archviceroy interjected. "You'd say *anything* to protect her."

"I want justice!" Daneysa raved as a physician hurried out into the night, led by a couple of openly weeping servants from the Seford household.

"You can't hold her for treason without proof," Navarre protested. "If there is a chance she's innocent—"

"How's this for *proof*." Daneysa withdrew a leather-bound journal from with the folds of her robes and held it high for all to see, her voice carrying boldly with accusation. "My sister found this in the rooms of Sinadine de-Arashi. She confessed she was afraid to come forward and asked I keep it safe until Ehrick's return. Inside are details about the palace and its defenses—all part of a plot to kill the emperling tomorrow at his coronation."

Navarre snatched the journal from Daneysa's hands and whisked through the pages. His heart slid from his chest, and bounced at his feet as he unfolded a coded letter, but it wasn't hard to sort out the message of the stonecat and the lone wolf.

Navarre slapped the journal shut. "Iereni found this in her rooms?"

"Yes."

"You'd stand before the God's Eye in judgement and swear to that fact?"

"Before the One God, Himself, I would so swear." Daneysa's voice brightened with fresh tears. "Sinadine must've realized my sister discovered her traitorous plans and sought to keep her silent. Now Iereni lays dead between us."

"She lives."

Daneysa faltered. "What?"

"I said," heat flared in Sinadine's eyes, bright as a newly forged blade, "your sister *lives*."

"But there's so much . . . how could she—?"

"There *is* a pulse," the physician confirmed. "It's faint, but there."

"And we are pleased to hear of it," the Archviceroy answered but he didn't look pleased.

"You, help me get her inside. You, bring me a fresh bowl of hot water and clean linen." The servants scampered to meet the physician's demands while Eban and another guard hoisted Iereni away.

"Take this creature to her rooms." The Archviceroy snapped his fingers. "She's to remain there under heavy guard."

Arms wrenched behind her back, Sirra raised her chin high, defiant and without apology or denial as manacles were clasped to her wrists. She didn't look to him as they dragged her away, or struggle or plead.

She was a warrior. Proud and fierce to the bone.

"Where is Ehrick?" Navarre demanded. "I must speak with him immediately."

"The emperling has been sequestered, for his own safety," the Archviceroy said, shoulders drawn like a general on the battlefield. "No one but Sir Rickard and I will be permitted to see him until we've reached the bottom of this sordid matter. The Privy Council will convene later tonight and determine her fate. As for you, Second Commander," he leaned in with a soft, cold whisper, "you're on thin ice. I suggest you watch your next step, lest it crack, and you fall through."

Seventeen stitches to close the wound.

Navarre had counted every single one, patiently watching the rise and fall of the physician's needle as the man worked deftly in the bright glow of his surgery. Nurses attended him, all the while, a bloody ballet.

Whoever had attacked Iereni had made a terrible mess of her throat, and the physician wasn't sure she'd live through the night, let alone the week, but even if she did there was a chance she'd lost the ability to speak. It would be impossible to know until the wound healed and the swelling abated.

For now, all he could do was wait. And pray.

When they were finished, Iereni was brought to the recovery room, dressed in sterile linens and wide-open windows, the floors scrubbed so clean he could smell the lemon in the wood. Kneeling aside her bed, Navarre took her limp hand and held on, firm but gentle. And willed for her to move.

*Please. Let me know you're still there.*

But those fingers didn't wiggle or tighten. Her lashes didn't flutter and her lips didn't draw into a sunny smile. So he watched the rise and fall of her chest, counting each steady breath. So long as she breathed there was hope.

So long as she *breathed* . . .

"I didn't think you were so close to my sister." Daneysa's voice floated around him. Thick, and cloying as her perfume. "Nearly six hours and they say you haven't left her side once."

Navarre didn't turn around, didn't pull his eyes from Iereni, and didn't pause in counting the beats in between those precious breaths. Not even when she sat down on the edge of Iereni's bed.

"Such a little thing," Daneysa sighed. "She's always been so slight. So small. A bird without feathers."

"Iereni's tougher than she looks."

Daneysa smiled. "Yes. I suppose she is." Liquid green eyes turned to his, rimmed red and swollen. "You must be exhausted." She stroked the line of his shoulders.

"I'm fine." He shrugged her off; annoyed she'd made him lose count.

"Honestly, Navarre, this is absurd. You're almost toppling over. Leave her to the care of the nurses and get some rest."

"No."

"I can appreciate we've always been informal, but must I remind you I am *Lady* Daneysa, daughter of the Marquisate of Seford?" Her tone sharpened, gone were the soft edges and gentle lines. "Now, for the last time, I want a moment alone with my little sister, so run along like the good little obedient *dog* that you are."

"I am Second Commander of the Imperial Guard. I answer to only to the First Commander, and Ehrick."

"She's *my* sister." Daneysa stomped a petulant foot. "If anyone should be holding vigil at her bedside it should be *me*."

"You swore a public declaration implicating Iereni as a witness to a possible act of treason, therefore, until she wakes and can speak for herself on the matter, you're not to be anywhere near her. Alone or otherwise. Now, you can either leave of your own volition," Navarre warned, "or I can order Eban to haul you back to your rooms and keep you there under guard. Which do you prefer?"

At the mentioning of his name, Eban entered from the hall, and crossed his arms.

Daneysa's lips thinned to a furious line over clenched teeth. "You will rue this day," she vowed, and stormed from the room.

"I don't think antagonizing the lady was wise," Eban noted.

"Daneysa is a brat and not to be trusted," Navarre snarled. "I won't have her near her sister, do you hear me? Day and night, Iereni is to be watched when I am not present."

"What will happen to Sina?"

Sighing, Navarre thrust a hand through his hair, disheveling dark waves. "I can't do a thing about it tonight. Tomorrow I'll speak with Ehrick—tell him everything—and try to restore sanity in the wake of this madness." Gathering Iereni's hand, he squeezed it gently, reassuring her he was still there. "Pray to God that it's enough."

# CHAPTER TWENTY-FIVE

## Sinadine

Minutes bled into hours, each one birthing an eternity. Not knowing was the hardest part, but silence was a gift even if it was a torment. No bells tolling. No screams of sorrow or shouts of grief in the corridors.

Silence meant Iereni was still alive.

I couldn't shake the image of Daneysa's tear ravaged face from my mind. Not only her lies, but that Iereni still breathing came as more of a shock then the thought of her sister being dead. Someway, somehow Daneysa was connected to the assassins and the Archviceroy.

Movement outside my door stilled my thoughts, my pacing, and they pushed open. Navarre entered, his features gaunt with exhaustion.

"Are you alright? Have they hurt you?"

"I'm fine. Iereni?"

"She still breathes, but the physician's concerned about significant blood loss. We won't know the extent of the damage until she wakes." He fastened manacles around my wrists and ankles, the chains linked to an iron belt at my waist. Anchoring my limbs so I could do little more than shuffle. "The Privy Council has assembled to judge you. Tell them the truth, Sina. All of it."

Daneysa stood in the doorway, eyes swollen but clear. "Step outside, Second Commander."

"The Privy Council is waiting. I can't—"

"I am here at Ehrick's behest," she interrupted. "You might not give credence to my authority, but I don't think you'd dare impugn his."

Navarre's fingers clenched into fists, but I gave him a subtle nod. I wanted this moment alone with her to look into her eyes and uncover my own answers. Resigned, Navarre looped my chains around the thick, marble column, drawn so tight I was forced down to my knees, and gave my hand a reassuring squeeze.

*Patience*, that touch said.

I nodded. *The stonecat is silence and strength.*

Daneysa's face remained a pained, emotional mask of a grieving sister until Navarre left the chamber and the barest hint of a smile took shape, like frost over water. So thin and translucent it was almost impossible to tell ice was forming before it was too late.

"Such a good dog, isn't he? Racing obediently to his master's side." She folded her hands before her, every bit the Marquisate's daughter in a gown of gold trimmed in purple. Empire colors. Ruling colors. "Ehrick has asked that I deliver a message. Swear your guilt before the Privy Council and he promises to be merciful."

"He can choke on his mercy."

Her answering laugh stroked across me like a dagger across a whetstone.

Bright. Sharp. And ringing with threat.

"Did you like your little gift?" She crossed to the foot of my bed and touched a hand to the polished oak post. "I went to great lengths to find the right box. Something . . . elegant and regal. Shame about the blood ruining the lining, but such things must be overlooked for the sake of *presentation*. And the sounds you made . . ." She whisked around to face me, a delicate hand fluttering to her chest. "I'd never heard true anguish before."

Understanding robbed me of speech, and quiet rage blanketed my bones, burning so hot it was cold. Were I not in chains, I'd have killed her with my own bare hands, punching my thumbs into her eyes—slowly—until the orbs popped and blood ran thick as her screams. But I leashed my rage and fury.

*The stonecat is silence and strength.*

Let her think she'd won. Let her think me subdued.

"Swear your guilt before the Privy Council," she said again. "Otherwise, he'll dismember the rest of your cadre until they're nothing but a pile of parts to feed to the birds in the aviary. And if you won't think of them, then think of Iereni." Her head listed to the side. "How easy would it be for me to go to her right now and pluck out a few stitches?"

Rage coiled inside me, a dark brewing cloud of seething black and grey poised to break into a horrific storm. "She's your sister."

"She's in my way. She's *always* been in my way," Daneysa snapped and stroked her hand across her belly as if smoothing out the violent wrinkles in her composure.

"Perhaps an explanation will better help you come to grips with circumstances, *hm*? My mother was a destitute widow when she married the Marquisate, with nothing to offer but a beautiful face and a firm body to offset the burden of an infant daughter. Me." She spread her hands, let them fall. "Thankfully she knew how to play those assets well and lured him to the altar before I was even a year old. Yet for all her talents, she couldn't secure my dowry or inheritance. Iereni has it all, you see. His name. His *money*. She holds the keys to forging her own legacy while I have nothing. No power of my own unless I fight and claw for it."

She paced in slow elegant strides, the fabric of her gown trailing like a river of molten gold. "My mother seeks to make an advantageous marriage for me to a general, perhaps, or a lowly baron. Someone decrepit and utterly useless. I'll waste away, rotting in the marriage bed." She made a disgusted sound and stamped a determined foot. "No. I will taste greater power and wealth. I will *rule*. Once you are executed for treason, and the treaty broken, Ehrick will be free to wed whom he chooses."

"You think he'll choose *you*?" I scoffed, aghast at all she'd revealed. The memory of Iereni bleeding in my arms and all for what? A child's fantasy?

"Yes. Because I know things that will crush his name to dust. He *needs* me."

"You're an idiot."

"An idiot who outmaneuvered *you*. A threat you never saw coming, even when she was close enough to kiss your lips." Lowering to her knees, Daneysa swept a tentative fingertip across my mouth. "I didn't want it to be this way. You weren't supposed to . . . *I* wasn't supposed to . . ." Her hand fell away, and she gathered a tense breath, released it. "All my life, I've played with hearts and emotions, never experiencing any of my own, then I met you and . . . how could I not? You're everything I've always wanted and never thought I would find.

"Fierce and strong and *beautiful* in your ruthlessness. You are perfect. If there was a way—if there was any other way—I'd be empress with you on the throne by my side and together we'd rule the world. Own it. Can you imagine such a thing?" Her smile softened with heart wrenching longing. "The freedom to have both power *and* love? But love doesn't protect women, Sinadine." Her smile fell away, and she dusted her hands on her thighs, clearing herself of any hope. "Only power can do that. So, whatever my heart may long for, I must be strong."

"Sisters before self, Daneysa. I thought I'd understood its meaning before now, but I see how blind I was to my own ambitions. My own desires. And what it cost me."

"Surely a warrior as fierce as you can understand that in the quest for glory, sacrifices must be made." Daneysa's eyes swam with tears. Regret. Remorse. "And like Iereni, you have the supreme misfortune of being in my way."

A smile split my face. Dark. Cruel. My mother's smile. "So do you."

Daneysa's eyes flickered with the first true spark of fear as I lunged—smashing my brow into the bridge of her nose—and her wet scream sang like a struck bell.

The door burst opened, and I laughed as the guards unfastened my chains, dragging me from her. A weeping, ruined mess in a puddle of crimson-stained gold. Her blood was still damp on my face when I was thrust before the Privy Council, into a large, circular room with high walls, fat pillars and narrow windows framed by faded velvet curtains.

"What is the meaning of this?" one of the Chancellors said, aghast. "Why is she brought before us so?"

"Apologies, my lords." Sir Rickard stood straight and proud. "But she attacked the Lady Daneysa moments ago."

"Heathen," the Archviceroy spat contemptuously. "She's as feral as a dog in the streets. If we ever needed proof of that, my lords, behold her thus."

I raised my chin, but inside I recognized too late my grave mistake. Of course Daneysa was sent to me, knowing full well I'd lose my temper and lash out, proving once again I was wild. Reckless. For all my grandmother's lessons on stealth and strategy, I once again failed when it mattered most.

"Let's not waste time with formalities on this creature," he said with the echoing bang of the judgement scepter—a long golden staff topped with the God's Eye. "Sinadine de-Arashi, Swordsworn daughter of the Acharrā, you stand in judgement before the court of the Privy Council, accused of the attempted murder of the emperling's own cousin, Lady Iereni of Seford, and the slaughter of thirty-one men of the Imperial Guard. Treasonous acts, all. How do you answer these charges?"

"Innocent."

Voices snapped in a whiplash of disgust, a chorus of disagreement that wrapped around the chamber like a cobressa circling her prey.

"You seriously believe I slew over thirty armed guards, singlehanded?"

The Archviceroy tented his fingers and leaned forward. The staff perched at his side. "As Swordsworn, who knows what you're capable of? Unless you confess to having accomplices? Name them, and we shall show you clemency."

"Rhys and Jasz were nowhere near the fighting. Their hands, their swords are *clean*." And I thanked the Spirits of my Sisters for that. These men could do what they willed with me, but my sisters would be safe—for now at least.

"Second Commander Navarre has already given sworn testimony of that fact before the God's Eye, otherwise they'd be in chains at your side," one of the Chancellors answered, his jowls trembling with the ferocity of his fervor. "But we will have justice here, so help me God."

"If I had tried to slit Iereni's throat with my sword it would've taken her head clean off," I countered. "I didn't do this. I am innocent."

"Alas, that is not entirely true," Archviceroy Henry flexed his steepled fingers. "Just this morning I received unfortunate news of Chancellor Reginald—found deceased in his apartments. The wounds you'd inflicted upon him had gone septic, poisoning his blood. A terrible, agonizing way to die. Plead innocence all you like, my dear, but we all witnessed your hand in this."

The Archviceroy's eyes gleamed like cold fire in his narrow face, and a soft laugh of understanding wheezed from my lungs, quickly chased by more, growing louder, bolder—ricocheting off the Privy Council chamber walls.

Reginald was dead. Another obstacle removed. Another thread elegantly cut.

*All things will reveal themselves in due course*, he'd said that morning I was brought to him and pushed to my knees. *Of that I am certain.*

"Come now, my lords, let us be done with this. The hour grows late and I tire of her offensive presence." Assent and agreement echoed as Archviceroy Henry rose, vestments slithering like sheets of blood as he plucked up the judgement staff and anchored it before him. "On behalf of Ehrick Torren, Emperling of the Great Bridian Empire, we, the Privy Council, find you guilty as charged. Confess, and you will be granted a swift execution. Deny, and you will be purified by pain." Grey eyes, cold as ice and stone assessed me without an ounce of pity. "Do you confess?"

Watery moonlight sliced across me and the scattered shadows of dancing flakes of snow that fell like frozen tears. The Spirits of my Sisters wept. I'd failed them. But I would not fail my sisters or my clan. I'd lashed out impulsively with Daneysa, a lesson learned too late.

*Sisters before Self.*

Shaking my head, I met his gaze and smiled. "Go to Hell."

"Very well. Then in a fortnight you shall receive your purification." The Archviceroy slammed the end of his golden staff, a hard crack like the snap of bones in a breaking neck. "May the One God, in his benevolence, grant mercy upon your soul."

The imperial prison ran like a spider's web beneath the palace, weaving towards the bowels of hell the Bridian's loved to speak of so often. Stone, slick with grime and damp lined the narrow cell walls, each sealed off with a row of iron bars covered in flaking rust. My chains were lashed to a wall, and I slunk down in a tight corner atop moldy straw that stank of piss and worse.

Torches cast golden shapes to dance in the dark, joined by a distant chorus of wailing and moans. Broken voices of prisoners so far gone they'd abandoned reason for madness, and I thanked the Spirits of my Sisters I wouldn't count myself among them for too long. A fortnight to wait, then I'd be dragged to the executioner's block, and I prayed to the First-of-Us for the strength to meet my end without fear.

Ehrick wanted me broken—I'd die before I gave him the satisfaction.

Footsteps slithered in the distance. Soft soled shoes, not the heavy boots of the guards.

"Damnable dead, I didn't think they'd take you this far below." Jasz stopped outside my cell, a torch in one hand, and a brown glass bottle in the other.

"How'd you get down here?" I asked, shielding my eyes against the bright wash of light flooding my cell. "The guards just let you come see me?"

"No. Rhys tried three times already. She's pacing the barracks and burning candles for your soul." Jasz notched her torch in a bracket on the wall. "I decided to find my own way."

"How?"

"You think you've been the only one running through the passages at night for weeks, learning where they lead and the secrets they contain?" She smiled settling down outside my bars. "I saw you sneaking about the grounds and followed."

I straightened with a scoffing breath. "How is it we never crossed paths?"

"When I realized you favored the night, I kept to the afternoons while you were busy training Iereni," she said slyly. "I wasn't sure what you were up to, but I thought maybe you were planning to run from your bloodoath."

"I would never." Running would've been a death sentence for her and Rhys. Then the emperling would either send an escort to collect three more or slaughter my entire clan. Knowing Ehrick and his pious uncle, it was safe to bet on the latter.

"Well, that's what I thought. At first." Jasz shrugged a shoulder. "But the days passed and you never left. Each morning I thought—today's the day she's done it. Today she's abandoned us. But you didn't." Her eyes flickered to me. "I'm sorry I doubted you."

"Why are you here?"

"You've just been sentenced to death for trying to murder the emperling's favorite cousin." She wiggled the bottle of spiced rum and uncorked it with her teeth. "Thought you could use a drink."

"No, *here*, Jasz. Why'd you take the bloodoath to serve the empire—with *me*? There's never been love between us. You could've been rid of me, but instead you gave up everything. Your life and freedom. Why?"

She took a slow, steady pull from the bottle before offering it to me. "The truth?" she asked, rum and spices on her breath. "I had no intention of doing it, but when you stepped forward so . . . selflessly I didn't have a choice." Her face pulled into a frown. "Nothing I'd ever do aside from joining you would bring the same honor. I could answer a thousand calls, and return with endless wagons of tribute, and still never rise from beneath your shadow."

A laugh slid out of me, warm as the rum settling in my belly. At the confused quirk of her brow, I told her about my aunt's threat, and my grandmother's intervention. She listened, her mouth falling open.

Then she laughed, too—long, deep—and pressed a hand to her face with a groan. "Damnable dead, I should've known you wouldn't take the bloodoath without serious provocation."

"For what it's worth, I'm sorry any hatred for me pushed you into this."

Jasz lifted the bottle. "I don't hate you. Not in the way you think." She took a long, deep drink, and swished the rum in her mouth before swallowing as if to wash some foul taste away.

The bitterness of truth, perhaps.

"I wasn't born into the clan, I was left outside the gates like trash. Part of me resented you for having such a distinguished bloodline and envied that connection to your roots. Knowing where you came from. You're the *last* bloodkin descendent of the First-of-Us and yet you've never taken that honor seriously. You're rude, and selfish, and I didn't believe you capable to lead us one day." She bounced her fist against her thigh. "I wanted it to be me. And I hated that it never would be."

"I wish it had. Maybe we both wouldn't be here now," I said, accepting the bottle again and kicked it back, guzzling the scorching warmth.

Jasz shifted onto her knees, fingers circling the bars. "We're going to find a way to get you out of here."

Choking on alcohol, I swiped a hand across my lips, moping stray amber beads running down my chin. "No."

"Sina."

It was strange, hearing my name on her lips, and the plea carried with it.

"No," I repeated, plunking the bottle at her side. Glass rang against stone and, bracing the bars, I squared myself with her. Our eyes level. "It's too late for me. But it's not too late to finish what we started. I want you and Rhys to flee—tonight."

Jasz snorted, incredulous. "You want us to abandon you to die?"

"The Archviceroy won't stop with just me. He wants us *all* dead. You must warn them, Jasz. They must know what happened here. Not just to me." Understanding pulled the lines of her face into a tight grimace. This was about more than me, more than us. "Promise me you will finish what we started." Reaching through the bars, I held out my hand and waited for hers to close around it.

Her grip confident and sure.

"By the Spirits of my Sisters, on the blood of my blood, we will kill Ehrick," she vowed, and tapped her fist twice to her chest. "Strength and honor."

I tracked her shape until she faded into shadows, leaving me alone in with the dark and that distant wailing, clutching her vow to my heart. By the hands and fury of my sisters, the skull wall would be brought down, and the dead avenged.

Knowing this gave me strength.

Acceptance.

Peace.

# CHAPTER TWENTY-SIX

## Navarre

Death prowled towards Navarre, a stonecat emerging from the dark.

Her eyes blazing embers of silver and blue in a world blanketed in snow. Wind roared around him, a deafening pitch, carrying with it the weeping of the dead and the howling of the living.

Her paws bloody and crackling with a power that shivered along the beasts glowing white-blue hide like lightning in a storm ridden sky. And the closer she drew, he could almost see the wind and snow passing through her translucent body. Something nested in her mouth—a head with long hair, dark as the shadows closing in around the edges of his world like ink.

*Move!* Navarre willed his body to run. To flee, but his limbs and head were unresponsive, locked in a state of bone deep fear. Frozen as a slab of ice. She stopped before him, so close he could feel the blast of her warm breath—an inferno in the bitter icy fury of the winter storm. Rank and fowl.

Her mouth opened in a terrible grin, and blood poured forth—endless. Vast. The head tumbled. Rolled. But Navarre couldn't look from her eyes or that red, ruinous fanged smile as the stonecat spoke—her voice cruel as the mountains, and savage as the snow.

*Night gathers, and the cold winds bring an end to the beginning.*

*Rise, Second Commander.*

*Rise!*

Navarre jolted, his world slamming down around him like a fist to a table. Gone was the snow and bitter cold. Gone were the burning blue eyes and iridescent silver fur. Gone was the river of blood, rising to swallow the world. And the head, tumbling from her jaws. He'd never got a clear look at the head as it spun to a stop at his feet. Only the shock of black hair . . .

Was it him?

Ehrick?

Someone else . . . ?

Toddrick stood over him, the fringe of his blunt bangs hanging in his eyes, cheeks pale and hands weighing on Navarre's shoulders. "S-sorry, milord."

"What's wrong? What is it?"

"It's the emperor . . ."

Navarre jerked upright, his feet kicking out from under the covers. "Is he—?"

"Fine, milord, fine—well, not fine. He's incensed. It's the Swordsworn . . . they . . . well, they—"

"Spit it out, Toddrick, for the love of God."

"They're *gone*."

Toddrick whimpered at the cold snap of Ehrick's voice as he shoved through the door, iron legs rattling with each lurching stride. The Archviceroy was with him, his face blazing as red as his vestments. Scuttling into a far corner, Toddrick pressed against the walls as if hoping to sink into the crevices and disappear from sight.

"Gone?" Navarre whispered.

"Gone." Ehrick wiggled his fingers like a conjurer performing an illusion. "Vanished into thin fucking air."

Navarre shrugged on a black robe, it clung to his sweaty skin, and belted it at the waist. "But they were under armed guard?"

"Apparently your men are either lacking in skill or discipline, Second Commander." Henry dashed an imperious hand. "Whoever was on duty last night should be hung from the palace gates for their ineptitude."

"Very well, uncle," Ehrick agreed. "Let it be a warning to the rest."

"Ehrick, please don't do this." Navarre pressed his hands together, beseeching.

"I want them found, Second Commander." Shifting on stiff legs, Ehrick held a fist between them. "I want them brought to me in chains—alive or dead, I don't much care. But for every day you fail, *someone* will suffer the consequence, do I make myself clear?"

"Sinadine is not a threat. Nor her clan."

His brother's eyes narrowed, smile grim. "Tell me you're not in love with her."

Navarre thrust up his chin. "I respect her."

"Then why would they flee like villains in the night?" Henry countered. "Innocent parties do not run unless they fear the wrath of their emperor's justice."

"You would want him to think that, wouldn't you?" Navarre sneered. Enough. He'd hoped for a moment of privacy—to catch his brother when he was calmer after the sentencing, but he'd waited far too long. It had to be now. "Brother, I need you to hear me; I renounce the Archviceroy as a traitor and the man responsible for the assault on Iereni."

In the distant corner, Toddrick muttered a soft, *'oh my'*, and promptly clasped a trembling hand over his mouth.

"Second Commander!" Henry bellowed.

Ehrick raised a silencing hand. "That is a grievous charge," he said gently. "You have proof of such guilt?"

Navarre winced. "Some."

"Then, let's have it."

Swallowing hard, Navarre offered a soft whisper of prayer before he let it all spew, every rancid detail from the events following their departure from the Acharrān mountains.

"Is that all?" Ehrick arched a brow.

"Is that *all*?" Navarre scoffed. "Clearly this proves that someone has been out to get us long before Sina ever set foot in the palace. And only days following our return, I discovered the barracks' payroll has been bled dry, and the person responsible for the theft stands at your right hand." Opening the drawer of a bedside table, Navarre presented the gold button into Ehrick's outstretched palm as he told him about the *Crooked Crow*, and the former Second Commander's clandestine meetings.

Ehrick turned the button over in his hand. "This is from a Chancellor's vestments. Not the Archviceroy."

"Chancellor Reginald is a known consort to your uncle. Together, they conspired to kill our father. They murdered the emperor in his sickbed."

"Slander." Henry spat. "I won't stand for it."

"I have a witness who will swear before the God's Eye." And that silenced the Archviceroy cold.

*There.* Navarre set his teeth in a lethal grin. *I've got you, demon.*

"That's enough." Ehrick snapped, bracing himself between the two men before facing Navarre. "I've listened to you, brother. Now listen to me. Our uncle did not kill our father."

"How can you possibly know that?"

"Because *I* did."

All righteous fury escaped Navarre in a staggered breath. "What?"

Ehrick and Archviceroy exchanged knowing glances before he continued.

"Do you remember when we were children, all the things we aspired to be?" Ehrick asked. "All our grand wishes and dreams?"

He did. Some nights they'd lain together in Ehrick's bed, wide enough to fit three grown men and far more comfortable than Navarre's narrow cot tucked in the servant's wing of the palace. Side by side, they'd dreamed out loud and wove wonderful tales of riding into battle or climbing the dais steps to sit upon the great Torren Throne.

The bastard and the lastborn who'd longed to show the world they had a purpose, and then one day those wistful fantasies had unexpectedly come true. Never once had he thought to question why or how . . .

Not until this moment.

"I never loved our father," Ehrick sighed. "Though I admired his strength and virility, he lacked sound judgement. Vision. Otherwise, he would've seen that I should've been named his successor. Not *Jaymeson,* or Rishard, or Jorge, or any of my other inept brothers. Brainless fools who would've only dragged the Bridian Empire down with them. But patience has always been my greatest attribute, a weapon I employed well, starting with Donathan."

Navarre shook his head. The coldness of shock and grief sharp along his skin, piercing his flesh like cruel teeth as he looked to his brother.

His calm and gently smiling brother.

"Don died in a brothel when you were *twelve.*"

"Yes, he did." Ehrick laughed, genuinely amused. "His weakness was always women and as the imperial heir, he was used to his opponents checking their strength and skill. All it took was a bit of gold in the right hand, and the rest fell neatly into place. But all my brothers couldn't die in brawls, no. That would not only lead to suspicion it also lacked . . . elegance." Ehrick rolled his hand before him like a conductor commanding a high note.

"Each death had to be carefully tailored to the individual. Rishard died from a broken neck falling from his horse. Jorge choked on a grape at breakfast. Wallace, poor lad, succumbed to the Black Fever during the summer plague four years ago. Xander—did me the grace of catching a bolt to the throat during the siege battle of Grigoy, so alas I cannot claim him. But on it went." His grin flashed, dark as the cloak of death he'd shroud himself in.

Accidents. Sickness. War. Each death had seemed so innocent and devoid of purpose, no one had stopped to question if there was a shadow hand pulling strings behind some dark, sinister curtain. But there had been a hand.

*Ehrick's* hand.

God's mercy. Seven brothers dead, and his father, too. He'd killed them all without tears or regret.

"I don't think you fully appreciate the effort it took to remove each of them so . . . stealthily. By comparison, killing father was the easiest and yet, it seems the most challenging part of my many machinations. Perhaps, in my arrogance I got a tad sloppy and failed to tie all loose ends. A thing I'll be sure to rectify swiftly, I promise you."

Navarre recoiled a step, horrified of the monster standing before him, a demon wearing his brother's skin. The brother he'd loved and cared for. The same brother he'd always believed had loved and cared for him. Who'd always treated him as an equal while picking off his elderborn siblings like fleas on a dog's back.

*And Iereni . . .*

Ehrick's grin flashed as if he saw the realization clear as morning sun rising in Navarre's eyes.

"They were your blood," Navarre croaked, voice hoarse with grief and misery. "Could you so easily dispatch of me?"

"Only if you give me reason to doubt your loyalty. To doubt *you*. But I know you, brother." Ehrick clasped a hand around Navarre's neck and hugged him fast.

The cool skin of his brow pressed against his.

"We came into this world together, I know your soul as I know my own and have given us both what we've always wanted—what we've always deserved and yet would never have been handed to us, otherwise. Our dreams are not dreams anymore, brother—I've made them reality. *All* of them."

Navarre tensed as Ehrick withdraw a small, golden scroll from his doublet, bearing the weight of a large, flat wax seal that swung like a pendulum. "I name you Navarre Torren. A recognized son of the empire. Approved by the Grand Patriarch at my behest."

Navarre's fingers closed around the scroll. He trembled and sank to his knees before his brother. His emperor.

*I am a Torren.*

*I belong.*

He'd been given a name. He should be happy. Elated. This was always his greatest wish and longing come true and yet . . . His belly soured. His guts twisted. His heart grieved.

"Why?"

"Because," Ehrick offered a tense smile, "I am unlikely to sire children, given my condition. Therefore, to ensure our legacy does not end, now that you are a recognized son of the Torren dynasty, it has been decided that you will marry the Princess of Oscano. And upon my death, you and your children will inherit the throne."

Dazed, Navarre's heart nearly stopped.

"You are stunned, I understand. See how gracious I am? How powerful? And this is only the beginning." Ehrick wove around him, too drunk on glory to see that the tremor in Navarre's shoulders wasn't joy, or gratitude, but disgust and hopeless rage.

"Yes, brother."

Ehrick clapped joyful hands together with a laugh. "Sinadine will die in a fortnight, after which you and the Princess of Oscano will be wed—and then, with all this finally behind us, we will claim our destiny. Together we are strong. Together we will move mountains and rip down the stars. The world will tremble under our shadow, it will shine in our gilded light. One world. One faith. That is our legacy as Torrens. History will remember our names and shiver in awe. We will be more than Gods, we will be Titans."

Navarre remained rooted long after Ehrick and the Archviceroy left the room, and wretched. Vomit splattering across the floorboards and his feet.

"Milord," Toddrick whimpered, helping him to the edge of his bed. "Shall I fetch the physician?"

Navarre shook his head. "I'd always known," he whispered, struggling around the bitter taste of bile coating his tongue. "Deep down, but I didn't want to see, I didn't want to believe." But he saw it now. The little things he'd dismissed and ignored.

The pups who'd froze to death one winter.

The stable girl who'd flinched every time Ehrick lurched by.

The servant boy who'd allegedly hung himself . . .

It wasn't the Archviceroy's influence that twisted Ehrick. Sinadine was right. The darkness had always been there, a malignant cancer rotting his soul. Only he'd been too blinded by love and loyalty to see the truth. Navarre pressed a fist to his lips. His heart unsteady, his lungs squeezing tight. God's Mercy, the weight of this terrible knowledge was going to break him apart.

Toddrick gathered a bowl, cloth, and pitcher from his bedside table, and cleaned the vomit from Navarre's hands and feet. "What are we going to do, milord?" he whispered, rinsing out the cloth in the basin.

Navarre took in his shining eyes and pale cheeks. It was perhaps the biggest mark of Ehrick's arrogance and power to make such a bold admission of guilt—of masterminding the demise of near an entire royal line—before not only him but Toddrick as well. And yet even if the pair of them went to the Privy Council it wouldn't matter a single damn.

Ehrick was emperor. The figurehead of a powerful dynasty, and as such he was beyond reproach. If there was ever a time to have brought him low it would've been before the crown was ever placed on his head, but now that it was there—it would take a force of nature to rip it from him. He was untouchable. No man could stop him.

No *man* . . .

"I need to find the Swordsworn."

"Milord," Toddrick gasped. "You can't mean to *help* the emperor?"

"Bring me my armor." Navarre struggled to his feet. "And find Eban."

# CHAPTER TWENTY-SEVEN

## Sinadine

GRANDMOTHER ALWAYS TOLD ME NEVER to spend too much time in the dark because it was easy to lose yourself. Isolation ate at the mind.

Darkness, the soul.

But as a child I never feared shadows. They were comforting and familiar and safe. I could sink into them and vanish—fade into nothingness. No sound or light or breath.

When my aunt had sent me to the pit, I'd weathered the fourteen days and nights watching the sky change, the light of the stars, awed by how brightly they shone. But here, within these stone walls covered in mildew and grime, there were no stars to comfort me. Only the haunting emptiness and the steady trickle of water. A maddening sound, that endless *drip-drip-drip*, wearing down stone and sanity.

The cell wasn't large, but I did whatever I could to keep my mind sharp and spirits high by working out or meditating, steeling myself for what was to come. Ehrick had tossed me into a dank hole so I would rot in misery and despair. He wanted me broken when I faced the denizens of the Imperial City. Little more than a mind-shattered husk to parade through the streets in filth and shame.

I would not give him the satisfaction.

The distant flicker of torchlight cut through the gloom, and I squinted as it sharpened, drawing closer—blinding as a sun after days of nothing but endless black. The rattle of the accompanying stride told me who my visitor was long before the bars on my cell groaned open and the emperling entered my cell, flanked by the First Commander.

Emperor. He was emperor now.

Evident by the crown haloing his head and the rich purple silks draped from his shoulders, a disguise to hide his true nature. But I saw him. A direwolf of death, teeth bared and waiting for his moment to strike for my vulnerable throat.

Sir Rickard set the torch he carried into the wall sconce, freeing his hands. "On your feet," he snarled.

Reaching for the winch, he hauled me up by the length of my chains coupled to a hoist in the ceiling until I was perched on the tips of my toes.

The raw skin at my wrists screamed against the tension and the sharp grooves lining the inside of the shackles, designed to discourage resistance or struggle, but I bit my lip to keep from crying out or showing any indication of pain.

"Thank you, First Commander, you may leave us."

"Sire, I don't recommend—" Ehrick angled a single look over his shoulder and Sir Rickard eased back a cautious step before bowing his head in acquiescence. "Sire."

"You're looking well," Ehrick said with all the joviality of a visiting friend once we were alone. "I trust they are feeding you?"

"Almost as good as your hounds," I answered. My voice sounded strange after so many days of disuse, but it didn't rasp or grate with the rawness of hunger or thirst. Meals came frequently, as did water. I'd meet my death in glowing health.

"That pleases me greatly."

"What do you want from me, Ehrick? You wouldn't be here unless you needed something."

"Too true." Ehrick chuckled darkly. "I sent Daneysa to do once what I should've taken the time to do myself. I've come to rectify that."

Understanding settled around my shoulders, warm and familiar as the weight of my grandmother's cloak. "You want my surrender." To kneel before him demurely and without protest as his mother had knelt before me when I claimed her head.

Even though I was a traitor sentenced to death, I could still make things difficult for him. He wanted to give the people a show of his position and strength, and the only way to do that was by breaking me.

Or coming to terms.

"A surrender of sorts," he agreed. Leaning firmly on his cane, Ehrick took a few slow steps until he was haloed in the torchlight before me. "First, you should know your cadre fled shortly after your trial which was a shock to us all. To think they'd abandon you?" He stroked the band of gold encircling his brow, etched with a fine hand, and set with a single diamond at the center to imitate the all-seeing God's eye. He tsked softly. "I thought Acharrāns possessed more loyalty than that."

A bittersweet surge of joy rose in my chest, but I smothered it like a spring lamb before its feet touched the ground lest Ehrick see the truth.

In the endless, quiet days, I had hoped Jasz had heeded my words and convinced Rhys to run. Knowing that they had gave me solace and comfort. One day they would avenge me, and I'd watch them from the stars as they did—lighting their path to retribution and glory.

I curled my lip over clenched teeth. "What would you know about loyalty?"

"More than you think," he answered. "I am profoundly loyal. Perhaps the most loyal Torren to ever live because *I* am willing to do whatever it takes to ensure the completion of my grandsire's vision."

"Did that include killing your father? Your brothers?" I searched the dark angles of his face for something akin to shock and perhaps offense at the accusation, but instead Ehrick merely tossed back his head and laughed, eyes shining with mirth.

"One-God, Himself, you are an unexpected joy." Planting his cane before him, he anchored it with both hands. "Bridians, I've come to find, are clouded by the infuriating short-sightedness of the able-bodied, but you, I dared hope you'd see my truth—a truth I only dared utter mere moments ago to Navarre, and you did not disappoint. It's . . . refreshing, I must admit." He raised his hand to his face and mimed removing a mask. "Like breathing clean air for the first time."

Numbness trickled down my arms like rainfall against the craggy sheet of mountain rock and I flexed my aching fingers, desperate to restore feeling.

With nothing but time and darkness, I'd worked it all out in the back of my mind—and I hated how obvious the answer was to the sordid puzzle. The Archviceroy might be a villainous man, but as I'd suspected Ehrick had skillfully manipulated him and everyone around him like a conductor in a grand orchestra. Using the threat of assassins to sow dissent and force his Privy Council to shatter a centuries old treaty, breaking ties with my clan so he could open up the gates of the Imperial Palace and forge new, prosperous alliances across the sea.

If only I'd been able to convince Navarre . . .

"Contrary to what you may think I wasn't motivated by hatred of my family. It was duty." Ehrick pulled his shoulders straight and proud. "My childhood was not easy, but if not for their neglect I would've been overcome by same the disease of privilege and comfort that infected my brothers. Alas, I am the last Torren left to shoulder the weight of an entire dynasty that is a whisper away from dying out. Sure, I may have put the noose around its neck, but it had to be done." He smirked at me.

Pleased to finally have an audience to share all that he'd carried inside his blackened heart for so long.

"Now I will complete my grandsire's vision of unity and I would like you to help me do it." Leaning firmly on his cane, Ehrick's voice enveloped me like twisting rope from the shadows as he wove around me in a slow, wide circle. "You could be a formidable weapon for change, Sinadine. Where others scorned you, I would set you free to do what you were born to do. So here is my first offer. Stand with me. Serve me, and you and Navarre could lead my armies together. You can swallow the world and forge it anew. The Sword and the Shield of the Empire."

Surprise caught me like a hand to the throat, cinching tight so I could scarcely breathe. Serve him?

Grandmother would have wanted me to say what he wanted her to hear. To bend but not break. Perhaps that would've been the smart path, and yet as I gazed in his gleaming black eyes my anger and pride and hatred rose too bright and too bold for me to contain.

"I'd rather die."

Silence fell, heavy and thick, before his smile spread like a slow opening wound.

"I can't say your answer displeases me. I've had such sweet dreams of your head mounted on my wall. Red gold with black diamonds for eyes and yellow sapphires for teeth. What a sight for the common denizens to behold." Firelight danced across his face, painting it molten like the metal he envisioned enrobing my skull. "Or perhaps I'll give it to Navarre as a keepsake."

"Come and take it then!" Snarling, I tugged on my chains and the little grooves of steel dug deeper into my already throbbing wrists. "I dare you to try."

Ehrick held the silence between us, and it took every ounce of patience I had not to scream in his face. I wanted him to lunge for me. To lose his temper and strike. Even chained I could take him down in several ways, I just needed him to drop his guard and get close. Instead Ehrick twisted the pommel of his cane, steel grating to stone, sharpening for the blow to come.

"Soon enough." His gaze skimmed across me, lingering with far too much awareness. "God, my brother . . . you should've seen the way he pleaded for your life like a mewling pup. It was for his sake alone I even extended an offer to spare your life at all. Personally, I don't get the attraction. But he isn't the only one taken with you, is he? The physicians say it was your name that Iereni whispered first when she woke though it was hard to make out given . . ." He sliced a long finger across the side of his throat.

A weak breath escaped me, the only outward sign of emotion I dared give him.

*Iereni lives.*

"This news pleases you. Good. Then let's proceed to my second offer. A week from now you will be executed. Face your death gracefully, and I'll allow her to live. You have my word."

"Why would I ever trust your word?"

"I don't kill without purpose," he said, almost incredulous. "At the time, she was expendable. Whether or not she has value to me alive now depends on you."

"Iereni means nothing to me." Difficult words for me to muster, but I hoped my callous answer would throw him off. I couldn't let him know that despite all efforts, I had grown to love her as a sister and would defend her as such. He'd already tried to kill her once just to frame me, and now sought to leverage her again.

Ehrick inclined his head. "Daneysa believes otherwise." He dropped an elegant hand to the length of chain suspending me, rings glinting like bloody teeth in the torchlight as they skimmed the steel links. "When she told me of your fondness for my cousin I was, admittedly, surprised. You didn't strike me as sentimental."

"I am Swordsworn." I grit my teeth against the tiny, sinister ripples of pain his gentle touch evoked, sending tremors that echoed in my joints. "It's my duty to defend the weak."

His fingers paused in their torment and the thin line of his lip curled in utter contempt. "Weak?" Ehrick bounced an infuriated fist against the taught length of the chain and a gasp of agony burst from the bite of sharp steel slicing deeper into delicate skin. "Acharrāns and their arrogance. I thought perhaps you saw the world with a little more perspective than your sisters, but you disappoint me, Sinadine."

Ehrick shuffled to the empty chair tucked against the rickety table perched near my cot, the only other bit of furniture in my cell, and sat down. His cane set against the table so that he could press his palms together in measured thought.

"The Salorcans have an interesting approach to wine," he began after a long stretch of strained silence through which I gathered my senses.

Breathing through the dizzying wave of agony that threatened to blacken my vision as warm rivulets of blood flowed from my wrists and ribboned down my arms like red tears.

"Stress the plant, and the stalk remembers. It can take a decade, sometimes more, but soon enough the grapes that follow are far more resilient. Floods, ice storms, droughts—they thrive all the same. Unlike my brothers, Iereni has proven herself resilient," he continued. "Otherwise, I would've finished what I started soon after her fall."

My head snapped up as Iereni's words stirred inside me. *I wasn't born this way . . .*

"Come now, you ascertained the truth of my father and brothers so easily, but had not stopped to wonder about little Iereni?" Pleased by my apparent horror, he closed his eyes, savoring the memory. "She was a case study, you see. Initially I'd explored my interests with lower risk subjects, but they offered little to no insight into assessing the ripple effects of consequence. No one cares if a mongrel vanishes or a kitchen maid dies, so if I was going to clear my path to the throne, I needed to aim a little . . . higher. She was meant to die, of course, but I miscalculated." Lips pursed, he brushed a stray bit of dust from his shoulder, annoyed by his own admission of failure. "Understandable, I suppose, given I was barely ten."

"She was a child!" Horrified rage swam in my blood, writhing and vicious with a fury I couldn't contain. Spirits of my Sisters, I wanted his screams ringing in my ears as the points of my thumbs gouged into the hollow of his throat.

Ripping him clean open.

"Suffering can visit us at any age," he answered, devoid of remorse. "Thankfully she was too young to remember it was me. But I see the truth every time I look at her. The graceless tumble of her body, the spinning roll of her flailing arms and legs, the velvet cry of her infantile voice . . . and it warms my heart."

I bit into an oath, and Ehrick assessed me with great interest. "The pretense of disgust is a charming effort, but I saw the look on your face after you'd attacked chancellor Reginald, and while you may have been provoked by his disrespect, his agony thrilled you." His chin dipped, discerning. "Not very Acharrān, is it? To savor the act of killing. The lust for blood."

A muscle ticked in my jaw and his grin broadened knowingly.

"You'll get no judgement from me. You should never feel ashamed for enjoying the very thing that makes you special, Sinadine, and death is who you are. Pain and chaos, these are lullabies to the darkness in your soul, and I know their melodies well. Therefore, if you would call me monster, then so are you, cousin."

The edge of my teeth set in a snarling grimace. "I'm nothing like you."

"I beg to differ. Yet violent and dark as we are, we are both protectors of the people, Sinadine, and we're both willing to do whatever it takes to see it done. Through me famine will cease, and wars will end. We will no longer be divided by boarders or belief. We will be one. True peace. Everlasting peace. I may have to burn down the world to see it done, but is such a future not worth a bit of cruelty to obtain? Can you honestly say that in your grand quest for freedom, you would not do the same?" He arched a brow. "Would you not do *worse*?"

I swallowed hard. Was he wrong? No. Rejected by my clan, I'd used the honing edge of their contempt like a whetstone to sharpen myself into a sword made of deadly Acharrān steel.

There was no throat I would not open if it meant serving my purpose. If I believed it just, blood would flow so deep and vast the palace would drown in it. Sisters above, and damnable dead below, the things I'd done—the things I would continue to do . . . I was a monster. But unlike him, I fought for my sisters. I would die for them. All of them.

I would die for Iereni . . .

I cooled the tempest of my emotions with a steadying breath then met his gleaming eyes with stoic calm.

"I will meet my death with honor and dignity but know this," I whispered in a rasp of quiet rage. "You're a dead man, *Wosturā*, until my sisters return to make it so."

Ehrick's teeth spread into a steady grin.

Unaffected and unafraid.

"I'd be disappointed if they didn't try."

# CHAPTER TWENTY-EIGHT

## Sinadine

THE SKY WAS GREY AS ASH when they dragged me out onto the stage, the plaza packed with bodies. Sir Rickard gripped my arm with bruising force, hauling me out from the church and into cold, biting air. The guards were dressed in leather and fur, but I wore only a red silk kubari. Same as the empress when I stood before her with sword and tears to take her head.

Her skull gleamed brightly in the wall in ivory gold with silver whorls and opal eyes.

"Look at them all," Ehrick whispered at my side. "More than we've ever received at the palace. Not even my mother's execution drew such a crowd." The grip of his fingers bit into my arm, belying the easy charm of his casually spoken words. "They've come to see the Acharrān girl who dared defy an emperor. Touching story. But it

384

ends today. And while they might've come for you, they will leave with a lasting impression of *me*. You will die a traitor, and I will rise—a legend."

Ehrick sauntered onto the terrace and the people cheered as he approached, waving a jeweled hand. Dressed in purple, black and gold, he was every bit the commanding Emperor. His oiled hair tied away from his lean face, all sharp cheekbones and deep-set eyes. But there was a color in his cheeks, a pallor of vitality I'd never seen in him before. Death and power brought strength to his bones and he drank in the fervor of the crowd.

He was enjoying this.

"Denizens of my great city," he called out, voice ringing true. "You've heard the whispers, and the read the reports in the newspapers. Today we are gathered to witness the death of a heathen traitor who plotted to end the great line of the Torren dynasty with a cutting stroke of her sword."

Sir Rickard wrenched me forward, and boos and hisses rained over me like acid, burning my skin with their derision. But scattered intermittently through the crowd I saw silent faces watching me. Their heads lowered in deference as they whispered prayers that soothed the thousand cuts of scorn slicing across me. I was not alone here.

My death would not go unwitnessed or unmourned.

Perhaps someone would sneak to a forgotten shrine tonight and light a candle for my soul, and speak the old words, guiding my spirit to the stars. Tipping my head back, I faced the swath of grey sky, the air cold with the bite of winter as snow and little pellets of ice bounced across the marble stage, pinging softly.

My soul ached for the mountains of home, the sweet scent of pine and xhixi trees. To hear the whistling cry of snow eagles and lilting howl of wolverines.

I hated that I would die here, so far away from all that I knew and loved.

*The stonecat is silence and strength.*

"Our great Chancellors have collected evidence of her crimes," Ehrick continued. "And even my sweet, dear cousin Iereni, who clings ardently to life has given voice to justice—naming her *true* attacker." He jabbed a finger towards me, roaring my name, and the violent hatred of the crowd rose to meet his rage, loud as waves crashing against stone cliffs.

Rickard pushed me to my knees before Ehrick and my kubari spread around me, baring my legs to the cold. They'd dressed my hastily, and the belt loosened around my waist so that it hung indecently on my body and the gleam in Ehrick's dark eyes confirmed that he wanted me like this.

Shamed, disgraced.

Archviceroy Henry approached, his blood red vestments vivid against the world of grey and white, and presented him with a sword.

*My* sword.

Sheathed blade in hand, Ehrick raised it high, and the mob roared. "I, Emperor Ehrick Torren, lastborn son of Edvard, eighth of his line, hereby sentence you to death by my own hand."

*The stonecat is silence and strength.*

Roars blended into cheers, and Archviceroy Henry exited the stage, escorted by the First Commander, to take his seat among the Chancellors upon the dais.

Eyes closed, I savored the cool kiss of wind across my cheeks.

*Spirits of my Sisters, grant me strength, grant me courage, and may I carry both with me in this, the hour of my death. I am prepared to leave this world with a true heart, and pray you find me worthy to join you among the stars.*

I concentrated on the hiss of my blade leaving its scabbard—that single sound drowning out all others. I could almost feel the metal singing through the air, screaming as it swung for my waiting throat.

I held true unto the last breath.

The last second.

Twisting—I rolled my head beneath the blade—and steel sliced through the air.

A lethal whisper.

Thrown off balance, Ehrick staggered, and I caught him by the arm. Looping my chains around the blade, I jerked once and, no match for Acharrān steel, iron snapped. He stuttered, a weak, disbelieving gasp as I shot up, driving the flat of my hand into the center of his throat.

Eyes rolling, gasping—he dropped like a stone.

In the space of a breath, blade in hand, I spun and sliced the legs out from the guard who rushed to stop me. Gutted the other before his sword cleared his sheath.

Jasz had been right to make this our strike point.

Too many people were packed into the courtyard, and even fewer guards were in position for my execution then what would've been for Ehrick's coronation. In his arrogance he'd cleared the dais, not wanting anything to detract eyes from his moment of glory.

A mistake that was going to cost him his head.

I dispatched the few guards easily enough. Then turned, dripping in sweat and gore, to face my true enemy. Slumped on the ground, Ehrick skittered away, his hands smearing blood against marble. Alarms blared, summoning the whole of the barracks and Sir Rickard frothed at the mouth, battling his way through panicked people to the stage.

No matter.

This wasn't going to take long.

"Y-you pr-promised," he struggled. His mouth a ruin of crimson, and eyes shining with pain. "You said—"

"I am Sinadine de-Arashi. To my clan I am the Stone-Claw. A Swordsworn daughter of the Acharrān and bloodkin descendant of the First-of-Us. To my enemies, I am the Dark One. A harbinger of death." Raising my sword, I pointed to him. "I will die on my feet, never on my knees, and before I leave this world—I'm taking *you* with me."

In the long, dank hours in my cells I'd plotted this single moment. I would die here today, but on my terms. This way Rhys and Jasz weren't at risk of being caught in the crossfire, and Iereni would be safe from Ehrick's threats. With the Emperor dead, my clan could handle the rest without me.

Sword raised, I loomed over him, a demon ready to drag him down to the depths of his burning Hell when the world shook. Exploded!

Once—*a vicious tremble!*

Twice—*a terrible blast*!

I barely had time to draw a startled breath when a third lashed out—brighter! Hotter! A surging wave of heat rolled above me in a near lick of flames, knocking me into spiraling tumble of earth and sky.

I reeled, head spinning, ears ringing, and hands unsteady as people screamed and smoke rose in thick, black plumes like demons from the shattered ruins of rubble and chaos.

Someone snatched hold of my manacles and dragged me to my knees.

"Sina!" Jasz shouted, her voice muted as if carried underwater. "Get up, now!"

I wobbled on weak legs as the manacles fell away and she thrust something into my hands. Long and cool and familiar as my own name. My sword. It grounded me like roots to the earth, holding me steady.

*Ehrick . . .*

My eyes searched through the chaos but he was nowhere to be seen in the writhing mob of panicked bodies. Rage spiked through my chest. *No. No. No—I had him!*

Guards swarmed the edges of the courtyard, fighting to get around the surging mass of denizens. Trapped. The main gate was a ruin of twisted iron, the stone walls collapsed, sealing everyone inside.

Chaos. Just as we'd planned for the coronation.

Rhys burst through the doors of the church, bodies at her feet, face slashed with lines of indigo woad and blood. Her white hair in braids. "Is she alright?" she demanded, hooking an arm around my waist. Her voice distorted by the sharp ringing in my ears, shrill as Taphne's singing.

"The final blast was too close," Jasz snapped, blood dripping from her sword. "I told you to set the charges further away."

"I did. I don't know what triggered the third explosion."

"We don't have time for this. Move!" Jasz ordered, and together, they hauled me forward.

My legs struggled to find their footing, but soon my head settled on my shoulders, and I matched their stride. The path to the underground tunnels was clear, and we flowed in practiced silence, knowing the route blindfolded. Jasz led the way with a torch she'd lit with a pocket lighter and above us the cries from the plaza carried down, like blood soaking into earth.

Behind us, the stomp of feet and the rattle of boots and armor. The guards were in the tunnels. It didn't matter. We had the lead, but as we neared a sharp corner, I knew something was amiss.

The smoke and dust . . .

Jasz slowed, stopped. "No." Rubble, sealed the entrance to a collapsed tunnel. The way out. "No," she breathed again, and then shouted it, her cry ricocheting off the walls. An echo of rage.

"It was clear this morning." Sweat dripped from Rhys' chin. "How—?"

"Ehrick," I answered. "The third explosion."

Jasz whipped furious eyes to us. "How could he know of our plans?"

"He didn't," I said. "But he must've set charges that were triggered by yours. He wouldn't have left anything to chance. This is his game."

"Guards at our back, a collapsed tunnel at our front," Rhys said. "What do we do?"

A clatter of sound to our left and we drew our swords, ready to meet our enemy, but the closer it drew my senses sparked with recognition.

It wasn't footsteps approaching. It was *wheels*.

Iereni rounded the corner and her eyes widened with relief at the sight of us. "Thought I'd find you here," she rasped, and pressed a hand to the side of her bandaged throat. Even after two weeks, it must still be tender. "Guards are close. We must hurry." She looked to each of us, urgent. "Come."

"To where?" Jasz pointed to the collapsed tunnel with her blade. "Our mounts—everything we need to escape—is at the Narrow Shore. We won't make it through the city, let alone the palace."

"There's another way." Iereni's eyes brightened. "I've used these passageways since I was a child. I know them better than anyone. It's how I slipped away for training. Come." She pushed her wheels hard and whisked past us without a backward glance. The end of the corridor met a short stack of stairs leading up.

Spinning around, Iereni held the railing with one hand and pushed her wheels backwards with the other, popping up one step at a time. At the top, she swiveled around and surged forwards. Each set of stairs cost time, and the shouts of guards were gaining ground.

Many of them.

Even if they didn't know the tunnels as well as she did, between her wheel tracks and our footsteps in the dust joining her, it wouldn't be hard for them to follow.

"Through here." Iereni panted. Rhys and Jasz struggled with cranking a wheel to open a heavy, slab of steel. The rusted chains screamed with each grudging inch. "Half a mile down this corridor and we'll hit the Narrow Shore."

"We need to close the gate behind us," I said. "Slow them down."

"There's no way to drop it from inside the tunnel," Rhys gasped.

Of course there wasn't. The gate was designed to keep unwanted people out of the tunnels, not to trap them in. The guards were so close now I could make out distinct voices amidst the thunder of boots.

Jasz drew her sword, face severe. "Then we make our stand here."

The tunnel was tight but if we formed in a single column, luring them inside, it was possible we could cut down enough of them to get clear.

"Iereni, get behind us," I ordered, steering her to the back of our line and tightened the belt of my kubari.

"They're too close. Too many," she panted. "We won't make it."

"Yes. You will." At the front of the line, Rhys whipped around. "Strength and honor, my sisters," she whispered and shoved Jasz into me—into the dark, tight tunnel. With a swing of her sword, the rusted chain snapped, and the gate slammed down, sealing the way.

Us on one side.

Rhys on the other.

"*No!*" Jasz smashed her fists against four inches of steel, screaming Rhys' name.

Through the thick weight of the door, I could hear the sounds of combat. She fought so we would live. If she died, the gate was strong but it wouldn't hold them back forever.

We had to move.

My arms closed around Jasz, holding her fast. The whites of her eyes shone bright in the dark—bright with grief and madness. All of which clawed inside of me.

*Rhys*. My sister. My friend. The moon that brightened my darkness.

"Let me go!" she raged. "Let me go!"

"Hear me now. *Hear me*," I said, strong with authority, but gentle with compassion. "Rhys fights for us now. We will avenge her." Cupping Jasz' neck—her pulse and tendons straining—I pressed my brow to hers. "Blood of my blood, I swear to you we will avenge her."

Jasz' ragged breathing slowed, and a sob of anguish pushed from her throat as she pressed her hand to the gate. "Strength and honor." The words were broken, but the fight left her body, and the calmness of acceptance settled into its place. Filling her blood and bones with the purpose of vengeance.

"Strength and honor," I answered.

Jasz scrubbed at her face, cleaning away tears though they still carried in her voice as she looked to Iereni. "Lead the way, little sister. We don't have much time."

Iereni wrenched her wheelchair around, arms pumping furiously down into the winding dark. The air was cleaner. Briny. And soon I could hear the rush of waves. The filmy glow of light broke at the end.

We'd made it.

The tunnel gave way to a final set of stairs dropping down to the cavernous shore with a wedge of grey pebbled beach. Three mounts were tethered in wait, their saddlebags heavy with provisions.

"Hurry," Jasz barked. "They'll come searching this side of the walls soon."

"Wait." Iereni caught my hand, eyes wide with pleading. "Take me with you!"

Jasz skidded at the bottom, her expression anguished. "Sina, we can't—taking a member of the royal family guarantees the entire Imperial Army comes after us."

"Please." Iereni's grip tightened on my arm, her knuckles white with terror. "He'll kill me," she whispered, tears in her eyes. "Please, Sina. You know it's true. You do."

I closed my hand over hers, unable to argue. Ehrick had said as much in the cells. Somehow, he'd know she helped us escape—and even if he didn't, he'd likely kill her out of spite. Leaving her behind was tantamount to a death sentence, and we'd lost too much already.

"She rides with me," I said and Iereni's face broke with relief.

"Sina—"

"I said she rides with me. Bring her chair." Hauling her over one shoulder, I hurried down the steps.

"There are clothes in the saddlebag. Dress quickly," Jasz said, and disassembled Iereni's chair, following her instructions, then lashed it to the back of her horse.

Stripping off the kubari, the wind snagged the red silk and carried it away as I dressed in the biting winter cold. Helping Iereni into the saddle, I mounted behind her as the cries of the city horns bellowed from the walls in long and harrowing blasts like the howl of direwolves in the night.

Telling all, far and wide, that fugitives were on the run.

"They'll have heard those horns for miles." Jasz gathered her reigns. "City Patrol will tighten their watch on the main roads."

"We'll take the merchant paths," I said, drawing my steed up next to her. "And we don't stop until we reach the Blue Wastes." That was a full day on horseback, and several more before we reached Home Mountain. Even with Imperial steeds, that was going to be a hard journey without rest.

The wind shifted and, kicking into a swift gallop, I watched the red silk kubari plummet to the distant horizon.

A red tear falling against a winter grey sky.

We raced well into the night, until we found a rise of rocks in the Blue Waste that acted as shelter from the heavy winds that would also conceal a campfire—a necessity if we didn't want to freeze to death in the night.

Drawing the horses inside the cluster of rocks, Jasz rubbed an ounce of kraken oil over the pile of bracken we'd gathered. She must have stolen some from the mausoleum while planning my escape. It wasn't much, but the oil would extend the life of the wood and hopefully burn throughout the night.

When we were done and all warming ourselves around the blue fire, I cut my eyes to Jasz as she speared a couple of jackrabbits on sticks. "I told you to leave me."

"Yes, you did."

"You swore an oath."

Passing the rabbits to me, she hooked her arms around her knees. "I promised *we* would kill Ehrick. You were part of that collective 'we'."

"So, you lied to me."

"Yes."

"It was stupid. You could've been killed, and if you listened to me Rhys wouldn't have been taken."

Her lips tensed into a thin line. "And I'll live with that regret, but we knew there was a risk, and both made our choice."

"I didn't want anyone to die for me."

"And we wouldn't let you die for us." Jasz answered. "We're sisters. Bound together by blood and oath."

I anchored the rabbits on a spit over the blue fire, their flesh crackled and spat as the fat dissolved and sizzled in the flames.

"It's more than that, Jasz. We knew by killing Ehrick there would be consequences, but his death would've disabled their hierarchy long enough for us to overthrow them. Now not only is he still alive, everyone also witnessed me try to kill him. It's the perfect excuse to *crush* us, as he's always wanted. He'll unleash the full fury of his wrath on our clan. All because you had to save my life?"

She dropped her gaze, swallowed hard. "Then let's hope your grandmother has done her part," Jasz said after a time. "If anyone can unite the clan for war, it's Avanthi de-Mazad." Confident in that belief, she plucked up a pebble and lobbed it with a lazy toss. "You're blessed to have such a grandmother."

We ate in silence, ears pricked against the wind for signs of danger. When done, Jasz slept while I claimed the first watch.

The fire had dimmed to a steady glow, but still emitted enough warmth, and if it failed, we'd huddle together until dawn.

Iereni silently watched the dying dance of blue flames licking across blackened wood, her gaze fixed on some distant thought. Finishing a sweep of the perimeter, I removed my cloak and draped it across her.

"The terms we made in exchange for training me . . . it was really about getting close to Ehrick, wasn't it? You were using me, right? To kill him?" she asked as I sat down, resting my sword at my side.

"Yes." The single word was heavy, dense, and hard to muster.

She turned her gaze back to the fire, her expression distant. "Did I ever tell you he was the one who made my chair?"

"No," I admitted. Surprised by this detail.

She nodded, the motion stiff as a dead limb. "Three years after my accident, he presented me with the first one, and then spent weeks with me as he figured out what worked, what didn't. Then every year after that he'd have a new one all ready for me to try out until we'd settled on the last design." The fire crackled and spit in the silence, and she released a steadying breath, digging deep to find the strength to keep going.

"When they told me you were sentenced to death, Ehrick forbade letting me see you but I wasn't going to let them take you without . . ." She shook away the thought, unable to speak the words. "I snuck into the passages and was coming to your cell but Ehrick got there ahead of me, so I hid in an empty one and waited for him to leave." She brushed a hand over her thin, misshapen thighs.

"The physicians said my legs hadn't broken in the fall. They'd shattered. The bone fragments were impossible to mend back together. I remember waking in the nights, screaming in pain—the *pain*. There isn't a day where I don't hurt. You have no idea how many times I'd wished to die." A tear broke free and raced down her cheek to dangle from her chin, a diamond in the firelight. "He did this to me."

She broke with a sob and my arms closed around her, holding her tight as she wept silent tremors of grief against my chest.

"I'm sorry," I said, devastated that she now knew the terrible truth. "I'm so sorry."

"I hate him," she said in watery whisper. "I hate him *so much*."

"He will pay for what he's done to you. For all that and so much more, he will suffer, he will bleed, and before he dies you will hear him beg for forgiveness." Drawing her back, I cupped her face. "This I swear to you."

Iereni's wet eyes lifted to mine and glowed like shooting stars in the night. "Strength and honor."

# CHAPTER TWENTY-NINE

## Navarre

"How goes your search?" Ehrick sat by the window, a heavy robe around his shoulders, fingers idly stroking an alabaster piece from a chessboard in play.

Three days had passed since the explosion in the palace courtyard.

The body count had been surprisingly minimal, caused mostly by a terrible third blast set beneath the grounds, collapsing a main tunnel that connected to the salt gate leading out to the Narrow Shore.

Navarre had been positioned on the imperial walls when it happened. Ehrick had ordered him kept far from the execution and pinned two men to his side to ensure he stayed at his post without issue. And he had, knowing full well Sinadine would not meet her end on that fateful morning.

After leaving his rooms with Eban, the pair of them had scoured the underground passages and found several tracks of footsteps in the dust but the clearest brought them to the lowest chamber of the mausoleum where Rhys and Jasz were burrowed in hiding.

They'd been careful, but not careful enough, and he'd told them as much. Jasz only shrugged, a gesture so similar to Sinadine it made his chest ache. She told him about what Sinadine had made her vow to do, but they had no intentions of leaving her to die.

That was not the Acharrān way.

"If you love her as we do, then you'll help us," Rhys had said, gripping his shoulders as her eyes swam with tears.

So he and Eban both hunkered down with them and well into the night they formed a plan. They hadn't had much time to sort it out and it took slow movements to gather all the supplies without triggering suspicion, leaving only a single night and a prayer to put it all into place. His role had been to move as many men as possible from the palace to the walls without tipping Ehrick off and he'd thought he'd gotten away with it, until he found out about the collapsed tunnel.

The one they'd marked for escape.

Ehrick had been on to them all along and counted on everything but Iereni slipping her rooms and showing them another way out. By now they would've cleared the Blue Wastes. He only hoped that he could keep Ehrick distracted with extending searches of the city long enough for them to get to Home Mountain, resupply, then push onward to Norland Harbor and sail far beyond his brother's reach.

"We've had some new leads to follow," Navarre said after clearing his throat, "and reason to believe they've been sheltered by a group of Acharrān supporters."

"That so?" Ehrick's lips quirked with a sardonic grin before moving a pawn up a square on the board. "Uncle will be sorely displeased to hear his campaign failed to root out all sympathizers."

The sun was bright today, the sky clear and light glittered off the fresh layer of snow blanketing the gardens beyond his bedroom windows, but Ehrick gazed listlessly at it like he wasn't seeing the glory of the day, the gardens, or the snow. He was seeing something else.

Something beyond Navarre's abilities to decipher.

Ehrick had sustained some injuries during the third blast that triggered an infection in his lungs, forcing him to bedrest. But nothing quite as severe as what had befallen the First Commander. Blown near twelve feet from the stage, a shard of iron ripped through his chest. The physicians and nurses worked tirelessly to repair the damage, but it would take months before he was on his feet, if ever.

It was still too soon to know for certain.

Navarre had seen many men survive similar injuries in combat, only for their bodies to give up. The Archviceroy, however, was barely grazed, and part of him wondered if his brother might have plans to remove his uncle as he had with Daneysa.

Within hours of the daring escape he'd accused her of playing a part in the treachery, an obvious lie but who was going to challenge the of the emperor? Ehrick sentenced her to imprisonment at Nabakza Tower, an impregnable fortress in the Norlands reserved for the worst of criminals. She'd wept and raged as they'd dragged her away, gagged and in chains.

Navarre had to tread carefully. There was no telling who else Ehrick would see fit to remove from the equation.

"I think it's time we entertain the possibility that your sources are leading you around like a dog chasing his tail." Ehrick moved another piece from the opposite side of the board. An obsidian rook. Studying the board for a moment, he claimed an alabaster knight and worked the smooth white stone figurine between his slender fingers while he decided his next move. "We should set our sights to Home Mountain."

"Sina would never go there, brother. She'd never put her clan in such danger."

"All the same, they have Iereni therefore no stone can be left unturned," Ehrick answered. "A battalion of two hundred infantry, and one hundred gunmen should be enough to bring me back their heads—and anyone who dares harbor them."

Navarre sighed. "Given the ragged state of the reserves only just returned from Zavora, even if we gathered all the guards within the barracks and the City Patrol, it would take weeks to assemble and organize that many men. Sina will have fled the empire by then and there's no telling where she'll go. I'd be trading my tail for smoke."

"I know," Ehrick replied in a lazy kind of drawl, like a cat bored with a trapped mouse between his paws. Ready to rip off its head. "Which is why I sent dispatches for conscripts the day father died and had them camped in Qadai awaiting my orders; our uncle left this morning to join them. He's most eager to spill Acharrān blood."

"There are *several* hundred Swordsworn there, at least another thousand in training who know how to fight, and their walls have never been breached." Bracing the table, he loomed over his brother— and God, how he wanted to seize Ehrick in his arms and shake him until some semblance of life or feeling swam back into his eyes.

Something other than the horrifying darkness that grinned out at him from oppressive shadows; a beast that had swallowed Ehrick whole, leaving nothing but empty bones stripped clean.

"You are sending good men to a needless death."

"Am I?" Ehrick dropped his leg from the windowsill, revealing a bronze hand resting casually at his side.

Navarre's heart shot into his throat. *Rhys.*

Ehrick set the game piece on the near empty board. An alabaster knight before an obsidian queen. No matter which way she moved, she was pinned.

The king immediately thereafter.

*Checkmate.*

<br>

Navarre left his brother, heart racing and chest tight. It took every ounce of self-control not to sprint to the barracks, to smile and maintain his composure and leisurely stride as he passed servants, guards and Chancellors.

But inside—inside he was a man on fire.

Qadai was a small city a scant ten miles from the Acharrān walls, and large enough to occupy a battalion, but why? Why would Ehrick put all this in place the day his father died? Endless questions rattled inside of his head like broken glass gripped tight in his hands—puncturing skin, and all the possible answers created one single bloody picture.

Sinadine was riding into a trap.

He burst into his office and Toddrick jolted in his seat with a startled, "*Oh my.*"

Eban halted in his pacing, his thumb between his teeth. A chronic nail biter when stressed, he'd chewed his fingers near to the quick over the last week. "Something wrong?" he asked as Navarre pushed the door shut and threw the bolt.

"Everything. Everything is wrong." Navarre gave them the quick, dirty rundown and Toddrick's usually rosy, round cheeks paled in horrified understanding.

"It's a trap," Eban whispered.

"I guessed as much, too," Navarre agreed.

"Well . . . what are you going to do, milord?"

"Todd, I want you to discreetly go to the storeroom and put together a bag of provisions for me. In an hour I'll sneak out to the harbor, take the fastest ship we have and warn her. Whatever Ehrick's planned—they don't stand a chance."

"I'm going with you," Eban said.

Toddrick popped out of his seat so fast his cheeks bounced. "Me too, milord."

Helpless Navarre dropped his hands. "It's too dangerous. These are men we've trained with, Eban. Men we know as love as brothers-in-arms. Are you prepared to fight and kill Trevor? Robin? Hugh and Wesley?"

"I will if I have to."

"And you, Todd, you've never held a sword in your life."

"I might not be a fighter, but my mind is my weapon. For instance . . ." Toddrick shuffled around the desk and pulled down a book of maps from the shelves. Flipping through the pages, he stopped abruptly on one of the Acharrān Mountains. "Here."

Navarre assessed the point marked by a plump finger capped with a nail bitten near to the quick. "What am I looking at?"

"It's the *small gate*," Toddrick answered with an aggrieved sigh.

A gate that, despite its name, was every bit as reinforced as the main one and near as large. Designed to give the Acharrāns clear access to the grove of sacred xhixi trees where they burned their dead.

"Alright. What about it?"

"Years ago, I read a book written by Professor Loren who spent a summer in the mountains with them, and he said that he discovered a cove, large enough that a ship could manage to make berth as close as fifty yards from the Small Gate."

"If that's true, it would save us almost a full day on horseback through the woodlands in winter," Eban acknowledged, and a scheming grin sliced across his acne-marked face. "That puts us at a serious advantage against the battalion. More than enough time to warn Sina and ride for all haste to Norland Harbor."

For the first time since leaving his brother's bedchamber, hope swelled inside him. Raising his eyes, he looked to the two young men who had already given him so much in terms of loyalty and service. Eban matched him in age, but Toddrick was all of seventeen and in a lot of ways, still just a boy.

Yet here he was prepared to die for what was right.

"You both should know that even if by some miracle we survive beyond this, we'll be fugitives for the rest of our days and hunted should we ever set foot on Bridian soil. Are you prepared for this?"

"I've always wanted to sail the twelve seas." Eban crossed his arms. "Todd?"

"Oh, well." Toddrick lifted a round shoulder. "I hear Oscano is lovely."

"There you have it Second Commander. We're going with you. To death or glory, as the Acharrāns say."

Navarre shook his head with a despondent laugh. "What are we waiting for?"

# CHAPTER THIRTY

## Sinadine

SNOW FELL LIKE FLAKES OF ASH. Slow. Drifting. Heavy.

A tremor of joy trickled through me, my heart near to bursting as I tipped my head to the sky and breathed a fresh, glorious breath of air. Far from the soot and misery of the Imperial City, here I could smell only pine and sap and the supple richness of moss and earth.

Tears swam and I let them flow with a smile.

I wanted to dismount from my horse and fall weeping to my knees, scooping up greedy fistfuls of snow and earth and press them to my nose, smothering weeks of soot and rot coating my lungs until all remnants of the Imperial city was scrubbed clear from every last inch of me. Until it was nothing more than a foul dream lost behind a blanket of all that was soothing and familiar.

Home. I was *finally* home.

Breaking the treeline I slowed my horse to a cantor as we neared the gleaming white face of the main gate where the warrior guarding our walls roared into the late sunlight.

One obsidian eye shattered.

"Something's wrong." Jasz roped her mare to a stop. "The gates are open."

We exchanged glances and, as one, drew our swords.

Iereni jerked in the saddle at the ring of my blade. "What's wrong?"

"These gates never remain open," I answered, lowering my voice as my eyes dragged along the high wall. No lookouts were posted, and I realized we hadn't come across a single scout as we rode hard through the woodlands. An egregious oversight in my haste to return to my clan.

My horse nickered, her neck lathered in sweat as I slid out of the saddle and handed Iereni the reins. "Wait here. If I'm not back to get you in twenty minutes, take this path to the main road and follow it north-east to Himeco. Sell the horses and get to Norland Harbor. I'll find you there."

"Sina . . ." she whispered, eyes widening, "let me come with you."

"Twenty minutes," I repeated as Jasz dismounted, tethering the horses to Iereni's saddle.

She nodded stiffly. I struck the horse on its hind quarters with the flat of my hand and Iereni guided the line of them into the safety of the trees. When she was out of sight, together Jasz and I slunk through the parting of the main gate and walked into wreckage.

The ripe stink of decay shot up my nostrils, a searing, foul burn that seared sharper than the cold.

Bodies were scattered everywhere. Those who hadn't died in combat were strung up and scorched—their blackened flesh marked with the evidence of torture . . . of all kinds. Some hung from the walls, some hung from the balustrade of the pagodas. All groaned and swayed heavy on the end of frozen rope.

Our family and friends. Our sisters. Women and children. Even the handmaids.

All left to rot like carrion in the winter sun.

I sank to my knees next to the corpse of a little girl, her sockets picked clean by crows and her mouth a ruin of rot and maggots. A tarnished silver bangle flashed on her left wrist.

*Taphne.*

Grief cleaved the ghost of a sob from my throat as my hand floated above the curve of her skull, crushed and broken from the stomp of a vicious boot. Even if I couldn't make out her features through the state of decay, there was no mistaking her misshapen legs, splayed like broken wings.

Determined, strong and brave Taphne.

The girl who climbed a mountain to bring me home. Who hungered for glory, a twin to my shadow, ever close, now lay twisted on the ground with a sword in her hand and blood on her blade.

Blood of the enemy.

She'd fought with pride and died a warrior's death long before it should have been her time.

My sobs burned with trapped screams as I folded over at her side. Rage, vicious and black, rose within me. Smothering sound, and light and reason.

Ehrick had slaughtered them. Weeks ago, from the state of the rot and the stench of bodies layering the mountain air in a greasy film of decay that coated my lungs, my skin, long before the crown had touched his head.

Perhaps even before I'd refused to bend the knee.

Damnable dead, I never should've left home. I should've been here to fight and die with them.

"Someone approaches," Jasz called out.

Swallowing my misery, it was a struggle to stand, but I found my feet and joined Jasz, ready to face whatever threat was emerging from the snow. Of course Ehrick had kept men close by to pick of any who'd managed to survive or later returned from a call.

Sword in hand, I let my rage flow through me, wild and free, prepared to cut the villains down like a sheet of ice breaking from the mountain when Navarre stepped out into the fading sunlight, his hands raised. Toddrick, his vassal, and Eban emerged with him. Their faces gaunt with wakening horror at what we'd just walked into.

"Sina." My name echoed in the space between us. "I got here as fast as I could. We should get inside," he said, careful to keep out of distance of my still unsheathed blade and his hands where I could see them.

"Did you know about this?" I demanded, gesturing to the decaying bodies strewn around us. My voice a ragged, hard rasp, filled with loathing, hatred and rage. I shook with the ferocity of it. A wild, vicious intensity, barely tethered to sanity or restraint. "Did you?"

"No." His eyes softened with misery. "Please, we don't have much time."

"Go on." Jasz touched my shoulder, squeezed. "I'll get Iereni and then seal the gate."

Inside the pagoda wasn't much warmer than outside, all the fires were out. Blood splashed across the floor and walls.

More bodies.

We entered Matron Lucera's room, and I snatched a kubari off the hook, wrapped it around my body, and belted it tight at the waist. Made of fine grey leather and warm black icefox fur, the hem and sleeves were woven with coral, turquoise and silver beads.

*Was.* Was her room.

"You wanted to warn me," I said, drawing strength from leather, fur, and the walls of home. "About what?"

His hand flexed between us as if he ached to touch me, and I ached to let him, but the ravages of grief were too bright, too raw. I was liable to kill him if he got close.

"A battalion is coming. Heavily armed. The same men I'm guessing who are responsible for this massacre. They will be here soon, Sina."

*Damnable dead.* "When?"

"Dawn, maybe. I doubt they'd strike ahead of that."

"Good."

Navarre jerked straight, stunned by my easy answer. "Good?"

"We will die as we were meant to die—in battle. Go home, Navarre. This fight isn't yours," I said, wrenching past him.

His hand caught my arm and held fast. "I won't let you do this alone."

"Are you really prepared to give up everything—your men, your status, your *brother*—everything you know and love, to fight against the Bridians who raised you?"

"Yes," he answered without hesitation then swallowed hard, pain shining in his eyes. "Ehrick killed almost everyone I've ever loved. My brothers. My father." He swallowed hard. "I'm with you."

Jasz cleared her throat from the doorway, dark eyes gleaming. "I found survivors."

Jasz brought us to the edges of the western ghat, leading up to the shrine, where the tracks started.

They were weathered, but thanks to the formation of the craggy rocks overhead, it was shielded from the snowfall.

The path was too rough for the wheelchair to manage so Navarre and I took turns carrying Iereni on our backs, winding up and into the shrine where the rattle of voices rippled through the corridors.

My aunt rose as we entered the inner chamber of the shrine where we'd all received our marks—it felt like a lifetime ago. Children and elderly were huddled together. Some played, some slept, and some sobbed into their blankets for mothers or daughters who would never return to them. A hundred, maybe a handful more, and few Swordsworn among them.

Not nearly enough to make a stand against the coming soldiers.

Anush scowled at the sight of me. Iona, too.

Rashni closed in, joined by many others. Navarre moved to block her path, but I stopped him with a swing of my arm.

"The stars foretold you'd been the ruin of us and they spoke true," Rashni snapped. Her white gold teeth glinting with malice, replacing the ones I'd knocked loose. "We should cast you from the walls. Leave you broken and bleeding for the wolverines."

Hands shoved. Voices clamored in agreement. Dark with pain and bright with fear, needing someone to blame for their misery.

Shaken, I held my ground, but I couldn't muster up the will to fight back. She was right. My destiny was to destroy all I loved, and yet I'd been stupid enough to think I had the power to change my stars.

How arrogant. *The stars don't lie . . .*

"That's enough." Elide's commanding voice rose beyond the circle of women, silencing the mob. They parted and she stood, regal and proud. Her hair knotted high around the woven bands of leadership.

Rashni whipped around, trembling with anger and tears. "This is her fault. All of it. The stars foretold—"

"I said that's enough. There's work to be done, injured and sick to tend to. You will all disperse now, or answer to me." Elide folded her hands before her, and for the first time in my life, she looked at me with compassion. And shame. "Come, Sinadine. Sit with me." She led us to the center of the chamber, to the round bronze brazier mounted in the floor.

A fire burned brightly. She sat down on a polished stone stool, and we joined her.

My aunt looked to Iereni, and then to Navarre at my side. "You are the one who returned the sword of Valan de-Nersu."

He lowered his chin in acknowledgement and respect. "I am her son."

"What happened here?" I asked, pulling her attention back to the subject at hand.

The proud line of her jaw wavered, and she faced the fire as if seeing it all play out in the flames. "The night you were taken away we drank in feast and celebration—to honor the courage of your sacrifices. We'd opened the wine barrels brought with the escort not knowing they were laced with a slow-acting poison. For days, we took ill. Some of us worsening. I thought it was a rash of fever; the symptoms were so . . . innocuous." Her lips pressed together, tight with regret.

And responsibility.

"Weeks later, riders came bearing the seal of the emperling. A strange, and unexpected visit, but I wasn't going to refuse him or his envoys."

"Ehrick was *here*?" Navarre gasped.

Elide nodded. "Yes. He apologized for not being present to honor us with his blessing and to rectify this he announced he would feast with us to celebrate a thousand years of peace. His men brought in more wine but this time, the effects were immediate. I'd elected not to partake, after having suffered from the first casks and not wanting to risk . . ." Her hand fluttered to a firm, round belly.

"They started frothing at the mouth. Convulsing. That's when I realized—too late. Those of us who were not affected, fought, but while we dined with the emperling a few of his men had opened our gates to soldiers waiting in the woodlands. It was a massacre. With so many of our Swordsworn weakened there was nothing we could do to fight back against such numbers. I gathered those I could and hid here, waiting for the men to clear out and our injured to recover."

"*Goddamn* him . . ." Navarre hung his head. "His trip to the Holy City was a cover. A lie."

"Grandmother?" I asked, my throat tight with sorrow. "Where did she fall?"

Elide's eyes flickered to me. "I'll take you to her."

My lungs squeezed tight as a fist, and refused to relax until we entered the antechamber, where the incense, and prayer candles were stored. Grandmother lay on a stack of furs, a cloth wound around her face and dried blood smeared where her eyes *should* be.

"We removed them a few days ago after infection spread," Elide explained.

I settled at her side, took hold of her hand. Her palm was warm, her calluses reassuring.

"You came home." Her fingers twined with mine.

"I did."

"And the Lone Wolf?"

I hung my head, tears spilling free, and they splattered over our joined hands. "I failed you. I failed all of you."

My prophecy was fulfilled. So many dead. Their bodies desecrated. Souls lost.

By killing Ehrick I thought I could stop this—all of this—from ever happening. What a stupid, arrogant fool. The stars didn't lie, and mine were clear at birth.

I was the *Dakuwan*. The harbinger of death and destruction. I didn't deserve to live.

The battalion marched for me and me alone. Perhaps it wasn't too late to save the few still breathing. Perhaps my sacrifice could grant them peace.

Grandmother sat up, imperious in her anger, and the hard crack of a palm to my cheek almost whipped me around full circle.

"Are you done riding the pity wagon, or do I need to strike sense into you again?"

Dazed, I blinked at her. "I didn't say anything!"

Another hard slap rang through my skull. *Damnable dead*, she hit like a hammer to an anvil.

"You didn't have to." She bounced her fist against my chest, above my aching heart. "It's here. Loud as thunder in the mountains. I won't have it. So, I'll ask you again, are you done with that childish nonsense?"

My lip slid into a pout. "Yes."

"Good." She dusted her hands together. Calluses grating. "You only fail when you give up. Have you given up, Sina?"

Had I? Two hundred men were coming for us, but even now, shattered to dust, beneath the throbbing pain lay an ember of defiance. The will to fight, though faint, hadn't quite extinguished.

"No."

"Then it's only a question of what you're willing to do. How far you're willing to go."

"I don't understand?"

"The last sickle moon," she whispered. "Tonight, it rises."

"That's just a story."

Her body shook with a jolt, and I flinched, bracing for another blow. "Have I taught you *nothing*?" she snapped. "There is power in our blood. Old and forgotten though it may be, it is there." Grandmother's hand closed over mine. Strong. Reassuring. And her confidence flowed into me, a river of bright warmth. "So long as the heart still burns there is *hope*."

Before I could find the nerve to speak, a lit arrow shot into the sky—raining a blast of sparks and smoke. Jasz was signaling trouble from the wall.

The Bridians. *They're here.*

Jasz paced the high wall, and waved her bow as Navarre and I stepped off the pulley.

"What's wrong?" I asked.

"See for yourself."

Wind howled, pulling at my braids as I peered down at the battalion camped below.

Navarre swore, disbelieving his own eyes. "That's more than two hundred men."

"Three hundred at least," Jasz agreed.

"Why did he lie to me?"

"Because he knew you'd betray him." I cast Navarre a sympathetic look. "This is what he does, misdirection and half-truths." And not only were there more men, but siege weapons as well. Trebuchets, ladders, and an iron battering ram shaped into a snarling wolf with a mouth that belched fire.

I was confident the gate would hold. Xhixi trees, like our mountain ore, was imbued with the energy of the star that fell millennia ago. Only Acharrān steel could bring it down. Our walls were another matter. There wasn't nearly enough of us to defend it from ladders.

Eventually they'd breach and we'd be swarmed.

"What's that?" I asked, gesturing to a white flag snapping in the wind, staked at least a hundred yards from the imperial encampment setup in the barren swath dividing our gates from the woodlands.

"It's a call to parlay," Navarre answered.

I gripped the hilt of my sword, so hard my knuckles whined. These were the same men who'd slaughtered near twelve hundred members of my clan. Every single one of them was going to pay for it. "Open the gate. I'm going down."

"I'll go with you. You shouldn't face them alone. It's too dangerous."

"He's right," Jasz said before I could argue the matter. "But before you do, there's something you should see."

Hooking the bow on her shoulder, she led us down the winding tower stairs to the weapons storeroom.

The narrow space was lined with rows of lances, bows, and quivers stuffed with arrows. Staffs and whips. At the end of the room, a rack of armor glinted in torchlight, with vambraces, made from Acharrān steel, strong enough to stop a sword or deflect an arrow, and draped in a gorgeous white stonecat cloak. The rubies dangling from black gold claws bright as fresh blood.

My heart kicked with surprise. "My cloak?"

"I grabbed it before we'd escaped and packed it with the provisions on my horse." Jasz scrubbed a hand over the back of her neck, flicking her long braid. "If you're going to greet the enemy, you should do it as a true Acharrān."

Pressing my brow to hers, I whispered my thanks and fastened the weight of it around my shoulders while Jasz tended to my face with a pot of blue woad.

Once I was dressed and ready, the gate groaned as Jasz worked the crank, opening them just enough for Navarre and I to step out to the where the flag trembled in the wind. The Archviceroy waited for us with Benj and one other man.

Stripped of his vestments, Henry was a cunning figure, lean and cagey and no stranger to wearing armor. "Second Commander, this is a most pleasant surprise."

"General Manderly," Navarre addressed the second man, ignoring the Archviceroy's remark.

"I'm sorry to see you're caught up in this, boy," Manderly shook Navarre's hand like old friends meeting for drinks instead of enemies about to go to battle. "And on the wrong side, no less."

"I was going to say the same to you, sir."

"Enough horseshit," Benj spat, his venomous glare boring into me with smug and brutal hatred.

"Indeed." Henry raised an imperious brow, his hand resting idly on the hilt of a sword topped with a snarling wolf pommel. "I bring word from his imperial majesty. Return Lady Iereni unharmed and lay down your weapons in surrender. Do so now, and we vow that those who swear themselves loyal servants of the empire will live to see the emperor's mercy."

"You will find no loyal servants here," I said, and with the lift of my hand, Jasz loosed a flaming arrow from the wall. It lanced the snow-dusted ground between the Archviceroy's feet. "Or mercy."

Henry stroked his tongue along the grinning edge of his teeth. "You have until dawn. Once the sun rises our battle will begin, and what's left of the Acharrāns will fall."

I smiled back at his threatening words, the beast caged inside of me purring with anticipation. "Sleep well."

Gathered around the fire, I shared my plan of attack. The Swordsworn listened, and I was grateful for their attention, even if it wasn't for my sake. We were united in grief.

"Is there no other way?" Anush asked.

"Even if we send the survivors fleeing for the coast, they won't get far enough. The battalion will give chase," I said, facing my sisters around the circle of fire, my aunt's features drawn in silence. "Not unless we can make our stand and hold them off, give them a fighting chance."

"Three dozen against three hundred are hardly comforting odds," Iona said, "but I will fight for our dead."

Elide's eyes found mine from across the fire. "If I'd listened to you before, I wouldn't have watched everyone I know and love die. I was wrong, and I won't make that mistake a second time. We must do something. I will fight."

"Not you," I said, nodding towards the mound of her pregnant belly. "You must protect those who can't protect themselves. If we fall, you'll be their last hope for a clean death."

Tension tightened the line of her jaw and a familiar gleam of challenge sparked in her eyes. My aunt didn't like being told what to do but gone was the woman who hated me without cause.

"We'll do it your way," she conceded with a tense nod.

"And I will join you." My grandmother crossed the chamber, firelight danced in the golden cuff beads decorating her silver hair, combed and freshly braided.

"You can't."

Her face snapped towards the sound of my voice, hand closing on the hilt of her sword. "They took my eyes, girl, not my spirit. Who are you to tell me when and how I will meet my end?"

"I will fight, too," Iereni spoke up, emboldened by my grandmother's words. "You trained me and I won't sit around waiting for them to slit my throat again like a cornered lamb."

A smile flickered across Elide's face and she offered me a helpless shrug.

Moving to Iereni's side, I tried not to picture Taphne's broken, rotting corpse dusted in snow. She had fought for her clan and died a warrior's death. Iereni deserved the same courtesy to decide her own fate. I would not deny her, or anyone, that right.

"If you're going to fight with us," I said, "then you will need a new sword."

"I'll see that she gets one," Elide affirmed, and I gave her a nod in thanks. "The rest of you know your tasks. Dawn will be upon us before long."

Everyone broke from around the fire, setting about to do what needed to be done.

Jasz circled the brazier and stopped at my side. Her dark hair painted crimson in the firelight. "I can't tell you how many times I've dreamt of a battle like this, but I'm afraid of what tomorrow will bring. I'm afraid we won't be enough."

"That's why I have to go," I said, strapping my scabbard to my hip. "Hold them for as long as you can." I gathered her shoulders. Squeezed. "And if I'm too late—make sure those bastards remember—*always*—the day they fought the last of the Acharrāns."

# CHAPTER THIRTY-ONE

## Sinadine

THE SICKLE MOON ROSE, A glowing smile against a midnight blue canvas. Tonight, was a time of great power.

A night when a bloodkin descendent of the First-of-Us could summon the souls of warrior gods. Our chances were futile, we'd all fight and die tomorrow. It was up to me to go to them and beg the stars that had once shunned me for help.

I prayed they would answer.

Grandmother stood at my side as I knelt before the prayerstone, cleansing myself with smoke from a burning stick of xhixi wood before my journey. It's scent both sweet and wild, I breathed it deep, and let the smoke fill my lungs with purpose.

"What if I can't do this?" I said softly. Only to her would I admit my doubts. My weakness. "What if they don't hear me?"

She smoothed her hands across my shoulders, her smile soft and wistful.

Proud.

"You are Sinadine the stone claw, fierce and relentless. They will listen because you will *make them listen.* And, whatever happens, come the dawn, we will face it together." She drew me into a fast hug, her strong, assuring arms holding me close and I gave into that offer of comfort and strength.

"It's time." Elide stood in the archway leading deeper into the shrine, a torch in one hand, and a sheathed sword in the other.

"Go." Grandmother kissed my cheeks. "There's not a moment to waste."

I left her by the obelisk where she sank to her knees and bowed, voice singing low in prayer.

"I wanted to give this to you." Elide raised the sword between us, and my breath snagged in my throat like a briar.

I stroked a hand across the lacquered scabbard, chipped in some places. There was no adornment or decoration aside from golden beads woven into the silk band of the hilt. I hadn't seen this blade since I was a child, speaking my mother's words into the cold snap of wind.

"Berséba was not an easy person to love." Elide smiled gently, tears thickening the usually stoic edges of her voice. "She didn't open herself to many, but I know her love for you was souldeep. Endless. Bersé would *never* have disavowed herself otherwise."

I steadied myself with a breath. "Thank you for giving me this."

"I should've given it to you long ago." Elide smoothing a hand over belly. "When she was pregnant with you—I was jealous that it was my younger sister who carried the future of our line. Who succeeded where I'd failed. When you were born cursed, I saw my hatred and envy as justification … I've wronged you in so many ways, Sina. Should we live beyond tomorrow, I hope you can forgive me."

I fastened to the sword to the belt at my waist, joining my own sheathed blade. "I already do."

Her smile spread, bright as the sickle moon hanging above us. "We need to hurry. There's not much time." Elide carried a torch lighting the path and we passed the spiraling rows of markers to honor our Acharrān dead inlaid into the heart of Home Mountain like stars in the night sky.

If I failed tonight we would be the last of them. There would be no markers to record our lives and deaths. The world would forget our names, and in time it would be as if we'd never existed at all.

"Why were the statues of the First-of-Us hidden away deep down here?" I asked as we reached the bowels of the shrine where a door gleamed made of the same steel as our swords, glistening silver-blue in the torchlight.

"I was told by the oldest of our matrons when I was child that this is where the star landed when the Acharrāns fell from the sky. It is here the stars energy remains strongest, and where what's left of the Heart still burns." Removing a key from a leather cord at her throat, she unlocked the door and nudged it open with her hip. It groaned, and together we stepped inside.

The chamber was wide, round and rough, as if chiseled by crude tools, but the floor was paved smooth with carved lines of an intricate knot at the center where a divot formed a multi-pointed star, large enough for a person to stretch out without ever touching the sides.

Above the center, a white dancing flame hovered and gleamed, haloed in blue and more dazzling than a diamond.

It was fire and ice, alive and pulsating with a light all its own.

And the closer we drew to it the air thickened. The Heart throbbed. And the weight of it pressed against my skin, my eyes, my ears.

So dense.

Tendrils of power wove through the cavern, and wrapped themselves around my wrists, my ankles and waist, beckoning me closer. The swords on my hip hummed, the mark on my back purred.

This was it.

My lineage. My destiny.

*Mine.*

The statues were as I remembered. Bright, gleaming, and pale as moonlight. Their features weathered but the runes on their bodies remained intact.

"I've spoken to them often." Elide approached the statues, her torch pale in comparison to that endless white flame. She brushed a hand across the arm of one of the stone figures.

Reverent. Wistful.

"They never answered my prayers. I hope they answer yours." She bowed deeply to the First-of-Us, whispering the old words of respect, and left me there in the pool of flickering white light.

Above me, the chamber spiraled higher and higher, a shaft that carved all the way to the surface where a faint scrap of sky could be seen and the glowing edge of the moon breaching the circle.

Almost time.

Notching the torch in the wall, I set to work, laying out my offerings and lit sticks of incense infused with cinnamon, myrrh, and ilang.

Sweet smoke wafted around me, spicing the air as the last corner of the grinning moon entered the circle and light funneled down into the chamber, amplified by sparkling facets of crystals that glowed with a bluish-white light that pulsed with the same flickering brilliances as the Heart.

Lifting the oathblade, I sliced my left hand and held it out over the abalone bowl and when enough was gathered, I marked each brow, following the groves of their name runes, and spoke their names aloud. Returning to the center of the circle, I spread my hands in supplication.

"Great Mothers, hear me. I summon you forward. I, Sinadine de-Arashi, the Stone Claw, your bloodkin heir, summon you."

An unseen energy rippled and carried with it sibilant whispers. Those glowing crystals shone brighter, like stars trapped in stone, and that energy I'd always sensed from the statues intensified.

The whispers grew louder. The Heart—scorching. And finally, a beam of light, bright as a waking sun, shot down in a single solid beam.

Gasping, I raised my forearm to protect my eyes from the blinding glare as a shape formed and gradually emerged moments before the blast of light melted away.

A figure of glowing, incandescent flesh—black as night—but radiant, with eyes and hair of liquid white.

"Well, that was a rush." She grinned, bearing fangs far more prominent that mine, and waved me forward.

I approached, cautiously, and shivered against the weight of her aura that cloaked the air. Every step closer was like running through water. "Who are you?"

"I am called N'jirah."

Hearing her name cleared the fog of amaze from my senses so that reality and understanding settled in like the shock of dipping a bare toe into cold water.

Though she was tall—much taller than me—she was far from the giantess warriors I'd been told of so often in my youth. Her features, carved of shadows and moonlight, were far too young to be who I was expecting.

She wore no kubari and no sword. In fact, I frowned at the state of her in wakening horror, she appeared no more than an Initiate . . . and she was alone.

"You are not who I called for. Where is the queen? Where are the others?"

N'jirah puffed up her chest. "I am who was sent."

"But you're a child!"

Her brow arched imperiously. "I'm older than you."

I recoiled in disbelief and outrage. "No. No, go back. Tell the queen the Pale Wolf rises again, and this time he will devour us all," I said, pushing strength into my bones as I met N'jirah's glowing gaze. "Her daughters need help. I need warriors."

"No." N'jirah dashed an unconcerned hand. "The queen can't be expected to save you from every petty squabble you mortals find yourselves in."

"This isn't a petty squabble. It's a slaughter!" I snapped, my voice cracking off the cavernous walls. "I don't understand . . . she fought for us once before, why would she refuse us now?"

"That was to neutralize a threat far greater than you realize." N'jirah narrowed moondust eyes. "One that would not have stopped at consuming your world, but others, as well. We are guardians of worlds, not caretakers you can summon to sweep dust from under your beds."

"There has to be something you can do." I staggered forward as she turned away. The dead—my sisters—must be avenged and I could not fail them, not when I was so close. "Her daughters are all near dead. Only a handful remain, and if you don't help us, they too will perish come the dawn. Who then will remain to worship you?"

"Such is life. We cannot be the solution you seek to solve every problem therefore this matter is yours, Sinadine de-Arashi."

"But—"

"We have given you all the tools you need." She spread her hands, back to me, and gestured to the mountains around us. "You have our steel. Our knowledge. And if you can't use both to save yourself then you're not worthy of calling yourself a daughter of the Acharrā."

Hope withered in my throat and with it all desire to be cautious or calm. I called for help, and instead of answering my plea, they'd sent me a grunt. An insult that showed an absolute lack of care or regard for our welfare.

A slap to the face I'd never expected from the ancestors I'd been raised to revere, and the shock of disappointment and heartbreak woke a kind of contempt I'd never experienced before this moment.

All my life I'd worshipped the stars and now when I needed them most, they'd shunned me once again.

Well, damn them all.

*If they won't listen*, my grandmother's voice swelled inside me, *make them listen.*

"Leave if you must." The quiet fury in my voice rang off stone with unveiled scorn. "But if you turn away from us now, know that if I survive the morning the first thing I'll do, once I've rid the Motherland of our enemies, will be to come back here and render these fucking statues to dust. I'll strike every mention of the First-of-Us from our books and I'll tear down these mountains with my bare hands, if needs be. No one will utter the name Acharrā again because if they would forsake us now, I am ashamed to call myself their *daughter*."

N'jirah turned to me, slow as ice forming on the peaks of the mountaintops. "You wouldn't dare."

I grinned. My mother's grin. "Wouldn't I?" Drawing my mother's blade, I let the light of wrath suffuse every inch of my being. "In fact, why wait? Let's start now." I rushed forwards with a battle-cry, steel arching for the gleaming white throat of the queen.

"Stop!" N'jirah screamed, throwing herself in my path.

My blade paused in its brutal stroke, close enough to kiss the surface of her skin and our gaze collided over the edge of steel. To my surprise, a cagey grin spreading across the shadows of her face, fangs gleaming like the point of the sword I'd nearly decapitated her with.

"You really are one of us, after all."

I raised the proud line of my chin. "We do not bow."

N'jirah's smile broadened with a laugh that rumbled deep in her chest as she pushed away the edge of the blade with the flat of her hand.

"Well . . ." she scraped a pensive thumbnail across the back of her nose, "summoning our warriors is out of the question. But there might be something I can give you. It comes with a terrible price, though. A price I am not sure you'd wish to pay once you know what it will take from you."

"Whatever it is, I'll do it."

A gilded brow arched over moondust eyes. "The consequences are—"

"I'll worry about the consequences later," I interrupted.

Eventually N'jirah nodded, then holding out her hand, light crackled in her palm. A ball of raw, primal energy. It pulsed and snapped and something inside of me roared in triumph.

"I can give you what is inside of me for a time, but as I said there is a price to pay and a balance to maintain. When your enemy is dead, place his head and heart at the feet of our queen before the first equinox and I'll return to relieve of your burden."

"That's in three months." I'd spent more than half that in the Imperial city and the advantage of surprise without success. Now I was hundreds of miles away and this time Ehrick would be ready for me. Waiting. To kill Ehrick—without the strength and fury of my clan . . .

I was just one girl against an entire empire.

"It's impossible. Give me a year, at least."

"This power I'm gifting you isn't meant for mortals," N'jirah said without remorse or pity. "Eventually it will consume you, breath, blood and bone. I'm afraid even three months may be more than your body can withstand, but it's the best I can do. And before you can even claim what I'm offering, a sacrifice of equal value must be made. Something you most hold dear."

"Sacrifice?" My brows furrowed in confusion. "Risking my life isn't enough?"

"No." N'jirah shook a despondent head. "The forces that govern us all demand a balance that must be struck. You're not afraid to die, but you *are* afraid to be alone. Truly alone. So to accept this gift you must sacrifice you're your soul—forsaking not only this life, but the one beyond, as well."

My eyes fluttered in disbelief.

For an Acharrā, the only purpose was to live with glory, and to ascend to the stars in death. Aside from my sword, it was the only other thing I'd ever wanted and now, to save my clan, I would have to surrender my soul to exile?

"This doesn't sound like much of a gift," I muttered.

"I can always rescind my offer." N'jirah pierced me with a glare. "What will it be, Sinadine the Stone Claw?"

*You only fail when you give up.*

*Have you given up, Sina?*

"Sisters before self." The words shot out of me like an arrow, and once set loose there was no calling it back.

My mind was set, the decision made. Rhys—if she was still alive—was counting on me. Whatever the cost, I would pay any price to avenge all those who'd died and protect those who still drew breath.

"I am the *Dakuwan*," I whispered, at last. "I have no place among the stars. Do it."

Something like surprise and pride moved across her features. N'jirah gathered my face in her cold hands and where she touched, I felt only the humming pulse of raw, brilliant power that humbled me to my core. Young, as she was, she was strong. I could see that now, and a very real whisper of fear wove around my usually steady heart.

"Then I give you the strength of stone." She pressed a finger to my brow. "I give you the purpose of pain. I give you the rage of tempests, and the wrath of a dying sun."

A hiss and burn scored from that touch, and for a single, bracing moment I lost all sight and sound and breath. When her finger lifted, the sear of a brand lingered in its wake. It pulsed and throbbed and *shone.*

"It's it done?"

She released my face to grip the width of my throat. "No."

The muscles in my neck stiffened in anticipation as gleaming fangs snapped at my throat. Her teeth sunk deep, and blood rushed from my body like water over rapids with great, dragging pulls that pulsed in time with my waning heartbeat.

A groan pushed past my lips and my fingers clasped the iron of her wrist. Powerful, unbreakable, and unyielding. I couldn't have dislodged her even if I tried.

And though I fought the urge to resist, the instinct to live was great and fierce as death closed in around my ankles, gathering up to my knees to then slither over my hips.

Spirts of my Sisters, I thought I knew cold, but this was brutal. Endless. I was ice and fire, life and death. The world swayed and only when the N'jirah withdrew with the last of my lifeblood on her lips, did I realize my body lay on the ground at her feet.

Weak. Empty.

Or almost.

Veins of light webbed across her midnight skin, glowing with vitality and the essence of life she'd snatched from me. Smoothing a hand across my cheek, her touch warm where I was frozen. So cold, I couldn't tell where my body ended and the icy stone beneath me began.

Slit her wrist with her fanged teeth, silvery white blood flowed and turned to light sliding past my lips. "Die," she whispered. "And be reborn again."

There was no taste, and I couldn't feel much beyond the kiss of energy on my tongue, but within moments something *moved* inside of me.

Slow at first. And then fast.

So fast.

My heart seized. My body shook. The world bottomed out beneath me, ice cracking on the lake, and I vanished into that dark pool—into death.

Into *light*.

# CHAPTER THIRTY-TWO

## Navarre

Navarre stood atop the Acharrān walls and gazed out at the rows of men. Trebuchets armed, ladders arcing forwards. The blast of a horn rallied the soldiers in long wailing notes.

"Sina's not back yet," Jasz commented, taking in the force assembling against them. "And I don't think they're going to wait much longer."

The soldiers roared their answer as Henry kicked his horse into a gallop, slicing before them, sword drawn to lead the charge. A billowing cloak streamed from his shoulders, red as the blood about to be spilled.

"How long do you think the gate will hold?"

"It's not the gate I'm worried about," Navarre answered. "It's those ladders. Sina was right. There's too many of them and not enough of us to keep them from scaling the walls. We've got minutes. Ten. Maybe twenty at most."

Sunlight spread across the horizon, chasing away the inky blue of night and turning the sky a deep cobalt. The Battle for Home Mountain was about to begin.

"Then we'll have to make them count." Turning to the courtyard, Jasz waved her hands, signaling the others to ready themselves.

Navarre lit the fuse and touched Jasz' shoulder. "Go."

She leapt from the scaffold and hooked an arm around the lift rope, she waited until Navarre joined her before unsheathing a dagger and, with a flick of her wrist, knocked the lever back. The lift lurched, groaned, and descended.

"It's not going fast enough." The count worked down in his head, seconds left and thirty feet to the ground. Twenty. "We won't make it."

Jasz unsheathed her sword. "Hold onto something." She slashed in a smooth stroke, and rope severed.

There was a moment of breathless weightlessness, and Navarre's stomach shot up into his throat as the lift plummeted the last ten feet and crashed at the bottom with a harrowing thud. Wood splintered and Navarre slammed to the ground with an *oof*.

Seconds later flames erupted overhead. The explosives they'd armed—half finished barrels of lantern oil, wine, brandy and rum—unleashed a wall of fire and belching clouds of smoke.

Cries of men sang from across the other side of the wall.

"That should slow them down," Jasz dusted herself off. Not that she needed to after landing on her feet with catlike grace.

Amparo loped over to them, hand on her hilt. "The next round of fuses are primed."

"Good." Navarre assessed the three towering pagodas, built entirely of wood, it would come down easily. He only hoped his guess was sound when gauging which support beams to blacken. At his careful instruction, small fires were set, and burned throughout the twilight hours, weakening the support beams of the center structure. There were only so many barrels left, and they had prioritized the bulk of them for the wall.

Leaving only a scant few to bring the pagoda crashing down, hopefully wiping out the bulk of the battalion while forcing the rest to funnel into the coliseum where they would rise to meet them. Giving them each a fighting chance until Sinadine returned. But if too many soldiers survived and the coliseum was overrun, they'd have no way out.

A dangerous plan, but it was the best one they had.

"Light the fuses!" Navarre shouted.

"We're destroying our home to save it," Cahira said with a sad shake of her head.

"A pagoda can be rebuilt," Jasz answered. "What's the point of it standing if none of us live to use it?"

"They've breached the walls!" Amparo flagged them as men flowed overhead and raced to the gears, activating the gate.

"With me!" Navarre called out and together they bolted for the coliseum. "Ready yourselves," he said. "And no matter what, hold the line."

Iona, Anush, and Rashni held the front with the most experienced of the Swordsworn. Eban, Jasz, Amparo, Cahira, were among the center, and Avanthi taking the rear with him, Iereni, Ro and Tiben, the oldest of the Acharrān children. Barely twelve, but they had a right to defend their home. Their lives.

The clamor of men rose, the ground trembled beneath the fury of their boots. The gates were open and in a moment the force of the charge was going to crash over them like a wave.

"Steady," Navarre said, eyes fixed on the center pagoda. "Come on . . ."

Seconds stretched into hours, into years, heart strained in his throat, he began to question, to doubt, until the first harrowing crack and boom shattered the dawn and that towering, elegant structure wavered. Toppled. Fell.

Men screamed as it crashed to the earth with such force the stone arches of the colosseum trembled. Dust and snow kicked up in a wave of debris, and Navarre bent over Iereni, shielding her from the rain of splintered wood and bits of stone.

Quiet. So very quiet.

It didn't last long. Vicious, angry roars rose to join the clouds of smoke. Too many voices. The pagoda hadn't taken out nearly as many as he'd hoped.

Jasz clapped a hand on his shoulder. "It was a sound effort."

"Hear them, sisters," Avanthi called, commanding attention—her proud voice sharp with age and virility. "They've come to snuff out our lives. No songs shall ever be sung, no stories of our great deeds will be shared over an open fire. The world will never know we fought and died here on this day." She lifted her head and smiled as if she could *see* the spread of stars that shone defiantly in the growing light. "The Spirits of our Sisters are with us. Today, we fight in their name, and tonight we will rise to join them."

The Acharrāns' drew their swords and loosed an answering battle-cry that shot fire into his blood. They were primed, charged and ready to face their deaths smiling.

"Sisters, get into formation," Jasz bellowed as men broke through the coliseum doors. "*Live with honor!*"

"*Die with dignity!*" her sisters roared in unison.

The first volley of imperial soldiers met with Acharrān steel, a rising chorus of swords and strangled cries as the wounded fell. Blood soaking into sand and snow.

Ro raised her bow, arm steady.

"Aim for the neck, underarms and eyes," Navarre instructed.

Tiben loosed the first arrow, its aim true—taking the first guard straight through the visor of his helm. He was dead before he hit the ground. Ro's arrow struck the second, not as cleanly, but Iona finished the job, slicing his throat open, and roared into charging her next opponent.

Navarre joined the frenzy with fast, sweeping arcs of his broadsword and ran his first man through. The soldier staggered, and his helmet tumbled free, ripping Navarre's heart from his chest in recognition.

Gavin Tibbs. They'd fought and trained as boys. Gavin, who smiled often and flirted with the milkmaids, who loved strawberries, could sing like a dream, and never bloody remembered to protect his left side. Gavin, whose dying body hanging from the end of Navarre's sword like a speared fish, his eyes glazing over.

"I'm sorry," he whispered as Gavin slumped to the ground. "I'm sorry." A foolish effort. Apologies were wasted on the dead.

Something shook through the world—through him. Something ancient, and dark and powerful. A violent chill that tore through him with the sudden and vivid memory of the stonecat emerging from the gale, carrying a head in her jaws, her eyes glowing and laughing as a sea of blood poured from her mouth.

Life and death. A beginning and an end . . .

"Second Commander."

Rough hands wrenched him to his feet and back to reality.

Avanthi de-Mazad held him fast, her eyes bandaged and unseeing yet somehow, she knew. "Rise," she said. And slashed her sword out, stopping a guard from taking Navarre's legs out from under him. With a hard twist she pushed him aside and re-entered the fray. Her movements sharp and swift, unhindered by blindness.

They had to hold the line—and it was failing as more guards pushed into the coliseum, more then he'd anticipated breaking through, driving them to the center.

At least a hundred men packed into the sandy arena and everywhere he looked all the saw was the faces of men and boys he'd once called friend.

The lines buckled, and Iona cried out as two guards sliced her through. Anush lay bleeding on the coliseum sands, her right leg missing and gushing blood. She'd be dead in minutes. They all would be if they didn't get to high ground before the circle closed.

*Brother, what have you done?*

"Fall back!" Navarre shouted. "Fall back. Take to high ground!" He found Iereni, struggling to hold her own against a guard and shoved his sword into the man from behind, driving through armor and bone. "You, help her." He snapped at Ro who stood by without arrows and the first glimmer of fear in her wide eyes.

She'd been so brave a moment ago, facing the enemy with steady hands, but now it was a world of blood and chaos, and to a child who'd never seen death—it was a miracle she and Tiben were still standing.

Both girls rushed to her side, and as they helped her with the wheelchair Iereni screamed, *"Behind you!"*

He moved with instinct instead of thought, dropping low and turning with the rising arc of his sword as Benj hammered down from above. A vicious stroke that would've cleaved him from clavicle to groin. The force of it shook up his arms, into his chest, and down into his knees. His muscles ached, his bones screamed. Benj outmatched him in size, but Navarre had agility and cunning.

"Hold men!" the Archviceroy called out, weaving around the dead and dying on horseback. "Hold fast. We've got them, now."

"Fight us," Amparo shouted and struck with a vicious swipe of her sword. Three guards pushed her back. There were too many of them for her to break through the circle of steel and shield and lance. All it would take was one word from Henry and they'd be slaughtered.

More helmets lowered from faces. So many men he knew and fought and trained with. These weren't faceless strangers.

"Men of the Imperial Army, many of you know me," he spoke loudly, holding up his hands and letting his voice carry in the silence of coliseum while the dying groaned. "The Archviceroy has led you astray. He is not worthy of your loyalty and service, please, brothers—lay down your swords."

Benj tossed back his head with a loud, barking laugh. "Us? Lay down our swords?" He held out his hands and more laughter circled the men. "We outnumber you, *bastard*. We've won and now you'll die, like the traitorous cur that you are." He slashed his sword towards him. "You drew against your men. Men who vowed to follow you into battle, men who placed their loyalty and respect on your shoulders even though you didn't deserve it, and you've pissed on us all by siding with the enemy. For that, I am going to enjoy spilling your guts."

"Steady, Lieutenant General." The Archviceroy dismounted and stalked towards Navarre, his features gleaming with the rush of battle, and thrill of victory.

"You'll have your chance soon enough. But first things first, where is *she*?"

"I'm right here."

Sinadine emerged from the shadowy crevice of the coliseum corridor, dark hair fanning in the breeze against her wane features, blood drying at the side of her throat. She moved in an unnatural gait, almost stiff and unsteady. Something was off.

Wrong.

His eyes peeled around her, seeking and searching, but it didn't take long for him to realize that Sinadine was alone, and his heart sunk low into his guts.

The surrounding army fell to silence and Benj sauntered forwards, face bloodied and smiling.

"I wondered where you were hiding." The Archviceroy angled his head, gentile in blood-splattered grace. "You have one last chance, girl, to do the right thing. Kneel and I'll make it quick, for you and your clan."

"You want my head?" Drawing two swords, she held steady. "Come and claim it, then."

The Archviceroy nodded to Benj. Broadsword drawn, he roared forward. Blade arcing overhead in a two-handed strike.

Sinadine twisted, slashed—a blur too quick for the eyes to follow—and his head tumbled to sand and snow. Smiling, she squared herself with the Archviceroy. "Will you send someone else to their grave?" she challenged. "Or are you man enough to face me?"

Grinning, he dragged a hand across his chin. "I'm *really* going to enjoy this." Removing his cloak, the Archviceroy descended from horseback and drew his gored blade.

Navarre tensed at the fierce slash of Henry's broadsword. He'd never seen him in combat before, and had to admit in this moment, he was truly formidable. All fury and hatred where Sinadine was smooth, easy confidence. She ducked and dodged, deflected and danced, without so much as touching steel to his blade.

*Keep moving,* Navarre silently urged. *Let him swing and miss. Wear him out.*

If she could kill the Archviceroy there was a chance he could turn his men, they were teetering on the edge. He felt their hesitancy in his bones. Sir Manderly watched the spectacle with an expression of resigned duty. He'd follow the commands of his superior, but if Henry died, leadership would fall to him and he was far more likely to hear reason.

Eyes back to the fight, Sinadine's swords arced and blurred, faster then he'd ever seen her move as she drove the Archviceroy into a frantic circle. Sweat dripped from his chin, his teeth clenched in disgusted outrage. She was toying with him. Several times her sword stopped a breath from his skin when she could've struck a fatal blow.

*What is she playing at? Why won't she finish him?*

The crunch of her fist into Henry's face sent a shock of cold disbelief to chill the blood of the surrounding men. They flinched, gasped and some even staggered back as the Archviceroy crumpled like a paper doll.

Sinadine sheathed her swords. One on either hip.

"What are you doing," Henry spat out a wad of blood and teeth as he struggled to stand. A livid bruise already forming on his jaw.

"You don't deserve the honor of Acharrān steel," she said, her voice changing and blending. Carrying many with it instead of one. "We're going to kill you with our bare hands."

On his feet, the Archviceroy drew back his broadsword, his battle-cry a vicious bellow as he charged, a man blood-drunk. Too blinded by his anger to see she'd *transformed*.

White light, dazzling and fierce, surged at the heart of her. Sinadine raised her hands, crackling with power—it arced from palm to palm, shone in her eyes and in the unholy darkness of her grin. She crossed her arms and blocked the fall of his sword with the Acharrān cuffs. They sang with each slice and stroke, and she spun into a kick, her foot slamming into his gut like she was going to punch straight through.

His sword clattered, fell. Blood splattered from his mouth with a broken, weepy groan. When his hands came forward to defend himself from the next blow, she knocked them aside with the flat of her hands, and even above his screams Navarre heard the snap of the joints.

Henry sank to his knees before her. Limp.

Eyes and hair blazing white, like the shock of power gathering inside of her. A maelstrom. A hurricane. Seizing him by his breastplate, Sinadine grinned in the face of his terror and *screamed* her wrath as a sheet of light shot up above her—moved, a beast rearing its head.

No, not a beast.

A stonecat.

"God in heaven." Navarre staggered, marking himself with the God's Eye as that creature of light roared its fury with her, and dove. Swallowing the Archviceroy whole.

Energy—an explosion that shook the world and shattered in a rain of silver fire—spears of lightning flashed like lethal arrows to the heart of every single Bridian soldier in a wave of power so great Navarre was swept off his feet.

Screams. Smoke.

Sinadine stood in the center of it all—fire and fury—and then silence.

Navarre struggled to his knees and rose to find nothing in the clearing haze. Near a hundred men and she'd reduced them to statues of ash. Some frozen in agony, and others crumbled into clouds of pale grey dust at the faintest touch of wind. An entire battalion obliterated.

Only one remained.

"Trevor," Eban croaked at Navarre's side.

The youth scuttled away, whimpering as Sinadine approached, her steps heavy and swift. She swiped the point of his broadsword aside with the flat of her hand and pressed a foot to his breastplate, pinning him like an insect to the ground.

"Please," Trevor panted, eyes squeezed shut and terror shaking him to his boots. "Please, mercy, *please!*"

"Open your eyes," Sinadine snapped, her voice once again the cool, brutal tone he knew. Her eyes no longer shone white, and her returned to its raven black as whatever power she'd summoned in those mountains went quiet within her bones.

"I want you to leave with a message," she continued as Trevor peered up at her through tears. "Tell everyone what happened here. Tell them you fought free women forged of stars and steel. We do not bow. We do not bend. We do not break." She pressed down harder, and Trevor gasped at the groan of concaving armor.

"And for your emperor, tell him to remember what I promised him. He will know only terror. He will know only pain. On the Spirits of my Sisters, do I swear such wrath and fury. His reign will be fleeting as an unguarded flame and before his time is done, I shall look upon his splayed corpse and smile."

# CHAPTER THIRTY-THREE

## Sinadine

I SAT ON THE FRONT steps, shaded away from the light. I didn't like the touch of it on my skin, or the glow of it in my eyes. Whatever was inside of me craved the solace of the night.

I twisted the silver bangle on my wrist. I'd had to cut it from Taphne's body, removing the hand, and in a strange way I could feel the echo of her in the silver. A comfort and a misery.

It took almost a week to tend to our dead, clearing out all the bodies with oxen and wagons to the valley before the grove of xhixi trees to burn atop a pyre. Our fallen sisters, and the guards not felled by my blast. Even if they were enemies, we would not show them the same inhumanity they'd bestowed on our clan.

Only one man would feel the truth breadth of my rage.

Once that was dealt with, we moved all the survivors from the shrine down into the communal hut which was well provisioned with medical supplies. By some sliver of a miracle, Anush survived her injuries, and with the aid of a prosthetic in time she would walk again.

Iereni rolled up to the steps, her new sword sheathed at her back.

"Let me see," I said, holding out my hand for the weapon. Without hesitation she removed it and gave it to me. I recognized the hummingbirds etched on the scabbard with jade beaks and ivory pearls in the hilt. "This belonged to Padma de-Inessa. She was a formidable teacher. A proud Acharrān."

I returned the sword to her and Iereni cradled it close. "I will try to be worthy of such a treasure."

"You already are."

Jasz approached, Navarre with her. "Sina. There's a wagon at the gates. And people."

"Let them pass. I will meet them." Riding from the step, I dusted the dirt from my kubari, a matron's robes.

Navarre stepped into my path. "Is that a good idea?"

I flexed my fingers, light and energy sparked in my palm. "What can they do to me?"

Reluctantly he backed away, an echo of fear in his eyes. A look I'd seen shared among the others, too.

I came from the mountains altered. Dangerous and what I'd done in the coliseum was not the Acharrān way, but those days were over.

A new era had to begin.

The gates yawned open, and I stood in the pathway as the wagons entered. Men and women with them, some on foot carried baskets strapped to their backs or perched on their heads. The wagons were stacked with crates and barrels. One trailed with pigs and goats, another with wicker cages filled with white feathered chickens.

An old woman hobbled towards me, leaning heavily on a bamboo cane topped with an orb of amber and dressed in a jade cotton kubari beneath a cloak of black mink. She sank to her knees, and bowed so low her brow touched the frozen ground.

"I am Zo Maidu, Uje of Qadai. Daughter of the Acharrā, we humbly come to pay tribute and ask that you forgive us our trespass against you and your sisters." As she spoke the other villagers dismounted or stopped where they stood and bowed just as low. "We could not deny the soldiers accommodation," she continued. "Many times, we tried to send a warning, but our birds were shot down. For every attempt we made, they killed two of our children. We lost many children."

I took her hands and urged her to rise and to face me. Her watery brown eyes, the whites yellowed with age, shone with grief.

"You are not at fault. None of you are," I said loudly so that all could hear.

"All the same, we wish to help restore what you've lost with this." Battling to her feet, she pushed heavily on her cane and swept out a hand to the wagons and baskets, crates and barrels. "Please accept our humble offering, and know that the people of Qadai are at your disposal."

Warmth spread through me, the first I'd felt in far too long. The last few weeks had called into question all that I'd believed and held dear, but here was proof that despite the efforts of the empire, we were not forgotten. We were not alone, and there was so much left worth fighting for.

"We're grateful for your generosity."

"Tomorrow, I will send men and women to help in rebuilding your great home. By the time the snow melts, everything will be as it was. On my honor as Uje, we will not fail you a second time."

"I'd hate for you to go to such an effort only for the emperor to send more soldiers to destroy it."

"Then we will rebuild it again," Lady Zo answered with a defiant stomp of her cane. "And again. As many times as necessary."

Smiling, I kissed both her papery cheeks and pressed my brow to hers, whispering the old words of respect. She dashed away a tear with a gnarled finger, twisted with arthritis. Together we unloaded the wagons, transferring the goods in the storeroom of the communal hut, and the livestock to the empty stables where we'd housed our fine Tehke steeds—stolen by the Imperial Soldiers.

As the sun began to set in the sky I climbed the steps of the pagoda to where my aunt busied herself organizing the chaos of her private office. Furniture askance and windows shattered.

I crossed the room and helped her right the upturned desk onto its feet.

"So much work to do," she sighed, looking around her. "But I have hope." Those eyes fell to me with a tender smile. "I never thought I'd live to say this, but you've given me hope, Sinadine."

"Don't thank me just yet." I faced the broken windows, as I had my final day home, and peered down at the laughing faces in the courtyard, gathered around flames and roasting meat.

"I hear that mind of yours racing." Papers ruffled behind me, and wood scraped over wood. "What troubles you?"

I'd spent the last few days asking myself the same question. While I had told everyone of what had happened in those mountains . . . I'd withheld on a few important details.

I'd been given the power of the stars, but less than three months to do the impossible. And though I was still saddened over the sisters we'd lost, I had a vow to fulfill. Time would not wait for me to mourn our sisters.

"If I'm going to storm the Imperial City," I said at last, "it's going to take more than the handful of us that remain, even with this gift I've been given, we'll need to gather reinforcements. Strengthen our numbers."

"How?"

"There are more of us out there who are willing to revolt against the Empire. Commoner or noble alike. But there's one person in particular I need to find."

My aunt drew to a pause and, understanding, she lowered to sit into the chair she'd tucked at her righted desk. "Berséba . . ."

I nodded.

"Where would you even begin to look for her?"

"I don't know," I crossed my arms as I paced in a slow, winding circle around the center of the room. "I was hoping you had some ideas."

"Well, if I had to guess . . ." Elide sighed. "Nabakza."

I paused mid-step. "Why would she be in the Imperial prison?"

"The Bersé I know would've raced to the Imperial City upon the announcement of not only your arrival, but most certainly your execution. That fact that she didn't can only mean two things."

"She's imprisoned," I answered. "Or dead."

Elide nodded solemnly. "If neither of those, then she might be on one of the northern isles. I'll send a couple of our fastest hawks tomorrow to find out, and if we're lucky we'll receive word in a week or two."

A start, but far too long for me to sit around and wait. Not with every day bringing me closer to the equinox.

"I'll ride for Nabakza in the meantime. While I'm gone, you will stay here and rebuild what was destroyed. But before I go, I need you to do something for me."

"What?"

I braced the edge of her desk and drew a short breath. "Disavow me."

Elide's mouth tumbled open with a gasp. "You can't ask me to do that."

"You must. Tonight, before the witnessing gaze of our guests, and then tomorrow you will also write an additional three letters, one to the emperor and two others to be delivered to the news distributors in the Imperial City, publicly advocating your allegiance to the throne so that word will spread across the continent that the Acharrāns intend to honor the treaty as they have for a thousand years, and that the girl who defied him is no longer Swordsworn."

Weary with the weight of emotions far too great to carry, Elide closed her eyes. "You can't ask me to do that. Not after everything we've already lost."

"You have to." Rounding the desk, I knelt at her side. "Ehrick's first attack was disguised as illness and the second was done under the cloak of secrecy, but to risk a third, without actionable cause after a public declaration of allegiance from you, would make him appear . . . unstable in the eyes of his people, and council." And Ehrick was far too smart for that. "He won't strike at you, again without serious provocation. Instead, he'll turn all his efforts to me."

"Disavowment is no small matter, Sinadine. Once done I cannot undo this. You understand what you're giving up . . . what you're sacrificing?"

Reaching between us, I gripped her hands firmly. "I'm already damned, auntie."

The silence weighed, and Elide's features softened in grief, her eyes searching mine for answers I'd never give. "What did you do?"

"Nothing that I wouldn't've done a hundred times over."

Tears fell in streaks down her face, a sight I'd never thought I'd live to witness. My aunt weeping for me?

"Why?" she whispered.

"Because I am the *Dakuwan*," I answered, as I had with N'jirah in the mountains. "I was born for this."

Her smile spread, warm and tender with pride. "I will never forget this sacrifice, Sina. You did what you had to, not for yourself, but for us and that is true leadership. For as long as we carry steel, I will not allow your legacy to die." Resting her brow to mine, Elide drew a deep and sobering breath. "We'll hold the ceremony in the morning."

"But—"

"In the morning," Elide interrupted, allowing no further room for argument as she swept hands across her cheeks. "Tonight, you will enjoy your last as one of us. I command it and until you are disavowed, I expect you to obey."

A startled laugh burst from me that ended with a watery smile. "All right."

We worked together in silence and once finished we made our way to the courtyard where our guests were gathered around the fire, sharing a meal of venison and wine with the clan.

We ate. We laughed. And once our guests departed to sleep for the night in our communal hut, I shared the details of what was to come for tomorrow.

"This can't be the only way." Jasz chucked a cleaned bone into the flames. "You can't surrender your sword!"

Echoes of sentiment circled the campfire and I looked to my sisters—the last of my clan. My grandmother leaned on her xhixi staff with Elide at her side and even sightless I felt her gaze and her reassurance.

"My path is set. My destiny has always been to destroy, so I will destroy our enemies and I won't rest until I have honored my vow," I said. "But each must search their own soul and decide for themselves, for once we start on this path there's no going back. And we cannot fail."

Jasz unsheathed a dagger, in lieu of the oathblade, and slit a thin score against her palm. A twin to the pale, healed scar already there. "Blood of my blood," she said, scattering drops in pledge. "I will follow you into battle, to death and glory."

Cahira took the dagger, scored her palm. Amparo as well. Down the line it went. Each echoing the words among them, and as I beheld those proud, noble faces, a kind of quiet and dark joy filled my heart.

A heart that beat with the strength and rage of the First-of-Us.

Accepting the bloody dagger, I scored my own palm and swore my vow, uniting us all in this dark mission.

"I should return to the Imperial City while you hunt for allies." Navarre gripped my bleeding hand in his. "I'd be of more use to you with eyes on the palace."

"Going back will be dangerous."

His eyes softened. "I know, but if necessary, I have friends who could help me hide."

"Miego?" He nodded and my fingers twined with his, our blood seeping from between our clenched fingers. I looked from him to my sisters—the last of my clan. "You are the daughters of the Acharrā," I said, anchoring my free hand on Amparo's shoulder. "And by the Spirits of our Sisters you will not be the last."

"*We* will not be the last," Jasz corrected with a resolute nod. "Behold the stars, *Dakuwan*, see how brightly they burn. Tonight, and always, they shine for you." She let loose a cry, and it rippled around the campfire, carrying into the night as more whooping shouts rose, fierce with joy.

The rising chorus of their love and pride brought warmth to the corners of my heart left untouched for far too long.

Tossing back my head, I joined them.

My sisters. My clan.

Armed with them by my side, and the power of the First-of-Us burning inside of me, we would fight the Empire unto our last breaths. And even though once I died my soul would fade into nothing, these were my last few moments of life, of purpose, and I would ensure every single one mattered.

If Ehrick wanted my head—then I would bring the wrath of the stars down upon his.

**THE END**

# EPILOGUE

## Ehrick

THEY CALLED IT THE FAULT—a fissure that had opened in the earth and spewed forth both fire and shadows that threatened to swallow the world whole.

No one knew for sure where it came from, or how it appeared, only that one day it ruptured and unleashed an army. Creatures of dark and depraved hunger that swept through the land, bleeding it dry. Smothering it like a violent fist seizing a vulnerable neck, choking out all life between vicious, clawed fingers, until the Acharrāns descended to battle it back. Stemming the flood and sealing what was left of its putridity behind an impenetrable steel door. A door, it was rumored, to be hidden deep beneath the foundations of the Imperial

Palace. An ancient secret left to moulder and rot in the shadows.

Forgotten.

Buried.

A secret that had once consumed his line of forefathers, almost to the point of madness with the desire to seize this source of ancient power for themselves, only to be met with complete and utter failure. A secret that Ehrick assiduously excavated after pouring through scrolls and old tomes seized from conquered nations, written long before his grandsire ever set foot on Tujinese soil. Most of the texts hadn't been formally translated, only ripped from the towering bookcases in the once grand citadels in the early years of conquest. An effort to ensure if the Torren's couldn't claim this power, no one ever would. And, much like the seal, all knowledge of the Fault was hidden away within the walls of the Imperial Palace.

Forgotten.

Buried.

Ehrick spent his nights siphoning knowledge from those delicate pages of lambskin and sedge leaves until one day he came across the first of many hints and whispers of where the seal may be. Whomever had documented its existence had also gone to extensive lengths to ensure it remained lost, planting a litany of dead-ends and false starts to throw off anyone eager enough to dig into the past.

But they'd failed to take into consideration one important detail: Ehrick had never come across a puzzle he couldn't solve and once he'd set his mind to a task, he had all the patience in the world to unravel the most complicated of threads.

This one was thin. Fragile. And easy to snap.

So he carefully plucked at until it unfurled, leading the way deep through the spiraling chasm of the catacombs. Miles deep. A complicated and winding pathway that would be easy to lose your way in and never resurface from. A nightmare without end.

His plan hadn't been to unearth the Fault for at least another ten years, but Sinadine . . . she was a variable he hadn't properly considered. And one that forced him to reevaluate the sequence of events, following news that not only was she alive, she was a thorn determined to root into his side and slither deep. Penetrating where he was most vulnerable.

The fact that she'd managed to survive the assault hadn't surprised him, but his only true regret was not being there to witness her shock and horror the moment she arrived home only to find her mountains little more than a smoking wreckage, littered with the bones of everything she knew and loved.

No matter, he'd deal with her soon enough.

His muscles screamed and his joints ached from what felt like an endless journey into the bowels of the earth, but at long last, Ehrick stood before the seal—round in shape and towering near twenty feet tall. It gleamed and shimmered blue as a newborn star, warmed by the soft light of the lantern.

*Finally.*

He pressed a hand to the seal and felt the humming pulse of magic trapped within push against the flat of his palm. Strong. Resilient. There was no key to unlock it, and no weapon could shatter its hold. The was only one way to open it . . . Stepping back, Ehrick drew the length of his mother's sword, plucked from her tomb, and held it before the seal. Sisters forged from the ore of the same mountain, it was said Acharrān steel carried more than magic, it carried the intention of the one bound to it, and while he was not his mother—he *was* her son.

"Open for me." A burning wish that filled his heart and roared in his blood. "I've come for what is mine. *Open for me!*"

Both sword and seal glowed and flickered in alternating pulses, responding to each other as if in heated conversation. But it didn't take long.

A slow groan, a steady yawn . . .

The seal rolled open, revealing a dark and cavernous mouth that flowed down into a pit so vast and dark the light of the lantern did nothing to penetrate the wall of endless black. This wasn't the darkness of shadows.

This was something else.

Stepping into the void, a wall of pressure settled on Ehrick's shoulders, and that weight clung to him like briars in a field, making his limping stride slow and unsteady. When he'd ventured little more than a hundred yards, Ehrick raised the gilded sword high overhead, its light shining far brighter than the lantern he'd brought with him, and scanned the cavern with walls made of glassy obsidian.

"Hello?" His words barely stretched an inch before they were flattened by the density of the air. "Hello!" he called out again, using the ferocity of his full chest, and this time his voice struck stone and ricocheted back, carrying with it another sound.

The rasp of an animalistic snarl, quickly joined by struggling movements and the click of claws as something emerged from the gloom. Too weak to stand, it crawled belly down on arms and legs thin as matchsticks, and reached for him with desperate fingers grasping at the air.

*<Feeeeed.>* Its sibilant voice croaked. The sound echoing inside Ehrick's head rather than filling the cavern around them. Weak as a dying man. *<Feeeeeed!>*

Ehrick stooped over the feeble figure of little more than blackened bones. It scuttled for him, frantic and starved, but unable to do more than paw at his ankle and flash blackened gums coated in filmy grim and the remnants of broken teeth.

Pitiful creature.

To imagine this had been one of legion, bearing the strength of ten men and capable of ripping throats clean open with a single snap of powerful jaws. Trapped for millennia, it had withered to a husk that could barely withstand a strong breeze, let alone the edge of a sword. If there were others still trapped down here, it was hard to imagine they'd be in a less insubstantial state.

How . . . disappointing.

This was not a weapon he could harness and unleash, but perhaps . . . perhaps it was something he could learn from.

"I was going to set you free. But now . . ." Lowering to his haunches, Ehrick stroked the dome of its smooth skull, from crown to chin, barely missing the nip of shattered fangs. "Now I have a better idea." Standing up, he drew back his sword arm and with a firm, clean stroke of steel to spine—the creature's head rolled to Ehrick's feet.

Spinning with eyes like blackened marbles in gaping sockets, gazing up at nothing.

Ehrick removed his waistcoat and wrapped the head in the swath of silk, inky blood oozing into the dark purple, as he cradled it like a beloved child born of his own flesh.

Sinadine called herself the *Dark One*.

She was about to find out what those words *truly* meant.